THE VINYL DETECTIVE

THE RUN-OUT GROOVE

Also by Andrew Cartmel and available from Titan Books

Written in Dead Wax
Victory Disc (May 2018)

THE VINYL DETECTIVE

THE RUN-OUT GROOVE

ANDREW CARTMEL

TITAN BOOKS

The Vinyl Detective: The Run-Out Groove
Print edition ISBN: 9781783297696
E-book edition ISBN: 9781783297702

Published by Titan Books
A division of Titan Publishing Group Ltd
144 Southwark Street, London SE1 0UP

First edition: May 2017
10 9 8 7 6 5 4 3 2 1

A CIP catalogue record for this title is available from the British Library.

Printed in the USA.

Did you enjoy this book? We love to hear from our readers.
Please email us at readerfeedback@titanemail.com or write to us at
Reader Feedback at the above address.

To receive advance information, news, competitions, and exclusive offers online,
please sign up for the Titan newsletter on our website:

www.titanbooks.com

For Ben Aaronovitch, comrade in arms.

Daily Chronicle

Saturday 21 January 1967

Singer Dead—Child Missing

NOTHING COULD BETTER illustrate the depravity of the current so-called 'psychedelic music scene' in Britain than the gruesome recent demise of the pop singer Valerie Drummond, alias 'Valerian'. Much has been written about this horrid occurrence (see lead story, pages 1–3) but not enough has been said about the fate of her infant son. True, he was an illegitimate child but that was not the little boy's fault. He was let down by those around him, a clique of selfish, hedonistic thrill-seekers for whom reality is not enough. Not for them the honest glow of daylight. They need the disturbing glare of so-called 'mind expanding' drugs. These drugs are actually mind *destroying*. They are the same mind destroying drugs that have already claimed the lives of other pop stars, such as Brian Jones of the notorious 'rock' group, the Rolling Stones, and many of Drummond's own intimate circle. When one contemplates the fate of that poor little boy, one can only shudder...

1. THE DISCOVERY

My friend Tinkler is about my age, considerably more plump, and has a face that suggests he is a member of some disreputable rank of the cherubim.

Today was his birthday.

"I beg your pardon?" he said, staring at both of us, hand theatrically on his chest. "A present, you say? For me? You mean you knew it was my special day?"

"You only mentioned it about fifty times. Anyway, Nevada found a record for you in a charity shop."

"What is it?"

"I don't know. She hasn't let me see it."

"A rare record," said Nevada. "A very rare record."

"Well, give it to me, then," said Tinkler.

She trotted into the bedroom to get the record—thoughtfully wrapped in elegant black and gold paper—and came back and handed it to me. "You can give it to him," she said. "I found it and I'm responsible for the wonderful discovery and I did all the hard work and paid for it and wrapped it and everything, but you can *give* it to him."

As I took the package, through the gift wrap, I caught a whiff of something penetrating but faint—spicy and musty.

I sniffed it.

It was the aroma of an *old* record. In fact, it was what a cardboard LP cover smells like after about fifty years.

I felt my stomach go hollow. "My god," I said. "I think it really might be something rare."

Nevada was staring at me. "You can tell by *smelling* it?"

Tinkler saw the expression on my face and immediately took the record from me. He began to unwrap it. Actually, "unwrap" is a considerable understatement. He ripped into it like the degenerate lord of the manor tearing at the bodice of the innocent chambermaid in a cheap romance novel. Bits of paper were flying everywhere.

Nevada watched, eyes gleaming. "I knew you wanted it, Tinkler, because you have a picture of it hanging on the wall. A framed picture of the cover, hanging on your living-room wall. That's how much you want this record."

Tinkler was now standing there, holding the LP.

It was hard to say who was more surprised, him or me.

It was *All the Cats Love Valerian*, the final album by the great British 1960s rock band whom those cats were said to love. It featured a cover photograph of the eponymous singer. Valerian was a wild child and prototypical hippie chick, completely nude and sprawled on an old Persian rug in a room full of antique furniture with cats climbing all over everything. It was a great photo and indeed the album had been banned at the time because of this image of

Valerian's provocative nudity—although some strategically placed antiques and the odd cat spared her modesty.

It was an incredibly rare item.

"Holy fuckaroo," murmured Tinkler.

"The Bard could not have put it better himself," Nevada said. Then, looking at me, "You didn't think it was the real McCoy, did you?"

This was true. "Well…"

"Never doubt me," she said complacently, picking up the cover and studying it. "Did the cats really love Valerian? She must have really loved *them* if she actually owned all this lot. I mean if they were her cats."

I went over to her. "No, it's just a photo shoot. It was a play on words."

"What was?"

"The title."

"How so?"

"Because all the cats *do* love valerian. It's the name of a kind of herb, and apparently cats just love it. They go wild for it. Rolling in it. Sniffing it. Eating it."

"Like catnip?" said Nevada.

"Exactly like catnip. Nip and valerian are the two drugs of choice for cats."

"Speaking of drugs," said Tinkler, "have you seen this?" He delved into his pocket and took out a scrap of newspaper. It was the front page of a tabloid with the headline STINKY STANMER COCAINE BUST across the top.

"My god," said Nevada.

"He's your neighbour, you know," said Tinkler.

"What do you mean?"

"He's in the Abbey." He nodded towards the window, and the garden beyond. Just over our back wall were the elegant white battlements of London's leading celebrity detox and rehab centre.

Nevada lowered the newspaper, which she'd studied carefully. "What? Why isn't he behind bars? I mean behind proper bars."

Tinkler shook his head. "I suppose no one was in a hurry to have a whimpering celebrity cluttering up the prison system."

I said, "I can understand that."

"What a shame," said Nevada. "I'd have thought they would have slammed him in the… slammer." She started striding back and forth. She seemed to be taking this personally. "Christ. He's going to be right next door? We'll never get rid of him." She glanced at me. "He'll be around here incessantly trying to chat me up and steal your ideas and generally making himself obnoxious."

Tinkler grinned. "Newsflash. If he so much as sets one toe outside the grounds of the Abbey they're going to rescind the deal and put him into a real, high-security prison complete with abundant scary cell mates and ample rape in the showers."

This put a different complexion on things. Nevada stopped striding and smiled a big smile.

"I just love the word 'rescind'," she said.

* * *

I duly wrote a post about the epochal discovery of *All the Cats Love Valerian* the next day, giving Nevada full credit for the discovery. When I finished, I pushed the button and the blog went live. In the kitchen I heard Nevada grunting with approval as she read it on her iPhone. Then she put on her jacket in the hallway and peered around the door at me.

"Who don't you doubt?"

"You."

"That's right." She blew me a kiss and headed out, going shopping. Charity shopping.

In a way, this was my fault.

I had introduced Nevada to the world of charity shops in the first place. I routinely trawled every one of these in southwest London in search of rare records, which was my business. In the course of accompanying me on a portion of this perpetual quest, she had come to discover that the shops weren't the malodorous quivering dens of parasitic insect life she had first supposed and, much more to the point, could be the source of some spectacular high-fashion but low-price acquisitions.

Now that we were living together she had taken to scouring them on a regular basis, and was always coming home with a bargain pair of Louboutin sneakers or a phenomenally inexpensive Dolce & Gabbana breechclout or something.

I returned to my blog and added a bit more detail. I gave some background about the band and Valerian herself, but I didn't mention her unpleasant fate or what had happened to her little boy.

More than enough had been written on these subjects already.

The phone rang. It was Nevada. "It's autumn," she said.

"Yes. I'd noticed."

"It's just perfect."

"What's perfect?"

"I've got an idea. For Tinkler's birthday party."

"Well?" I said. "Spill the beans."

"It'll be a surprise. For you as well as him. And Clean Head. For everyone."

I said, "I don't think Tinkler can take any more surprises."

I woke up in the middle of the night, instantly aware that something was wrong. Fanny moaned in complaint as I shifted under the covers. The little opportunist was huddled up to me, for my body heat. Which was odd, because she'd been favouring Nevada of late. I rolled over in bed and reached out for Nevada.

She was gone.

I fumbled for the alarm clock and held it close enough to my face to read. It was three in the morning. The godforsaken hour when hope fails, the frail and elderly die, and—apparently—your girlfriend goes missing.

I called her name and checked the bathroom and kitchen, but I already sensed that the house was empty. I pulled on some clothes as I searched the other rooms, increasingly anxious.

Then, suddenly, I knew where she'd be. I went into the kitchen again and opened the curtains, peering out. There she was. I put on my shoes and a scarf—it was a cold night—and went out to join her.

My little house is in a small square of similar buildings on the raised concrete platform of a large housing estate, the kind London's councils built before they knew better. It's been much improved over the years, and what is now a large sunken basin adjacent to our houses, full of low buildings, fir trees and winding footpaths, was once an underground car park and the estate's giant boiler room. You can look down into this basin over some railings at the edge of our square.

That was where Nevada was standing now.

I went and joined her. She glanced at me, then took my hand and resumed staring downwards. "I couldn't sleep," she said. Her hand was cold.

"Bad dreams?"

"Bad memories."

The basin below was lit by high streetlamps. Their amber glow gave it a slightly eerie cast. It was the kind of light that would have made a puddle of blood look utterly black.

There was no blood down there now, of course. It had been washed away long ago—in an uncharacteristic burst of efficiency by the local authorities.

I looked at Nevada's face and realised, with astonishment, that she was scared. This was doubly strange because she hadn't been scared at the time. Indeed, she had saved both our lives.

Later, looking back at this moment, I couldn't help wondering if perhaps it wasn't the past that frightened her. Not what had happened but in some inexplicable way, what was yet to come…

I felt her shiver and I wrapped my arms around her.

"Don't worry," I said, holding her tight. "It's all over now."

I didn't know it was just beginning.

2. DINNER PARTY

While I did all our day-to-day cooking, Nevada liked to prepare the occasional elaborate dessert for a special occasion, and it turned out this was the birthday boy's surprise.

"I'm going to do a tart. A tart for Tinkler," she announced one morning. Shortly thereafter she started purchasing and assembling ingredients, which for some reason was a protracted and clandestine business. Finally she was ready to start cooking.

The tart, prepared under conditions of strictest secrecy, was smelling good by the time our guests showed up on the night of Tinkler's party. First to appear was an elegant apparition in a white trench coat with a bottle of wine under one arm and a long thin cardboard tube under the other.

This was Agatha DuBois-Kanes, better known by her now firmly affixed nickname of Clean Head. We had met her, a beautiful mixed-race woman with a shaven head, in her capacity as a taxi driver, piloting one of London's fleet of storied black cabs. But on this occasion she had got one of her colleagues to chauffeur her to our place. No driving for her tonight.

"I fully intend to get blotto," she said, handing me the bottle of wine as she kissed me. She smelled good. I was about to ask her about the cardboard tube when the doorbell rang again. It was the birthday boy himself, resplendent in a Hugo Boss jacket, Paul Smith sweater and Woodhouse trousers, all of which Nevada had found for him at various times in her charity shop excursions. I wasn't surprised to see him dressed to the nines. Tinkler had a doomed passion for Clean Head.

Supper went well and, as usual, I began to relax as soon as people had hungrily cleaned their plates and asked for second helpings. "What is this cheese?" said Tinkler. "I think I've conceived an unnatural infatuation for it. Can a man love a cheese? Would we be happy together?"

As the evening progressed I provided the music, selecting the records. These were mostly jazz and Brazilian— sometimes Brazilian jazz—and Nevada made sure the wine glasses stayed full. We took a little break between the main course and dessert, allowing Clean Head to give Tinkler his birthday present, which of course is what the cardboard tube turned out to be.

It contained a poster of the Rolling Stones. A moody black and white shot of them in their surly heyday, circa 1968—*Beggars Banquet* era—by the great rock photographer David Wedgbury. It was a perfect gift for Tinkler, and so thoughtfully chosen that I began to wonder if his passion was entirely doomed after all.

Then, with much ceremony, Nevada carried in the tart.

It was a beautiful confection of almond pastry, with a glazed surface of sliced apricots. It was also oddly thick. "This is a very special tart," she said coyly, setting it on the table.

"*You're* a very special tart," said Tinkler. For which he got kicked under the table.

"It is special," persisted Nevada, taking out a pie cutter, "because it has an utterly unique ingredient." She drew a careful line across the glazed fruit with the cutter, dividing the tart neatly in half. Then another line the other way, forming a perfect cross.

The tart was now divided into quarters. She set about subdividing each of these. When she was finished, it was divided into *sixteenths*.

She carefully insinuated the point of the pie server under one of these tiny wedges and began to prise it out. "You've got to be kidding," I said. Nevada smiled triumphantly as she lifted out the first miniature serving of tart. "Tinkler isn't going to settle for a portion that small," I said.

She handed the plate to Tinkler. "It's a very special dessert."

"So you keep saying." I was looking at the slice. I could see the inside of the tart now, and there was a curious brown layer under the yellowish apricot slices. "Those aren't berries."

"Who said anything about berries?" Nevada was smiling at me.

"Or apples. You weren't picking berries on the common. Or apples." I stared at her. I finally got it. "You were picking mushrooms."

Magic mushrooms.

"That's right." She extracted another slice of the tart and put it on a plate. "It's exactly the right time of year. And the common was positively dotted with them." She handed the plate to Clean Head, who accepted it eagerly.

"So it's *that* kind of party," she said, lifting her fork.

Tinkler was staring at the minuscule slice of hallucinogenic dessert on the plate in front of him. Saying nothing, which was odd.

"That's why I can only serve you these little teeny slices," said Nevada. "Because larger ones would cause your skull to go *ka-boom*." She selected a third slice, put it on a plate and handed it to me.

I stared at it. The brown layer underneath the apricots was disconcerting. Not to say sinister. "It's going to taste a bit weird, isn't it?"

"Magic mushrooms taste like shit," said Tinkler, with the manner of a man who knew.

"Don't worry, boys," said Nevada. "I soaked them overnight in sugar and Cointreau." She served herself a slice. Clean Head had already started, spearing dainty chunks of tart and devouring them with evident relish.

"I'm sorry," said Tinkler, lifting his fork glumly, "but I have a confession to make."

"You're not going to say you can't eat it," said Nevada.

"No, of course I'll eat it. But it won't have any effect on me."

"Do you want a bigger piece?"

"No." He shook his head gloomily. "It won't do any good."

"What do you mean?"

"I've taken mushrooms, I've taken ecstasy, I've taken acid—"

"Tinkler, you dark horse!"

"And I'm immune to hallucinogenic drugs."

"I'm sure it will be completely different when you try some of Auntie Nevada's hand-picked fungi."

Tinkler shrugged. "I'm not so sure." He picked up his fork and started eating. I looked at my own serving with hesitation.

It wasn't that I didn't want to eat the dessert my own true love had prepared for me with her fair hands. It's just that I don't believe in tampering with my brain chemistry— numerous cups of high-end coffee aside.

I twirled my fork in my fingers, stalling for time.

The wedge of tart stared up at me, beginning to look very vivid against the bright red plate. It was like the emblem of some drug-crazed Mod. It looked positively lethal. I wondered if I could sneak it into the kitchen under some pretext and pitch it into the bin without anyone being the wiser. I glanced across the table at Nevada.

She knew me far too well for any such knavery.

Now she watched keenly as I pressed my fork into the tart and took the first mouthful. It was much better than I expected. In fact it was good. You could taste the mushrooms, just about, but they merely provided a kind of background meatiness to the flavour.

I found I was actually enjoying it and polished off the rest while Nevada watched with approval. I told myself that perhaps, like Tinkler, the mushrooms would have no effect on me.

* * *

I don't know how long it took the drugs to come on, because the first thing that went was my sense of time. Indeed, my whole *perception* of time changed. Instead of a continuous flow, it began to arrive in discrete intervals. It was like the difference between a sine wave on a graph and a square wave. Separate moments arrived as individual snapshots.

I only realised just how far gone I was when I started talking to the cat.

Fanny had come in through the cat flap, evidently curious about what was going on with the grown-ups. She settled down on the floor and I went over and knelt beside her. My hand felt like it was sinking into her warm fur as I stroked her back. I could feel every individual hair, like a living filament with a delicate electrical charge.

She tilted her little head and stared up at me. Her eyes were enormous. I gazed into them and they were like the green and yellow landscape of an exotic planet. I could see details—oceans, mountains, plains.

And then she started talking to me.

Fanny spoke in a soft, attenuated, echoing voice. It was a pleasant enough voice, but strangely not in any way feminine. But then I realised, why should a female cat sound like a female human?

I hadn't considered this before.

She didn't move her lips when she spoke, of course. Cats don't have lips like ours, anyway. The words just appeared over my head, somewhere above my pulsing brow centre.

She said, "You know when you're having a bath and I come and scratch on the side because I want to have a drink from the taps?"

"Yes?"

"Well, sometimes you don't hop out of the bath right away, and I can't clamber in and get my drink."

"It's not so simple," I said. "I mean, I get out as quick as I can, but I still have to pull the plug and the bath has to drain. You can't just clamber in while there's still bath water in there. You'd get your paws wet."

"Well, it just isn't good enough," said Fanny.

"What about this," I proposed. "While you're waiting I could turn on the tap in the bathroom *sink* and lift you up to drink from it?"

There was a snort of suppressed laughter and I looked up to see Tinkler standing over me holding a long cardboard tube to his lips. It was the tube his Rolling Stones poster had come in and he was speaking into it. The tube gave his voice an eerie, echoing tone.

So Fanny hadn't been talking to me after all.

It had been a cruel hoax.

"You drug-addled halfwit," he said.

According to what I'd read, there should have been no hangover with magic mushrooms. But like so much pro-drugs propaganda, I found this was wildly wide of the mark. Or at least, I was the exception to the rule.

The next day I felt like the inside of my skull had been sand-blasted. And the world seemed a strange place. Everything looked normal, but slightly off, as if overnight the size and shape of familiar objects had been subtly altered.

I managed to make my morning coffee, deploying the familiar but somehow unearthly implements. Nevada joined me, chopped up some raw Aberdeen Angus beef with the kitchen scissors and served it to the cats as their breakfast. She moved to the sink to wash the scissors and suddenly stopped and gave a little cry.

I went to join her. She was looking at the metal pie dish that, last night, had still contained three quarters of the magic mushroom tart.

It was now completely empty, except for a few crumbs.

Nevada spun around to stare at Turk and Fanny who were busy demolishing their breakfast. She said, "Do you think the cats could have eaten it?"

I went and looked. "Only if they used a fork and a plate and put them in the sink afterwards." Nevada and I looked at each other.

"Tinkler," we said, simultaneously.

Nevada picked up her phone and dialled his number. As soon as he answered she said, "Tinkler, how could you?" She put her hand over the phone and looked at me. "He said he was *peckish*."

She resumed speaking into the phone. "Peckish or not, your fucking head will explode." She checked her watch. "Will *already* have exploded. What? Christ." She listened for a long time then hung up.

"It seems that when he got home, late last night, his boss was waiting for him on his doorstep. Apparently there was some kind of crisis at work. Some sort of super important database had failed or something and they needed Tinkler to go in and fix it. So he did."

"He did? He fixed it? After eating all those magic mushrooms?"

"Yes. And apparently he did such a great job his boss is now buying him a champagne breakfast."

"I guess he really is immune," I said.

I took my coffee outside and sat in our back garden. I was sitting there when the doorbell rang.

I heard Nevada go and answer it. There was a man's voice and a woman's voice—not Nevada's—and then Nevada's voice again. Two people at the door. It could only be the Jehovah's Witnesses or some other equally enthusiastic sect, proselytising on the doorstep. I sighed and rose from my chair. Underneath, where she had been sheltering in my shadow, Fanny gave a little squeak of alarm at being suddenly and cruelly exposed to the fearsome naked rays of the brutal British autumn sun.

I went in to help Nevada. It seemed unfair to let her deal with these callers on her own. And there was always the terrifying possibility she might invite them in for coffee or something.

As I stepped through the back door I heard a woman's

voice, soft and tentative, saying, "Is this the correct address for the Vinyl Detective?"

And a man's voice; brusque, peremptory and brooking no opposition. "We want to hire him."

3. THE CLIENT

Nevada had indeed invited our visitors in. She was standing with them in the sitting room in the uncertain configuration of strangers who have just met. The couple definitely didn't look like any Jehovah's Witnesses I'd ever seen.

The man had an abundant crop of grey hair so pale it was almost white, combed and styled with narcissistic care. His eyebrows were darker, thick charcoal hyphens above emphatic greyish blue eyes. He gave the impression of disciplined good health and carefully cultivated athleticism. He must have been at least in his sixties, but he seemed powerful, vigorous and forceful.

He was neatly turned out and was dressed, as Nevada would later remark, as if he had just looted a branch of L.L.Bean.

The woman was a quite different proposition. She was perhaps twenty years younger than him, but beefy and solid-looking. Despite being smaller she must have weighed considerably more. Her big amiable face was like a cylinder on which various features had been stuck—jutting ears, a snub nose. She was dressed in grey and pink tracksuit bottoms and a matching sweatshirt with a large slogan that read YOUR SUSHI'S GETTING COLD.

The tracksuit was clean but very rumpled and, along with her brown hair, which hung down in irregular strands, gave an impression of disorganisation that contrasted sharply with the man's chiselled neatness. His shoes were brown patent leather and polished to an improbable mirror gleam. Hers were white trainers, new but already muddy and scuffed, with the shoelaces loose and flopping in the currently fashionable manner.

He was buttoned down and squared away; she was shambolic.

The only common denominator between the two of them was the fact that strapped around their waists they both wore what we call a bum bag and the Americans call a fanny pack. Whatever you call it, it's not exactly a fashion statement.

They had identical bright red ones.

The man looked at me as I came in. He said, "My name is John Drummond and this is Lucille Tegmark." There was no offer of a handshake and he seemed to deliver this latter piece of identification reluctantly, as though unhappy about being associated with the woman, but making the best of it.

She smiled at me. "Lucy," she said, correcting him. She had a trace of an accent that I couldn't immediately identify. On the other hand, he definitely sounded American.

Fanny packs it was, then.

Nevada was grinning at me. "They're looking for you."

"I know. I heard."

"They want to *hire* you." As Nevada said this I noticed the man wince as if, having actually caught sight of the famed Vinyl Detective in the flesh, he was having second thoughts. That was fine with me.

"Won't you sit down, please," said Nevada, who had suddenly become hostess of the year. And, before I could stop her, she added, "I'll get you some coffee. We've just made some. It's nice and fresh."

"Smells good," said the man, as though reluctantly conceding a point in a negotiation. "Thanks."

"Thank you," said the woman, and promptly sank into one of our comfy leather armchairs. The man gave her a look of tired disgust, then walked to the dining table, pulled out one of the wooden chairs facing it and sat down. I noticed he'd chosen the least comfortable seat in the room. Even at this early stage in our acquaintance this struck me as absolutely characteristic of the guy.

I wondered if L.L.Bean manufactured any hair-shirts. If so, he would certainly be their top customer.

He sat in the chair stiffly, leaning back slightly, as if to place himself as far as physically possible away from the woman.

And from me.

Fanny had followed me in from the garden and instantly gone into concealment. Now she emerged from her hiding place under the unoccupied armchair, where she had been sheltering just in case our visitors had turned out to be, for example, a Mossad hit squad with the wrong address. She wandered over to the man and sniffed at his shoes.

Without looking at her, he lowered his powerful, hairy hand and tickled her under the chin. Fanny luxuriated in the attention, the treacherous little trollop. Meanwhile in the kitchen Nevada was clattering around, looking for cups and generally making coffee-serving sounds.

"Thank you for the hospitality," said the woman—Lucy Tegmark.

"No problem."

"We missed breakfast," said Lucy, shooting a look at the man, who ignored her. "We were in such a hurry to get here." She kept looking at him and he kept on ignoring her. "I'm certainly looking forward to lunch."

"There's a place nearby we can recommend." Nevada leaned around the kitchen door. She smiled at me. "Isn't there, darling?" She was holding in her hands a tray that had leaned against the wall in my kitchen unused for approximately the last ten years. She was wiping it with a sponge, as well she might, since it was covered with the dust of ages.

Apparently she had decided that our guests were of such a calibre that they would be insulted if they weren't served refreshments on a proper tray.

"Thank you," said Lucy. "That would be great." She looked at the man, who continued to ignore all her cues. "And thank you for the coffee," she said. "Doesn't it just smell delicious?"

It certainly did, because it was the pot I had just prepared and it was the good stuff—some of the last of my dwindling supply of *ca phe cut chon* beans from Indo-China. The one time in my life when I'd actually had money, had in fact very briefly been extremely wealthy, I'd managed to treat myself to a few small luxuries before the shit had hit the fan and the money had vanished like the abstract fantasy it basically was.

One of those luxuries had been the coffee beans. If I'd been given any choice in the matter, I would have slipped into the kitchen and decanted the remainder of that pot of coffee into a thermos and hidden it from view until our guests had safely departed, all the while making them some instant. Come to think of it, even the jar of organic Ecuadorian shade-grown freeze-dried instant coffee was probably better than they deserved, particularly the man, who was now giving me a look with his cold little blue eyes, as if sizing me up as the slacker I so manifestly was.

He said, "We've come about that record. *All the Cats Love Valerian.*" The baroque title sounded strange coming out of his military mouth. "We read about it on your website."

"Your blog," Lucy Tegmark corrected him.

"I'm sorry," I said, with an immense feeling of relief— maybe we'd be able to get rid of these two without even having to serve them coffee, "but that record's not for sale." Although the thought of the look of scandalised horror on Tinkler's face did almost make the notion worthwhile. "In fact we gave it to a friend as a gift."

"We're not looking to buy the record," said the man. "We want to talk to you about her."

"Her?"

"Valerian," said the woman.

"Valerie Anne," said the man firmly. "Valerie Anne Drummond." A faint little alarm bell began to ring in my head, a sense that I was missing something, or had forgotten something very important.

"Her and her son," said Lucy. The man shot her a look of pure hatred. She couldn't have been unaware of it, but she merely smiled complacently, as if it was what she had come to expect, and perhaps even enjoy. She just sat there letting his hostility wash over her.

I said, "The little boy who went missing?"

"We don't need to get into that," said the man tightly.

Lucy chuckled. "The Colonel here seems to think we can employ you to do a job for us without actually telling you what that job *is*." She hitched around in the chair so she was looking at me. "We need your help," she said simply.

I went and sat in the chair opposite her so she wouldn't have to contort herself. I said, "We're talking about Valerian's son, the little boy who disappeared just after she died?" It had been a cause célèbre at the time, and a huge scandal.

"Or disappeared just *before*." She looked at me. "No one knows exactly what happened. That's why we want to hire you." She glanced at the man. "If the Colonel here can bring himself to allow you a full briefing."

I wasn't sure I wanted to be fully briefed. She turned back to me. "We want you to look into his disappearance."

"I find vinyl," I said. "Rare records. Not missing persons."

At this point Nevada, who had been eavesdropping in the kitchen, came hastily bustling through with four cups, the sugar bowl and a petite jug of milk perched on the freshly washed and gleaming tray. She made a major production of serving everyone. The Colonel gave her a genuine flash of a smile as she set the cup down before him. He leaned over the cup and inhaled with pleasure and approval, as well he might. "Smells great," he grunted. He looked up at her and his icy blue gaze actually seemed to warm for an instant. Nevada beamed proudly as if the making of the coffee had actually had something to do with her.

"I find records," I repeated, before things got too cosy. "I don't—"

Nevada came to me and took my hand. "Let's just hear what the people have to say, honey." Her tone was all sweetness, light and reason. She gave me her big eyes and, although I knew she was working me, I was putty in her hands. I sighed and sat back in my chair.

"All right," I said. "Tell me about it." Nevada smiled a delighted smile and perched on the arm of the sofa, legs crossed, elbow braced, chin attentively on her hand.

I sighed and looked at Lucy Tegmark. "So, tell me all about it," I repeated.

She seemed suddenly uncertain. "Where should I start?"

"Well, why don't you start by explaining how you come into it? You and the Colonel."

"Don't call me that," said the man.

"What?"

"The Colonel. I'm not a colonel. I'm not in the army and I never was."

Lucy smiled at me. "It's true. But he's *always* talking

about his *father*. How the old Colonel would do this, or do that—everything from the proper way to butter a slice of toast to the correct method of making sure you're not short-changed by a taxi driver. Anyway, he talks about the Colonel so much I started calling him that. I suppose it's a nickname. And it stuck."

"No it didn't," said the man stubbornly.

I said, "So what do we call you, then?"

"John," said Lucy merrily. "Johnny. Jack."

"Mr Drummond," said the man, tightly.

Drummond.

The faint alarm bell in my head got suddenly louder. Now I knew why it was ringing. I would have put it together a whole lot sooner if my brain hadn't been addled by the magic mushroom tart my beloved had poisoned me with. I must have been staring at him because suddenly his cold little eyes were beaming directly into mine. I searched his face for a family resemblance. I could detect none, but I was certain all the same. "You're a relative," I said.

"She was my sister."

Nevada leaned forward. She said, "Valerian was your *sister*?"

"Valerie Anne. Yes."

4. VALERIAN'S BROTHER

"That's why we've come to see you," said Lucy Tegmark.

"That's why *I've* come to see you," said the Colonel. "She's just along for the ride."

She glared at him. "I am as much involved in this project as you are. I am just as committed to it. Just as emotionally invested."

"I don't think so," he said dryly, and I had the sudden surprising impression that he might be right; that this apparently emotionless man sitting at my table, petting my fawning quisling of a cat, might be a hell of a lot more 'invested' in this than she was.

Maybe it was just the residual psilocybin in my system, but it seemed for an instant that he'd spoken a profound truth, and everybody sitting here listening to its echo in the quiet morning sunlight knew it. He had somehow put us all to shame.

But especially Lucy.

She turned to us, apparently eager to make up lost

ground. "Of course I'm not *family*, but I am passionately interested in this story. In discovering the truth of it and putting it in the public domain."

I said, "You're a journalist?"

The Colonel snorted. She shot him a look of unadulterated hostility; for the first time he'd managed to get under her skin. "I'm a writer," she said. "I don't know that I'm qualified yet to be called a journalist. My *father* was a journalist. Monty Tegmark." She sounded proud.

The Colonel grinned mirthlessly. "Journalist is stretching it a bit," he said. "He was a stringer for a sleazy Fleet Street tabloid." Suddenly, under the American accent, I could detect English tones and intonations. He must have grown up here if he was Valerian's brother. A local boy, after all.

Lucy Tegmark shook her head. She had regained her composure and didn't seem stung by the remarks. It was as if she was on firmer ground here. "My father was a very respected professional. He was held in high esteem by all the national dailies."

"The point is," said the Colonel, growing impatient at this encomium, or perhaps just nettled that he hadn't been able to rile her sufficiently, "he left behind a cache of useful information. Documentation."

"About what?" I asked.

"Valerian," said Lucy. "My father knew a great deal about her. He went on tour with the band, wrote a whole series of articles."

"During the period when…" I was going to allude at

this point to Valerian's grisly demise—but then I realised that her brother was sitting right here at my table, looking at me. Near enough to reach out and touch, in the unlikely event that anybody would want to touch him.

So instead I said, "When her boy went missing."

"During and before," said Lucy. "Dad was one of the first newspapermen to discover Valerian, to discover the band. So he had access to them from the start. He was writing about them when they were still on the pub circuit. He followed their rise to fame, charting it, writing profiles of all the band members, interviewing them…"

"He was working on a book," said the Colonel.

"And now I'm working on that book," said Lucy Tegmark. "I want to write the masterpiece my father never completed. But I want it to go further than just being a mere biography of Valerian, a tale of her music and her band and how she lived and died." I noticed a barely perceptible tremor go across the Colonel's face at the word *died*. I knew what he was thinking and I didn't blame him.

It wasn't just the fact of her death. It was the way it had happened.

Lucy hadn't noticed. She was still droning on about this hypothetical book she was planning to write about Valerian, concluding by saying, "But the most important single thing I want to do is to resolve the question of her son's disappearance."

Yes, I thought, *that's going to be easy*.

I looked at the Colonel and said, "And she's interviewing you for the book?"

"No. I'm bankrolling the operation."

"So how do I come into it?" I said. "You're bankrolling her and she's researching it. What do you need me for?"

Lucy shifted in her chair. "I'm not an *investigative* journalist. I see myself as pulling the book together from a rich diversity of sources and writing it in a single authorial voice, once we have all the facts we need in front of us."

"So you want me to do the investigating?"

"They want you to be their legman," said Nevada happily. "He'll be a very good legman. He's got nice legs."

Lucy and the Colonel went out to have a bite of lunch while Nevada and I talked.

"I'm not sure I want to do this," I said.

"Did you hear her say money is no object?"

"Did you see the look he gave her when she said it?"

"Well, look or no look, we need funds."

I said, "I find records. I don't find people."

"You did a pretty good job of finding somebody last time."

"That was just a side effect of looking for a record. It was a happy accident."

"So why shouldn't there be another happy accident?"

I shook my head. "That little boy didn't just vanish into thin air. Somebody *took* him."

"Who?"

I shrugged. "Presumably the sort of people who take little boys. He was probably dead within twenty-four hours of being abducted. And that's if he was lucky. Any accidents in this situation aren't going to be happy ones."

"Poor kid," said Nevada. She stood up. "Well, just think about it. They won't be back from lunch for a while."

She smiled at me and then went out into the garden to use the phone, which was suspicious in itself. I went to the window. I could faintly hear her out there, just the buzz of her murmuring confidentially as she occasionally glanced my way. She was obviously up to something. She came in looking pleased with herself and walked through to the kitchen.

A minute later Turk came clattering in through the cat flap. She hurried over to the sofa to say hello to me. I held my hand in the air and she put her front paws on my knee and stretched up and brushed her head against my palm. She studied me for a moment, her extraordinary turquoise eyes gleaming on either side of her scarred nose. She was more of a roughneck than her sister, and that scarred muzzle gave her a piratical look. After a moment she turned away and hopped up onto the coffee table. She loved to lie stretched there for hours on end like a very large and furry ornament. Now she looked at me and flopped over on her back, legs akimbo and the white fur of her belly exposed for rubbing.

Only I wasn't looking at her fur. I was looking at the red plastic collar fastened around her neck. "Honey," I called.

"Yes?"

"Honey, you know we agreed that we wouldn't give the cats collars, because they're probably uncomfortable, and there's the remote hazard of them getting snagged on something?"

"Yes, yes, yes," said Nevada, coming in. "I remember all that. What on earth are you talking about?"

I pointed at the table. "Well, then, why did you put a collar on Turk?" She stared at the cat, and I stared at her.

I said, "You didn't put the collar on Turk, did you?"

"No."

Nevada bent down swiftly, examining the collar. "There's something under it," she said.

"Something *under* it?"

"A piece of paper," she said. "A note." She caressed Turk's head and then slipped her hand down to the collar and carefully extracted a folded square of white paper. She opened it and examined the other side, which was covered with writing.

"What is it?"

Nevada handed it to me. It read:

GREETINGS HIPSTER!

I HOPE YOU DON'T MIND ME USING FANNY TO SEND YOU MY LITTLE MESSAGE. FANNY MAIL! HA HA. SOUNDS A LOT MORE FUN THAN FAN MAIL! ANYWAY, NOW THAT I AM STAYING NEXT DOOR TO YOU I THOUGHT IT WOULD BE RUDE NOT TO SAY 'HI'. I CAN SEE YOUR HOUSE FROM HERE, AS THEY SAY. THAT'S RIGHT, I AM STAYING IN THE ABBEY. JUST A SHORT STAY FOR A BIT OF R R. I NEEDED A BREAK, SO HERE I AM. IT'S A GREAT PLACE. THE FOOD IS FANTASTIC. AND MY FELLOW GUESTS ARE AMAZING. SO MANY MUSIC GREATS. IT'S LIKE THE MERCURY AWARDS BUT WITHOUT THE CHARLIE,

HA HA! WHICH IS WHY I'M WRITING TO YOU. YOU WOULDN'T BELIEVE THE STORIES I'M HEARING IN HERE. THE GOSSIP, THE TIPS. AND THE CONTACTS I'M MAKING ARE MIND-BLOWING. IT'S THE MOST VALUABLE NETWORKING EVENT I EVER ATTENDED. I'VE GOT SCOOPS, EXCLUSIVES, INTERVIEWS THAT ARE SOLID GOLD. ENOUGH FOR A DOZEN TELEVISION PROGRAMMES. BUT I CAN'T USE ANY OF THEM! THERE'S NO INTERNET ACCESS HERE, NO PHONES, NO LETTERS ALLOWED IN OR OUT. THAT'S THE RULES. AND THERE'S NO CHANCE OF SMUGGLING ANYTHING OUT WITH THE STAFF. THEY'RE REALLY STRICT ABOUT THAT. SO I'M WRITING TO YOU, OLD CHUM. HERE'S THE DEAL. YOU BECOME MY PIPELINE! I SEND THE STORIES OUT TO YOU ON FANNY HERE (DO YOU LIKE HER COLLAR? I CHOSE THE NICEST COLOUR, HAD MY PA SEND IT TO ME) AND THEN YOU PASS THE STORIES TO MY OFFICE. I WILL MAKE IT WORTH YOUR WHILE. YES, MONEY AT LAST. I'LL SEND MY PA'S DETAILS ON THE NEXT NOTE. THANKS FOR YOUR HELP.

YOUR FRIEND, STINKY

P.S. GIVE NIRVANA MY LOVE.

We stared at each other. Nevada said, "Nirvana?"
"Apparently he thinks that's your name."
"The fucking halfwit. He can't even tell Fanny from Turk."

"He just guessed about the cat's name. He knew he had a fifty-fifty chance of being right. And he'd look smart if he got it right."

"He could never look smart."

I took out a pen.

"What are you doing?"

"Composing a reply." I turned the note over and wrote: *My cats hate you. How did you get close enough to one of them to put a collar on her?*

Nevada read over my shoulder and snorted with amusement. We folded the note up again and tucked it back under Turk's collar. Just then the doorbell rang, causing Turk to jump up, leap off the table and flee out of the cat flap in the back door—perhaps to relay our message to Stinky in the Abbey. While the cat was hastily absconding Nevada went and let our visitors in. "How was your lunch?" she said, ushering them into the sitting room.

"The burger wasn't bad," allowed the Colonel.

"The burger was fantastic," said Lucy Tegmark. "I saw how delicious it looked—I'd ordered the fish—"

"She likes to think she doesn't eat meat," said the Colonel, "but she eats more meat than any apex predator."

"He refused to even let me try a little piece of his burger."

"I'm not letting her eat the food off my plate," said the Colonel truculently, as though she was some kind of vile household pet.

"Well, so you liked your meal," said Nevada, pouring oil on the troubled waters.

"Yes. It was good. Thanks for the recommendation," said the Colonel. He looked at me. "I understand you're concerned because we haven't got a record for you to find?"

I could feel Nevada's gaze boring into the back of my head like a laser beam. "Well," I said, "I suppose, you see, it's normally my—"

"We've got a record for you to find," said the Colonel.

"What?"

"Don't misunderstand us," said Lucy Tegmark, interrupting the Colonel. "We still need you to discover what happened to little Tom Drummond. That's our ultimate objective. To discover the fate of the missing child. But the first step in doing this involves you finding a record."

"Oh, does it?" I said, glancing at Nevada. "It suddenly involves me finding a record, does it?" Nevada didn't meet my eye. She was too busy looking studiously innocent.

"It's a very rare and difficult to find record," said Lucy earnestly.

"I'm sure it is. What is it?" I was entirely certain this was something Nevada had cooked up on the phone with them, to make the deal more amenable to me.

"The 45rpm single," said the Colonel, "the one that was released to coincide with *All the Cats Love Valerian*. Do you know about that?"

I stared at him. Of course I knew about it. But I was surprised that he did. "Sure," I said, "it's even rarer than the LP. There's probably only a handful of copies still in existence." Despite myself I felt a familiar excitement stirring.

"Why is it so rare?" said Nevada.

"Because it was withdrawn from sale," I said. "Suppressed. They pulled it off the market before it even hit the shops."

"That doesn't sound like a particularly clever marketing strategy."

"They'd abandoned marketing strategies at that point. Valerian was dead and her son had gone missing and the record company was in damage limitation mode."

"What damage were they trying to limit?" said Nevada.

"Well, there was a rumour that Valerian had recorded a hidden message on the A-side of the single."

"What sort of a hidden message?"

I opened my mouth to say something about black magic, child sacrifice and ritual cannibalism, but I suddenly shut up.

The Colonel was staring at me hard.

It struck me for the first time in a non-abstract way that this was actually Valerian's brother, sharer of her flesh and blood, standing here in front of me. I felt a fleeting, enormous aftermath of the hallucinatory drug in my system. It burst on me like a giant flashbulb going off, lighting up everything in the room.

This bitter, hard and hardened man staring at me... he had once been a child and had grown up with her.

So I'd better steer clear of any off-colour remarks about how his sister was rumoured to have killed her only begotten son in a satanic ritual and then *eaten* him. Luckily, I was saved by Lucy Tegmark. She said, "At this point Valerian was being accused of witchcraft, of black magic, all kinds of occult nonsense. She's supposed to have recorded some kind of incantation or black mass or something. If you play the record backwards you can hear it."

"That's just one of the stories," I said. "There's a load of urban myths. No one knows the truth of it. The one persistent theme is that the hidden message alludes to the little boy's… disappearance."

"So it could be a valuable clue," said Nevada.

"Yes."

Nevada shook her head impatiently. "So, why don't we just listen to it and find out?"

"The single was recalled and destroyed. The record company panicked and snatched them back from the shops and melted them all down."

"Not *all* of them. Surely."

"All right, not all of them," I said. "Not every copy."

Nevada went over to the only shelf in the room that wasn't covered with books, records or cushions for the cats. It was the shelf where I kept my laptop and the wireless router. "Then surely someone somewhere has put a recording of it online."

"Oh, yes," said Lucy Tegmark. "There are plenty of them."

Nevada hesitated, turning away from the laptop. "Plenty?"

Lucy nodded. "Dozens. All different."

Nevada came back and sat down beside me. "So they're all fakes?"

I said, "Well, there's a maximum of one that might not be a fake."

"But no one knows which one that might be?"

"Exactly."

Lucy smiled. "So you see, the only way we have of finding out the truth is by getting a copy of the record and playing it ourselves."

Nevada grinned happily and turned to me. "And that's where you come in."

I looked at her. She had me. I looked at the Colonel and Lucy. They had me, too.

This is what I did.

And the truth was, I actually wanted to hear this record myself.

I wanted to find it.

5. MERCY KILLING

Lucy Tegmark handed me a sheet of paper. "These are details of people from my father's research. People who knew Valerian well or who were present at the time of the little boy's disappearance. Names and addresses and phone numbers."

I glanced at the sheet. There were only eleven people listed on it. Something of my disappointment must have registered in my face because the Colonel said, "Don't worry. There's more where that came from."

Lucy nodded. "There's a wealth of information in my father's papers."

"Well, it would be useful for me to have it," I said. "All of it. Anything you've got."

She kept nodding, all the more emphatically. "We're getting the papers copied for you."

"We're having them scanned," said the Colonel. "Onto a USB memory stick for you. And for us. It will be a damned sight easier than carrying around a huge wad of photocopied pages." He gave Lucy a look. "What would have made sense would have been to scan all the documents onto a USB memory stick in the first place." He really loved using that technical designation; I guess it made him feel young and with it. "Instead of photocopying all the damned things."

I could see that he'd managed to get under Lucy's skin. "How did you expect me to get them scanned in Morocco? They don't have the facilities there."

He snorted with contempt. "Of course they do."

"They're not as readily available."

"Of course they are."

"It was difficult enough getting the papers photocopied."

"Difficult for you," said the Colonel. "For you everything is difficult."

"You were in Morocco?" said Nevada hastily, the dove of peace flying bravely into the crossfire, olive branch firmly clutched in beak. She smiled dazzlingly at Lucy. "I bet it was beautiful."

"I live there," said Lucy Tegmark, staring coldly at the Colonel. "I've lived there virtually all my life. So I ought to know how problematical it is to get a large cache of documents digitally scanned."

"Nonetheless," said Nevada, still bravely trying, "it must be beautiful."

It went on like that for a while, with the Colonel and Lucy at each other's throats and Nevada doing her best to keep things civilised and calm. It was a relief when the two of them finally left. As soon as they were gone, Turk came trotting in.

She was a little shy of visitors and often lurked outside

until the coast was clear. She entered warily and then, as soon as she was certain it was just us here, she hopped up and lay down on the coffee table.

It was Nevada who spotted that she had a note under her collar.

She gently teased it out and showed it to me. It was the same note we'd sent back to Stinky, but with a new annotation. Just under where I'd written *My cats hate you. How did you get close enough to one of them to put a collar on her?*

It read:

FRESH SALMON.

And, pathetically:

PLEASE HELP.

Nevada read it with me then said, "Hang on just a minute." She went and rummaged in a drawer in the kitchen and came back clutching a thick-tipped red marker pen. She took the note and wrote across it in large letters, FUCK OFF STINKY. "Should I sign it *Nirvana*? Oh dear, I don't seem to have left enough room."

She folded the note and slipped it back under Turk's collar. Turk seemed to be getting used to the routine. "Good girl," said Nevada. "What a good girl. Our little postal pussycat."

* * *

I immediately got busy. I made some phone calls about the record, Valerian's great lost 45. Despite its enormous rarity I had a pretty good idea of someone who might have a copy—Freddie Fentyman, known universally in the record-collecting community as Freddie Forty-Five.

Having arranged the earliest possible visit to Freddie and his frankly huge collection of singles, I got on with the list of names Lucy and the Colonel had prepared for me. They included Valerian's publicist, her business manager (a woman—unusual back in those days), her lead guitarist, and a famed 1960s photographer who'd done a lot of work with the group.

This list had been compiled from sources long before the days of the Internet. Indeed, the London area codes on some of the telephone numbers were obsolete by decades. This didn't fill me with confidence about the up-to-date accuracy of the document as a whole, and sure enough it turned out that three of the people on it were long since dead and four had vanished. Of the remaining four I managed to track down some kind of contact number for three of them.

The first one I tried was Nic Vardy, the photographer who had shot the original cover for *All the Cats Love Valerian*. He had been one of the great photographers of the 1960s and I'd always admired his work. I was looking forward to meeting him, regardless of whether he had any useful information about the disappearance of Valerian's son.

Vardy was based in London—good man—and both his studio phone number and residential number were available from directory enquiries. I left him what I thought were friendly yet businesslike messages on both, but I got absolutely nowhere. I also tried email and leaving a message on the comment section of his website.

No response of any kind.

In the end I gave up and tried the other numbers, which belonged to the publicist, one Jack Welland, and the lead guitarist. The guitarist proved as much of a frustrating dead end as Nic Vardy.

But I eventually got lucky with Welland. The residential number I had been calling always went straight to voicemail after half a dozen rings, and I duly left messages but they went unanswered.

I kept trying, though, and finally got a different recording on the voicemail. Instead of inviting me to leave a futile message it offered an alternative number to ring. A mobile this time. I jotted it down, hung up, and immediately dialled the new number.

Welland answered on the first ring. I was so eager, having finally pinned him down, that I could hardly speak. But I managed to tell him I wanted to talk to him because I was researching Valerian for an article I was writing for my music blog. This was the story I'd decided on.

I wouldn't have thought it was such a big deal, but I was gratified to hear that he was virtually breathless with excitement at the prospect of being interviewed, and he instantly agreed to see me. Having set a date and time, I was willing to wrap up the conversation, but he wouldn't let me off the line. "You know how we met? Me and Valerian? We both bought our boots from Stan the Man in Battersea!

I met her over a pair of pointy-toed boots!" He was now breathless with nostalgia. "I knew her really well, Valerian. I know things about her, things nobody else knows."

I felt a little hollow thrill of anticipation.

I said, "Like what?"

"Like the father of her little boy. I could give you a fair idea of who that was." I could hardly believe what I was hearing. But then his voice changed. "Poor little boy," he murmured. "Poor little kid. What happened was so terrible…"

I could sense him beginning to have second thoughts, so I said a hasty goodbye and told him we'd be there to interview him as arranged. I briefed Nevada, who began to have fantasies about how much we could invoice the Colonel for.

But when I rang Welland's mobile the night before to confirm our appointment I got a new recorded message, in a new voice—an elderly woman. She said she regretted to inform the caller that Jack Welland was now deceased.

She gave the date and time of his demise in a dry, detached voice, and then the message stopped. The shock must have showed on my face as I hung up. "What is it?" said Nevada.

I told her. "He was going to tell us something. Something of vital importance. And now he's dead."

"I know what you're getting at," said Nevada calmly. "But don't you think you're jumping the gun a little?"

"No."

Just to prove her point Nevada insisted on calling Welland's mobile to get more details. I told her it was just a recorded message, but she persisted. And the next day she actually managed to get through to someone: the woman who had left the recorded obituary notice.

"It's Welland's mother," she told me. "He was no spring chicken himself, so she must be, let me see, at the very least in her eighties. But she's sharp as a needle. And do you know what she told me?" Nevada gave me an ironic look. I asked her to go on.

"Welland was in a hospice. Terminally ill. Some kind of respiratory condition. He was due to go any time."

So he hadn't been breathless with excitement.

And there was nothing suspicious about the circumstances of his death.

That seemed like that. Then, two days later, I was on a train between Putney and Barnes and I noticed a newspaper lying abandoned on the seat opposite me. The headline that caught my eye was MERCY KILLING AT HOSPICE?

The story went on to detail how the apparently natural death of a terminally ill patient at a hospice in east London had been discovered to have in fact been an unlawful killing. The patient—Jack Welland, of course—had been suffocated with a pillow.

This was only discovered because a medical student was working in the hospice to earn some extra money. He had seen the body and recognised what were described in the story as the 'telltale bloodshot eyes' and also noticed that the deceased's dental bridge had been dislodged, as if someone had forced something over his face. Tiny rips in the pillow of the victim (he had been promoted to a victim by this point in the article) matched the metal work on the bridge. He'd had his mouth open wide and had been struggling as the pillow was held over his face.

Terminally ill as he was, Jack Welland had been in no hurry to die.

6. LAST RESORT

That night in bed Nevada said, "There's something fishy. And before you worry, that's not a remark about anyone's personal hygiene."

"Not even the cats?"

"Not even the cats." She rolled over and we curled together, the long, lithe, nude length of her warm against me. "It's about this record," she said.

"Valerian's single?"

"Yes. You made such a song and dance about how rare it is…"

"It is. It's almost impossible to find a copy. It's difficult enough locating a rare album, but a single is much more problematical."

"Why?"

"Singles are smaller. They often don't come in a picture sleeve, but just a generic wrapper, or if you're really unlucky just a blank paper sleeve. And they don't have a spine."

"Spineless, eh?" said Nevada.

"Yes, literally. So they're constantly being misfiled or misplaced. Even people who think they know what they have don't know what they have. The land of the 45rpm record is the land of chaos."

"So I begin to see."

"For all these reasons, singles are ten times as hard to find as LPs. And when the record is rare to start with, as in the case of Valerian…"

"It's almost impossible to find."

"Yes."

Nevada rolled over, leaning on her elbow and looking at me. "And yet," she said. "And yet I don't sense any hopelessness in your voice."

"Don't you?"

"Not even any fashionable cynicism."

"Oh dear."

"In fact what I sense, when you expound at such great length on just how fucking impossible it is to find this record of Valerian's, is quiet *confidence*."

I smiled in the darkness. She could see right through me. "That's because I think I know someone who's got a copy," I said.

"Well, why haven't we gone to this person and obtained the record?"

"Because he's currently out of the country. But he's due back soon."

"Excellent," said Nevada. She was silent and I began to drift off to sleep. Then she said, "Do you really think he was murdered?"

For a second I didn't know who she was talking about. Then it came back to me. Jack Welland, with the pillow pressed down over his face as he struggled in his hospice bed. Someone had stolen what few days he had left.

I had told Nevada all about it.

Now I shook my head, lying beside her in the dark. "I don't know. I mean, I'm damned sure he was killed by someone. I just can't be sure..."

"Whether it's got anything to do with our case?"

I said, "We're calling it a case now, are we?"

"Yes."

I went back to the list of names that Lucy and the Colonel had given us. The only real leads I had left were the elusive photographer and the guitarist. Theoretically at least, I had phone numbers for both of them. But there was no luck with either. The bastards just wouldn't get back to me. It was like running into a brick wall.

And, unlike searching for records, when you need to speak to a particular person, you can't respond to failure by going out in search of another copy.

I was soon frustrated and seething with subdued rage. No one likes to be ignored.

My mood didn't go unremarked by Nevada. "Don't worry," she said soothingly, taking the sheet of paper, by now covered with my scribbled emendations and the occasional angry obscenity. "Let me have a go." She studied the list. "Both blokes," she said, and smiled at me. "Let me work my charms."

This seemed like a good idea, not least since I'd run out of alternative strategies. The next day she began working the phones. By mid morning she was as pissed off as I'd been. "What is it with these people?" she said. "Do they think they're too good to talk to us?"

We went to bed that night in matching moods of gloom. The following morning I woke up to hear delicate slurping sounds from the direction of the bathroom.

"Turk's drinking from her bowl," said Nevada, lying beside me. "Isn't that sweet?" Fanny would only drink from a running tap but Turk liked to go to her bowl first thing in the morning, when she had returned from a busy night of rodent hunting. She often followed up her drink by triumphantly bringing a dead mouse into the bedroom and presenting it to us—or rather, showing it to us and snarling if we made any move to take it from her before she had disembowelled it and, if we were lucky, devoured it from the end of its perky nose to the tip of its cute little tail.

This morning she didn't have a mouse. But she did have a slip of paper under her collar. Nevada sighed and extracted it. "It's Stinky again, of course," she said, reading the note.

"What does he have to say?"

"Just the same as before. Begging us to act as what he calls his pipeline for what he calls his scoops. He's offering you what he describes as handsome sums of money and he's still calling me Nirvana."

"I could never take his money."

"I'm so glad you said that." Nevada rolled over and kissed me. Then she wadded the note and threw it into the corner.

Turk went streaking after it, found it and started batting it around the floor with her paws. "Anyway," said Nevada, "you've already got a paying job. Finding a missing person."

"At this rate we'll be lucky to get paid," I said. "Judging by the lack of responses and my complete failure to get an appointment with any of those fuckers, I'm never going to—" I fell silent, suddenly thinking.

Nevada was looking at me. "What is it?"

"Stinky," I said.

"What about him?"

"He can help."

"You have to be joking," said Nevada, sitting up so she could look down at me and make sure I was not, in fact, joking.

"No," I said. I began to grin. The notion was growing on me. "God help us, but we can use his help."

"What help? How?"

"I hate to admit it," I said, "but he has an entrée into a world that is closed to us."

Now Nevada was smiling as she stared down at me. "The world of music."

"Rock and roll," I said. I sat up beside her. "It might just work." We got up and found some paper and a pen and between us composed the note over breakfast. "Tell him we don't want money," I said.

"We want access to his contacts," said Nevada.

"Right. And we want this personal assistant of his to be at our beck and call."

"Brilliant. I've always wanted someone at my beck and call. The only thing is, I don't feel entirely happy about the other side of the deal. Being his conduit for god-knows-what salacious gossip and celebrity tattle. Who knows what malicious blether he intends to spew into the world?"

"Well," I said, "the only way he can get any writing out is past us. If we don't like what he writes we'll just change it or discard it."

"You mean we exert editorial control?" said Nevada, and grinned. "Well, that's a different kettle of cat biscuits. Of fish. Of fish-flavoured cat biscuits."

When we were finished with the note we folded it up and tucked it under Turk's collar. We got Stinky's reply—and his eager, not to say obsequious, consent—in a note that came back that afternoon.

"By return of post," said Nevada. "Or rather, return of puss." She caressed Turk and poured her a bowl of biscuits while I rang Stinky's PA.

The following day we had our first appointment.

7. DOCKLAND DUCKS

Nevada spent two and a half hours choosing what we were going to wear to our meeting. Half an hour was devoted to me, two hours to her.

I said, "Am I to interpret this as a measure of our relative importance?"

"You're to interpret it as a measure of how much more fucking clothing I have than you," said Nevada, frowning furiously at three different tops spread out on the bed. She discarded one and added two more. I was scrupulously saying nothing but I might have glanced at the clock. She turned to me and said, "Don't you think it's important that we look the part? I mean, we're supposed to be media achievers at the cutting edge of contemporary culture."

"Since we're also supposed to be working for Stinky Stanmer you might have slightly overstated the case."

Finally she chose a top and her ensemble was complete. Now all we had to do was feed the cats, brief them, and then get out the door.

Briefing the cats had begun as a joke by me. Sometimes when I was going out I'd tell the cats where I was going and what time they could expect me back. However, Nevada had latched on to this and now it had become a matter of official policy, with the force of law. You don't go out without telling the cats.

Nevada poured biscuits into their bowls. "Now, girls," she said, "we're going out to Canary Wharf and we may not be back until late—if I can convince this cheapskate to take me to a movie." Fanny and Turk sat looking up at her. Fanny was stationed on the floor by the refrigerator, Turk sprawling on the counter by the sink. They might even have been patiently listening.

On the other hand, perhaps they were hoping that the strange noises would lead to more food.

"And perhaps a little light shopping," added Nevada, putting the bag of cat biscuits back in the cupboard.

"No shoes," I said.

"You don't have to worry about that. There are no charity shops in Docklands." Then she stopped and smiled a sunny smile, perhaps contemplating the inevitable collapse of capitalism. "At least not yet."

We strolled across the common and caught the train to Waterloo, then walked through the cavernous modernist spaces of the station to the gleaming entrance to the Jubilee Line, the newest and shiniest segment of London's underground railway. "You know what I like best about the Jubilee Line?" said Nevada, as we descended to the eastbound spur.

"The fact that it features sliding Perspex doors that seal the passengers on the platform away from the track and thereby prevent annoying suicides that slow everybody down?"

"No, but that's now my *new* favourite thing about it."

The train carried us east into the heart of Docklands. We got out at Canary Wharf and rode the long escalator up into daylight. Turning away from the water, we walked through Jubilee Park, a small green rectangle of grass and trees that had been mercifully spared by the skyscraper enthusiasts. Nevada took my arm.

"This is where I'm proposing we have lunch afterwards. Get some sandwiches and eat them here."

"So long as we're not attacked by pigeons. Or bankers."

We walked across Grime Street—a reassuring name amidst this mass of gleaming glass and polished steel—and back towards the water. We walked along Montgomery Street paralleling the water, then crossed it, past another block of glass skyscrapers to Cartier Circle, a rather more appropriate name for the neighbourhood.

I was wondering about property prices as we came to a large open expanse of water with houseboats tethered in it and, facing the marina, a small residential street.

"How much do you suppose it costs for one of these bijou residences?" said Nevada.

"I was just wondering exactly that."

"Nic Vardy can't be hurting for a few bob."

"Photographing the rich and famous must have worked out for him."

"The rich and famous and album covers," said Nevada.

We came to the house on the corner, which was Vardy's address. Actually 'house' doesn't quite describe it. It was a sizable two-level apartment occupying a large part of the first two floors of—wait for it—a glass skyscraper.

It had floor-to-ceiling windows, some of which were sealed from view with floor-to-ceiling blinds in primary colours. This gave the place the look of a Mondrian canvas from the outside while offering, from the inside, a dramatic view of the water.

We checked the address we had against the number of the front door, which was a big slab of pale wood varnished to reveal the beauty of its grain. There was a peephole at eye level and a bell just below it.

Nevada and I looked at each other. She straightened my lapel and gave me a brisk kiss and then we rang the bell. It echoed in the depths of the house. We waited. Then we waited some more.

"Do you think we should knock?" said Nevada.

"On the principle that he might have some kind of selective deafness that renders him unable to hear the doorbell, but able to hear a knock?"

Nevada shrugged. I knocked. Nothing.

"Well, we're early," said Nevada.

I checked the time. "No we're not."

"Well, we're not late. Which by the standards of these people is early."

"Which people are these?"

"The fashionable people," said Nevada. "They're fashionably late."

I checked the time again. "Well, if he doesn't get a move on he's going to be unfashionably late."

Nevada sighed and we waited. And waited. What else could we do?

We wandered to the edge of the water and stared out over the marina. "It's a lovely day," said Nevada in a determinedly cheerful voice. I could tell that, deep down, she was as doubtful as I was that this fucker was going to turn up for our appointment. I gazed out at some birds splashing happily in the water. At least they were enjoying themselves.

I said, "Should we phone him?"

"Give him a little longer."

We gave him a lot longer. I began to get pissed off and Nevada set about distracting me. "Shall we see a film here afterwards? They have a cinema at West India Quay. We can choose a film to see." She took out her smartphone. "Let's see what's on."

This was a clever move, because there was no way I was going to let her choose a film without my input. Nevada shared my love of movies but, fatally, she was a sucker for anything esoteric, pretentious or subtitled—any two out of three would do. This penchant of hers had led to many an enjoyable shared experience in the cinema. It had also, on occasion, led to us sitting, interminably sitting, through what I now liked to recall—indeed only could recall—as the Sicilian movie about goat milking with the giant vegetables.

"Here, let me see what's on," I said quickly.

But even bickering about our choice of film could only occupy so much time. Soon enough we found ourselves again standing outside Nic Vardy's empty house, waiting in the cold breeze blowing off the water. I gazed out at the marina to hide my anger.

"Ring him," I said, finally.

Near the houseboats, the birds were busy ducking and diving. A lone man leaned against the railing watching them. "No reply," said Nevada. "Went straight to voicemail." A passenger jet trundled high overhead, leaving a glistening white vapour trail. "What should we do?" The man moved closer to the birds and something gleamed in his hands. At first I thought he was feeding them, but then I realised he was holding a camera. He was photographing the birds. "Should we wait?"

I turned to Nevada and shrugged. "What else can we do?"

The birds, perhaps disturbed by the man's attention, lifted, flapping from the water, flew a short distance and settled in the water again, virtually at our feet. They were sleek black birds with white trim and striking red-orange beaks with white tips.

"Aren't they lovely?" said Nevada, eager to forestall any suggestions from me that we should just go home and call it a day. Which I was indeed just on the verge of offering.

I watched the birds with her for a while. "We've got some ducks like that on our estate," I said. "They swim in Beverley Brook."

"They're not ducks," said a voice. "They're moorhens." We turned to see the man standing there. He had walked the length of the marina and joined us. He was dressed all in black with a neat black corduroy cap. His hair and Van Dyke beard were also jet black, and dramatically angular, giving him a cultivated satanic appearance. The camera was hanging on a strap around his neck. It was an old-fashioned but very expensive- and professional-looking analog camera.

A camera.

Finally I put two and two together. "Nic Vardy," I said.

"Of course," said Nevada, "Mr Vardy."

"We had an appointment," I said. But before I could indicate my displeasure at being kept waiting, Nevada took his hand and said, "We are *so* pleased to see you."

"Sorry, I'm running a little late," said Vardy over his shoulder as he walked to the door of his house. As off-hand apologies went, this one took the cake. He was more than a little late, and if he'd known he was running late why had he paused to photograph waterfowl? These and other thoughts ran through my mind as he opened the door and we followed him inside. Nevada must have sensed my mood because she shot me a warning look as he closed the door behind us. Despite the austere glass and steel of the place, it was warm and snug inside.

"It's the white spot at the tip of the beak that gives them away," said Vardy, taking off his cap and coat. He looked at me in case I didn't get it. "The moorhens." He hung up his cap and coat then turned and walked upstairs and left us to decide whether we should also take off our coats and hang them up or scamper immediately after him. We followed him up the stairs and into a long lounge with a wide window overlooking the water. The white wall at the back of the room, facing the window, was hung with photographs in chrome frames. All of these, I assumed, were his own handiwork.

Vardy settled onto a green leather sofa, sprawling in the centre of it with arms spread wide across the back. This left us to sit in two red leather armchairs, spaced widely apart, facing him. *Divide and conquer*, I thought. We unbuttoned our coats and sat down. We were sitting either side of him but Vardy continued to stare straight ahead, through the window, not looking at either of us. Apparently we weren't sufficiently important to make eye contact.

"So, how can I help?"

Well, for a start by looking at us when you talk to us, I thought. But I didn't say anything. I didn't trust myself to. Instead I took a cue from our host and avoided looking at his face, studying the wall behind him. To my surprise, considering the number of celebrities Vardy had snapped over the years, all of the photographs were of animals.

Birds, in fact.

"Well," said Nevada, "as you know, we're researching a programme for Stinky Stanmer Enterprises, concerning the singer Valerian."

"Valerian?" said Nic Vardy. "Why?"

"Well," said Nevada, "because she's a fascinating figure in the history of rock music. Of British rock music." She flashed me a look to make sure she wasn't getting any of this too wrong. "A great singer. A great British singer. And a fascinating personality."

"I mean, why now?" said Vardy.

"Why now?" repeated Nevada.

Vardy sighed, a tired, disgusted sigh as though he was watching someone take a piss off one of the houseboats into the beautiful blue water of his marina. "There has to be a hook. You people always have to have a hook for these things. What is the occasion?"

"The occasion…" said Nevada, desperately playing for time.

Vardy shook his head. "You people love anniversaries. There's no anniversary coming up; not of Valerian's birthday, not of the formation of the band…" He obviously had a very good memory for dates and Nevada had just strayed into quicksand.

I did a quick calculation in my head. "It's the anniversary of the album being released," I said. "Their last album. *All the Cats Love Valerian*." Nevada gave me a quick look of profound gratitude. And of course it was also the anniversary of Valerian's death. But something stopped me saying that.

Vardy considered this, then nodded. "All right, so what do you want from me?"

"Your thoughts and memories," said Nevada.

He turned and looked directly at her for the first time. He smiled. It wasn't a pleasant smile. "My thoughts and memories."

"Concerning Valerian," I said. "You knew her quite well."

"I wouldn't say that." He was staring out the window again. He shook his head. "I wouldn't say that at all."

"But you took all those marvellous pictures of her," said Nevada. "Like that wonderful cover photo for *All the Cats Love Valerian*."

Vardy shrugged. "Just because you take someone's

picture doesn't mean you know anything about them. In a way, you know less about them after you've photographed them. Because in the act of taking the photograph you've abstracted something. You've taken something away."

This was clearly a pet theory of his, and I hoped that by airing these cherished vapourings he was beginning to open up to us. But he immediately fell silent again.

"I really love that photo," said Nevada, gently nudging him back into conversation. But he just smiled a thin smile and stared out at the water. "I believe it was banned," said Nevada. "The album was banned because of that cover image."

"That's right."

"We're particularly interested in the final weekend of her life," I said. He turned and stared at me. Ah, eye contact at last. I could see that Nevada wasn't sure I should have said this, but what the hell. There seemed little point pussyfooting around, not least since the bastard didn't appear inclined to give us any help anyway.

"Why?" he said.

"Because it obviously ties in with the recording of the last album," said Nevada hopefully. Vardy looked at her, then at me. He was grinning aggressively now. He glanced towards the stairway, the exit, and I realised we were on the verge of being invited to leave the house.

"So," he said, "it wouldn't be anything to do with a lurid desire to rake up a lot of old muck and slime about how she died and what happened to her poor kid, to put it in this programme of yours and exploit it all and wring out the last fucking drop of blood and pain and suffering?"

There was a long, tense silence during which Nevada and I looked at each other. I took a deep breath and turned to him and said, "Well, of course that's exactly Stinky's angle, because that's the kind of pinhead he is." Vardy had been moving forward on the sofa, shifting his weight as he was about to come to his feet. But this stopped him in his tracks.

"Pinhead?" he said.

"Oh yes," said Nevada, nimbly joining in. "What an insufferable jerk."

He looked at us, a little bewildered, and settled back down onto the sofa. "I thought you said you work for him."

Nevada smiled. "Work *with* him."

He stared at me. "What exactly do the two of you do?"

"I'm the senior researcher," I said.

"And I'm the producer," said Nevada. Of course she had to be one rung up the ladder from me. He was staring at her and to my amazement and relief I could see that he was beginning to buy it.

"But don't you have to…" he gestured vaguely with his hands, "at least *pretend* to respect him, his opinions, Stinky Stanmer?"

"Oh no, we're very forthright about that," said Nevada. "We're more like independent consultants for Mr Stanmer rather than his wage slaves."

Vardy shook his head, grinning happily. "I assumed if you were working for the guy you would at least have to pretend to respect him."

"Not at all," said Nevada breezily.

"But I'm afraid we still have to pursue the angle of the

last weekend of her life," I said.

Nevada nodded, right on cue. "They're very insistent on that. Stinky and his cabal. You know the disgusting bloodlust of these people. They always want to sensationalise."

"Although we're going to strongly recommend to the network that we don't go that way," I added.

Nevada nodded again. "That's right. We'll do our best to curb his vile impulses. You know what Stinky's like."

Vardy nodded like he did. He looked at us and got to his feet. "Okay. Let me see what I can dig out. Follow me. Can I get you something to drink?" We followed him, Nevada beaming at me and silently mouthing the words, *Something to drink.*

We had evidently all bonded over our hatred of Stinky.

Vardy's work room was south-facing and full of light. There was a desk at one end with a computer on it and the rest of the room was crowded with the kind of low table-surfaced cupboards with flat drawers, called plan chests, that you find in architectural practices. The walls in here were also lined with photographs of birds.

Now that I had a chance to look at them more closely I was impressed. They caught quite strikingly the magnificence of these creatures, freezing them in moments of characteristic motion and casual splendour. They were beautiful.

At the far end of the room, incongruously, there was a locked glass case with half a dozen expensive shotguns in it. Vardy caught me looking at them and said, "I was a kid from the East End who got rich very quickly and fell in with the wrong people." He grinned at me. "Bankers and stockbrokers and managing directors. I started smoking their cigars and drinking their whisky and going with them to their houses on the weekends. The green wellies brigade. And we used to go shooting. I loved getting up early and the fresh air and the cold and the feeling of excitement. And those birds looked so beautiful, flying, just before we knocked them out of the fucking sky." He shook his head ruefully. "I hated killing the birds, but I loved everything else about it. Finally the penny dropped and I realised I could keep the bit I loved and get rid of the bit I hated."

"By photographing the birds instead of shooting them," said Nevada.

"That's right, shooting them with a camera." He sighed. "You would have thought a fucking photographer could have worked that out a little more quickly." He touched the lock on the glass case. "Never shot one since. Not a living animal." He turned to us. "Still do a little skeet shooting, though."

"I hope you wear your ear defenders," said Nevada.

He smiled at her. Nevada's nefarious charm was finally starting to penetrate his defences. "Yeah I do," he said. "Now, let's see, Valerian…" He prowled between the rows of plan chests, checking the labels on the drawers. "I've had some interns in here, sorting everything out. The big project these days of course is making digital scans of all my slides and negatives. So I've got some young and enthusiastic help." He suddenly turned and squatted by one of the chests, then shook his head. "Nope." He rose and continued prowling.

"You don't have to show us the photographs immediately," said Nevada. "You could just talk to us about those days…"

"I *do* have to show you the photographs, darling," said Vardy. "Otherwise I won't be able to remember anything to talk about. It's a funny thing. They say smell is the strongest stimulator for memory, but for me it's definitely a visual thing." He paused, then crouched down again. "Here," he said, pulling out a drawer. "Valerian."

We went over to join him. "That's odd," he said. Looking over his shoulder we could see the white surface of the empty drawer, with just one photograph, about eight by ten inches, lying face-down in it. "They should all be in here." I felt my stomach shrink into a cold knot.

Vardy shut the drawer again and checked the label. "No. Definitely in here." He pulled open the drawer again. Still just the one photo. He looked up at us with a contrite little smile. "One of my interns must have moved them."

"Why would they have done that?" I tried to keep my tone casual, but paranoia had by now become an occupational hazard. Vardy shrugged.

"Oh, they might be in the middle of scanning them. Like I told you." He moved to shut the drawer again, but Nevada stopped him. "May I have a look?" she said. She indicated the one photo lying face-down in the drawer. He picked it up and handed it to her.

It was black and white, a head and shoulders shot of a smiling woman with an elfin face, turning to look at the camera, caught in a moment of surprise.

Her pale hair was streaming around her face and she looked young and beautiful.

"She's lovely, isn't she?" said Nevada. He nodded and she handed the photo back to him. "And that's the only photo of Valerian you have to hand?"

"That isn't Valerian," said Vardy. "It's her sister."

"Her sister?" Nevada looked at me.

"Cecilia," I said. "She used to play piano in the band and sing backing vocals." I didn't add that this was before her slide into mental illness. They'd been an ill-fated family.

"They look a lot alike," said Vardy, putting the photo back in the drawer and sliding it shut.

"Why didn't you tell me Valerian had a sister?" said Nevada.

"It didn't come up."

"Surely we should be interviewing *her*?"

"She died a few years ago."

"Even so, I should have known that she once existed. I was in grave danger of looking like a fool in there." She glanced behind us at the marina and the street with Vardy's house on the corner. We were taking a stroll back through Harbour Quay, heading for Canary Wharf, with the wind whipping cold off the water around us. I noticed that the moorhens had scarpered.

"Don't worry," I said, "once he realised the depth of your loathing for Stinky you could do no wrong."

"Yes, he seemed like quite an agreeable chap once we established that common ground." As reluctant as I was to agree with her after his initial rudeness, Vardy had indeed ended up being quite affable. He'd dug out some bread and cheese and even a bottle of what Nevada had identified quietly as a very good wine—already opened, I'd observed, and resealed with a vacuum stopper, but nonetheless a very good wine.

And he had seen us off with a promise to find the photos or send us the digital scans. "Meanwhile I'll dig out my contact sheets," he'd said. "Those should jog my memory." He'd even waved goodbye and hadn't slammed the door behind us.

"Not a complete shit, anyway," I said.

Nevada grinned. "You're still angry at him, aren't you?"

"I'm slow to forgive."

"Still, an interesting bloke, you must admit."

"He's very well preserved, for his age," I allowed. "His hair and loathsome little goatee are still black."

Nevada snorted at my designation of his goatee. "He dyes it."

"Really?" I said. "You're kidding."

"No. Not short of vanity, our Mr Vardy. So what now? Do we wait for him to dig out his photos and jog his memories? Or do we move to the next name on our list?"

"Neither," I said. "We go after the record. Valerian's notorious lost single."

"The one you said you know where there's a copy of it?" She paused. "Is that even a sentence? Not in English."

I nodded. "The guy who might have a copy is back from abroad. We'll go and see him."

"Excellent. And this is the record with the satanic incantation recorded on it backwards?"

"That's the one."

Nevada took my arm and gathered herself more closely to me in the teeth of the chill wind. "So, do I need to bring my crucifix and holy water?"

"It couldn't do any harm."

8. THE SINGLES BARN

"Here's what I want for driving you," said Tinkler.

Nevada shook her head sadly. "I thought you were doing it out of the goodness of your heart."

I said, "I knew there had to be a condition."

"Just so we're absolutely clear on this," continued Tinkler, "I'm only doing you this enormous favour because I expect to be handsomely rewarded in return."

"Exactly what kind of reward do you expect, handsome?" Nevada was leaning forward from the back seat, towards where Tinkler and I sat in the front, so we could hear her over the roar of the engine and howling of the wind that battered the little car.

"Well," said Tinkler, "I was thinking along the lines of you asking Nic Vardy for an original print of his photo for the cover of *All the Cats Love Valerian*."

"Us asking?"

"Yes. My god, *I* couldn't ask him. I don't know him."

"You want an original print?" I said.

"I'm going to frame it and hang it on my wall," said Tinkler happily.

I shook my head. "You don't know what this Vardy character is like."

"He's a brilliant photographer."

"He's a right difficult bastard is what he is."

"Don't worry," said Nevada. "I'll have him wrapped around my little finger in next to no time. Just you wait and see."

"Then you can ask him for me," said Tinkler.

"Let me get this straight," I said. "You just expect Nic Vardy to give you one of his original photographic prints?"

Tinkler frowned thoughtfully as he drove. "It's hard to say exactly what constitutes 'original' in the context of a photographic print. Wouldn't you agree?"

"And you want this in return for driving us?"

"That's not all," said Tinkler. "After you get the copy of 'Butterfly Dreams'—"

"Is that the name of the single?" said Nevada. "The title, I mean?"

"Yes."

"'Butterfly Dreams'. I like it."

"Millions of stoned hippies would no doubt have shared your opinion, if only they'd been given a chance to listen to it," said Tinkler. "Anyway, when you get it from Freddie Forty-Five I would like it for myself. When you're finished with it."

I said, "What do you mean, when we're finished with it? We're buying it for the Colonel."

"Yes, but he wants it—you all want it—so you can hear whatever secret sinister message is recorded on it, right?"

"Right, okay, but—"

"So when you're finished listening to the message, let me have it and I can listen to the music. The music that comes before and after the sinister message. I mean the *whole thing's* not a sinister message, is it?"

"No, I guess not."

"So I might as well make use of the parts you're not interested in." Tinkler slowed for a red light. He was grinning placidly, evidently pleased with the elegant nature of his own logic.

"You want to add it to your collection, I assume."

"Oh yes," he said. "So, are we clear? When you're finished with the record, give it to me."

"*Give* it to you?"

"Well, the Colonel won't need it anymore and he can resell it to me at a really knocked down rate. Or, preferably, as I suggest, give it to me gratis. In any case, I'll be happy to take it off his hands. Your hands. Anybody's hands."

Nevada sighed, "We'll see what we can do, Tinkler."

We drove out of London past the art deco elegance of the old Hoover Building and droned up the M11 towards Cambridge, turning off at Saffron Walden. Then we wound around the secondary roads, passing through smaller and smaller towns and then finally villages. We cruised past autumn fields and an old church, finally ending up on a winding rural lane.

"We're here," I said.

We drove in through a narrow wooden gateway between hedges with a sign on the side that said ST JUDE'S COTTAGE. As we crunched up the driveway we saw another sign that said THE SINGLES BARN.

Then one that said TRESPASSERS WILL BE GOOSED.

The gravel drive ran in a straight line from the gateway then opened up in a broad circle around a patch of unruly long grass with a pond in the centre of it, reflecting the milky afternoon sky. An elegant old Victorian park bench, painted green, looked out on the pond. We parked in a paved area on the left of the farmhouse. Over on the right, beyond some gardens, was the barn.

I say 'gardens' plural because the place was a patchwork grid of them. It had once been farmland but now the fields around the dwellings had been subdivided into small units of hand-cultivated land. Some were planted with flowers and decorative shrubs, still showing a surprising amount of colour this late in the year. Others were devoted to fruit or vegetables. They were all irregular, interlocking shapes, like a jigsaw puzzle with its pieces set loosely together. Crazy curves of gravel paths led between them. The effect was less that of an ornamental garden than a very bohemian kibbutz.

We got out and stretched our legs.

"This is brilliant," said Nevada, looking around. "I love this place. Can we explore?"

"Actually," I said—and just then her phone rang. She checked the number and showed me. Nic Vardy.

"I'd better take this," she said, moving away from the car.

Of course… I remembered we'd given Vardy our numbers yesterday and asked him to get in touch when he'd succeeded in finding some of his photos of Valerian and/or managed to jog his memory of events of that last fateful weekend when Valerian had died and her little boy had vanished.

I'd never actually expected to hear from him again, so this was a result. While Nevada was talking I went to the door of the farmhouse and knocked. Tinkler came and hovered at my shoulder. "Is no one in?" he said anxiously.

"Give them a chance," I said, and knocked again.

"Aren't they *supposed* to be in?"

"Yes." I knocked again. I was beginning to have a terrible sense of déjà vu.

"I don't think they're in," said Tinkler.

"No." We turned away from the front door and walked back onto the driveway. Nevada finished her call and looked at me. "That was old dye-job Vardy."

"So I gather."

"He's managed to dig up a few pictures, just a few so far, but he's sending them to us."

"That's nice of him," I said.

"They're not actually of Valerian."

"No, of course not."

"So, no nudes?" said Tinkler despondently.

"No," said Nevada. "And before you ask, no I didn't have a chance to ask him about your print. The time didn't seem right."

"Fair enough," said Tinkler, stretching and yawning.

"He told me they weren't actually pictures of Valerian

herself," Nevada continued, "but they were all, as he put it, relevant. Ah, here are the images now." She watched her phone for a moment, then showed it to us. The first picture was the one we had already seen of Cecilia, Valerian's sister. The next one was of a very skinny and very hairy young man in a tie-dyed tank top intently playing an electric guitar. It was a moody black and white shot, full of energy.

"That's a classic." Tinkler studied it happily.

"Who is he?" asked Nevada.

"Eric McCloud," I said. "Lead guitarist in the band. Valerian nicknamed him Eric Make Loud and he adopted it. That's what he's called himself ever since."

"Except now he spells Erik with a 'k'," said Tinkler. "Because he thinks it makes him sound more like a Teutonic heavy metal guitar god."

"Is he a complete tosser?" said Nevada. "He sounds like a complete tosser."

Tinkler shook his head vigorously. "On the contrary. He is a guitar god. He played with Zappa."

"Oh well, if he played with Zappa," said Nevada, scrolling through the photos on her screen. There were six more shots of Erik Make Loud in action, taken at various gigs. She moved through these quickly then stopped at the next image, which was of a gravestone in a rural churchyard. It was covered with bouquets of flowers, candles, photographs, scraps of writing, condolence cards, toys, dolls and teddy bears, wine and spirit bottles and sad little offerings of food.

"This one is self-explanatory," she said. "Her grave,

yes? The poor thing. And they've turned it into a shrine, her fans." She looked at me. "Where is this?"

"Canterbury," I said. "That's where her family came from. The Drummonds."

"And it's where the band came from," said Tinkler. "They were part of the Canterbury scene."

"It's so sad, isn't it?" she said, peering at the picture.

"We have a shrine like that near where we live," I said. "In Gipsy Lane. For Marc Bolan."

"Except that's to mark the spot where he actually died," said Tinkler.

"Or at least where his car crashed."

"All right, anyway, so that one's self-explanatory." Nevada flipped to the next photo. "But what is this?" She showed it to me. Another moody black and white composition, a study in contrasts. But this one was a landscape shot of a mammoth gnarled oak tree looming in shadow, as full of sinister character as anything ever drawn by Arthur Rackham. Nevada looked at me. "Why has he sent a picture of a tree?"

A sound suddenly arose on the other side of the farmhouse, in the direction of the barn. It was a furious, diabolical honking, quite savage and almost machine-like in its intensity. For a moment none of us knew what the hell was happening and then, dashing along the winding path between two vegetable plots, came the rotund white shape of a goose, wings spread wide in a display of aggression. It ran off the path and onto the driveway and came straight at us, running with big flapping steps of its clumsy feet, neck extended and head held high.

We began to back away as it came surging and flailing towards us. It honked again, a nerve-shredding shriek like a steam whistle on steroids. It sounded angry.

"Holy shit," said Nevada in alarm. We all turned and fled, taking shelter on the far side of Tinkler's car.

"They weren't kidding about getting goosed," said Tinkler.

The goose came to a wary halt beside the car, peering around at us with its long neck extended. Its gaze looked strangely cross-eyed, which did nothing to diminish the alarming nature of its appearance. Or rather, *her* appearance.

"Hello, Gwenevere," I said, "don't you remember me?" I took a tentative step out from the shelter of the car and moved towards her, hand extended. *See? I come in peace.*

She surged forward, bristling with hostility, and I jerked back.

"Evidently not," murmured Nevada.

We stayed put, the three of us huddled behind the minimal shelter of Tinkler's car, and Gwenevere began to behave like she'd cornered us there. Which, thinking about it, I suppose she had. She strutted around, keeping an eye on us, never venturing far from the car and the spot where we cowered. After sizing us up from a variety of angles, that eager, watchful head extended on its long neck, she settled down into a rhythm of patrol. She was on guard, marching around us in an exaggerated military fashion for all the world like a Nazi stormtrooper; it made you realise how accurate the term 'goose stepping' was.

"Can we get into the car?" suggested Nevada.

"I think the moment we begin to move, she's going to charge at us."

"This is just like that novel by Stephen King," said Tinkler. "Except it's a stupid goose instead of a huge rabid dog."

It's interesting to speculate how long we would have stood there, three grown people, frozen, surrounded by a single goose. But then there was the rumbling of an engine, and a once bright yellow but now very grubby Volvo estate nosed through the gate and turned into the driveway. Freddie and Magda were grinning at us through the mud-spattered windscreen. I suspected that it was not the first time they'd come home to a scene such as this.

They parked their car beside the pond and got out and wandered towards us in a leisurely fashion.

"So she got you cornered, eh?" said Freddie. He was dressed in his usual corduroys—baggy maroon trousers and a mustard-coloured jacket. I couldn't see if his shirt was corduroy, but if he'd managed to find one it would be. Corduroy socks and undergarments didn't bear thinking about. He still had the silly Edwardian mutton chop sideburns he affected. I was amazed that Magda tolerated them.

The goose backed away from us until she was standing between Freddie and Magda and then, never looking away from us, she began to make a low, conversational gabbling sound, as if she was reporting back to them about our conduct.

"Is it safe to come out?" said Nevada.

"Sure," said Magda, "her bark is worse than her bite."

"Her honk is worse than her hit," said Freddie.

"Come and give me a hug," said Magda. She was a plump,

freckled woman who wore an assortment of hand-knitted jumpers, long Indian-looking skirts and woolly hats, often all at once. She came from Munich and after living in England for years her German accent was faint but still in evidence. I went and hugged her, breathing in the scent of apples. I wondered if it was shampoo or actual apples. She released me and looked at Nevada. "And this is your new lady friend?"

"I keep him out of trouble," said Nevada.

"Come, you have a hug too. When Gwenevere sees us hugging she'll know you're friends and she'll leave you alone." Nevada seemed a little sceptical, but willing to try anything. She emerged gingerly from our hiding place behind the car and gave Magda a hug.

"Do I get a hug, too?" said Tinkler.

"Yes. Even you."

The ridiculous thing is, it seemed to work. As soon as Magda and I had broken our clinch the goose came over to me and leaned against my legs. She made a few gentle gargling sounds, craning her head to look at me as though to say, *Sorry about that. No hard feelings.*

"I hope you weren't too inconvenienced," said Freddie. "Or frightened."

"You told me you were going to be at home."

He shook his head. "I know, I know. We had to pop out for supplies. We were planning on getting back before you arrived and Gwenevere sprang on you. She's better than any watchdog, eh?"

"She certainly is," said Nevada, keeping a wary eye on the goose.

Freddie stroked Gwenevere's sleek head. "We've had a problem with local kids breaking in. Probably on a dare, raiding the garden, that sort of thing."

"Like apple scrumping," said Magda, savouring the odd English idiom. "Just kids having fun. Harmless."

"It won't be so harmless if they break into the barn and get at my stock," said Freddie. "Anyway, Gwenevere makes short work of them whenever they come around."

"I'll bet she does," said Nevada.

Magda opened the back of the Volvo and began to take out trays of small green plants. They'd evidently been shopping at the local garden centre. As she took them out Freddie hastily said, "Let me show you around the place," in a transparent attempt to avoid helping his other half with the unloading. He led us down the same path from which the goose had so recently and so furiously emerged. The barn loomed towards us over rows of bamboo poles covered with what looked like string beans.

It was a tall, modern structure of pale, unstained wood. It stood on the site of an original farm barn but had been rebuilt from the ground up. Above its wide doors a looping red neon sign read SINGLES BAR. A large yellow neon N in a completely different font completed the name. The unpowered neon tubing appeared pale and sickly in the daylight. At night it looked great.

"Oh, the singles *barn*," said Nevada. "I get it."

"Duh," said Tinkler, making a drooling cretin face, and Nevada punched him on the arm.

"So that entire structure," she said, "is full of singles."
"Yes," said Freddie proudly.
"And our Valerian record is in there somewhere."
"Yes."
"I think I will leave you gentlemen to it," said Nevada.

9. BUTTERFLY DREAMS

While Nevada went off to explore the gardens and presumably bond with Magda, Freddie let us into the barn. There was a proper security system in place with a key punch on the wall beside the barn door. He keyed in the number and a big lock clunked open inside and we spread the twin doors wide. It was dry in the barn, as it needed to be, and just a little cooler than room temperature, thanks to the heating system Freddie had embedded in the concrete floor to drive the damp out of the place.

Our search wasn't as much of an ordeal as I'd feared. The barn was pretty much full of singles, untold tens of thousands of them, but they were well organised and properly catalogued. All we had to do was laboriously manoeuvre down from a shelf the three boxes of Valerian 45s and look through them. We each took a box.

Tinkler went through his, sorting the singles like a professional blackjack dealer shuffling cards in a casino. He was obviously energised by the thought that the single might end up in his collection.

But it was Freddie who found it.

It was in a plain white sleeve with a hole at the centre to reveal the original pale blue label and white horse logo. I slid it out of the sleeve and went out in the daylight to check the vinyl. It was perfect. "It looks unplayed," I said.

"Well, let's go and fix that," said Freddie, grinning. We trooped back towards the farmhouse, keeping an eye out for Nevada on the way. I spotted her sitting on the bench by the pond. Then I saw the white shape of the goose on the bench beside her and my stomach went cold. Gwenevere had her long neck extended, her sharp head hovering beside Nevada's face, bobbing slowly up and down like a cobra waiting to strike.

Nevada sat there unmoving, hunched and paralysed as the goose probed towards her face.

I started running towards them.

But I had hardly gone three steps before I got a better look and realised that I'd got it all wrong.

I'd thought Nevada was frozen with fear. But if anything she was frozen with sheer pleasure. I could see now that she was smiling in mesmerised delight as the goose took her long black hair, strand by strand, and ran it carefully through her beak.

She worked methodically and gently, moving around Nevada's head. Nevada looked up at us as we joined her. "She's combing my hair," she said.

"Gwen likes you," said Freddie.

The goose made happy little sounds as she worked.

"She's been talking to me," said Nevada, "doing a lot of squonking and squanking."

"I've done a lot of squanking myself," said Tinkler, "over the years."

"No smut," said Nevada sternly. "Not in front of the goose."

We waited until Gwenevere had finished with Nevada's hair and then we all started for the farmhouse, the goose cheerfully following us. I showed Nevada the single.

"So that's it?" she said.

Freddie nodded. "Do you know why it's called 'Butterfly Dreams'?"

I said, "Does it have something to do with an ancient Chinese philosopher?"

Freddie laughed. "You're way ahead of me."

"Oh, of course," said Nevada. "Butterfly dreams."

"All right," said Tinkler, "what the hell are you all talking about?"

"The story goes something like this," said Nevada. "Once there was a Chinese philosopher who fell asleep—"

"It was Chuang Tzu, actually," said Freddie.

"Okay," said Nevada.

"He was a contemporary of Meng Tzu."

"Good old Meng Tzu."

"And he's widely regarded as the greatest Taoist philosopher."

"I meant to say." Nevada was starting to get a bit tight-lipped. I recognised the signs.

"Except for Lao Tzu, of course," added Freddie.

"Well, moving right along here," said Nevada, "he had

this dream. He dreamed he was a butterfly."

"Was he smoking opium?" said Tinkler.

"I don't know," said Nevada, who was by now thoroughly exasperated.

"I think he probably was," said Tinkler.

"Just listen! Anyway, he had this dream and then he woke up and he found himself thinking about it, the dream, pondering on it philosophically, its philosophical implications, and he ended up wondering if he was a man who dreamed he was a butterfly or, in fact, and this is the meat of it, a butterfly who dreamed he was a man." Nevada paused and looked expectantly at him.

"That's the stupidest thing I've ever heard in my life," said Tinkler. Then, "Why am I the only one who hasn't heard of this fucking Chinese philosopher?"

"Chuang Tzu," said Freddie.

Freddie had a proper listening room, which was situated at the back of the farmhouse and ran the length of the building. It was a rectangular space with the speakers at the far end, firing down the long axis of the room to a sofa and some armchairs at our end.

"Aren't those speakers like yours?" said Nevada. "Only bigger."

"Yes," I said. "Mine are Quads and those are stacked Quads."

"Well, don't go getting a set. We won't be able to see out of the windows."

"Don't worry," I said, "I won't. It's a mod."

"A Quad mod?"

"Yes, an unofficial modification. I'm not sure I approve."

"But they sure sound good," said Freddie, smiling. Tinkler nodded happily in agreement, the hypocrite—he had a pair of Tannoy horns at home. Freddie showed me his amp, a very respectable Copland integrated tube model, connected to a lovely vintage John Michell phono stage. But I was more interested in the turntable he was using.

"What the hell is that? Is that one of the original singles players?"

Freddie bobbed his head. "That's right. An RCA J-2 45 player with the thick spindle."

"Ah, the thick spindle," said Nevada. "How the young lady of today yearns for that."

It was clearly Freddie's pride and joy. "And it's got the rare red spindle cap!"

"Of course," I said. Nevada couldn't think of anything prurient to say about that, though I could see her trying.

Freddie had also modified the J-2 so it used a modern playing arm that could be fitted with an assortment of interesting cartridges. I noticed at the moment he was running a Sumiko Blue Point Special. He switched on the Copland and took the record from me and lovingly fitted it on the turntable. He set the turntable in motion and carefully lowered the stylus into the run-in groove.

Warm music immediately filled the room. It was a standard—Gershwin's 'Summertime'. "This is the B-side," I said. Freddie nodded. "But the hidden message is supposed to be on the A-side." Freddie shrugged. Then I shrugged. "Okay," I said. "No problem. We'll listen to this first." It was no hardship. Valerian's extraordinary voice probed the beautiful contours of the song, turning it from a lullaby into something else, a folk ballad from a lost world.

"Doesn't she have an extraordinary voice?" said Nevada.

Freddie nodded doubtfully. "Though I still say Janis has got the edge on her." One of the two big clichés about Valerian was that she was the English Janis Joplin. This was only superficially true. She had something of Janis's bluesy edge and knack for wracked distortion, but she also had an instinct for unconventional sound shapes and rhythms, like a great jazz experimenter.

The other big cliché about Valerian was that she was the female Jim Morrison. And when you considered her penchant for dark poetry, her charisma and gift for offending society—not to mention her rapacious drug use, sexual excesses and her extraordinary early end—there seemed a little more truth in that.

'Summertime' came to an end and Freddie turned the record over. We all leaned forward. 'Butterfly Dreams' began.

It was a minimal production, just acoustic guitar, piano and backing vocals filling in the spaces around Valerian's singing. The lyrics were spare, obscure, allusive. Her voice moved from sexual intimacy to outer-space abstraction. She slowed words down, broke them into fragments and stretched them to the breaking point.

She sounded like a cross between the much-cited Janis Joplin and the jazz goddess Betty Carter. And despite the enigmatic poetry, or perhaps because of it, it created an eerie mood. It lingered, yet it had swing. It had both strangeness and charm.

What it didn't have was a hidden message.

With the simple instrumentation and the sparse vocals, there was nowhere for anything to hide. Nothing was buried in the mix. Freddie's speakers revealed every note and syllable.

No hidden message. Backwards or forwards or sideways. No trace of anything.

We all looked at each other as the song came to its end. *So much for that*, I thought. *One more urban myth bites the dust.*

And then the stylus reached the run-out groove.

The run-out groove exists at the end of a vinyl recording to protect the needle, to prevent a noisy and potentially damaging excursion into the paper label at the centre.

The idea is that the stylus rides there in a blank groove in the vinyl, endlessly and harmlessly, with no more noise than the occasional subdued thud, until the lazy audio enthusiast gets up and lifts off the tone arm. But, apart from the endless loop structure, a run-out groove is just like any other microgroove on the playing surface.

And there's no reason that it can't have something recorded on it.

As we hit the run-out groove Valerian's voice suddenly came back, a warm whisper, intense and intimate, saying,

Love is this…

Love is this…

Love is this…

We all looked at each other again. Nobody moved. We sat and listened, as though expecting something to be revealed, even though we all knew that it was only those three words, could only ever be those three words, repeated over and over again. We wouldn't hear anything different from what we'd already heard.

But we *did* hear something different.

It grew on you. The very repetition of the words began to have an almost hypnotic effect. Valerian's voice was soft, sultry, and infinitely intimate. Suggestive and erotic. A lover whispering in your ear. I began to realise why someone might have wanted this banned. Any prurience was entirely in the mind of the listener.

But, in a way, that was the most powerful place for it.

Love is this…

Love is this…

Love is this…

I looked at Nevada and she raised her eyebrows and fluttered a hand towards her neck in an 'I'm too hot' gesture. Tinkler leaned over and silently mouthed something. I had no idea what he was trying to say, but it was clearly pornographic.

Freddie was just sitting with his hands folded between his knees, staring intently towards the speakers as if he expected Valerian to emerge from behind them and start to perform a strip tease.

But even the intensity of that sweet, insinuating voice, promising untold sensual pleasures, began to wear thin. I was on the verge of suggesting we switch the record off; after all, it was just three words, repeating forever. Unchanging.

Then the strangest thing happened. It was not unchanging. It changed.

Not the words themselves. The sequence of them.

Up to now there had been no question that Valerian was whispering "Love is this," leaving the listener's mind to invent the exact details, but it was nonetheless a statement of erotic pleasure, an unequivocal declaration. But suddenly she was saying something different. Not "Love is this, love is this, love is this", but...

Is this love?

Is this love?

Is this love?

It wasn't a statement. It was a question. Without doubt, this was now the true intent of the words. It wasn't pleasure. It was pain. She wasn't describing the joys of communion. She was begging to know if such a thing existed. To identify what she was suffering and give it a name.

Is this love?

Is this love?

Is this love?

It was eerily as if her intonation had changed, although I knew that was impossible. We were listening to exactly what we'd been hearing before. What had sounded like erotic bliss now sounded like emotional torment. Instead of a statement by an accomplished temptress it was a desperate question by a disturbed and despairing girl.

I looked at Nevada. She'd got it too. It was utterly eerie.

The hair on the back of my neck and arms was standing up in atavistic reaction. And then the meaning shifted *back* again. Without any warning, smooth as silk, the voice was back to its warm insinuation of carnal delight. The pain and longing and questioning were gone.

The meaning shifted back and forth. It was like watching a bicycle wheel spinning and then, at a certain point, the motion of the spokes suddenly seem to reverse and start moving in the opposite direction.

Love is this… Love is this…

Is this love? Is this love?

"Well," said Nevada. "I've got goose bumps. Which is very appropriate. Where's Gwenevere?"

That broke the spell. Freddie got up and carefully lifted the needle from the playing surface. He took the record off the turntable and put it back in its sleeve. Then he cleared his throat. He seemed a little reluctant to look at us. I understood why. We'd all been through something strangely intimate together, something secret and almost shameful. It had been like peeking under someone's sheets. But it had also been like looking under their bandages.

"Okay," said Tinkler. "That really did my head in."

Tinkler and Nevada were waiting for me outside on the driveway after I finished talking to Freddie. I understood their need to get out in the fresh air. Nevada looked at me as I came out of the farmhouse and said, "So there is a hidden message after all."

"Yes."

"But it's of no use to us in our quest."

I shook my head. "I don't see how it can be. It doesn't tell us anything."

"It certainly tells us about her state of mind," said Nevada. "The poor girl."

"Well, I'm going ahead on the assumption that the Colonel still wants us to secure the record for him, so I've discussed purchasing it with Freddie. He's agreed not to sell it to anyone else until we check back with the Colonel."

"But the Colonel may not want it now. After all, whatever else it might do, it can't be said to shed much light on the little boy's disappearance."

"True," I said. "That's why we have to check with him."

"How much does he want for it?" said Tinkler. "Freddie?"

"He asked for twelve hundred pounds."

Tinkler jerked as if stung. "You're kidding. That's completely out of order."

"He's just drawing a line in the sand. He had to say something. I haggled with him a bit but there's no point really getting down to particulars unless we know the Colonel wants it. If he does, I'm going to try to get Freddie down to three hundred quid."

"That's more like it," said Tinkler.

Nevada put an arm around me and said, "My negotiator. Why can't you be like this with the household budget?"

"Anyhow, I'm sure we can get it for no more than five hundred."

Tinkler kicked at the gravel despondently. "But if the

Colonel doesn't want it, our trip has been a complete waste of time."

"Not a complete waste of time," said Nevada. "We got to meet Gwenevere the goose." She scanned the gardens around us. "I wonder where that girl has got to?"

"There's something else." I took out the piece of paper Freddie had given me with his ungainly angular writing on it. I suspected he was trying to make even his handwriting Edwardian. "Apparently there's a place nearby we should visit. A house called Catherwood. It's the last place Valerian lived. Freddie knows the people who live there, two brothers, Timothy and Gordon Treverton, and he says they knew Valerian at the time. Maybe they can tell us something."

Tinkler looked at me. "You want to go there now?"

"No, tomorrow."

"What, you want to drive down to London, then drive back tomorrow?"

"No," I said. "We can stay the night. He's recommended a pub with rooms and he says the food is very good."

"Which is crucial," said Nevada happily. She put her hand on Tinkler's shoulder and said, in her best wheedling tones, "You don't have work tomorrow, do you?"

"No, I'm off for the rest of the week, but we can't just..."

"Oh yes we can."

"But..."

"Oh, go on, Tinkler."

Tinkler sulked. "We have to stay in a pub?"

Nevada said, "The place is probably packed with simple-minded little rural harlots who would just love to have sex with a big city boy like you."

Tinkler paused. "You think so?"

"Of course. You know how inbred they are in these parts."

So we bundled into the car and set off in search of the pub in the dying light. Nevada consulted Freddie's scrap of Edwardian script so she could phone ahead to make a reservation. As she looked for the pub's number I said, "We'll need two rooms, a single and a double."

"Or just one double room with a locked chest at the foot of the bed, where we can keep Tinkler as our gimp," said Nevada.

"That's never going to happen," said Tinkler firmly. "Not unless you *pay* me."

The pub was called the Black Ox. It was a handsome old coaching inn and the food was almost as good as Freddie had claimed. After dinner we sat in the bar, which was mostly filled with old geezers, though there was the occasional middle-aged couple, and their dogs.

"No harlots," said Tinkler sadly. Then he perked up. "I wonder if there's porn in the bedrooms?"

The next morning we rose early, as agreed, but despite much hammering on his door, Tinkler refused to get up and join us for our visit. His door opened a crack, just enough to hand us the car keys, and then closed again as he went back to bed.

"Too much porn," said Nevada.

We went out to Tinkler's car, wiped the condensation off the window and set off. I drove. Despite its age the car handled well and we plunged along curving country roads as the sun came up. Nevada was humming happily but I felt a growing tension as we neared our destination. We wanted to learn something about Valerian, and I was afraid we might.

After all, 'the last place she lived' had been a euphemistic way of saying 'the place where she died'.

10. STRAWBERRY HAT WEATHER

As we drove, I told Nevada about my conversation with the Colonel. "I rang him last night while you were taking your two-hour bath."

"Nonsense," she said. "I wasn't in there more than one hour and fifty-eight minutes, one hour and fifty-nine minutes, tops. The tub had claw feet. They're my weakness, tubs with claw feet. For some reason they're always much harder to get out of. So what did he have to say, the Colonel?"

I slowed as we approached a crossroads. These little country lanes were well stocked with blind corners, and I didn't want us rammed amidships by someone in an overpowered four-wheel drive racing to or from a horse show. "Well, first off he was appalled that we were feeding Turk and Fanny dried cat food."

"He was what? How would he even know that we do that?"

"Because he was there when Clean Head served them their supper. He dropped by our place on the off-chance we'd be home."

"Do you think he's lonely?"

"I think he wanted an excuse to get away from Lucy."

"Ah," Nevada leaned back in her seat, "now that makes sense. I can imagine he'd rather spend the evening waiting in the cold rainy night outside our front door than be with her."

"Yes, he's not mad about the girl."

"Or vice versa."

"Anyway, besides our cats' diet, we also managed to talk about the record. And he still wants us to go ahead and buy it."

"Even though the supposedly hidden message doesn't tell us anything?"

"He said at least it proves all that nonsense about black magic and orgies and cannibalism is not true. If he has the real record in his possession he can refute all that."

"Good point. Refute. Indeed."

We drove in through the gate of Catherwood House and onto an oil-stained grey flagstone driveway. It wound through a stand of trees towards the house, which loomed on a rise of land overlooking us. I immediately saw it on our right— the tree. It was a tall, gnarled oak covered with bundles of flowers, some synthetic and bright, others real and dead, and ribbons, scraps of paper, photographs, items of clothing and numerous other offerings.

"There it is," I said.

"What?" said Nevada.

"The tree where she hanged herself." I pulled the car

over and stopped. Nevada followed me out, pulling on her woolly white hat with the strawberry on it. The air was already biting with a premonition of winter. It was definitely strawberry hat weather.

"Valerian hanged herself?"

I turned and looked at her. "Yes. How did you think she died?"

"An overdose."

"So why did you think Nic Vardy was sending us a photograph of a tree?"

"I had no idea. No, wait, I'm sure I read it somewhere that she died of an overdose."

"Read it where?"

"On the Internet."

"Well, then," I said, "it must be true." I walked over towards the tree. The grass was wet and muddy underfoot and thick with dead yellow leaves. It had been a few years since anybody had tended these grounds. Nevada followed, picking her way carefully.

"No," she said, "it was definitely on some respectable website. From some reputable source. Here, look…" She took out her phone and began searching for the page. She obviously wasn't going to let it go. I stared up at the tree.

The various notes and handwritten cards that remained attached to it had been sealed in plastic folders to protect them from the weather. These had then been nailed or stapled to the bark of the living tree, which seemed a little callous to me.

"Here you go," said Nevada. "It's this article about

the twenty-seven club, you know, all those rock stars who died at the age of twenty-seven. And how Valerian was one. And it compares her to Jimi Hendrix and it says," she peered at the screen, "Valerian... just like Hendrix... at twenty-seven... died of an apparent drug overdose... Oh." She stopped and looked at me. "It's ambiguous. I see, the overdose bit is still talking about Hendrix. The subordinate clause is ambiguous. Because they've put the commas in the wrong place in the sentence. The silly buggers have put the commas in the wrong place."

"Always a danger."

We walked up the leaf-strewn driveway to the front door of the house. Stained glass set in the green wooden door stared into empty darkness. One diamond-shaped pane of the stained glass was gone and had been neatly filled with brown cardboard. I pressed the doorbell set in the flaking paint of the jamb. We listened, but it was impossible to tell if anything was ringing.

There was also a heavy metal knocker on the door, so I tried that, loudly and at length. Nevada and I looked at each other. She shrugged.

"No one in?"

"How could it be any other way?" I said. "We're three-time losers. Why can't anybody answer the fucking door at our first fucking attempt?" We wandered back down the steps onto the driveway. I turned to stare back at the house. A floral curtain seemed to stir in one of the high windows that looked down on the drive. Was it moving? I stood and watched while Nevada strode back to the tree. The curtain moved again. Then again. It was twitching in a breeze that was evidently getting in through the ill-fitting panes. I turned and went to join Nevada.

She was standing in front of the tree with her phone in her hand. She turned to look at me. "At least we can take a photo of this tree. It may not compare with Nic 'natural lustre' Vardy's work, but it will certainly be of more recent vintage." She peered at the moody old black and white photo of the oak. "Do you suppose this was taken when it happened?"

I looked over her shoulder. "I imagine so, because there aren't any offerings on it yet."

Nevada frowned at the picture. "You're right. No flowers, no poems. This must have been taken just after it happened."

"Hang on a second," I said, "let me see that." I took the phone and looked at the photo, then at the tree, looming against the damp morning sky.

"It's not the tree," I said.

"What?"

"It's not the same tree."

"How can it not be the same tree?"

I handed her the phone. "Look at it," I said. I left her comparing the picture to the tree and walked back towards the house. This time I ignored the front door and turned along the footpath, towards the left side of the building. There were several large oaks here, bulking like solid grey shadows on the overgrown lawn. I wandered around them, getting my shoes soaked, until I came to the one closest to the house.

Its long branches extended almost to the windows on

the top floor, like the hands of a supplicant reaching for someone's shoulder.

I stared up at the tree and then I went back and got Nevada. "Come and see this," I said. We compared the picture on the phone to the twisted oak beside the house. "It's the same one."

"Yes," said Nevada, looking from the photo to the tree. "You're right. It is. Shall I photograph it?" I was going to reply but then I realised that someone was looking at us.

Standing in an open doorway at the side of the house. A man.

He was tall and thin, with a deeply lined face and hair that at first glance looked dead white but on closer inspection turned out to be extraordinarily pale blond. I made a note to ask Nevada later if it was a dye job. If it wasn't, maybe I could ask him what his secret was, because he was clearly in his sixties. He wore a long-sleeved sweater with a design of grey and lemon-yellow diamonds and had a navy-blue scarf tucked into the neck of it. I presumed he was one of the Treverton brothers Freddie had mentioned.

"Can I help you?" he asked mildly.

"We tried the bell," I said.

"Oh, it's broken," he said. "It's been broken for yonks."

"We also tried to knock," I said, perhaps a little pointedly, because Nevada stood behind me so he couldn't see her nudge me in the ribs.

"We're so pleased to find you in," she said. "We wanted to have a word."

"A word? Really? About what?"

I saw Nevada suddenly dry up. She hadn't quite fully worked out her spiel yet, the poor thing. So I stepped in. I pointed at the oak tree. "This tree, for a start. It's the one, isn't it? Not the one by the road, but this one."

He stared at us. He had unsettling pale eyes or, as Nevada would say later, "He's got that nasty sort of *Lord of the Rings* evil elf look about him. Bit big for an elf, though." He just stared at us and said nothing.

"We're making a documentary about what happened," said Nevada. She'd evidently decided to revive our Stinky Stanmer cover story. That was fine with me. The man looked at her. "What happened to Valerian," said Nevada. He kept on looking at her. "For television," she said.

It was as if the mention of television had decided him. And not in a good way. He had come a few steps out of the house. Now he turned back towards the door. "If you'll excuse me, I have things to do. Photograph the tree if you must, but I do ask you not to photograph the house." He was obviously about to go back inside and close the door on us, in every sense.

Inspiration struck. "Freddie said we should look you up."

He paused and looked back at me. "That's right," said Nevada quickly. "He's written us a note of introduction." This was embroidering the truth lavishly; what he'd done was written us some directions.

"Freddie who?" said the man.

Nevada looked at me. She only knew our corduroy-clad friend as Freddie Forty-Five. "Fentyman," I supplied.

The man looked blank, then seemed to relax a little

and said, "Oh, Freddie Forty-Five."

"He said he knows you fairly well."

"Freddie? Oh, yes, I suppose so. Gordon and I have seen him at the county show a few times. And he always has a stall at local boot fairs and village fetes and that sort of thing. Still flogging records in the age of the compact disc. Or trying to." He looked us over again, as if making sure we weren't too grubby. He seemed to have reluctantly accepted that he had to invite us in. "I'm Timothy. Gordon is upstairs."

As soon as we got inside I realised why he was wearing a scarf. It was as cold as a tomb in here. It actually felt colder inside than out, as an unheated house often does, if only because it engenders a chill sense of injustice—indoors really should be warmer than outdoors. The house was gloomy and full of shadows, but only because there were no lights on.

The walls and furnishings were pleasant pale colours, faded pastels and off-whites. If the place had been properly illuminated it probably would have been bright and cheerful, in stark contrast to the glum autumn day outside. As it was, the house's interior formed a continuum with the icy grim morning beyond the windows.

And a little central heating wouldn't have hurt.

Timothy began opening cupboards. "Do you drink tea?" he said. I had to admire the fact that he didn't seem to like us and clearly didn't want us here but, on the strength of our mutual acquaintance with Freddie, felt he had to make us a cup of tea.

"Can I help?" said Nevada.

He ignored her and set a box of teabags down beside the sink, then ran water from the tap into the spout of a chrome kettle so covered with dust that it had achieved a matte effect surface. If he was going to be rudely reticent I felt I could be rudely forthright. "That *is* the tree out there, isn't it? The one beside the house?"

He sighed and switched the kettle on. "No one ever noticed before." He went to the kitchen table, a square of lime-green linoleum on a wooden frame, and pulled out three chairs. Evidently we were supposed to sit. We did, choosing the two chairs closest to each other. Despite having pulled out one for himself, he remained standing.

"You see, when it happened," Timothy said, "we started to get this constant stream of visitors. It was like they were making a pilgrimage. I suppose that's how it all gets started. Saints and shrines and pilgrimages and so forth." He gave a little barking chuckle. "Although it's very odd to mention her in the same breath as a saint."

"Valerian?"

"Valerie Anne." He looked down at us, his pale eyes showing, more than anything else, disgusted mild irritation. "I knew we shouldn't have let them stay at the house."

"Them?"

"Valerie Anne and her son and her sister, and whatever members of their entourage happened to be around at any given time."

"Why *did* you let them stay?" said Nevada.

He shrugged. "Our families had been friends, or at least been friendly, ever since we were children. Our father and

Old Man Drummond were on quite close terms. So, when she came to us years later and said she needed a place to escape to, somewhere in the country, to hide from the press and her fans and all that, we agreed to lend her the house." He smiled thinly. "Rent it to her, actually. She could afford it."

The kettle boiled and he made us tea. "There's sugar, but no milk."

"That's fine," said Nevada.

"Were you here when it happened?" I asked.

He shook his head. "No. My brother Gordon and I were in Switzerland. But it was all waiting for us when we got back: the whole ghastly business. Of course, people being what they are, everyone wanted to see the tree in question. They came and made their little offerings. They took pictures. They had picnics. Some of them rutted like wild beasts, right there under the tree."

"How awful," said Nevada.

"That wasn't the worst thing," Timothy said. "The worst thing was when they came peering in our windows. Like we were specimens in a zoo. So we did it. I don't know who came up with the idea, but it was a damned good one. We waited for a nice dark night, then we did it. My brother and I." He smiled at us, fondly remembering a past triumph. "We took everything off the tree, all the bouquets of flowers and the wretched little doggerel poems and the stained little knickers and we moved them to that tree by the road." He chuckled nostalgically. "And we fastened them to that tree there and, sure enough, the next irritating party of pilgrims went unquestioningly to that one instead. Business as usual, but all the way over *there*. Out of sight and out of our hair. And they've been going to that tree ever since." His smile faded. He looked at me bleakly and I could fill in the blank. *Until now.*

He shook his head. "No one else ever noticed we'd moved it."

I said, to make him feel better, "We had a photograph of the real tree."

"They're all *real* trees." He looked towards the front of the house, and the cluster of woods by the road, where they'd perpetrated their fraud. "It just isn't the *right* one. It was a harmless enough deception." He turned to us. "I'm sure many a famous shrine has been similarly shifted, for similar reasons."

A voice called, from somewhere deep in the house, causing me to jump. Despite the talk of a brother, I'd begun to think of him as alone in this cold, dark place. He got up wearily. "Excuse me," he said, and went out the kitchen door.

Nevada looked at me for a split second, then got up and started snooping. I stayed put, partly because I have a higher set of moral standards and partly to keep an eye out for him in case he suddenly came back.

Nevada wandered through into an adjacent room joined to the kitchen by an arched, open doorway. I heard her moving around in the shadows as I listened for our host to return. Then she called to me, "Come and see this." I got up and went into the adjoining room. It was a dining area with a small, oval table and two very uncomfortable-looking antique chairs. At least someone had had the good sense to put a fat, tattered, old floral cushion on one of them. Nevada was staring at a wall covered with framed pictures of all shapes and sizes. "Look at this."

I went over and joined her. It took me a moment to sort out the various images, and realise that they were all of the same two people. Two boys or, in some of them, two young men. They were all outdoor shots and in many of the pictures the boys were in shorts or serious-looking open-air gear, including rucksacks, silly hats and what looked like wooden staffs. In a couple they were on skis and moving across snow. No shorts in those shots. In the background of almost every one of them was a mountain, or mountain range.

The images had a strange kind of Hitler Youth, strength-through-joy vibe to them. Something about all that fresh air and mountain scenery and the vigorous clean-living lads. The fact that they were both blonds also helped. Nevada tapped one of the pictures, of the two boys in what looked like scout outfits. "It's him, Timothy," she said.

I looked at the other boy, identically dressed, identically blond. "And his brother Gordon?"

"Must be."

I noticed the rucksacks at their feet, with long coils of rope spilling out of them, and belatedly recognised it as mountain-climbing gear. Suddenly all those magnificent peaks in the background made perfect sense.

Almost all of the photos pertained to mountaineering. There was one of the two boys canoeing, and a couple of them with bows and arrows. "I did archery at school," said Nevada, looking at the pictures. "I was something of a whiz at it."

I was about to say that I was entirely prepared to believe this when I heard movement in the hallway. Nevada heard it, too. We both hurried back into the kitchen, getting there just in time to hover politely by the table as our host came back in. As if we'd risen to our feet on hearing him return, out of sheer good manners.

Timothy looked pissed off. "Gordon would like to see you."

Gordon Treverton was waiting for us in an upstairs corner room with windows on both outside walls, letting in the cold north light—and a good portion of the cold north wind. I say waiting, but he didn't look like he had anything else to do, or ever did much else, than just sit here.

He had an armchair with a little folding table set up in front of it. On the table was a square metre of brown card, on which was set out a half-completed jigsaw puzzle. He had the same colouring as his brother but he looked shrunken, more frail, under the shawl and blankets that covered everything except his head and arms. I tried not to look at his hands, which were knobbly claws, as red as a boiled lobster. His brother had said something about arthritis as he'd led us up the stairs and left us here.

There were no other chairs in the room, just a couple of cushioned foot stools. Nevada and I each perched on one and looked at the man and his jigsaw puzzle. He was smiling at us, quite happy to have some company, apparently. "Timothy tells me you want to know about the hanging tree."

Nevada nodded, "My name is Nevada Warren, and I'm producing…"

He cocked a misshapen hand to his ear and said, "Warren? I didn't quite catch the first name?"

"Nevada."

"Sorry?"

"*Nevada.*"

It occurred to me that his brother might have mentioned the deafness when he was briefing us about the arthritis. But the old boy had apparently got it now, because he said, "Like Brooklyn Beckham?" I glanced quickly at Nevada, waiting for the explosion.

But she was on her best behaviour, and cutting him a lot of slack. She smiled a beautiful smile and said, "It means snowfall."

The man cocked his head again and returned his hand to his ear. "Snowball?"

"*Snowfall.*"

"Snowball?"

"Snowfall!"

"Snowball?"

Nevada fell helplessly silent and Gordon looked at me and grinned. "We're having a snowball fight!"

Nevada took a deep breath. "Anyway," she said, or shouted, "we're making a programme about Valerian." The man nodded, listening, but kept looking down at his jigsaw puzzle. There was a large wooden spoon lying among the puzzle pieces. And I noticed that his left hand had a pale band wrapped around it, of what looked like masking tape.

"I see," he said. "And under whose auspices is this programme taking place?"

We looked at each other, hesitating. I took the plunge. "Stinky Stanmer."

"Oh, Stinky Stanmer!" He looked up. "I listen to his programme on the wireless. Wednesday evenings, isn't it? I adore him."

"He's very adorable," said Nevada.

"Well, then tell me, what would you like to know?" Suddenly he seemed able to hear perfectly well. Stinky had wrought a miracle, just through the mention of his miserable name.

I said, "Your brother told us that you were childhood friends of the Drummonds."

"Yes, yes, that's right. Our father always sought to cultivate Colonel Drummond. You see, Daddy always wished he'd fought in the war, but he couldn't because he was hopelessly asthmatic. So he rather hero-worshipped Colonel Drummond who really *had* fought in the war." I suddenly twigged that we were talking about the real Colonel Drummond here, the father of our client.

He nodded, as if confirming something to himself, and said, "He fought in the North African Campaign and was much decorated for his efforts." He chuckled, a harsh rasp. "Daddy was very impressed by his medals." He looked up at us. "Personally, I never liked Colonel Drummond. He was a bastard to those poor girls, you know. Especially after their mother died and there was no one to protect them from his Victorian notions of child rearing. No wonder they ran away the first chance they got. To join the circus, so to speak."

"The rock and roll circus," said Nevada.

Gordon grinned happily and nodded. "Of course, Colonel Drummond really hated that. Long hair, loud music, promiscuity and drugs. All his hatreds rolled into one, you might say. And it really got to him when they became successful, the girls. Because of the publicity. Everybody knew Valerian was his daughter, and what she was getting up to. Remember that story about Marianne Faithfull and the Mars Bar?"

Nevada looked blank but I nodded. I'd tell her later. Or, better yet, let Tinkler tell her.

"Well, when that story first got started, it was about Valerian! It was only after she died that it became attached to poor old Marianne Faithfull. And then there were all those reports of her stripping off during her concerts, and all the men, the male groupies, the orgies." He smiled at Nevada, his eyes glowing. "You've heard of Messalina?"

Now it was my turn to look blank, but she nodded. "One of the benefits of a classical education."

He chortled and nodded. "Yes, well Colonel Drummond had a classical education, too. So when he read an article in the *Telegraph* comparing his little Valerie Anne to Messalina, he knew exactly what they meant." He shook his head happily. "He knew how many men a night in her bed that *meant*." He glanced up at us, to see if we were following. "So he hated her for that. And he hated poor Cecilia as her accomplice. But what he really hated was that they had succeeded. His daughters had run away from him and succeeded in creating a life of their own, and he had no part in it, in that life or that success."

He paused and I thought he was lost in memory, but then I saw he was actually studying the jigsaw puzzle spread out before him.

He lifted his left hand and lowered it carefully so that the edge of it touched one of the pieces that was lying scattered, waiting to be used. I realised that the masking tape had been wrapped around his palm sticky side out, so that the piece adhered to it. He lifted the piece and held it over the growing corner of the puzzle that was complete. The picture on the puzzle wasn't clear yet, but I could see the blue of sky, and some grey and white masses, perhaps clouds.

He looked up and smiled at us. "There's an art to it. I have to rub the tape against my jumper so it loses a bit of its stickiness. It has to lose just enough. It needs to be sufficiently sticky to pick up the jigsaw piece, but not so sticky it won't release it..." He gently shook his hand and the piece fell down near the assembled section of the puzzle. He chuckled happily. He looked like a small boy. I had to admire the way he had triumphed over his crippled hands. "And absolutely it mustn't be so sticky that it tears a portion of the image from the jigsaw piece. We have to preserve the image. After all, that's what it's all about."

He moved his right hand towards the wooden spoon that lay beside the puzzle and picked it up. Gripping it clumsily in his twisted talon, he manoeuvred it over to the newly selected piece and used the spoon to nudge it into position and press it into place. He studied it with satisfaction, then looked up at us again.

"Preserve the image, eh? That's what Colonel Drummond wanted to do, at all costs, but thanks to Valerian there was no chance of that. He was furious with her. Refused to speak to her or acknowledge her existence. Hers or her sister's. Which broke Cecilia's heart. She wasn't as strong as her sister, or as hard. Maybe that's why she eventually lost her marbles. She wanted her daddy back, god knows why. But there you have it." He shook his head.

"They were only reconciled when she had a baby— Valerian, I mean."

I considered his words, trying to wind my thinking back into a 1960s mindset. I said, "Why would an illegitimate child help? I mean back in those days it was a big thing, wasn't it? A major social stigma."

"Oh yes," he nodded merrily. "You're quite right. It was not the done thing! It was utterly scandalous. So of course it initially made things worse. And yet it did eventually bring them back together. Drummond and his daughters."

"Really?" said Nevada. "Why?"

"Ah, you see, Old Man Drummond always wanted a male heir."

"But he had one," I said, thinking of our client and how unhappy he would be to have his existence denied. "He had a son."

"Oh yes, but Johnny was a big disappointment to Colonel Drummond. Just like everything else." He chuckled. "Especially after Johnny was arrested for taking part in the anti-Vietnam protests at the US Embassy in London. Now that really was the final straw! Long hair and beads and a criminal record. In addition to photographs in the paper of Johnny wrestling with two policemen—and doing quite a good job, by the look of it—as they dragged him off to the paddy wagon."

Nevada and I exchanged a look. Who would have suspected our 'Colonel' of such a colourful background?

"So Old Man Drummond disowned him, totally. Just like he had the girls." He smiled at us. "And then there were none, so to speak. And I suppose the old man finally realised what he'd done. He was going to die, bitter and alone, with no one to follow him. Especially no *bloke* to follow him. He thought the male line was at an end. Quite a big deal for one of these military types, you understand."

"We understand," said Nevada.

"But then the baby, this criminally, disgustingly, illegitimate baby turns out to be a boy." He studied us, then began to smile slowly. "And the hard old bastard just melted. He began to let Valerian and Cecilia back into his life."

"But not Johnny?" said Nevada.

Gordon shook his head ruefully. "No. I suppose the old man had to draw the line somewhere."

"But there was a reconciliation with his daughters," I said. "With Valerian."

"Yes, thanks to little Tom. Valerian's son." He suddenly stopped. "That poor little boy."

"Did you know him?"

"Yes, he was a lovely little chap."

"Do you have any idea what happened to him?" I said.

He seemed suddenly guarded. "Why would I know anything about that?"

"I mean, if you were to make a guess."

He shrugged. "Kidnapped by gypsics? How should I know? All I know was that when his grandson was taken, that was the end of Colonel Drummond. With one daughter a suicide and the other one in the madhouse, all that scandal and heartache, it killed him stone dead."

We were all silent for a moment. He studied the jigsaw puzzle. I looked at the corner that was completed with the blue of sky on it and I realised that the other colours weren't clouds. They were mountains.

I said, "Your brother told us you were away when Valerian... died."

He nodded absently. "Yes. In the Alps, climbing." He looked at the mangled claws of his hands. "I think that was the last time we did the Alps."

He dropped his hands and smiled brightly. "But we heard all about it when we got back. Apparently she walked out the bedroom window with the rope around her neck. She used one of our climbing ropes, which she must have found somewhere. There were always plenty of them lying around. She put it around her neck and went out the window. The tree had branches that grew all the way to the house back then, poking almost inside the window. And you could just step outside, onto the branch. Which is what she did. It always reminded me of Peter Pan for some reason. Someone walking the plank, I suppose, on a pirate ship."

He looked at us, his eyes bright. "We trimmed the branch

when we got home. Cut it right back—as if there was some danger of someone else doing the same thing. As though it was some kind of perennial hazard." He leaned back in the chair, his eyes suddenly dreamy. "The branch has grown back now, of course. Someone could go out again if they really wanted to."

I looked at him and suddenly wondered if he was mad. It was a very uncomfortable thought. I cleared my throat. "What happened afterwards? After the suicide and the disappearance of the boy?"

"Ah well, as I said, Colonel Drummond died pretty promptly. And Johnny had left the country. Went to America, of all places. I suppose they didn't hold a grudge against him for trying to burn their embassy down. Very broad-minded, the Americans. So that only left Cecilia. Little sister. Last of the Drummonds." He sighed wistfully. "I read in the papers a few years ago about how she'd died in the madhouse. The poor thing. Completely gaga and her brain apparently burned to a veritable cinder by repeated applications of the old electroshock therapy."

Then he fell silent, staring blankly ahead, as if something had just occurred to him. "My god..." he whispered.

"What?" said Nevada.

He looked at us, then down at the jigsaw. He moved a piece of the puzzle diagonally from one side of the tray to the other. "That piece goes *there*! At the bottom left-hand corner. It doesn't belong at the top right-hand corner at all. My god. I should have seen it all along..." He wobbled his head happily.

I heard footsteps on the stairs. Timothy appeared in the

doorway. "Come on, Gordon," he said. "You mustn't tire yourself out by talking too much."

Gordon smiled at his brother and said, "Did you know that this delightful young lady is called Snowball?"

Timothy escorted us out. In the hallway there was a table piled high with jigsaw puzzles, stacked in their boxes. There were dozens of them. All mountain scenes, of course. Above them was another framed photograph. In the Alps, the two blond brothers, lost boys from a lost age.

As we drove back to the pub I glanced across at Nevada. "What would you like for lunch, Snowball?"

"Fuck off."

11. LUNCH

Tinkler said, "So were they deformed yokels with shotguns and rocking chairs?"

"No," said Nevada. "They weren't like that at all. They were, or at least one of them was, an evil pale elf in a really hideous sweater."

"I wish I'd met this guy," said Tinkler.

"You will insist on sleeping in."

"I stayed up late watching a documentary about the blue whale," said Tinkler.

Nevada gurgled with laughter. "I'll bet."

I slowed down as we approached a point where the narrow lane twisted and disappeared around a blind corner. I didn't trust these country roads. I briefly applied the horn, letting anyone coming from the other direction know that we were here and that approaching at high speed on a road that wasn't wide enough for two vehicles might lead to an unpleasant experience for all concerned.

"You know what?" said Tinkler.

I eased off the brakes, coasted around the corner, saw that no one was there and picked up speed again. The road ahead was clear. I glanced at Tinkler in the mirror and said, "What?"

"They might still have some records there. At the Evil Elf's house. Who knows what they might have. They could have all kinds of albums that Valerian's people left behind. It could be a treasure trove."

"It could be," I said. I kicked myself for not thinking of it.

"They might have a copy of the Artwoods' first album, the original Decca issue, with the Mod cover." Tinkler's voice had softened rhapsodically.

He was right. "We're going to have to go back," I said.

"Not today," said Nevada firmly. "Today we just pick up the record from Freddie, after you have haggled with him in a masterful fashion and generally fleeced him on the Colonel's behalf, and then we say an emotional farewell to Gwenevere the goose and drive back to London where our little darlings are waiting for us and you will, with a bit of luck, cook us a mouth-watering supper."

"With a bit of luck," I said.

"Can I come too?" said Tinkler. "My mouth is watering just because you said mouth-watering."

"He's not a bad cook," said Nevada complacently. "Of course you can come too."

Freddie's place was coming up on the right and I signalled and turned. Freddie was standing in the driveway, waiting for us.

I knew right away something was wrong.

* * *

I got out of the car and hurried towards him, Tinkler and Nevada following.

Freddie looked at me, red-eyed and angry. "Last night someone broke into the house." A principal component of my shock at hearing this news was the realisation of just how unsurprised I was. On some level, I had been expecting something like this.

"They stole the computer," he said.

"That's terrible," said Nevada.

"Was there anything embarrassing on the computer?" said Tinkler. "You know, any, ahem, adult websites bookmarked or anything?"

Freddie looked at him bleakly. "It doesn't matter about the computer. The computer can be replaced."

Tinkler cleared his throat. "You're insured then?"

Nevada was looking at Freddie strangely. "What's wrong?" she said. "What else happened?"

"When we woke up this morning and saw what had happened we couldn't understand how they'd got in without us being alerted. Gwenevere is better than any alarm system. And then of course we found that they'd…"

"What?" said Nevada. "Oh Christ. No."

Freddie shook his head, tried to speak for a moment and couldn't. I realised his eyes were red because he'd been crying. "Yeah," he said hoarsely. "They killed Gwenevere. The bastards killed her."

"They did, did they?" said Nevada and I saw real rage

flare in her eyes, and then reduce to a dangerous smoulder, suggesting her rather large and resourceful intellect was busy at work.

I realised glumly that all this didn't bode well for whoever might have killed the goose, if we ever happened to bump into them. It was wise on such occasions to recall that my honey pie knew how to use a gun, and where to get hold of one.

The question was, would she be mad enough to use it?

I looked at Freddie and said, "Look, Freddie, I really hate to ask you at a time like this, but I need to know. Did they take the record?"

"What?" Freddie gave me a disgusted look and turned away from me as though in sudden physical pain. He waved his hand in the air. "I don't know. Everything's a mess. They totally turned over my office. They stole the computer."

"I know. You said."

"And a phone. Magda's iPod. The telly from the kitchen. You know, the usual stuff." Freddie looked at me. I think he was a little contrite about his previous reaction. "I really don't think they were after your 45. I think it's just buried under all the other crap. They really turned the place over."

"You must sleep pretty heavily," said Tinkler.

"All the real upheaval took place in my office, which is in a separate building and at the other end of the farmhouse from our bedroom. We didn't hear a thing. But that doesn't mean ninjas crept in under cover of darkness and stole your copy of 'Butterfly Dreams'." He was starting to sound angry again. "I really think it's still in there somewhere, just buried under all the other crap."

I had my doubts about this theory, but I sensed I couldn't press him any further. He shook his head and said, "I just don't feel like digging it out for you right now, if you don't mind. Under the circumstances."

"No, of course," said Nevada. She took my arm and stood looking at Freddie. "How did they do it? To Gwenevere?"

"They garrotted her," said Freddie. "Put a wire around her neck and pulled it tight, sliced right through her throat."

We all looked at each other. "They garrotted the goose," said Tinkler. Nevada's face had gone a perilously pale shade but she just nodded, apparently calmly.

Then the door of the farmhouse banged open and Magda stepped out.

Nevada and Magda took one look at each other and then flung themselves together, sobbing in each other's arms. I looked at Tinkler in astonishment and we backed slowly away, as men tend to do when suddenly confronted by a powerful display of female emotion. As if backing away from something that might explode or throw off dangerous radiation.

I said, "They only met yesterday."

Tinkler shrugged. "They bonded over the goose."

Even Freddie had backed away to a safe distance from the two sobbing women. He looked at us. "You're going to stay to lunch," he said.

"Jesus, Freddie," I said. "I don't see how we can under the circumstances." But he was shaking his head stubbornly. I said, "I mean, Nevada won't want to eat anything after what she's just heard." Nevada broke her clinch with Magda and looked over at me. She wiped her eyes. They were both wiping their eyes.

"You must," said Freddie.

"Well, I suppose..." said Tinkler, who was always thinking about his stomach. I shot him a furious look, but he just shrugged. "I need to drive back to London. I've got low blood sugar. I need a meal. You wouldn't want me to drive back to London with low blood sugar, would you?"

"I can drive to London," I said. "My blood sugar is fine." Nevada came over to join us. I looked at her. "You don't want to eat anything, do you, honey?"

"You must," said Freddie.

"Oh yes, you must," said Magda, joining us. Her eyes too were painfully red.

"Well, if you insist," said Nevada. It was becoming clear to me that for some reason it was emotionally important to Freddie and Magda that we joined them. Maybe they didn't want to eat alone.

"I guess it's fine," I said.

"Great," said Tinkler. "What's for lunch?"

"Roast goose," said Magda. We were all silent for a moment. I couldn't decide which was weirder, whether she was serious or she was making a hideous joke. Then I looked at Freddie and realised they meant it.

"You've got to be kidding," said Nevada.

Magda and Freddie were both shaking their heads, in utter accord. "No, we are not kidding," said Magda. "How else can we make her death less senseless, less meaningless?"

Freddie was nodding in fervent agreement. "Someone

wasted Gwenevere, but we can't let her go to waste. It would be a crime."

"You're serious," said Nevada.

"This is the only way for her death to have some meaning," said Freddie.

"We loved her," said Magda. "And this is the last way we can make that love mean something. The last way we can express it."

"It seems quite a sensible notion to me," said Tinkler.

"Shut up, Tinkler."

"I'm just saying."

Lunch was, as you might imagine, a rather odd affair. The first thing that has to be said is that Gwenevere smelled delicious and my mouth watered in a treacherous fashion. We all sat around the big table in the kitchen. Tinkler had grabbed the seat nearest the Aga, where it was warmest. I was beside Nevada who was beside Magda. Freddie sat opposite me and he began the meal by pouring a glass of red wine and holding it high in front of us.

"Thank you and farewell, dear friend," he said, and then Magda commenced to carve the roast bird, which was golden, done to a turn. The skin crunched juicily under the pressure of the knife. There were tears in their eyes as we began eating.

Nevada refused to eat any. She looked at me. "But you go ahead," she said.

She seemed to mean it.

I took one small slice, as a token to appease our host,

then passed the platter along to Tinkler.

I carefully ate one symbolic mouthful of goose. It was delicious and I was a little regretful to leave it at that, but I wanted to respect Nevada's feelings—feelings that I shared—for the poor fucking goose.

Meanwhile Tinkler tucked in happily, helping himself to seconds.

After all that malarkey about blood sugar I ended up driving us back to London with Tinkler lounging in the back seat. I think one of the principal attractions of having his own car was for him to be able to loll about as a passenger while others chauffeured him around.

I looked at Magda and Freddie waving in the rear-view mirror, standing outside the farmhouse, shivering in the cold, then I turned onto the main road and they were out of sight.

"Can you believe we just did that?" said Nevada.

"Well, it made them feel better about losing her," I said.

"By eating her?"

"Well, you know what they said about her always being part of them now." And part of me, I suppose. And definitely part of Tinkler, who had eaten an enormous amount of goose meat and was now torpid as a result.

"Yes, very poetic and moving," said Nevada. "But poor Gwenevere. It still involved roasting her and cutting her up and eating her."

Tinkler leaned forward. "Not just that. She also had her liver made into pâté."

"Really?"

"Yeah, Freddie spent all morning doing it. You fry onions in butter…"

Nevada shuddered and cut him off with a wave of her hand. "That's so disgusting. The whole episode is disgusting. It's enough to make one want to go vegetarian. Forsake meat for good."

"The cats wouldn't stand for that," I said.

"No," said Nevada, her tone softening. "That's true. The disreputable little carnivores would not approve. I wonder how they're doing?"

"He made it with brandy," said Tinkler.

"Made what with brandy?" said Nevada.

"The liver pâté."

Nevada paused, then looked back at him and said, "Tinkler, you didn't."

There was silence in the back of the car. Then, "Well, it was twenty-year-old Armagnac."

"You *didn't*."

"I couldn't let it go to waste! It sounded delicious. They didn't want it." He reached in his pocket and produced a small jar with a hand-lettered paper label on it.

"And it comes in an attractive ramekin."

12. CUSHION

They say you can't train a cat, but as soon as I slipped the note under Turk's collar she turned and trotted for the cat flap and thrust herself out into the back garden. I went to the window and watched her hop nimbly onto the rear wall and then over it, heading for the Abbey.

She knew the presence of the note meant she could seek out Stinky and receive a reward of fresh salmon or king prawns—Stinky had made some kind of arrangement with the Abbey's kitchen. Perhaps they thought he was a recovering seafood addict.

Whatever he gave Turk, she must have eaten it quickly because she was back five minutes later with his reply. Unusually for Stinky there was no absurd attempt at trendy salutation followed by a combination of name dropping, sexual boasting and social condescension, with Nevada's name incorrectly rendered at least once as Nirvana.

Instead, just a phone number.

Half an hour later Nevada came in the front door, keys

jingling, and said, "I got the French bread you like but they didn't have the cheese you asked for. I had to wing it. If you don't like it, blame the chap at the cheese counter." She set the shopping bags down on the table and I came over to inspect the substitute cheese; it was fine. She kissed me. Her hair was cold from the outdoors. "As for wine," she said, "don't get me started. The way these people carry on you'd almost think there were other wine-producing countries than France, and other regions of France than the Rhône valley. I mean they've got racks and racks of stuff from Australia and New Zealand and Chile and the United States and Italy and Spain. But try looking for a decent Rhône red. They didn't stock a single thing by Paul Jaboulet, can you imagine? Luckily I got a Chapoutier." She proudly unwrapped the bottle and handed it to me. Like her hair, it was cold from her walk home.

"Shall I pour us some now?" I said.

"Why don't you do that?"

As I opened the wine I said, "Do you know what we've lost in the era of the mobile phone?"

"The ability to communicate meaningfully?"

I poured the wine. "Well, that too of course. But I was thinking of dialling codes."

"Dialling codes?" Nevada took a glass and we sat down on the sofa.

"For the local exchanges. Time was, you could look at someone's number and know in what part of London they lived. That's the beauty of a landline." I handed her the piece of paper Stinky had sent me. She turned it over in her hands.

"What's this?"

"You know all that trouble we were having getting through to Valerian's guitarist?"

"Erik Make Loud. Erik with a 'k'. That just kills me— 'kills' spelt with a 'c', by the way."

"Well, I'd tried all the numbers that Stinky's PA managed to dig up, and none of them were any good. They were all mobile phones and I couldn't get anything but voicemail. So it occurred to me that an arch ligger like Stinky might have the number for Erik's personal direct line."

"And he did? Excellent!" Nevada kissed me. "As loath as I am to admit it, Stinky does seem to have his uses. And have you noticed how glossy Turk's coat is? That's all the fish oil she's getting."

"But look at the dialling code," I said, "on Erik's number."

Nevada frowned at the piece of paper. "It's the same as ours."

I chuckled. "That's right. We've been chasing all over London looking for the bastard, and here he turns out to live just up the road."

"So we can go and see him? I mean, just pop over and visit?"

"Yes. I phoned him, or rather his housekeeper, and made an appointment for us to go over tomorrow."

"Excellent," said Nevada. "Remind me not to take the piss out of him about his name."

The doorbell rang and I went and admitted Tinkler. Rather promisingly, he was carrying a bag with the logo of an expensive delicatessen emblazoned on it. "A wine and cheese party," he said. "How fashionably retro! Can we have fondue next?"

"Hello, Tinkler," said Nevada, and kissed him.

Tinkler ostentatiously removed his jacket. It was the houndstooth silk one that Nevada had found for him in an Oxfam shop in Hammersmith. Underneath it he was wearing the black John Smedley roll neck she'd found in Twickenham. Dressed to the nines again, I noticed. He was handing me the jacket when he froze.

He was staring at the coffee table where we had spread the photographs. "Where did you get those?"

"They came in the post this morning," said Nevada. "From Nic Vardy."

"My god," breathed Tinkler. He settled heavily on the sofa, knees spread apart, and bent forward to study them.

"Yes," said Nevada, "he may be a hair-tint cheat but he's quite good at snapping a photo."

Tinkler picked up a shot of Valerian standing holding a microphone, a spotlight behind her head. A halo of sweat and curly hair surrounded a face that was both angelic and demonic, frozen in the ecstasy of song. It was a black and white shot, like all the others.

He rifled through them feverishly. "These are great! He *gave* them to you?"

I said, "He included a note about how everything is going digital and, since that's the case, maybe we'd like these duplicates of his prints that he's managed to dig up."

"Maybe you'd *like* them?" said Tinkler.

"They were addressed to me, actually," added Nevada demurely.

"Have you asked him about my autographed print yet?"

"No, Tinkler, but we shall." Nevada sat down beside him and looked at the photographs. "You know what is strange about these?"

"No," I said.

"No, what?" added Tinkler.

She picked up the photographs that Tinkler wasn't monopolising. "There's lots of shots of everybody in the band…"

"Yeah. Aren't they great?" said Tinkler.

"Except Valerian's sister. Everyone except Cecilia."

"Oh, that makes perfect sense."

"Really? Does it? Why?"

Tinkler handed his sheaf of photos to Nevada. "Well, you see Cecilia played the piano. And a lot of these gigs they had, especially in the early days, were at venues that were too small even for the smallest upright piano."

Nevada shook her head. "So poor Cecilia was left out?"

"She became sort of a back room presence," said Tinkler. "Like Ian Stewart in the Rolling Stones."

"Who's Ian Stewart?"

"Exactly," said Tinkler.

I sat down on the sofa with them, looking at the photos. I picked up a particularly striking shot of Erik Make Loud. "We're seeing him tomorrow," said Nevada.

I nodded. "He lives just up the road," I said. "In Barnes."

"Good gravy," said Tinkler. "That close? One would have thought we'd be able to hear the howls of reverb and distortion from here."

"Time for me to go and assemble a green salad," said

Nevada. She looked back over her shoulder as she headed for the kitchen. "By the way, you needn't have got all dolled up, Romeo. Clean Head can't make it."

Tinkler's face fell. "Why not?"

"She's working. We'll have to have a separate summit with her later."

"Is that what this is, a summit?"

I went and sat down at the dinner table and he joined me, carrying the delicatessen bag. He opened it and took out a jar of cornichons, little French pickled gherkins. "I thought I'd contribute these," he said.

"Thank you."

"They'll go very nicely with this." He took out another jar. It was the pâté Freddie had made from Gwenevere's liver.

"Jesus," I said, glancing towards the kitchen. "Did you have to bring that?"

"Why?" said Tinkler. "It's not still a sore spot, is it?"

"Not still a sore spot? The poor fucking goose was only killed yesterday."

"I just thought, you invited me around, wine and cheese…"

"We invited you around because it's important that we talk. And anyway, we didn't invite you. You invited yourself."

He paused in the act of opening the jar of cornichons and looked at me. "Important that we talk? Why? What about?"

"Look," I said, "we don't want to make the same mistakes we made last time. The last time something like this happened."

"And what mistakes were those?" He popped the lid off the jar.

Nevada came back with a salad bowl and set it on the

table. She sat down and said, "It took us too long to realise that the opposition had us under surveillance."

Tinkler chortled. "The opposition? Don't you think that sounds a little paranoid?"

Nevada reddened. "Paranoid?" she said in a threatening tone that suggested at the very least a long, loud, sarcastic and very eloquent refutation of poor Tinkler. She'd been on a short fuse ever since the goose.

"But there *was* an opposition," I said. "And they were dangerous."

"They may well have bounced you down the stairs on your noggin, Tinkler," added Nevada.

Tinkler rubbed his head and did his rueful look, which he was rather good at. "But those people are gone, aren't they?"

"Sure, but this is a new situation and there's no reason to assume that there won't be some new form of opposition, that they won't be at least as dangerous, and that they won't be on to us just as quickly."

"What do you mean, on to us?" said Tinkler.

Nevada sighed. "Isn't it obvious?"

I said, "Whoever robbed Freddie's place was obviously looking for the record."

"*Our* record," said Nevada.

"And they got hold of it before we did."

"You think the robbery was all about the record?" said Tinkler.

"Of course."

"But they took Freddie's computer, and Magda's iPod, and…"

"That was all just camouflage," said Nevada.

I nodded. "They tore the place apart to hide the fact that they were after the record."

"Okay…" said Tinkler, stretching out the first syllable, obviously unconvinced.

I took a deep breath. "Look," I said, "we have to assume there is an opposition—"

"Not paranoid at all," murmured Tinkler.

"And we have to assume that they're on to us."

"*They*," said Tinkler.

"And we have to try and work out who they are."

"That's right," said Nevada. "So we're drawing up a list."

"Ah, a list. Are you checking it twice? It's getting on for that time of year."

I ignored him. "And on it we're putting the names of everyone who might have known that we were going to Freddie's to buy the record from him."

"And we want your contribution," said Nevada.

"And Clean Head's?" said Tinkler. "You don't trust her more than me, do you? I mean, you don't think I'm any more likely to be the leak than Clean Head?" I couldn't help noticing that the man who had been so breezily proposing paranoia only moments earlier was now thinking in terms of avoiding the blame for being the leak.

"Yes, we are going to talk to Clean Head too, and find out if she might have mentioned it to anyone, or if anyone might have found it out without her knowing about it."

"If they found it out without her knowing about it, she wouldn't know about it," said Tinkler. "It's like at the airport where they ask you if anyone could have tampered with your bag without you knowing about it."

"Anyway," said Nevada in exasperation, "right now she's not here but you're here, so we're asking you."

"To tell you anyone I might have mentioned the record to? Anyone who might turn out to be the 'opposition' and have stolen it?"

"Yes." Nevada took out a pen and a sheet of paper and was looking at him in a businesslike way when the doorbell rang. I went and opened the front door.

It was Freddie and Magda. He was wearing a plaid cap and tweed jacket. No corduroy, I realised with a mild shock. He was looking sporty and well turned out. At his elbow Magda was in some kind of brocaded black jacket with a yellow silk scarf at her throat. She was holding a large, beaded red bag. *That* was corduroy, I noticed. Her expression was solemn, but Freddie looked like a man who had to keep reminding himself that he shouldn't be jaunty. "Can we come in?" he said.

"Of course. Good to see you. This is unexpected." I escorted them through the narrow hallway into the living room where Tinkler and Nevada were sitting. Apparently in my brief absence hunger had got the better of Tinkler, because he had the jar of pâté open and was spreading a liberal quantity of pinkish goose liver onto a piece of bread. As we walked in, he set the jar back down on the table. At the centre of the table actually.

It couldn't have been more featured if we'd shone a spotlight on it.

Magda took one look and did a slow 180-degree turn

and walked back out again. I heard the front door close behind her. Freddie and I looked at each other. "Should I go after her?" I said.

Freddie shook his head. "No, she'll be fine. She'll wait in the car and—oh shit, the bag." He hurried after her, out the door. I looked at Nevada who was glaring at Tinkler, who was still frozen halfway through the motion of lifting the incriminating morsel of bread and goose liver to his mouth.

"Tinkler!"

"What?" he said, reluctantly setting it back down on his plate. "How could I know they were coming? You didn't tell me."

"We didn't know," I said. "We had no idea they were coming."

"Although now that they're here," said Nevada, "they can help with the *list*." She tapped her pen on the piece of paper. The door opened behind me and a sudden gust of cold air signalled the return of Freddie. He shut the door behind him and came in, taking his cap off. He had a large square cardboard envelope under one arm.

"I'm sorry about that," he said. He looked at the open jar of pâté, then at Tinkler, and said, "No, you go ahead."

"Oh, really? Are you sure?" said Tinkler. He picked up the bread with the thick coating of pâté on, and bit it in half, happily groping for a cornichon as he did so. He ate the rest of the bread, crunched the cornichon, and began to spread more pâté on another piece of bread.

"Well, we certainly weren't expecting you, Freddie," I said.

"It was an impromptu visit. Magda has these people in London who buy the cushions she makes. And yesterday when Gwenevere…" He paused tactfully. "Well, we wanted to use her feathers for something, just as we used every other part of her if we could. So Magda made a little cushion and stuffed it with the goose feathers. But she didn't want to keep it in the house. It reminded her of Gwen. So we came down to London to sell it today."

"Ah," said Nevada.

"Here," said Freddie. He took out his phone and showed us a photo of the cushion in question. It was a lovely little piece of work, with the silhouette of a goose embroidered on it. *She must have stayed up all night doing that*, I thought.

"It's beautiful," said Nevada.

"It was a good idea, really, coming down to sell it. We made enough money to cover the cost of the trip to London and more."

Nevada looked at me. I knew what she was thinking. There's money in these cushions. "And also," said Freddie, "it gave me a chance to deliver this." He handed me the cardboard envelope.

"What is it?" I said.

"Your record."

"My record?"

"'Butterfly Dreams'," said Freddie patiently. Tinkler was beaming at me. I refused to meet his eye as I opened the envelope and took out the record. Sure enough, it was the single. Freddie was watching me. "So," he said, "we hadn't actually settled on a price…"

"Okay," I said.

"How about five hundred?"

"How about four hundred," I said. I could see Nevada out of the corner of my eye, holding her breath.

"It's a very rare disc," said Freddie.

"It is," I agreed. "And it's in very nice shape. But it has had the centre punched out of it."

Freddie nodded. "Yeah, good point. Pity that. I think it might be a juke box copy." He sighed. "Okay, we'll call it four hundred and fifty."

"Four hundred and twenty-five."

"Okay," said Freddie, and he shook hands with me in the manner of a man who was getting twenty-five pounds more than he expected. I could have pressed him harder, but it wasn't my money and I felt obscurely guilty about the goose.

"I'll get our client to transfer the money to you tomorrow," I said.

"Great. Make sure it goes into the Singles Barn account, the business account." Freddie paused. "Well, if you don't mind, I'd better make a move. Magda's waiting in the car…"

We said our goodbyes and watched him leave. Then we all looked at the record he'd left on the coffee table. Tinkler was chuckling. "'It was all just camouflage'," he quoted. "'*They* tore the place apart to hide the fact that *they* were after the record.'"

"All right, all right, all right."

Nevada was staring at me. "So they didn't steal the record?"

"I guess not."

"And it was all just a coincidence?"

"I suppose so," I said. And then it occurred to me. "Unless…"

"Unless?"

I looked at the record. "Unless they've replaced it with a fake," I said.

"Oh boy," said Tinkler. "The dizzying heights of paranoia."

I picked up the record. The label looked kosher, pale blue with the logo of the Uffington white horse. Examining the vinyl told me nothing, except that it was in excellent condition. "We have to play it," I said.

"Can you?" said Tinkler.

Nevada looked concerned. "Why wouldn't he be able to?"

Tinkler grinned. "Your boy doesn't have a thick spindle," he said.

Nevada smiled back. "That's an unwarranted canard."

It was true, though—because of the large hole punched in the middle of the single I couldn't play it on my machine without some form of adapter. How annoying of Freddie not to have provided one. Not like him. Then a thought struck me. I picked up the cardboard envelope and shook it. There was a rattling sound. I reached inside and fished out a small black shape. A 'spider'-style plastic adapter. Tinkler was watching with approval. "All that for only four hundred and fifty pounds."

"Four hundred and twenty-five."

"Who's counting? Let's play it."

"Okay." I inserted the adapter into the big hole in the centre of the 45. Nevada came and studied the record as I did so. "Isn't that horse the ancient chalk one?" she said. "From the Berkshire Downs? From the hillside?"

"Yep." I snapped the adapter into place.

She studied the pale blue label. "So why didn't they make the background green? Like a hillside."

Tinkler said, "They were taking so much acid they probably thought it *was* green."

I went to the turntable and put the 45 on the platter. It looked remarkably small and vulnerable there. I reached for the controls, then hesitated. "What's the matter?" said Tinkler.

"The Garrard," I said, "I've never played it at 45. Only 33."

"So what? There's the speed-changing control. So change the speed."

I peered down at my beautiful turntable. "But what if it makes it go wrong?" I said. "What if it damages the belt, or…"

"It's a Garrard 301," said Tinkler impatiently. "It's built like a Russian T-34 tank. It was designed to be played at three speeds and give untold decades of service to myriad stalwart audiophiles all over our great empire."

"All right," I said. I flipped the switch and changed the speed to 45 with a reassuringly well engineered click. I started the turntable spinning and lowered the stylus into the run-in groove. Then I went back to the sofa and sat down with Tinkler and Nevada. We all listened to the song. It was 'Butterfly Dreams', all right.

But what I really wanted to hear was the run-out groove.

The song ended and the needle slid into it. And Valerian's soft insinuating breathless voice began.

Love is this.
Love is this.
Love is this.

We listened to it until the meaning reversed itsclf, from a statement to a question and back again, and then we switched it off. We looked at each other.

It was unquestionably the same record.

"You are now leaving the city limits of Paranoia Heights," said Tinkler. "We trust you have had a memorable visit."

13. FLOOD PLAIN

The next morning we fed the cats then set out for Erik Make Loud's house. We went on foot because it was a pleasant walk, splashing through the fallen leaves of Vine Road, strolling past the playing field on the common and pausing at the railway crossing. Both the railway crossings, in fact. "We managed to catch both bloody trains," said Nevada. "I don't mean actually *catch* them," she added.

"I know what you mean," I said as the train finally thundered by. When it was gone there was an electronic ratcheting sound and the red and white striped barriers creaked up into the air. We walked across the tracks, then along the footpath that led us into a grid of residential roads. Emerging from a side street, we turned the corner where the old police station used to be.

Across the road was the pond and a stretch of park that featured a boot fair once a year. I had many fond memories of records found there, including some immaculate Duke Ellington ten-inchers and a rather nice June Christy on Capitol.

The pond itself was pleasant enough, too, with an assortment of lively waterfowl that it would have required a Nic Vardy to correctly identify. "Our photographer would be in his element here," said Nevada. "Old false plumage Vardy."

"I was just thinking that," I said. "And that reminds me, do you think that other guy dyes his hair?"

Nevada took my hand as we waited to cross the street. "What other guy?"

"The Evil Elf."

"What was his name, incidentally? We can't go referring to him by that outlandish soubriquet indefinitely. Or can we?"

"Timothy," I said. "Timothy Treverton. Brother of Gordon with the arthritis and the jigsaw puzzles."

"The poor bastard."

The traffic stopped for the lights and we crossed the road. "No, his hair is totally natural as far as I can tell," said Nevada, "the old Evil Elf." We walked past the Bull's Head, a famed music venue that had featured luminaries from Tubby Hayes to Michael Garrick. I'd once attended a memorable gig there by an American singer called Ree. Ree was the granddaughter of the great Rita Mae Pollini, and third-generation jazz royalty. Two streets away from the pub was the house where we'd found the dead body of Ree's bass player and had to fade carefully away before the police arrived.

I made a point of not reminiscing about any of these episodes with Nevada. Ree was still a sore point with her. Clean Head had once told me that she referred to Ree as 'his whore in Hawaii'. *His* meaning *mine*. "She likes the alliteration," Clean Head had said, needlessly. It was true Ree was now living on the Big Island and that we had once dated. And it was also true that I had a standing invitation to visit her there.

Which I could accept only at considerable risk to life and limb.

We walked along with the river on one side of us and a row of white houses on the other. "You know what surprises me about Barnes?" said Nevada. "What surprises me is that there is not more riverside frontage. You know, houses right on the river with river views. I mean, look how far all these houses are back from the river. Someone has failed to make use of prime real estate worth billions."

"That's because the Thames has a nasty tendency to flood," I said. "You see where the houses start? That's pretty much the point the flood waters reached the last time the Thames breached its banks."

"Breached its banks?" said Nevada. "It's amazing how serious that sounds." We crossed the street, moving from the river side to the residential side, and approached Erik Make Loud's house.

It was set well back from the pavement. We actually walked across a black cast-iron walkway above what looked like a narrow concrete moat before we reached the front door. As far as I could see the 'moat' ran all the way around the house, as if in an attempt to separate it from the world.

The door itself was tall and white and imposing with a button below a vertical letter slit set high in it. I was reaching to push the button when Nevada stopped me.

"Here, let me try," she said.

I stepped aside. "Sure, but why?"

"Whenever you ring the bell, no one is in. Let me see if I have more luck."

She pushed the button and there was an efficient-sounding electric buzzing within the house, followed immediately by footsteps resonant on a tiled floor. Nevada turned to me.

"You see?" she beamed, just as the door opened with an expensive-sounding click. The woman who looked out at us was squat and stocky, with a flat, suspicious face. I later learned she was, or had been, a Korean national. She was wearing black ski pants and a navy-blue blazer over a Fair Isle sweater and, incongruously, a string of pearls.

"We have an appointment with Mr Make Loud," said Nevada brightly.

"For Stanmer Productions," I added. We were just making up these company names as we went along.

"I know," said the woman. Her accent, if anything, suggested Birmingham. "I spoke to you yesterday." She checked her watch, presumably to make sure we weren't early—or late—and said, "Wait here please." She showed us in, or at least a little further in, shutting the door and then disappearing deeper into the house. We cautiously edged forward as we waited. There was a long strip of rush matting just inside the door leading to a hallway lined with tiles so pale green that they were almost white. Those windows set on either side of the door and a skylight above us made the entrance hall uncommonly bright and welcoming.

In front of us there was a mirror hanging above a low bookcase full of volumes on the history of World War Two. On either side of us the walls were decorated with striking rock posters by some of the finest artists. I recognised Rick Griffin, Alan Aldridge and Martin Sharp. Mounted behind non-reflecting glass in ebony frames, they featured acts like the Doors, Pink Floyd, Hendrix and Cream. On closer inspection I saw that the paper of some of the posters was ivory-coloured with age. They were originals. Beautiful and worth a fortune.

I made a note not to tell Tinkler, otherwise he'd be around here with a crowbar.

"I can't believe I said 'Mr Make Loud'," said Nevada.

The woman came back. "Erik will see you in the guitar room."

"Excellent," said Nevada.

The guitar room, as it transpired, was in the basement with views from its tall barred windows of the interior of the concrete moat and, just visible at the top, a glimpse of daylight. It was indeed a room full of guitars, hung on the walls and free-standing on custom-made mounts on the floor. I was no expert but I recognised some vintage Fender Stratocasters. Dotted among the guitars were armchairs, dining chairs, sofas and settees. There didn't seem to be any focal point in the room. It reminded me of a showroom at a music shop. We found a couple of seats that allowed us to watch the doorway and settled down, or tried to settle down, while we awaited our host.

He came thumping down the stairs, trotted through the door and looked at us and then away from us, around the room. It was as though we were a disappointment and he was hoping that someone else might have come to interview him. He was barefoot, in jeans worn to exquisite paleness and thinness, so that they almost looked like they were fashioned of some delicate white muslin. He was deeply tanned and in very good shape for his age. He obviously worked out. Thick muscular arms emerged from a sleeveless Hawaiian shirt—something I'd never seen before. He had a lion's mane of grey hair and a small earring. His dark face was lined and serious-looking with a bulbous nose, which, if it had been a less healthy outdoors colour, would have unambiguously signalled a heavy drinker.

Finally, having surveyed the room carefully, he turned to us. It came to me that perhaps he'd been counting the guitars, to make sure we hadn't stolen one while we were waiting.

"What a lovely room," said Nevada when he finally focused on us. "What a magnificent collection of guitars."

"Yeah," said Erik wearily. I could see his attention draining away already.

So could Nevada. "I hope you've taken measures to protect them in the event the river floods," she said.

He looked at her with a glimmer of increased interest. "Yeah, that's why we had the moat built."

Ah, the moat, I thought. *That will do a lot of fucking good if five million tons of Thames Floodway fails.* Maybe the doubt showed on my face because he added, "And anyway, Bong Cha is under strict instructions to move everything upstairs if there's any threat from the river."

"Bong Cha?" chuckled Nevada.

"Yeah, my housekeeper."

"Bong Cha." She gave me a mischievous look. "Perhaps she'd be the perfect girlfriend for Tinkler."

I doubted it. Tinkler had long since been spoiled by magazines full of naked supermodels. "She certainly has the name for it," I said.

"It doesn't mean what you think," said Erik Make Loud. "Apparently it signifies 'superior daughter'."

"Funny," said Nevada, "I always thought that was me." Her bright aphorism just hung in the air. Erik yawned. Nevada smiled bravely, but I could feel the whole interview slipping rapidly south. He turned away from us and wandered to the window, the better to stare out at a concrete wall. Apparently that was of more interest than us.

With his back to us he said, "So Stinky sent you."

"That's right," said Nevada. "I'm senior development executive at Stanmer Multimedia." Another spurious promotion, I noticed. Soon she'd be running the company. Whatever it was called.

"And I'm producing the documentary," I said, thinking that I might as well get in on the act.

He swivelled his head to look at me. "The documentary?"

"About Valerian," said Nevada.

"Okay," said Erik mildly, "okay." He looked back out the window.

"About Valerian and your involvement with her. I mean, musical involvement," said Nevada. "That is to say, your involvement with the band."

He turned away from the window and looked at us.

"You want to know about my involvement with Valerian?"

I could see that we'd hit an unfortunate note and Nevada could see it, too. "Well…" she said, hastily backpedalling.

Erik Make Loud strode towards us, his voice heavy with sarcasm. "My involvement with her was that I had to use the toilet on the band bus after she did and breathe the stink of her shit. I breathed the stink of her shit for four years in that band. Four years in a career that has spanned fifty years." He actually said 'spanned'. "I've played with dozens of bands and hundreds of musicians. But all anybody wants to talk about is Valerian. It was all over a lifetime ago, but all anyone asks me about is Valerian." We'd hit a sore spot all right. He gave us a baleful gaze. "Well, if you're asking if I fucked her, I didn't. I'm one of the exclusive few. Sorry to disappoint you."

He turned away from us, staring out the window again. Nevada looked at me and I shrugged. I had the uncomfortable feeling that our interview was at an end. This was confirmed when he cleared his throat and said, "Listen, I don't have much time and I really don't know if I want to talk to you."

"Sorry?" said Nevada.

He kept his back to us but his shoulders rose and fell. "The thing is, I don't *need* to talk to you."

I said, "But yesterday when I spoke to you on the phone—"

He turned and looked at us. "That was yesterday." He shook his head and started towards the door. Nevada and I exchanged a look. Things weren't going according to plan. "We only want a few minutes of your time."

He wheeled and stared at us. "*My* time. That's right. It's

my time. You're talking to *me*, not to Valerian."

"We understand that," said Nevada mildly.

"Do you? Do you even know who I am?" I wondered if he was going to tear his shirt open and start beating his chest.

"Of course we do." Nevada could see it all slipping away but she wasn't giving up without a fight.

"Really?" He gave us a mirthless grin. "I don't think so. You're a couple of iPod kiddies. Music begins and ends for you with pirated MP3 files. You think rock music is wankers like Blur and Oasis and, and—" I could see him struggling for a more contemporary reference. "The Kaiser Chiefs," he finally spat out. "Elbow. The flaming Flaming Lips." He came and loomed over us. "You don't know the first thing about real music. You don't know the first thing about me."

"I know you played with Zappa," said Nevada.

That shut him up.

He stared at her. "Zappa?" he said.

"Of course," said Nevada. "Everyone knows that."

He looked at us both blankly, then turned and wandered in an apparently random fashion among the guitars, coming to a stop by the wall. He reached out and slapped something on the wall and I realised there was a small intercom discreetly fixed there. "Yeah, listen," he said into the intercom, "how about some drinks?" Without waiting for a response he turned and threaded his way back towards us, picking up a wooden chair as he went by. He set the chair down in front of us and sat on it.

"So, Zappa, huh?" I was hoping to god he wouldn't ask what album he'd played on. Nevada had no idea and neither did I; it was a shame Tinkler wasn't here. I wondered if I could slip out and surreptitiously phone him. "Frank was already sick by the time I was playing with him," said Erik, sounding regretful and nostalgic. "But we did some nice sessions. Some of them were kind of like soirees, you know, musical evenings. He'd sit there and listen while I played and a bunch of other guys played. One time I was there with some Tibetan nose flutists. He loved it. He loved it all. He was getting weak, but still he was in the studio every day. And he used a bunch of my stuff."

There was a tactful knock on the door, or at least the doorway, and Bong Cha came in with a tray. On it there were three glasses with ice in them, a glass bowl full of additional ice and a large jug of clear liquid with a wedge of lime in it. I suspected it wasn't water. She came over to us and stood there holding the tray, giving Erik a pointed look. He belatedly hopped to his feet and went off to get a small table, which he set in front of us. Bong Cha put the tray on it, scowled and left.

It was obvious who was in charge in this household.

Erik poured drinks and handed them to us. I took a cautious sip. Blueberry vodka. The breakfast of champions. "Here's mud in your eye," he said, and drained his glass. "Come on," he urged, "are you going to drink with me, or what?"

Nevada and I exchanged a look. In for a penny... I tilted my glass and swallowed half its contents. It was cool and pleasantly fragrant and seemed quite innocuous. I set my glass down on the tray and Erik suspiciously checked the level in it, then reluctantly accepted that I'd been a good boy.

He topped it up and handed it back to me. I took another sip.

A warm fuzzy feeling was gradually developing behind my eyeballs. Erik rcfilled Nevada's glass, and then his own, which he proceeded to drain almost immediately. He was knocking them back like a trooper. I wondered if I'd been right about his drinker's nose after all. "So, what can I tell you?" he said.

"Well," I said, "anything you remember, especially from towards the end, about Valerian."

"Towards the end?"

"When she died, and the little boy…"

He waved his hand in the air. "I wasn't around when any of that shit happened. None of the band was. We were all here in London recording, just around the corner in fact, at Olympic Studios."

"You were recording, but she wasn't with you?" said Nevada.

Erik snorted. "By this point in her career she thought she was Frank Sinatra or something. We laid down the instrumental tracks all ready for her. For her royal highness." He snorted again. "And boy was she high. Practically all the time. That was part of the problem. It got so we didn't know if she'd show up for a gig. And we're talking about important gigs. Major venues. Not Eel Pie fucking Island anymore. Anyway… she just wanted to come into the studio and do the vocals in one take. So we were down here in London, sweating away, while she was swanning around in that country house she was renting."

"So you don't have any idea what actually happened?"

He shook himself like a wet dog. "I know exactly what happened. She jumped out of a tree with a noose around her neck."

"To her son, I mean," I said. "You don't have any idea what happened to the boy?"

He shook his head. "I've always had my suspicions," he said darkly.

"Really?" said Nevada.

"Oh yeah. Oh yes. I mean, look at the freak show she was hanging out with. There was that business manager of hers. He was banging her. And that toady of a publicist. And that newspaper man. And that useless fuck of a bodyguard of hers. I mean, where was he when he was needed? They were all banging her." He poured himself another drink, splashing the vodka into the glass and dropping in ice cubes one at a time with savage precision. "And that fucking psychiatrist of hers. The shrink. And then there was…" He paused and looked at us. "Have you ever heard of John Blacklock?"

We shook our heads.

"Oh yeah, oh yeah," he said, nodding, warming to his subject. "You should really look into him. Yeah, Blacklock. I've always had my suspicions."

"Who was he?"

Erik laughed. "Okay, you have to remember that this was the era when the Beatles were hanging out with the Maharishi. All the other bands were doing similar things. You weren't anyone if you didn't have a guru or yogi or spiritual advisor." He spat the words out. "But Valerian being Valerian she couldn't get some nice friendly smiling Asian gentleman.

She had to go for John Blacklock, that snake."

"But who was he, exactly?"

"A fucking Irish fucker. Ireland's bog-trotting answer to Aleister Crowley."

"So he was some kind of black magician?" said Nevada.

Erik nodded. "Self-styled shaman to the stars." I remembered the constant rumours of Valerian's involvements with the dark arts and felt a small stirring of disquiet. But then I reflected that 'Butterfly Dreams' was supposed to have been stuffed with satanic messages, and look how that had turned out.

"So you think he might have taken the little boy?" said Nevada.

"Sure."

"Why? I mean, do you think he—"

Erik shook his head, shrugging off the grisly implications. "No. Not that I'd put it past the snake. But I always reckoned that he might have been the boy's father."

Nevada and I looked at each other. "Really?" said Nevada.

"Sure. He was banging Valerian. Everybody had a go at her except me, but he was in the saddle at the crucial time." Erik Make Loud paused and belched decorously.

I said, "Do you have any idea why Valerian might have done it?"

"Done it?"

"Killed herself. Was she under any particular strain, or was she depressed or—"

"Valerian?"

"Yes. Anything you can tell us about her on that weekend."

"I told you, I wasn't there."

"Around about that time then. Was Valerian—"

He snarled, "Valerian, Valerian, Valerian." He chanted the name in a high-pitched, effeminate voice. "It's all about Valerian." I uneasily sensed a return of his earlier surliness with the additional unwelcome component of booze sloshing around his rock star brain.

"Or her sister, Cecilia," said Nevada hastily. "Is there anything you can tell us about her?"

He calmed down immediately. "Cecilia Drummond," he said reminiscently, as though tasting the name. "Now, she was a sweetie. And, if you ask me, the more talented of the two sisters. Cecilia never got the credit she deserved for what she contributed to the band, and the songs. I think a lot of the songs that had Valerian's name on them were as much Cecilia's work as hers. And she was a proper musician, Cecilia. A lot of the chords in those songs could only have come from her. Lovely little voice, too. Not strong, not a blues shouter like her sister. But very frail and pure. Just lovely." He sighed and refilled his glass.

"The trouble with Cecilia was that her instrument, the place where she could really shine, was the piano. And a lot of gigs she couldn't play because there was no piano on the bandstand. She never played electric keyboards, didn't even like using an upright; always preferred a grand or baby grand. A purist, I guess. So she became almost like an auxiliary member of the group."

"Like Ian Stewart in the Rolling Stones," said Nevada.

Erik stared at her in surprise. "Exactly like that!" He

thumped his thigh with his fist and grinned. "Exactly." His bulging eyes gleamed fondly. Nevada smiled modestly. Butter certainly wouldn't have melted in her mouth. He got up and strode to the wall and slapped the intercom again.

"We need something to go with the Absolut," he said. "How about fixing some caviar? The real stuff, not the lumpfish roe. And use the proper sour cream, not the ordinary cream. If we haven't got any, go out and get some. The little supermarket around the corner has it."

He came back and sat down with us, grinning. The caviar arrived, on another tray, with sufficient dispatch to suggest that a foray to the little supermarket around the corner hadn't proved necessary. The housekeeper withdrew after giving us all a coldly disapproving look. Since Erik hadn't been excluded from this, I didn't feel too bad about it. And the caviar was very good, served with small blinis as well as the sour cream. Erik sampled the latter with suspicion.

"I think she used ordinary cream with some lemon juice in it," he said. "What do you think?"

"I don't think I fucking care," said Nevada. "You don't mind if we stuff our faces?"

"Not at all." He turned to me. "How do you like it, sport?"

I liked everything fine except being called sport. "Nice blinis," I said.

"Home-baked with buckwheat flour. Bong Cha does have her uses."

The caviar went stereotypically well with the vodka and we drank—and ate—considerably more than was good for us. But this seemed to put our host in a jolly frame of mind. He lolled back in his chair and regarded us fondly. "Do you want to hear something really weird about Cecilia Drummond?"

"Yes please," said Nevada, polishing off a blini heaped with caviar, then taking a neat little sip of her vodka. "Absolutely." She peered into her glass. "No pun intended."

"Okay. So after Valerian died and all that shit hit the fan we were left with a band without a singer." He peered at us. I could see the impact of the drink in his eyes but he still sounded entirely lucid. "Worse than that, we were left with a band without a name."

"You could have continued calling yourself Valerian," hazarded Nevada.

"We could have, if we'd been the kind of ball-less wonders who are forming reunion bands even as we speak and touring the world to wring the last penny out of a dead horse." This seemed a substantially mixed metaphor but I said nothing. "So anyway, the first thing we had to do was come up with a name. Mickey who was the drummer said, 'Let's go about this scientifically. Our old name was Valerian and now Valerian is gone. So what are we left with?'" He looked at us expectantly. "Nothing. That's what we were left with. You take Valerian away from Valerian and there's nothing left. A blank title. So Mickey said, why didn't we call ourselves that. Blank Title. So we did."

He looked at us proudly. Indeed he had some reason to be proud, Blank Title having gone on to considerable chart success and even managing to break America.

"Blank Title was a hell of a band," said Erik happily. "And we all still get along. We're all still mates. Every few years we reform. I wouldn't be surprised if we reformed again. I bet you could sell a lot of tickets to a Blank Title world tour." I wondered if this wouldn't be wringing the last penny out of a dead horse, but I kept my mouth shut.

Erik suddenly fell silent and looked at us blankly. "What was my point? I was going to make a point."

"You were going to tell us something really weird about Cecilia Drummond," said Nevada. I was impressed by the way she'd kept her eye on the ball, despite all the vodka she'd put away.

"Oh yeah, right, anyway—hey that ties in with exactly what I was talking about. Blank Title, right. When we last got back together and recorded an album, when was it, last April? No, the April before that. It was at Olympic Studios in fact..." He seemed to have lost his thread again. He stared blankly into his glass.

"Yes?" said Nevada helpfully.

"You know, it really *was* weird," said Erik. And I realised that he hadn't lost his thread at all. He was overcome by memory. "You see, we were doing this song that we'd written. It was called 'A Song for the Sister'. It was all about her. Cecilia. About the way we felt about her, and what had happened to her and everything. That poor kid got such a raw deal."

He shook his head and topped up his glass. "And we wrote this song about her, and we were recording it, and then we looked up and standing in the control booth there was this woman. Just standing there. And none of us recognised her. And we all thought, who the hell is that? She wasn't there a minute ago. So we wrapped up the track and went in to see who it was. I was pissed off with Joey, the engineer, for letting a stranger into the session and I was going to give him a bollocking, but then he whispered to me." He looked up at us, his eyes bright with the booze, but not just with that. "And he told me who she was."

"And who was she?" said Nevada.

"Cecilia," he said. "It was so weird. Here we were recording a song about her and she just turns up at that exact moment. Turns up out of nowhere. Apparently she'd hitch-hiked up from Canterbury. She never did that. Never came to London. But for some reason she did this time, and walks into Olympic Studios at just the moment when we were recording that song, of all songs. None of us recognised her. She'd changed so much." He shook his head. "She was such a mess. I can't imagine anybody picking up a hitchhiker who looked like that. But she got here."

I was staring at him. A sudden chill had wormed its way up my spine. The world had ceased to make sense and I needed to put it back together again. Nevada was staring at me. "You say this was Cecilia Drummond?"

"Yeah. Cecilia."

"Here in London. A year and a half ago?"

"Around about then, I guess."

I said, "But she's been dead for twenty years."

Erik stared at us for a long moment. Then he chuckled. "Oops," he said. He looked at the glass in his hand as though someone had placed it there without his knowledge. "That's right."

"What do you mean, 'that's right'?" I was eager for the world to make sense again.

"I guess I let the cat out of the bag." Erik chuckled. "Oh well, I suppose it had to come out sometime."

"You mean she's not dead?" said Nevada.

"That's right."

"Well, what the hell is going on?" I said.

Erik sighed and poured the last of the vodka into his glass. "Like you said, it was about twenty years ago. Some tabloid newspaper ran a story about how Cecilia had died in a loony bin. It was a big deal, you know, a chance to dig up all the shit from the past and sell a few papers. All the other papers jumped on the bandwagon. The story was everywhere." He chuckled again and grinned at us. He looked like a mischievous kid. "But it was wrong. The fuckers had got it wrong. You see, what happened was that some woman called Drummond with the same initial as Cecilia—C. Drummond—had died in a psychiatric hospital in Kent and some reporter had put two and two together and got twenty-two." He shook his head fondly. "The dumb fucks."

"And no one discovered it was a mistake?"

"Well, we did." Erik smiled happily. "Me and the boys in the band. Of course we did. The only people who really cared about her."

Nevada shook her head. "But you never told anyone else?"

"Well, at first we were going to." Erik looked at us slyly. "Then we thought, why? It would just mean *more* hideous fucking publicity. And the way things were, Cecilia could actually be left in peace. When you think about it, it was a blessing in disguise. So we just let everyone go on thinking she was dead. And it worked."

We all looked at each other. "Holy shit," said Nevada.

"You didn't tell Nic Vardy about her?" I said.

"We *especially* didn't tell Nic Vardy about her. He's a photographer. What would he have done? Taken her picture. That's the last thing any of us wanted, the state she's in."

The cold air sobered us up as we walked back through Barnes. Nevada huddled close to my side, sheltering from the wind. She said, "I had planned to scoot across the bridge to Hammersmith and do the charity shops. But after all those revelations…"

"And all that vodka."

"And all that vodka, I don't know if I'm up for the charity shops." She took my arm and looked up at me. "Do you mind if we just go home? We can check on the little demons."

I shrugged. "Fine with me. I've got to get back anyway. The Colonel is due soon. He's coming over to collect his single."

"And pay for it."

"He's already paid. Freddie texted me to say thanks, the money had arrived."

"That was efficient," said Nevada. "Yes, we'd better get back. The Colonel is likely to be on time." Then she suddenly gripped my arm hard and stopped dead. "My god. We're going to have to tell him about his sister."

"Absolutely not."

She stared at me. "But she's alive. She's his one surviving relative. He has to know."

"She was alive eighteen months ago when Erik Make Loud was cutting his album. Who knows what's happened since then?"

"What do you mean?"

I said, "Erik told us he's not in touch with her on any kind of a regular basis. For all we know she's dropped dead of a heart attack or something in the meantime. Do you really want to take that chance? Tell the Colonel that his one surviving relative is still alive, and then discover she's kicked the bucket?"

"No, I suppose not. Not when you put it like that." She looked at me. "But do you really think that's likely to have happened? Her kicking the bucket?"

"We're not taking any chances," I said. "We're going to confirm Erik's story, and see her in person, in the flesh. And when you and I have seen that she's actually alive, then we'll tell him."

The Colonel certainly was on time, ringing the bell on the dot, standing outside our door looking pink and scrubbed in his full L.L.Bean winter regalia. The weather had really turned cold. I brought him in and Nevada made coffee—the second-best stuff—while I showed him the record and played it for him. I expected him to display some kind of a reaction to the eerie chant in the run-out groove—after all, this was his dead sister. But for all the expression I could discern on his face, he might as well have been listening to refrigerator noise. So I put the record back in its sleeve and we talked business until Nevada brought the coffee through.

She sat with us at the table and Fanny came to join us, hopping into the one empty chair, which happened to be beside the Colonel. He reached down and patted her gently on the head as we talked. I told Nevada about the deal we'd struck. "I mentioned that a friend of ours is interested in acquiring the record when the Colonel—"

"Mr Drummond," said the Colonel, pausing sternly in his massage of our cat.

"—When Mr Drummond is finished with it. And Mr Drummond has agreed to sell it to Tinkler for two hundred pounds." This was a good deal for Tinkler, and for the Colonel for that matter, and I was proud of having struck it.

"Providing your friend will sign an agreement giving me access to the record whenever I need it, to show to the media or whatever." He gave Nevada a steely gaze. "I assume this friend is reliable?"

"Oh, absolutely," said Nevada.

"Now," I said, "I think you have something for us."

The Colonel frowned and looked up from stroking Fanny. "Something for you?"

"You said you'd bring over the documents. Lucy's father's material about Valerian. The photocopies she brought over from Morocco."

"Oh, that," said Colonel, and resumed his attentions to the cat. "I'm afraid I can't help you with that."

"Why not?"

"It seems that Lucille," he intoned the name with heavy sarcasm, "managed to screw things up."

"What do you mean? What happened?"

"She took them into this printing place to get them scanned and there was some kind of mix-up. Before they could scan them they lost them. Apparently they were handed over to someone. A customer. The wrong customer. And they went off with them and now the printing place doesn't know where they are and disavows any responsibility for losing them. This is just so typical of that woman."

He seemed almost happy in his bitterness. "So typical. She insisted on choosing this print shop to look after it, and they've gone and lost them. Just let someone walk in off the street and waltz away with them."

Nevada and I looked at each other.

"Welcome back to Paranoia Heights," she said softly. "We hope you enjoy your stay."

14. ROCK PUB

"I think Tinkler suspects something," said Nevada, over the noise of the traffic.

"I'd be surprised if he didn't," I said. "You were carrying on like Mata Hari."

"Well, it's just that I have no gift for intrigue." I showed what I thought of this proposal with a snort. "All right," she allowed. "Under normal circumstances I do have a certain gift for intrigue. When it's called for. But not when it involves pulling the wool over poor Tinkler's eyes. Isn't that an odd expression? I'll have to look up where it comes from. Wool over the eyes. I mean he is our friend and everything."

We waited for a gap in the steady stream of cars and then walked across Rocks Lane. It was a cold night with a high white moon. A full moon. Turk would be out hunting. I hoped she was okay.

"'And everything' is right," I said. "If Tinkler found out we were going to one of London's legendary rock pubs, to see a pop goddess who has been presumed dead for two decades…" We paused and crossed Queen's Ride. The traffic grew thinner as we moved away from the main road.

"And what's worse, it's in Putney, this legendary rock pub. I mean it's in Tinkler's back yard. His stomping ground."

"He doesn't have a stomping ground. He doesn't stomp. In fact, he doesn't get out much." Tinkler's idea of an adventurous evening was smoking dope and sitting in front of his hi-fi. It has to be said, it is a very good hi-fi.

"Still, it does seem a bit of a betrayal," said Nevada.

"If he'd known we were going he would have insisted on coming along. And we don't want to freak Cecilia out. With any additional attention, I mean."

Nevada shrugged. "It sounds like she's fairly thoroughly freaked out already." We turned off Queen's Ride and went left, walking down Gipsy Lane.

"Also he would have pestered Erik Make Loud for an autograph."

"That's a point," she said. "He would have wanted Erik to sign that copy of *All the Cats Love Valerian*. That rare prize which I found for him."

"Hell no," I said. "Tinkler will want to keep the cover pristine."

"Oh."

"He would have wanted Erik to sign a piece of paper especially designed to slip inside the album without damaging it."

Nevada sighed. "Ah well, it's all academic. Since we didn't tell him where we're going." We slowed down now, both because the footpath narrowed here and because we were approaching the shrine that marked the spot where Marc Bolan had died in a car crash. It looked ghostly in the moonlight, a weather-beaten little affair. It obviously still received considerable attention. "His fans are just as dedicated as Valerian's," said Nevada, looking at it as we walked past. "Although he doesn't have a giant oak tree devoted to him."

"A giant, spurious oak tree."

"Very spurious, yes." Nevada turned and looked at me. Her face was pale in the moonlight, her dark eyes huge. "What was all that business about the Mars Bar? You know, the Evil Elf's brother. What he told us."

"Gordon Treverton."

"Yes. What was he talking about?"

"Well, I was going to get Tinkler to explain, but since we're deliberately avoiding him…"

"Only for this evening."

"To cut a long story short, the police made a drug bust, bursting in on Valerian when she was in bed with some guy. Her tour manager, I think. And it was said they found him in the act of eating a popular brand of chocolate bar, out of her… intimate apertures."

"Nicely put."

"But then after she died the whole story promptly migrated to Marianne Faithfull and Mick Jagger." Which said something interesting about the nature of urban myths. "They were also caught, allegedly *in flagrante*, during a drug bust."

"I see. I think. How extraordinary."

"And now it's your turn."

She looked at me, smiling. "Is it?"

"To explain something to me."

"Oh."

"Who was Messalina?"

"Oh, that. Have you never seen *I, Claudius* with Derek Jacobi? Well, you must. We'll have to download it. Or I've got a copy of Graves's book somewhere. No wait, damn it, I lent it to Clean Head. It was a Penguin edition. That's why I haven't got it back. You have to watch that girl. She's very nice and all that but she will steal your Penguin paperbacks. She has a particular weakness for the Penguin Modern Classics series. It's a character defect."

"And Messalina?" I said.

Nevada took my hand in hers. The fabric of our gloves squeaked. "Well, she was a notorious trollop. She was Claudius's wife and she was unfaithful on a sort of industrial scale. She is, I suppose, what in an earlier and more innocent age we would have called a nymphomaniac."

"You don't hear that term much anymore," I said.

"Perhaps because it's been assimilated into ordinary standards of behaviour. I've certainly done my part to contribute to that tendency."

"Haven't we all?"

"Anyway, Messalina. The story goes that she once challenged Rome's leading prostitute…"

"This is ancient Rome we're talking about here."

"Yes. You have to picture them all wearing sandals and in Messalina's case not much else. So she challenged ancient

Rome's leading professional prostitute to see who could, ahem, 'service' the most men in a single night. Messalina won by a country mile, so to speak. The prostitute fled with some harsh words about what an insatiable, depraved slut Messalina was."

I let the implications of this sink in. "So Colonel Drummond," I said, "I mean the real Colonel—Valerian's father—he had to read about that in the newspapers. How his daughter was British pop music's answer to Messalina?"

"Yes," said Nevada. "He had to read it over his breakfast marmalade, as it were." She looked up at me. "Nice, huh?"

"Not very."

Nevada squeezed my hand tight. "We're going to meet Cecilia Drummond."

"That's right."

"What are we going to say?"

"I don't know."

"We can ask her why her sister hanged herself."

"If she *did* hang herself," I said.

As we walked through the door of the pub, into the welcome warmth and smell of beer, Nevada said, "Erik was very insistent we shouldn't refer to him by name."

"I remember. You said."

"He doesn't want to be mobbed by his fans. A natural anxiety, I'm sure."

We spotted him immediately, sitting at the bar. He was wearing a blue and white striped jacket and straw hat, for all the world as if he'd been hanging around since the boat race last spring. He was even wearing sunglasses, despite it being an autumn night, and indoors. Apparently this was his idea of incognito.

He was chatting up, or trying to chat up, the pretty girl serving him. She was smiling tolerantly as she waited for the foam to settle on his pint of Guinness. "And a gin and tonic, please, love," he said as we joined him. "Might as well get them in before the show starts," he commented, grinning at us. "So you made it, eh?"

"Thank you for tipping us off about this," I said. "It's a perfect opportunity." He didn't seem to hear me. Maybe he was a man embarrassed by gratitude. Or made deaf by stadium rock.

Nevada smiled at him as she unwound her scarf. "Can you believe I've never been here?" she said, pausing to unbutton her coat. "I mean, we live around the corner, right in the neighbourhood, and I've never been here."

"Spoiled a perfect record, eh?" said Erik. He peered around, perhaps trying to see through his sunglasses.

Like the Bull's Head in Barnes, and a million other music venues the world over, the Half Moon consisted of a large front room that was a saloon bar with doors at the back that led into a dedicated music area. But the music wasn't in the back room tonight. Instead, one corner of the pub had been kept clear of customers—not a difficult challenge given the sparseness of the crowd—and featured an acoustic guitar poised upright on a stand, a stool, and a hand-lettered placard on a music stand that read ALL THE WAY

FROM CANTERBURY... THE SPIRIT OF THE JAGUAR.

"This is perfect," said Erik. "You can meet Ambrose, her manager, and decide what you want to do about an interview." He peered at us over his sunglasses. His eyes were surprisingly clear for a man who was drinking Guinness and gin. "You can go down and see them in Canterbury or whatever. I didn't feel right just giving you Cecilia's address. But you can meet here, on neutral ground, and take it from there."

"What did you tell her?" I said.

"I didn't tell her anything." He sipped his drink. "I spoke to him. You have to speak to him. Ambrose. The amazing Ambrose Smith."

"What did you tell him?"

"I mentioned that you were from Stanmer Productions and he got very excited." He smiled at Nevada. "Don't worry about getting an interview. He'll probably take your arm off in his eagerness. Ambrose would do anything for publicity."

I said, "If he's so eager for publicity why isn't he cashing in on her real name?" I nodded at the placard on the music stand.

Erik nodded and leaned in closer to me. He smelled of expensive aftershave. He spoke in a low voice. "Me and the boys had a quiet word with him, when we found out he was involved with Cecilia. We've told him he can do that if he wants—tell everyone she's alive. But if so, he has to be prepared for a lot of publicity. Including publicity about how he was her psychiatric nurse before he became her boyfriend and business manager. Which puts him on very dodgy ground both ethically and legally. When we put this to him he eagerly agreed that maybe certain sleeping dogs should be left well alone."

"So now they're trying to make it under the name 'The Spirit of the Jaguar'?" said Nevada.

"Yeah."

"Is it South American music?"

"No."

"So what's the relevance?"

"Relevance is the least of their fucking worries," growled Erik.

"But what about now?" I said.

"What about now what, sport?"

"What if *we* reveal who she is." Nevada gave me a what-the-hell-are-you-doing look. "In this documentary we're researching for Stinky," I said. And Nevada got it. Our cover story required this question. "I mean we can hardly dodge around the issue if it's a documentary about Valerian."

Erik Make Loud shrugged and sipped at his gin and tonic. "It has to come out some time. Just so long as it's not exclusively for that little bastard Ambrose to cash in on. He's cashed in enough as it is. Look at that." He nodded at the guitar.

"Very nice," said Nevada.

"Hand made," said Erik, "by Brook in Devon. Beautiful guitar. Much too nice for that silly sod. He's got ten thumbs. He should be playing a plastic banjo."

Nevada frowned as she adjusted her hair tie. Her black hair had grown long since I'd first met her, and it looked good. "And you're suggesting that he fleeced poor Cecilia to pay for it?"

"Oh yeah, she picks up all the bills, or at least her trust fund does." He lifted his pint of Guinness again.

"She has a trust fund?"

Erik wiped the foam off his upper lip. "Yeah, after Valerian topped herself and Cecilia was committed and rendered, you know, unfit to look after her own affairs, her father was put in charge. He was the next of kin. And he made sure all of the money that came in, all Valerian's royalties and all Cecilia's royalties, went into a fund to look after her care. I think he realised he wasn't much longer for this world himself."

"That was good of him," said Nevada.

Erik shrugged. "Not really."

"What do you mean?"

"The condition of the trust is that it only pays out a pittance. A bare living for Cecilia." He grinned. "Just a bit of the interest generated by the capital. Barely enough to keep her in medication and Ambrose Smith in guitars and gold teeth. Meanwhile untold fucking wealth is piling up behind the scenes. And she never gets to get her hands on it." He stared into the dark depths of his pint. "Like a teenager who never grows up."

"What happens if she gets better?" said Nevada.

"She isn't going to get better."

"What happens when she dies?" I said.

"All the money goes to some military charity designated by the old man. Plastic poppies for plastic heroes, or something like that." Erik shook his head ruefully. "You can imagine how pleased Ambrose Smith is about that. Oh look, here he is now."

A man was moving towards the corner of the pub reserved for music tonight. He was in his thirties or perhaps early forties. It was hard to tell. But, either way, decades too young to be with Cecilia. Classic gigolo stuff. He had an odd golden skin tone and I couldn't identify his origins, which were obviously mixed race. He had an afro and freckles and was wearing a camouflage-pattern jumpsuit, the bagginess of which only emphasised the emaciated leanness of his frame, and highly polished oxblood Doc Marten boots. He picked up the guitar, sat on the stool and began to strum away.

It became immediately evident that Erik hadn't been exaggerating. Ambrose Smith couldn't play the guitar, or at least not very well. His music was hesitant and stilted and his sense of time was way off. There were even some titters from the crowd, which he ignored or perhaps genuinely didn't hear. He certainly seemed to be concentrating on his playing.

Then the pub fell silent. Emerging from the women's toilets came a strange figure. Pale-faced and lank-haired, she was of medium height but stupendously fat. Her dress, if you could call it that, was black and decorated with silver crescent moons. It had a cheap, shiny look and might have been made out of fabric intended for a children's tablecloth. She had a preposterously large, red plastic flower clipped in her hair and was wearing splayed and battered red velvet slippers. She slopped across the pub to the corner where the freckled man sat playing, as if wading through a shallow swamp.

He flashed her a smile as she joined him. Literally flashed. The man's mouth was full of metal. I understood now what Erik meant about spending money on gold teeth. She stood beside him as he played, inert and massive. She made no move to do anything, and I began to wonder if indeed this was the act—that he thrashed ham-fistedly at the guitar while she towered in silence beside him. A thoroughly modern piece of performance art.

But then she began to sing.

At first it wasn't clear whether she was making any noise at all, or if the noise was coming from her. The pale lips in her broad, pasty face were barely parted. But the sound kept getting louder, and sharper, until it was like something a cat might have made in a moment of torment, or ecstasy. Everyone in the pub was staring at her, even the bar staff, standing transfixed in mid-motion of pouring drinks.

Suddenly the noise turned into song. Instead of inchoate sound, words were emerging. Soft and loud, harsh and gentle, a stream of words apparently unconnected, in such sharply varying pitch and intonation that it was like someone tuning a radio and spinning through stations, though without the intervening static.

But all the time the voice was riding the tune that was coming from the guitar, and compensating for its deficiencies. It thickened the chords, tightened up the rhythm, made the effect more tuneful. Turning it into music. Thanks to the voice it was definitely music, real and urgent and unearthly.

It wasn't easy to listen to, though. It was as if something had been unleashed in the pub, and people couldn't decide whether they were scared of it, or drawn to it. The vulnerability that shimmered in the voice, threatening to break through at any moment, gave tension to the stretched purity of every note. And her sense of time was extraordinary, the way she could draw out phrases was utterly unsettling, as though disdainfully showing that the idea of time itself was nonsense.

She sounded strikingly like her sister, though more raw and damaged. The years had not been kind.

When she finished there was stunned silence. Sometimes such a silence comes just before a tumult of applause. Not this time. There was some sparse clapping, including from our table, but for the most part just more silence, a grieved and injured stillness from listeners who seemed angry about what they'd been exposed to. And what it had made them feel.

"They won't be knocking the Arctic Monkeys off YouTube any time soon," cackled Erik, shaking his head. But he was clapping.

Ambrose came bustling over to our table, holding his guitar by the neck in one hand and Cecilia by the wrist with the other. She followed him neither willingly nor reluctantly, but like a mindless mass being moved by random forces. He sat down with us and she sat beside him. He grinned all around, showing us his gold teeth. There were a lot of them. She didn't look at us, but just gazed vacantly into the middle distance. There was a dismaying blankness to her face, as though a big hand had passed across it and wiped it clean of personality.

"The flower looks really good in your hair, doll," said Ambrose. He kissed her on the lips with a swift predatory motion. "Nice one." He might as well have kissed a statue for all the response he got. What little signs of life she had shown while singing had submerged again, utterly and profoundly. Ambrose hitched around in his chair so he could direct his smile at Nevada and me. "So you're with Stinky Stanmer, eh?"

"That's right."

"And you'd like to talk to us?"

"Yes, about Valerian," said Nevada. "We're working on a programme about her." She looked at Cecilia. "And her sister, of course."

"That's great," said Ambrose. "Isn't that great, doll?" He kissed her again, on the cheek this time, and she swayed a little under the pressure of his lips but otherwise showed no reaction. "They want to talk about your sister."

"Uh, if that's all right," said Nevada, watching this freak show.

"Yeah, yeah. You can come down to Canterbury, can you? To see us?"

"No problem," I said. We exchanged phone numbers and then Ambrose Smith left, guitar in one hand and singer in the other. A young couple were coming in through the pub door as they were going out and they recoiled physically from Cecilia. She gave no sign of even noticing this. The door swung shut and they were gone. We looked at each other.

"Maybe it was just a bad night for her," said Nevada.

Erik laughed. "A bad night? This is as good as it fucking gets."

* * *

"Erik Make Loud, you lying bastard." We looked around to see Nic Vardy standing beside our table.

"So you got here," said Erik. He looked at us. "When I told you about Cecilia I had to tell old Nic, too." Vardy pulled up a chair and sat down beside us, close to Nevada, I noticed.

"The lying, lying bastard. All these years, letting me think she was gone." But he didn't seem terribly angry, and Erik just shrugged casually.

"You know how it is, mate. Did you catch the show?"

"Oh yes."

"What did you reckon?"

"Oh, straight to the top of the charts. Definitely."

"You take any pictures?"

Vardy shook his head. "The only one in here worth photographing is that girl behind the bar." He looked at Nevada. "Present company excepted, of course."

"Yeah, she's cute isn't she?" leered Erik, his eyes on the barmaid. They then proceeded to discuss the woman's merits. I glanced at Nevada, who rolled her eyes. I was impressed at the laddish persona Vardy had taken on in Erik's presence. Maybe this was what you did if you were a good photographer. Imitate your subjects, so they relax in your company. But it was tedious to listen to, and I was just wondering if we could make our apologies and slip away when Vardy got to his feet again.

"Well, I just dropped in for a quick visit," he said. "Places to be." He waved to us and left. Erik sighed.

"I felt bad about keeping him in the dark. So once I told you two…"

"We understand," said Nevada.

Erik drained the last of his Guinness. "I'd better be going myself." He grinned. "Bong Cha will be worried if I'm late."

"We'll see you off the premises," said Nevada. We followed Erik and were almost at the door when a familiar voice called out.

"Erik Make Loud! What an unexpected pleasure."

We turned to see Tinkler sitting on a bar stool, smiling like the Cheshire cat, with a whisky in front of him. He looked at Nevada and me. "Oh, and look! My old friends. What a surprise."

"You know this guy?" said Erik.

"Yes, I'm afraid so," said Nevada.

"It's a real privilege to meet you, Mr Make Loud." Tinkler ostentatiously moved the empty stool beside him, indicating that it was available for occupancy. But Erik wouldn't even look at him directly. I was beginning to realise that this was a rock star habit. If you weren't interested in someone, just pretend that they don't exist.

"I'd better make a move," he said, turning for the door. Tinkler didn't seem troubled, or offended.

"I recently acquired a copy of *All the Cats Love Valerian*," he said, casually. "With the original blue label and the nude cover."

Erik paused in mid-stride and turned and looked at him. "Fucking hell, those are as rare as hen's teeth."

"Indeed."

He drifted back towards Tinkler, who remained sitting nonchalantly on his stool. "I haven't even got one myself," said Erik. "The ex-fucking-wife got all my copies. Find it on eBay, did you?"

Tinkler shook his head and smiled suavely. "No, in a charity shop, as it happens."

Erik settled down on the stool beside him and stared at Tinkler. "You're kidding."

"No."

"How much did you pay?"

"Fifty pence," said Tinkler. This was, indeed, what Nevada had paid for the LP in a charity shop in Hammersmith.

"You're kidding! You bastard." Erik began to laugh helplessly.

"Yes," said Tinkler, "this is the kind of bargain you can find if you have time to scour the charity shops." He looked at Nevada and me. "Unfortunately my friends here don't have time for that kind of thing. Being high-flying media achievers."

"Fifty pence!" cackled Erik. "You want a drink, mate?"

"I wouldn't mind," said Tinkler offhandedly. Erik slapped him on the back.

"I suppose you want me to autograph it for you, the album?" he said.

"Oh, I wouldn't put you to that trouble," said Tinkler. He took a piece of paper out of his pocket. "It would be quite sufficient if you were to sign this." He handed the piece of paper, and a pen, to Erik Make Loud, who promptly signed his name.

"Who should I make it out to, mate?"

"Jordon Tinkler please. Jordon with an 'o'."

"Like that bloke who played for Birmingham?" said Erik.

"Exactly."

"What position did he play?"

"Midfield."

"That's right!"

Nevada stared at me. "I can't believe it," she said. "They're bonding over football."

But the conversation had already moved on. They were now discussing the cover photo of *All the Cats Love Valerian* and Tinkler was drawing relaxed reminiscences out of him in a way we had never achieved. "Never was there so much pussy on one album cover," reflected Erik Make Loud philosophically.

"That's right," said Tinkler happily. "Pussy!"

Nevada and I edged up to the bar beside him. "How did you know we were here?" I whispered.

"Clean Head told me."

I looked at Nevada. "Oops," she said. "Loose lips sink ships."

"There is no escape from me," said Tinkler. "And by the way, I'm coming with you."

"Coming with us when?"

"When you go down to Canterbury to see Cecilia Drummond."

I said, "What makes you think—"

"Oh come on," said Tinkler, and sipped his whisky.

15. CANTERBURY

The Colonel looked like a man who'd seen a ghost. Which I suppose in a way he had.

He set something down on the table in front of us. It was a sealed plastic bag of the kind you use to store food in the freezer. Inside it was a cotton swab. "DNA sample?" said Nevada. The Colonel nodded grimly. "You think it might not be her?" Before he could answer, the waitress came and took our order. Nevada and I each asked for another coffee. The Colonel ordered nothing.

We were in a little café near Canterbury West station where the coffee was surprisingly good—particularly surprisingly since Ambrose Smith had recommended the place. We had come in on the train that morning—despite his threats, Tinkler had stayed at home; it had been too early a start for him—and Nevada and I had waited tactfully here while the Colonel went for his reunion with his sister. Under the auspices of Ambrose of course.

As soon as the waitress was gone, the Colonel said,

"That bloated monstrosity? Are you surprised that I doubt it's my sister? That distended bag of flesh?"

"Ah, she is a big girl," said Nevada diplomatically.

"She's revolting. How could someone let themselves get like that? I tried to count her chins but I couldn't. I literally couldn't, because they were wobbling too much. She wouldn't look me in the eyes and I couldn't stop staring at all those grotesque, disgusting chins."

Yes, that must have been a jolly family reunion, I thought.

"That coffee smells good," said the Colonel abruptly.

"We'll get you one," said Nevada.

"No, don't bother." But Nevada was already looking for the waitress. He turned away and sighed with exasperation.

"You need something," said Nevada. "You must, after seeing her for the first time in—how many years?"

"Over forty," said the Colonel. "Over forty years."

I said, "And for twenty of those years you must have thought she was dead."

Nevada winced at this bluntness but it didn't seem to trouble the Colonel. He just shook his head pugnaciously, like a man coming to a conclusion, and said, "I'm still not convinced it's her."

Nevada nodded at the plastic bag with the swab in it. "Well, you'll soon have proof one way or another."

I said, "Do you have a sample of the real Cecilia's DNA on file somewhere?"

He shook his head. "No."

"So what will they do?" said Nevada. "What will they test it against?"

"Him," I said.

The Colonel glared at me. I'd spoiled his explanation. "That's right," he said. "They test me and then they will be able to determine if this sample came from my sister."

"How did you get it?" I said. "Did you swab her mouth?"

He held up the bag and looked at the little white swab with an expression of distaste. "No, her keeper did that for me. While I watched."

Nevada snorted. "Her keeper. That's a bit harsh."

He shot her a look. "Do you think so?"

"Perhaps not." Nevada looked at me and I nodded. Perhaps not indeed. Poor Ambrose hadn't won many friends among us.

"That's exactly what he was, though," said the Colonel, "like some kind of keeper who has got hold of a rare and precious animal."

"A cash cow," suggested Nevada. Then, hastily, "Not that I'm calling anyone a cow."

The Colonel grinned nastily. "No, but she is. You're right. She is a cow. A disgusting, fat cow." I could see that Nevada was getting nervous about what she might have unleashed. She looked again for the waitress, who was still busy on the other side of the café.

"But you must have had a feeling," she said, while she kept watch on the waitress.

"A feeling?" said the Colonel, as if he'd never heard the word before.

Nevada caught the waitress's eye and waved. "About whether or not she was your sister. You must have had some kind of response or reaction."

"She didn't say a word to me. She didn't talk at all. I tried speaking to her, introducing myself, asking her questions. But I eventually gave up because she didn't say anything. Not a word. Maybe she can't. She just sat there looking at me, with those eyes of hers." He shook his head. He actually sounded a little freaked out, or as much as a buttoned-up man like him would allow himself to be. "It's like there is no one at home behind that fat face."

The waitress was working her way over towards our table. "All right," said Nevada. "You didn't speak to her, but you must have had some kind of *feeling*." It seemed she wouldn't let go of this line of enquiry, but I could have told her that the Colonel wasn't the kind of man to talk about his feelings, unless they were ones of vociferous disapproval.

I said, "She didn't say anything to you?" He shook his head. "So you just sat there in silence?"

"No, that would have been preferable. But that Ambrose character kept talking. And then she started singing."

"Singing?" said Nevada.

"He made her do it for me." The Colonel grinned mirthlessly. "Perhaps he thought I wasn't getting full value. Like getting his trained monkey to perform for me." He lowered his eyes. "But when I heard her…"

"Yes?" said Nevada.

"I began to think it might actually be her." He shook his head, as if disgusted with himself for even entertaining the possibility. "But even then, there was something about it that wasn't quite right. It sounded like her, but…"

"It sounded more like Valerian," I said.

He stared at me. I felt that I'd finally got his full attention. "Yes," he said. "That's right. How did you know?" Nevada was looking at me.

"That night when we heard her in the pub. I thought that then. The way she was singing, bending notes and stretching time, it was what Valerian used to do."

"Is that significant?" said Nevada.

I said, "Well, if you were going to coach someone to pretend to be Cecilia Drummond you would have to go to the records. And those records feature Valerian a hell of a lot more prominently than Cecilia. And when the two sisters sing together, Cecilia is often just there in the background, buried in the mix."

Drummond was nodding his head eagerly. I couldn't believe we actually agreed about something. "That's right. If you tried to research the records, you might well end up sounding like the wrong sister." He chuckled at the thought, as if we were already exposing some swindler. "Anyway, we'll soon know." He patted the pocket where he had his DNA sample securely stowed. He looked entirely happy, a man at peace. Ah, the comforting certainties of science.

The waitress finally arrived and Nevada flashed her a smile. "We'll have another coffee, please," she said quickly, before the Colonel could countermand her order.

When she left he said, "What do you know about this Ambrose joker?"

"Just what we told you. Apparently he used to be her psychiatric nurse."

"But how did he get his hooks into her? She's twice his age. I'm going to look into this bastard's background."

"Good idea," I said.

The Colonel sighed and relaxed. Losing its characteristic frown, his face became strangely smooth. He seemed content at last. Perhaps it was having a definite plan of action, and one that might ruthlessly expose someone's legal and moral shortcomings. "I think it is her, though," he said suddenly.

"What?" I said. This seemed a dramatic volte-face.

The Colonel wouldn't look at me. Instead he was gazing steadily at Nevada. "You know you kept asking me if I had a feeling?"

"Yes."

The Colonel stared down at the table. "Well, I didn't exactly, but I did notice something. When we sat down to eat together—Ambrose Smith insisted we have tea and cakes; very generous of him considering that it's Drummond money that's funding him, every penny of it. We're keeping him very nicely—anyway we sat down together, and there was something about how she ate. The fat woman. She was almost choking because she was eating too quickly." He looked up at us. "It was something she'd always done as a child. Cecilia. She was always impatient, always greedy." He shook his head and chuckled. "She was rake thin, Cessie. We always joked that she should be big as a house the way she ate." His smile faded. "Now she is." He looked at us bleakly. "Maybe," he added.

Nevada put her hand on his arm. He looked at her but didn't ask her to remove it. He really quite liked Nevada.

"So you might have found your sister."

"No," said the Colonel. He stood up abruptly, his chair scraping back against the floor. "She is not my sister," he snarled. "Whatever the DNA proves, that thing is not my sister. Not anymore."

I began to realise that Nevada wasn't going to be able to get the Colonel his coffee after all.

"Wherever Cecilia is now, she's not there. Not resident in that thing, that empty husk of lard."

He shook his head and left.

The Colonel caught a train back to London but we stayed on, as planned. We'd arranged to give Cecilia an hour to recover after her meeting with her brother before we went to interview her. So we drank another coffee, and we were just paying and getting ready to leave when we saw Ambrose peering in the window and grinning. He waved to us and pushed in through the door and came and sat at our table.

"I'm glad I caught you," he said.

"We were just coming to you," I said.

"That's why I'm glad I caught you." He winced and pressed his hands together in a prayerful gesture. "I wonder if we could postpone it?"

"Postpone the meeting?"

"With Cessie, yeah." He smiled. "It really took it out of her, seeing her brother after all these years, as you can well imagine, and I thought it was best if she just had a little lie-down for the rest of the day."

I was furious. We had come all this way especially. Nevada gave me a warning look, so all I said was, "Well, I guess you know best."

"Thanks, yeah, thank you for being so understanding. You see, I do know best, as you say."

I sighed. "Back to London, then."

"Yeah, we'll rearrange the interview. Come back any time."

"We will," said Nevada, and we moved towards the door. But as we did so he grabbed my arm. I turned back and looked at him. He was surprisingly strong. I suppose if he'd been a psychiatric nurse that might well have been a requirement.

"There's just one thing I don't understand," he said slowly. He had stopped smiling. "You say you're working on a documentary."

I felt my heart begin to beat raggedly in my chest. Nevada was staring at us. But I kept my voice calm. "Yes?"

"Well, then, why didn't you have some cameras there?"

"Cameras?" said Nevada.

He nodded. "Yeah, to record the big moment. When the brother and sister meet each other for the first time in decades?"

I said, "We'll restage it for the programme."

He let go of my arm. "Oh yeah. Of course." He nodded. "Great idea. Restage it."

We arranged a time to come back for our interview with Cecilia and he patted me on the shoulder and then insisted on shaking hands as we said goodbye. His palm was sweaty. I tried not to hold this against him, and failed.

When we got outside Nevada said, "Nice save."

16. BABY GRAND

On our second visit to Canterbury to interview what Nevada insisted on calling the 'happy couple', we drove down in Tinkler's car. We'd told him firmly that he couldn't join us when we went to see Cecilia, but he assured us he wanted to visit Canterbury anyway. His motives were pretty obvious— it was a Sunday and Clean Head had decided she fancied a visit to the old cathedral city, as well.

Being Clean Head, however, she had to do the driving. This involved first sneering at poor Tinkler's little blue car, apparently because it was an automatic. Her disdain didn't prevent her from getting us out of London in record time and flinging us onto the M25, bound for Kent. "Quite nippy, though," she allowed. She looked at Tinkler, who had his head out the window in the slipstream like a happy dog.

"Do you mind winding that up," said Nevada. "It's getting a bit breezy back here."

"Sure," said Tinkler, shutting the window and settling back in his seat. He gazed adoringly at Clean Head who was merging with traffic, moving us from the slow lane to the medium lane and then the fast lane in a smooth flow of manoeuvres. The car was quite nippy, as she said, but I couldn't quite free myself of the notion that it might fly apart at any moment. This was mostly because it belonged to Tinkler, though, rather than any intrinsic judgement on the machine.

"Have you given it a name yet?" said Nevada.

"What?"

Nevada patted the roof. "Your car."

"Yes," said Tinkler. "Kind of Blue."

"Is that because of my abiding love of the Miles Davis album?" I asked.

"No, it's because it's kind of blue." It was indeed, an odd metallic shade that must have given his sister Maggie a negotiating advantage when she'd been beating the price down.

"You realise this really isn't a Volvo?" announced Clean Head.

"Yes it is."

"Oh no." She shook her head, smiling. I could tell she was bursting to tell us something.

"It says Volvo on the outside," said Tinkler. "And the inside. There, look. There."

"Oh, it's been rebadged as a Volvo all right," said Clean Head. "But it's actually one of the last DAFs. They were a Dutch firm with some very interesting technological ideas." She patted the gear lever. "And did you know you had a Variomatic transmission?"

"I didn't know I had a transmission."

"It's a belt drive system. Quite revolutionary, no pun intended." She cursed at a slow driver, slipped into the middle lane and proceeded, quite illegally, to overtake him and remorselessly bury his dwindling reflection in the distance. The engine roared. "It's a continuously variable system. And it works in reverse. In fact, you can drive as fast backwards as you can forwards."

"No need to demonstrate that just at the moment," said Nevada quickly. The little car shook, shouldering against the slipstream as we continued to fly down the motorway, obliterating all competition.

"And, of course, it gives you optimum torque," said Clean Head.

"I knew that," said Tinkler.

The happy couple lived at a narrow, terraced house in Castle Row near the city wall. The door sprang open as soon as we knocked and Ambrose Smith gave us his big, gold smile. "Welcome," he said. "Come in. We've been expecting you." He stood back and we had to brush past him to get inside. The house was tiny. We stepped from the front door straight into the living room. This would have been a comfortable, cosy space if it hadn't been almost completely filled with a gleaming red-lacquered baby grand piano. Nevada and I looked at each other, thinking exactly the same thing.

How the fuck did they get that in here?

"Be right back!" exclaimed Ambrose brightly, and he

trotted into the back of the house where I had glimpsed a kitchen.

"It's nice and warm, anyway," said Nevada, taking off her coat.

"And so spacious," I said, trying to edge my way further into the room.

Nevada chuckled. She touched the baby grand's gleaming top. "This is a lovely piano."

"They probably have to keep the place warm for the sake of the piano," I said. Certainly it dominated the room, and indeed most of the ground floor of the house. It was jammed into the room with two armchairs and a sofa. They had all been upholstered in the same white fabric, with a rather tasteful black pattern on it, which on close inspection turned out to consist of the repeated silhouettes of little horned goats. Nothing odd about that, then.

I thought of the dress Cecilia had been wearing when we saw her sing. With the crescent moons on it. There was a sound in the back of the house and then Cecilia came out of the kitchen, her pale face looming in the shadows as she approached us. She completely filled the small hallway, brushing against both walls as she advanced, and she briefly filled the entire doorway, cutting off the daylight as she came in to join us. Nevada and I moved around in an intricate little dance so she could get into the room, edging into the narrow space between the piano and the chairs.

As Cecilia popped into the room, clearing the door, it became obvious that Ambrose was standing behind her and had indeed been pushing her. Rather than having come into the room of her own volition he'd basically propelled her in as if he'd been shoving a trolley. We all stood in the small room trying not to stare at each other, except for Cecilia, who was focused on some interior landscape to such an extent that her gaze had been emptied.

They were at one end of the piano, the keyboard end by the sofa. We were at the other end, by the armchairs. "Please sit down," said Ambrose, proceeding to sit down on the sofa with Cecilia. Or rather pressing her down onto it and then sitting beside her. Nevada and I sank down into the armchairs, our knees under the piano.

His gold smile gleamed in the gloomy room. "Well, very nice of you to come down and visit us."

"Is Cecilia, ah, prepared for the interview?" said Nevada. Sitting on the sofa staring blankly into space, Cecilia didn't seem prepared for much of anything.

"Oh yeah. Yeah, yeah, yeah," said Ambrose. "Aren't you, doll? You're ready." Cecilia gazed placidly at him, or in his direction, and said nothing. Ambrose cleared his throat. "Well, go ahead. Ask any questions you want."

Nevada and I looked at each other. "All right," I said. "Cecilia…" The woman didn't look at me. "What was it like touring with your sister and the band?"

"Cessie didn't tour much," said Ambrose quickly. "She mostly worked in the studio. Didn't you, doll?"

"Listen, Ambrose," said Nevada brightly, "as a general rule could you please try and avoid answering on behalf of Cecilia? Thank you. It makes for a better interview that way."

"All right," said Ambrose with a mournful look, "but I

can't guarantee that she'll want to answer you."

"Then why are we here?" I said. "Why did you agree to an interview?"

"Oh, we can still have an interview. You just ask me the questions and I'll ask Cessie. On your behalf."

Nevada leaned forward, or at least as far forward as she could get before she was pressing herself against the piano. "You'll ask Cessie? You mean later?"

"Yes."

"When we're not around?"

"It'll be a good system. I'll get back to you with the answers."

"It won't be a good system, Ambrose," I said.

"Oh no, it'll work fine. Won't it, doll?" Cecilia continued to say nothing and not look anywhere in particular in the room, her empty gaze wandering lazily, passing across us with no more attention than it accorded the furnishings or the wallpaper. "You just ask me, I ask her, and I tell you. In an interview situation. Or I could just do it direct to camera if you like."

"You?"

"Yes?"

"Direct to camera?" said Nevada.

"Like a talking head sort of thing. Or I could be like the MC. Guiding the viewer through the documentary."

"That's very kind of you to offer," said Nevada firmly. "But no."

"The thing is," I said, "it's Cecilia we're interested in."

"Exactly," said Nevada.

"Not you."

"Not you *per se*," said Nevada.

Ambrose shrugged. "Well, I'm afraid I can't guarantee when Cessie might be inclined to talk to you. She's not always feeling that communicative. And we don't want to pressure her, do we?"

"This isn't proving very satisfactory, Ambrose," I said. He shrugged again and said nothing. His lips were shut tight and his face was stubbornly set. I could see we'd reached a stalemate. I turned to Nevada to see if she had any good ideas but suddenly she looked away from me. She was staring across the room. I followed her gaze and saw that Cecilia had abruptly struggled to her feet. Ambrose looked as surprised as we were when she turned to the piano and sat down. Her hands sank out of sight onto the keyboard.

And she began to play.

It was beautiful and subtle and fluent. The music just seemed to flow out of her, coming from nowhere, transmitted through her fingertips. It was a classical piece, something theatrical and teasingly familiar. Mozart, I guessed. At first just a note here and there, building up a pattern, setting a tempo, then settling into the piece with smooth assurance. She played in a minimalist way, dotting notes at exact intervals that should, by rights, have been too slow but instead seemed to milk extra emotion from the music. She remained on the beat yet somehow put a lot of space into the music, with the discrete pointillist notes growing into a bigger picture, the complexity and pace accumulating as it went along.

Because I'm a barbarian, it reminded me of Count Basie. She must have played for fifteen minutes. None of us said anything or moved. Perhaps we didn't want to break the spell. Then she stopped. The silence seemed to vibrate around us. Cecilia sat placidly at the piano, unmoving and apparently spent. I looked at Nevada.

"Mozart?" I said.

She nodded. "*Don Giovanni.*"

"The Beethoven transcriptions," said a voice. We all turned and looked at Cecilia. Nevada and I were too shocked to reply. We'd become accustomed to the notion that Cecilia couldn't speak—even though of course we'd heard her sing.

If anything, Ambrose was even more shocked than us.

Finally Nevada cleared her throat and said, "Perhaps you'd like to play something else?"

"Oh no, no," said Ambrose. "Cessie mustn't overdo it." But Cecilia had already leaned towards the keyboard and begun to play. Ambrose glared at us. Nevada had made a connection with her, and he didn't like it. He moved over to kneel on the floor beside Cecilia, who continued to play, apparently quite unaware of him. "Mustn't overdo it, doll. Come on now. There's a good girl."

He was grinning all the while he spoke, as if to sustain the illusion that this was all just a casual, friendly conversation. He rose from the floor and stood beside Cecilia. She kept playing. More Mozart, I think.

Clearly, she didn't want to stop.

Abruptly he reached down and lifted her left hand from the keyboard. But her right hand kept playing. He let go of her left hand and gently lifted her right hand, but now her left hand resumed playing. Then he went back to her left hand and lifted it, with the predictable result; the right hand resumed. This went on for what felt like an embarrassing length of time. Finally he lifted both her hands at once, plucking them off the keyboard, and held them tight, hugging her from behind.

He chuckled and smiled at us to show that this was just an affectionate tussle between a couple, rather than a man imposing his will on a woman who might as well have been a stranger. Cecilia stared at us, her face expressionless, her hands stilled.

It reminded me of the way a cat will accept an unwanted embrace, silently enduring it until she can squirm free.

"I'm afraid you have to go now," said Ambrose, smiling politely at us.

"I don't think so, Ambrose," I said. "We've come all this way, twice, and you're sending us away with nothing."

"Oh, no, no," he said. "No, I'm not." He gingerly released Cecilia who sat there, unmoving. Reassured by this passivity he leaned down and picked something off the floor under the sofa. It was a sheaf of notepaper, ruled and handwritten. "I'm going to give you this." He lifted the papers and smiled, as if we should admire them.

Cecilia suddenly started playing again. Ambrose sighed and set the papers on the piano, turning back towards her. "Now, doll," he said, "I thought we had sorted this out—"

There was a bright, chiming sound that harmonised with the music coming from the piano. For a moment I thought Cecilia must have pressed a switch—or perhaps a pedal—to activate another instrument. Then I realised it was the doorbell. Ambrose was gazing towards the front door. "Who could that be?" he said. He turned and looked at us, as if we might know. He seemed to think we'd brought someone with us. I just shrugged, though I had an unhappy fluttering in my stomach as I reflected that it might be Tinkler, ignoring all our injunctions.

Nevada leaned over to me and whispered, "If that's Tinkler I'll kill him."

Ambrose was still staring towards the door. Cecilia kept playing, either genuinely oblivious to everything else or just ignoring it. The sound of the piano in the room was amazing. It was a salutary experience to be reminded of what a real musical instrument sounded like in a real environment, at close quarters. This is what every hi-fi nut aspired to, after all. I was impressed with Cecilia's lightness of touch and delicacy of playing. In a room this size it could easily have been an overwhelming, deafening experience. Point-blank piano. But instead it was sheer pleasure.

The doorbell rang again, and once again randomly fitted in with the contours of the music. I almost laughed. It was such an absurd situation, with Ambrose still sitting there, making no move to answer the door and staring at it—I thought—a little fearfully.

The piano kept playing. The doorbell kept ringing. Then the doorbell stopped. And the front door opened. Now, the only person I knew who was rude enough or arrogant enough to walk into someone's house uninvited was currently ensconced in rehab on a cocaine charge. So I was quite interested to see who this newcomer might be.

He was a small, neat man in a pale-green tweed suit with a bald, pink head and a trim little silver moustache. His eyes gleamed as he smiled at us. He looked alert, prosperous, precise. His first words were, "You must forgive me."

Cecilia stopped playing.

I could see our host didn't recognise him. Ambrose pulled himself to his full height and began to walk towards the uninvited stranger. Suddenly he was tall and quite intimidating. But the little man didn't back away. He just continued smiling in an attempt to defuse the situation and said, "I am so sorry just to barge in but I was ringing the bell—"

"I know," said Ambrose. "We heard you."

The little man sighed. "Well, that's just the thing, you see. I couldn't be sure you *had* heard me." He nodded at Cecilia and smiled at her. "Not with that beautiful music playing. I was standing outside listening to it and it was a genuine pleasure. I could have stood there all day. But I'm afraid I finally had to ring the bell." He took a further step into the room, which wasn't easy, and moved towards Cecilia.

Ambrose moved to block him.

"You play as wonderfully as ever, Cessie," said the little man.

"All right," demanded Ambrose. "Who are you?"

The little man was looking at Cecilia. She gave no sign of seeing him. He said, "Dr William Osterloh." He turned and smiled at Nevada and me. "But call me Bill." I noticed that Ambrose wasn't included in this invitation.

"Doctor?" said Ambrose. He sounded simultaneously both more and less suspicious.

"Yes, Bill Osterloh." He was looking at Cecilia. "You remember me, don't you, Cessie? I travelled with you and the band many times, when your sister and I were having our sessions."

"Sessions?" I said.

He turned and smiled at me. "Ah, the ambiguity of language. I take it you were thinking of sessions in the musical sense. As in 'a session in the studio'." He twinkled at me, bright eyed. That was indeed exactly what I had been thinking. He shook his head and chuckled. "No, not so." He turned and looked at Cecilia. "Cessie did those sort of sessions and so did Valerian." Ambrose was watching him warily. "And in between those Valerian and I would fit in *our* sessions." He turned back to me. "My sessions."

I said, "You were her psychiatrist."

He smiled. "Psychologist. But yes, her shrink." He nodded at Cecilia. "You remember me, don't you, Cessie?" She was staring blankly, face inclined a little downward, perhaps looking at the keyboard, and giving no sign of having heard him. She seemed completely buried inside herself again.

"Okay, right," said Ambrose. "What exactly do you want here, Doctor?"

"Want?" said Osterloh. "Nothing." He was looking down at the piano, at the papers Ambrose had set there.

"Here, I'll take those," said Ambrose, abruptly snatching them up. Dr Osterloh looked at him. He didn't seem offended.

"I have only just learned that Cecilia is still alive," he said. *News travels fast*, I thought. "And I was so *pleased*. I simply had to come and look her up and tell her in person how pleased I am that she is alive and well." He looked at the great pale bulk of the woman hunched over the piano, and I thought, *She's alive all right, but I don't know about the rest of it.* "Such wonderful news."

"Well, that's very kind of you, Doctor," said Ambrose and he smiled a mouthful of gold. He seemed to have settled for his standard unctuous approach. "But it's time for Cecilia to have a little lie-down."

Osterloh's eyebrows raised in polite concern. "Really? Is there something wrong with her?"

"No, not at all. She just gets a little worn out."

Osterloh smiled. "There's no reason why she should. A strong woman like her. Perhaps you'd like me to make an assessment." He leaned towards Cecilia, turning an enquiring smile on her as he began to peer into her eyes.

"Oh no, Doctor," said Ambrose hastily. "That won't be necessary. No. Come on now, love. Come on, doll." He coaxed Cecilia up from the piano stool and began to lead her towards the door.

"Goodbye, Cecilia," said Nevada. "Thank you for playing the piano for us. It was lovely."

"Yes, it was," I said.

Ambrose turned and gave us a strained rictus of a smile. "Isn't that nice, doll? Wave goodbye to the people from Stanmer Productions. We'll be seeing them again soon." He actually lifted one of her hands by the wrist and made her wave to us—a clumsy, flapping, limp-wristed gesture. Dr Osterloh watched in fascination. Ambrose propelled Cecilia out of the room. Osterloh turned to us.

"You are working for Stinky Stanmer?"

"*With* him," said Nevada. "Working *with* him. I'm the executive commissioning producer of his documentary department."

And I'm the king of Siam, I thought.

"So you're working on a documentary," he said.

"Researching one," I said. "You must have known Valerian very well, Doctor."

"Yes."

"Even in the last days of her life."

He nodded, his eyes bright and alert, gauging me. "Especially in the last days of her life."

"Perhaps we can talk to you, then," said Nevada, "in the course of researching our documentary."

"Of course," said Osterloh, taking out a business card and handing it to her. "I hope you do." He turned to me. "And perhaps you'd like a copy of my book."

"Your book?" I said.

"Yes, *The Sovereignty of the Self.* I have some autographed copies in the boot of my car. Would you be interested in buying some?"

"What is the book about exactly?" I said. I was hoping he wouldn't say the sovereignty of the self.

"It's an enquiry into method," he said. "And an ontological statement. It's regarded in some quarters as a modern classic."

"I'm sure it is," I said, "but we have to be quite focused in our research. Does it have anything about Valerian in it?"

"No, I'm afraid it doesn't."

"Well, we'll have to give it a miss."

His silver eyebrows went up. "Are you sure? I still have several hardcover first editions I could let you have at a very advantageous price. Considerably less than they fetch on eBay."

"No, but thanks."

He shrugged. "All right. But don't complain to me when they're gone."

There was a sound from the hallway and Ambrose came in. "Cessie's having a little nap." He looked pointedly at the good doctor.

"I should be getting along," said Osterloh. He nodded to Nevada and me, smiled enigmatically at Ambrose, and went out the front door. He closed it firmly behind him but Ambrose insisted on opening and closing it again, apparently to make sure he was gone. Then he turned and looked at us. "Now, let me give you these." He handed me the papers. They were covered with angular, untidy handwriting in peacock-blue ink.

"What are these, exactly?" I said.

Ambrose smiled modestly. "Well, we knew you were coming down, coming all this way to interview us, and we wanted to make sure you had something worthwhile, worth your journey. So I spoke to Cessie, and discussed various topics we thought would be of interest to you. About Valerian. And I took down what she had to say."

"You took it down?" said Nevada.

A golden smile. "Yes."

I stared at the papers. "So you wrote this?"

"Yes, and—" He fell silent. I turned and saw with a jolt of surprise that Cecilia had emerged from the back of the house. Her big face was pale in the shadows.

"Do you want to know the truth about my sister?" she said.

For a moment we were all too startled to respond.

Then Ambrose moved to her hastily. "Doll. You shouldn't be up. You should be in bed." She ignored him, staring at us with those strange, blank eyes.

"Do you want to know the truth?"

"Yes," I said.

"Doll—"

"She took it to the grave with her," said Cecilia. "That's where it is. All of it."

"Okay, that's enough. Back to bed, you." Beaming with false bonhomie, Ambrose literally pushed her out of the room.

"That's where it is now," she called as he forced her back down the hallway. Then there was silence. He was back a moment later, the horrible false smile firmly fixed on his face.

"Thank you for coming. Best of luck with the documentary. But I think you need to be going now. Goodbye."

As we walked away from the house Nevada said, "She spoke. She actually spoke to us."

"Yes."

"I didn't know she could."

"Neither did I," I said. "But while we were sitting in there it suddenly occurred to me that she might be doped to the eyeballs."

Nevada stared at me. "What?" Then, as it sank in, "You mean we just witnessed a lucid interval, when the drugs were wearing off?"

"Or maybe he got the dosage wrong." I shook my head. "I don't know why I didn't think of it before. Maybe she's like fucking Einstein and he's just keeping her doped up."

"Christ, yes."

"He's a psychiatric nurse," I said.

"So he'd have access to the drugs," said Nevada.

"And that would explain why he was so eager to get rid of Dr Osterloh."

She glanced at me. "You mean, before he had a chance to properly assess her and suss out what was going on."

"It's a theory, anyway," I said. I took the papers out of my pocket and studied them. "Oh, come on."

"What is it?" said Nevada.

"It's just the Wikipedia entry on Valerian. He's copied it verbatim." I showed her the papers.

We dumped them in the first bin we came to.

17. BRIC-À-BRAC

We met Tinkler and Clean Head as arranged and headed back to where we'd parked the car.

"Did you find things to do?" said Nevada.

"Absolutely," said Tinkler. "We went to the cathedral—"

"You went to the cathedral?"

"Of course," said Tinkler primly. "We couldn't come to Canterbury and not see the *cathedral*." He glanced at Clean Head. "And then we went to see the Westgate, and the castle, which isn't really a castle at all."

"It's Norman ruins," said Clean Head. "It's fantastic." She was the real culture vulture. Tinkler was just along for the ride. And of course he had an ulterior motive—he could hardly take his eyes off her.

"So he hasn't dragged you around the charity shops looking for records?" said Nevada.

"Of course not," said Tinkler virtuously. "I've been very well behaved. We've done the historical sites and had tea and scones at a nice little tea and scone place and visited an antiquarian book dealer where we found some rare Penguins."

"I got a couple of Graham Greenes," said Clean Head with satisfaction. "The three-and-six editions. With the full colour Paul Hogarth cover art."

"And we went to a shoe shop," said Tinkler.

"A shoe shop," I said.

Clean Head nodded. "I have to say your boy has been very good. Patient. Considerate. Never pestered me to go and do his thing."

"I'm an ideal travelling companion," said Tinkler. "And shopping companion. Patient. Considerate."

"Would this have anything to do with it being Sunday afternoon and the charity shops all being shut?" I said.

"Well, there's that too," said Tinkler.

When we got to the car I saw there was a note under the windscreen wiper, a small sheet of pale green paper. Tinkler spotted it too, and hurried to examine it. "How dare anyone put something under my windshield wiper?"

Nevada looked at me. "Is it a ticket?"

"No," said Clean Head, with the air of one who knew. "They come wrapped in waterproof plastic."

"Also, everybody has got one," I said. There was a piece of green paper on the windscreen of every car parked in the street. They couldn't all be illegally parked. Tinkler had picked up the sheet of paper and was reading it. He gave a low whistle and handed it to me.

It was a handbill, printed on green paper.

House Clearance Sale. Bric-à-brac, records, magazines etcetera, all from the 1960s. Plus much vintage clothing.
Clearance as the result of a recent bereavement.
Everything must go.

Underneath this, handwritten in ballpoint pen, was an address.

Nevada and Clean Head were reading it over my shoulder. I looked up to see that Tinkler had scurried down the street and was working his way back along the row of cars, plucking the green pieces of paper from every windscreen. He was grinning broadly when he got back to us, with a fistful of them. "What are you doing?" said Clean Head.

"Guaranteeing we don't have any competition," said Tinkler. "We don't want anybody else turning up." He happily folded the handbills and stuffed them into his pocket.

"A bereavement," said Nevada. "Isn't that sad?" Then, after a moment, "Much vintage clothing!"

"Fuck the vintage clothing," said Tinkler. "Take us to the vintage vinyl."

"Maybe they'll have some books," said Clean Head.

"Never mind the books," said Tinkler as we pulled up outside. "We're going to separate these hapless gap-toothed hicks from their rare LPs."

"What happened to the perfect companion and perfect shopper?" said Clean Head sardonically.

"He's been carried away by the thrill of the chase," said Nevada.

"So I see."

I must admit the thrill of the chase had got to me a bit, too. My heart was thumping a little, just a ragged edge of excitement. Who knew what we might be about to discover? Maybe the dear deceased had been a jazz fan.

Perhaps a set of Tubby Hayes originals on Fontana beckoned.

It was a large detached house in its own grounds near the Dover Road on the outskirts of Canterbury. We'd driven down residential streets and past a church and a small private hospital on our winding way as the daylight faded, bickering incessantly about the GPS, but eventually we'd found the place. We parked in the street outside and approached on foot. There were apple trees reaching over the low stone wall, and a gleaming new tarmac drive led in through the open gateway. Inside, the drive forked and split in two around a patch of well-tended rose beds. One branch led to a garage with its green-painted wooden doors firmly closed. We followed the other branch to the front door, past a trickling water feature of a Grecian lady with an urn constantly replenishing a pond where goldfish darted. Turk would have enjoyed keeping an eye on that.

A notice on the door read CLEARANCE SALE in large letters written on a sheet of the same green paper that had been used for the handbills. It was taped to the door and fluttering in the wind. "It looks like it's the right place," said Tinkler, rubbing his hands together happily. He trotted forward, ahead of us, and jammed his thumb on the doorbell.

"His childlike excitement lightens the heart," said Nevada as the doorbell sizzled.

"No one's coming," said Tinkler.

"Don't just lean on the bell continuously," said Clean Head.

"Yes, it's rude," said Nevada. Tinkler let go of the bell as if it had given him a shock. No one came to the door and we couldn't discern any activity within. Tinkler looked disconsolate. I knew how he felt. That flyer had really got my hopes up, too. He looked at me.

"No one's home."

"Hello!" We all turned to see an elderly lady coming around the side of the house. She was spry and well turned out, dressed in jeans and green wellies and a brown and white roll-neck sweater. She wore big, clumsy gardening gloves and was holding a bunch of sad-looking roses in one hand and a pair of muddy garden clippers in the other. "I almost didn't hear you. I was around the back." She peered at us happily. "Have you come for the sale?"

"We certainly have," said Nevada.

"I'm sorry I wasn't waiting inside to greet you," said the lady. She wiped her forehead, which was damp with sweat. She'd obviously been hard at it in the garden. She radiated vigour and good-natured health. "I was cutting back the roses."

"The roses are lovely," said Nevada.

"Yes, they're beautiful," said Clean Head.

Tinkler caught my eye and silently mouthed the words, *Fuck the roses.*

* * *

The woman introduced herself as Mrs Beatty and insisted on making us a pot of tea, which she served with a homemade lemon and poppy seed cake, which was really very good. Tinkler and I were champing at the bit to go and rifle through her records—and presumably Nevada felt the same way about the vintage clothing. But the formalities had to be observed.

"So do you have a lot of stuff to get rid of?" said Tinkler. "I mean, to sell."

"Oh yes. Far too much," said Mrs Beatty. "I have to seriously declutter my life." She smiled bravely. "This is all because of Robert," she said. As she mentioned the name a shadow passed over her face and she paused.

"What happened?" said Nevada, in that shockingly direct way that women sometimes have, and often get away with.

Which is what happened here. Mrs Beatty immediately opened up to her and gave a moving account of the death of her husband of fifty-seven years from cardiac occlusion. She presented the facts with precision and detachment, keen with dry-eyed regret. She'd obviously lost the partner of a lifetime, and I felt a bit bad about finding myself automatically doing the arithmetic—working out what age old Robert must have been when he popped his clogs and therefore what kind of records we might find in his collection.

Nevada praised Mrs Beatty on the quality of her flyers and Mrs Beatty nodded and smiled, happy to be appreciated for her ability to use a computer and printer. They spoke briefly in French, and the little old woman listened with approval as Nevada expounded to us on how bric-à-brac came from the phrase 'à *bric et à brac*', which means 'at random'.

Luckily this led us back to the topic at hand: the sale. "I need to get the keys," said Mrs Beatty, "for the various rooms upstairs. Everything is stored in the rooms upstairs, all the clobber I need to get rid of. I've kept it stored there and locked up since Robert passed away. I suppose that seems silly to you."

"Not at all," I said and she smiled at me and shoved another piece of cake my way and then went over to a cupboard and took down a key. "This is for the room with the clothing," she said and I watched Nevada do a very good imitation of someone who didn't actually want to snatch a key from the hand of a frail elderly lady.

Instead she said, "What sort of clothes, exactly…"

"Oh I kept everything, dear," said Mrs Beatty. "I don't really know why. Did I think I was going to be young again? Anyway I kept it all. All the lovely dresses I got from Carnaby Street and the King's Road. Biba and Hung on You and Granny Takes a Trip." I could see Nevada almost begin to salivate as the woman enumerated these legendary boutiques. "Let me show you," said Mrs Beatty. "Come upstairs with me."

"There's no need for you to come along," said Nevada.

"Oh, it's all right, dear. I need to get the other keys from upstairs. Then I'll leave you in peace."

"I don't suppose you have any books?" said Clean Head suddenly.

"Books?" said Mrs Beatty.

"Paperbacks. I don't suppose you have any Penguins?" said Clean Head.

Mrs Beatty stared at us and blinked. "Why, you know," she said with a note of surprise in her voice, "that's the most extraordinary thing. We actually have masses of books. I just didn't think of putting them in the flyer. There are paperbacks of all kinds. Robert had loads of Penguins. And he kept them all in immaculate condition." Clean Head's face lit up and I found myself hoping Robert had given the same care to his record collection. "They're right next door. Would you like a look?"

Clean Head immediately got to her feet and Tinkler rose with her. "I'll help you look," he said. She gave him a sceptical glance.

"Aren't you itching to delve through the vinyl?"

"Oh, that," said Tinkler in his best offhand manner. "That can wait." He shot me a look. "But if you find any classic British rock, it's mine."

"Maybe," I said as Mrs Beatty led him and Clean Head out. A moment later Tinkler's head popped back around the edge of the door. "Or classic British R&B," he said. Then he disappeared. I looked at Nevada.

"What's with him?" I said. Nevada grinned.

"He could see he was losing brownie points for being such a record-hunting fanatic."

"What's wrong with that?" I said. "I'm a record-hunting fanatic."

"Yes, but you didn't spend the morning going around

Canterbury Cathedral and the tea shops trying to prove to Clean Head that you're actually a well-rounded human being. Now he's trying to make up for lost ground, by taking an interest in what she's interested in."

"So he intends to seduce her over a pile of Penguin paperbacks?"

"Yes," said Nevada. "And if they find some Modern Classics it might work. Because she'll get hot."

Mrs Beatty and the others were gone a long time and we sat there at the table in the warm little kitchen sipping tea. Nevada flipped idly through the pile of flyers that Tinkler had left on his chair. "The *accent grave* over the 'a' in bric-à-brac is a nice touch," she said. "I like a woman who knows her diacritical marks."

Mrs Beatty looked in and said, "Did you want to see the clothes, dear?"

Nevada got up. "Yes, please."

Mrs Beatty smiled at me and looked back. "I just have to find the key for the record room and I'll be right back." They went out. She didn't come right back. I heard footsteps upstairs. Then silence.

Time passed and I sat at the table, feeling left out and a little odd. It was very warm in the kitchen. Sweat prickled on the back of my neck. I yawned and stretched. My blood pounded in my ears. I felt a little light-headed, as if I might be coming down with a cold.

I thought about going upstairs to look for Mrs Beatty, but it seemed a bit weird to just wander around someone's house uninvited. I wished I had a book to read. Perhaps I should go and find Tinkler and Clean Head and the Penguins.

But I didn't want Mrs Beatty to come back and find me gone.

With nothing else to read, I found myself looking at one of the flyers again, one of the many Tinkler had stolen. It was exactly like the one we'd had on our windscreen, except for one thing.

There was no handwritten addition on the bottom of it.

No address. No way of finding the house. I looked through the others. None of them had the address on them. Just ours.

That was odd.

What was also odd was the way the green paper of the handbills had begun to glow. It was a faint but intense luminosity that actually floated above the paper. The colour and the paper had become separated. I spread out the handbills on the table and looked at the glowing placards of colour that floated in the air just above them. They seemed to move with my breath. My breathing was very loud.

Then I looked up and saw Mrs Beatty standing in the door of the kitchen. She was smiling and holding a key. "Would you like to see the records now?"

"I don't know," I said.

"Oh, come now." She smiled at me. "Why ever not?"

"I feel a bit strange."

"There's a great deal of jazz," she said. "Robert had a splendid collection. And it's all in superb condition."

"All right," I said. She led me out of the kitchen. The shadowy house suddenly seemed huge and I was glad to have someone to guide me through it. I followed her up the stairs, my body making stiff rhythmic movements of arm and leg like a mechanical toy as we climbed each step. There seemed an awful lot of steps. The wooden staircase creaked under us, the noise of it flying around in the air to all the corners of the house, like a flight of startled birds. Then we were in a dim, carpeted upstairs hallway. I paused. Mrs Beatty turned and looked at me, smiling.

"What is it, dear?"

"I'd like to see Nevada. My girlfriend."

"Of course. Right this way." She turned to a door on our right and opened it. "The records are in here." It was a bedroom with a tall chest of drawers on the far wall, gleaming strangely in the last daylight coming through the window. "The records are in that cabinet," she said. "Go and have a look and I shall get Nevada for you." The chest of drawers seemed very tall and very far away. The room was full of shadows and I didn't want to go into it.

"No," I said, turning around. "I'll just wait out here."

"I'm afraid that won't be possible, dear," said Mrs Beatty. There was a man standing beside her. He was broad and stocky with short, dark hair and a pair of glasses with heavy, square, black frames. I was startled by his sudden appearance and was completely unprepared when he put his hand against my chest and shoved me through the doorway. I stumbled back into the room and they slammed the door. I heard the sound of it being locked. The key turned with an intricate metallic click.

The sound went on for a long time, echoing in my head.

I turned around and looked at the room. I went to the chest of drawers and opened it. It was full of sheets and smelled of lavender and damp. No records, but by now I hadn't expected there to be any. I went to the door and tried it. I couldn't open it. I hadn't expected to be able to. The brass doorknob felt very strange in my hand. Endlessly slippery. And the coldness of it seemed to cling to my palm even when I took my hand away. There was an odd rectangular glow at the other end of the room and it took me a moment to work out that it was the window.

I went and stood at it. For the first time I noticed there were bars fixed outside the glass, vertical steel bars. I stared through them. I could see the corrugated tin roof of a shed in the next garden, just over the wall. A charcoal-grey cat was sitting on it, enjoying the last rays of sunlight. I stared intently at the cat, trying to will my thoughts into its head. To send it a message to relay to Turk and Fanny. Tell them…

Tell them what?

We're not coming back.

I saw movement in the darkening garden below. It was Mrs Beatty and the man with the spectacles from the hallway. They were walking quickly, voices raised. They were arguing about something. I couldn't hear what they were saying, and in a moment they were gone from sight. The light fled the sky and the window grew dark. All I could see in the glass was the ghostly reflection of my face and the dark lines of the bars. When the segments of my reflection began to separate, like strips of fabric someone was cutting away, I turned quickly from the window.

My heart was beating so hard I could feel the blood pulsing and stinging in the tips of my fingers. I was having trouble breathing. I sat down on the bed and the springs in the mattress creaked and rang endlessly. I sank into the softness of the mattress until it began to absorb me, then I stood up hastily.

I tried to think. The window was barred. The door was locked. My thoughts travelled in great circles, as though they were coming to me around the circumference of the Earth. And they kept repeating themselves. The window was barred and the door was—

The door opened.

Tinkler was standing there. He had a halo around his head and his hair seemed to be moving in slow motion at the probings of a gentle breeze, but it was Tinkler. He said something and it took me a minute to put the words together.

"Come on. Quick."

I was out of the door and moving with him down the carpeted hallway. The hallway seemed a lot longer than I remembered it. It seemed to go on forever. We kept walking and walking, but there was always still more carpeted hallway.

"Where's Nevada?" said someone. I realised it was me.

"With Clean Head," said Tinkler. "They're in the car. Now we've all got to get out of here. Before they get back."

"They drugged me," I said. "I was drugged."

"No shit. We all were. I think she slipped something in the tea. Or that fucking lemon and poppy seed cake."

As we came to the top of the stairs I caught the scent of something, intense and raw and rank. It burned my throat as

I breathed it in. "What's that smell?"

"Petrol. They were splashing it everywhere, and then they ran out of it. Not enough to finish the job. So they rushed off to buy some more petrol."

"Splashing it everywhere?" I said. "Why? Were they going to set fire to the place?"

"That's right. With us locked up inside it."

"They were going to kill us."

"No shit, again."

Someone wanted me dead. It was not the first time, but the shock was undiminished. The house creaked around me as I put my foot on the staircase. I froze. It was as if a vast gulf had opened up. I didn't want to take another step in case I fell in. Tinkler was staring at me. His face seemed to pulse, growing larger and smaller according to the beating of his heart. Or maybe it was the beating of *my* heart.

"What's the matter?" he said.

"I'm scared."

"Oh, for Christ's sake." He took my hand and led me down the stairs. When we got to the bottom he looked down at my hand in his. "There is absolutely nothing gay about this," he said. "Remember that." What I was remembering was my father, walking with him hand in hand and feeling safe. We walked together through the maze of the dark house. I didn't know my way, but I could see in the dark. The house was huge. Every room led into another house, or perhaps it was just the same house from a different angle.

"Was everyone locked up?" I said.

"Yes. But I got them out."

"How did *you* get out?"

"I had to unscrew the hinges on the door."

"How did you unscrew them?"

"With my Swiss Army knife."

I said, "You own a Swiss Army knife? What are you doing owning a Swiss Army knife?"

"I got it free when I bought twelve giant Toblerones."

The front door opened and suddenly the cool, beautiful smell of night air was in my face. We stepped outside. I was suddenly hungry. "Can I have one?" I said.

"One what?"

"One of the giant Toblerones?"

"I don't *still have them*. This was years ago. That LSD has addled your brain."

We walked across the tarmac that gleamed like black ice and out of the gate and into the street. Tinkler's car was there under the sodium glow of a street lamp, crouching like an animal. Clean Head was sitting in the front. Nevada was in the back. She stared at me and started waving at me through the window. We tried to open the door and get at each other, but neither of us could figure out how to operate it. Tinkler snarled with impatience and opened it for us. I climbed in with Nevada and she seized me and began kissing my face. "You're here!" she said. Her lips were cool and I could smell the night in her hair.

Tinkler had the front door of the car open and was leaning in towards Clean Head. "Move over," he said.

"I want to drive."

"Move over!"

Clean Head sighed and folded and unfolded her long limbs elegantly as she slid over the transmission hump and gracefully exuded herself into the passenger seat. *She must do yoga*, I thought.

"Why do you get to drive?" asked Clean Head sullenly.

"Because I'm the one who's immune to hallucinogenic drugs." Tinkler twisted the key, gunned the engine, and we accelerated away into the night.

18. LAMB

The Colonel had a shopping bag from Harrods Food Hall tucked under his arm as he came through the door in a blast of cold air. He was wearing a duffel coat with a green and blue scarf at the neck and a black and white tweed cap. I didn't blame him. The weather seemed to have skipped autumn and gone straight to winter in London this year.

He took off his scarf and coat and hat, but kept hold of the bag until he set it down on the table and sank down in a chair opposite me.

As soon as she spotted him, Fanny, who had wedged herself underneath one of the armchairs, scrabbled her way out and came trotting over. I could see the Colonel trying not to look at her as she approached, but as soon as she was within reach he leaned over and began to stroke her on the head, working all the way down the smooth fur to the tip of her tail.

He looked at me as he stroked her and said, "So you weren't able to get any kind of a lead on who these people are?"

I shook my head. "The only person who knew we'd be in Canterbury that day, and who might conceivably have some reason to get rid of us, was Ambrose—"

"That gold-toothed bastard," said the Colonel. I could see he liked this hypothesis. "He wants Cessie all to himself. He feels threatened. I wouldn't put it past him."

"But it couldn't be him."

"Why not?"

"Setting aside my doubts that he could organise something that elaborate, there's the fact that this was an ambush carefully tailored for Nevada and myself." I described the handbill with its enticing promise of vintage clothing and vinyl. "That was the work of someone who knew us." Knew us disturbingly well.

"Well, let's go back to Canterbury and try to get to the bottom of this," said the Colonel.

"We did. We went back the next day—the day after next, rather. We actually spent the next day recovering from whatever drug it was they slipped us."

Indeed we had spent the day in bed. When Tinkler dropped us off on our return from Canterbury we had still been awesomely stoned. The night sky had looked like a cheap theatrical backcloth above the illuminated white shape of the Abbey, where a light in one of the upstairs rooms had glowed with a particular, singular intensity.

I'd 'known' instantly this must be Stinky's room and I could feel his eyes on us as we hurried to our front door, pursued by the endless clattering echo of our own footsteps, and by Tinkler. He saw us safely through our front door, said, "Remember, you're not allowed to have psychedelic sex," and then drove off to take Clean Head home.

Unfortunately we let Tinkler down. Watched respectfully by the cats, whose eyes were four tiny, glowing, golden-green mirrors in the darkness, we had lain in bed making love slowly, endlessly and tenderly, spurred on by the certainty we had almost died. Finally as the dawn light was coming through the window, in slow solid blocks that pulsed as they arrived, we came to a halt. I lay exhausted on top of Nevada.

She bit my neck gently and whispered something in my ear, so quietly I could hardly hear. But as I drifted off to sleep, the soft repeated syllables had slowly soaked into my brain:

Love is this.

Love is this.

Love is this.

The next day when Tinkler saw us he shook his head disgustedly and said, "You had psychedelic sex, didn't you?"

"Anyway," I said to the Colonel, "we didn't get back to Canterbury until the following day." Nevada was looking in anxiously from the kitchen where she had gone to start making coffee—she was under strict instructions to use the second-best beans—as soon as she'd seen the Colonel outside our gate. She was always concerned that I might get into a fistfight with the irascible old bastard, or something.

There was certainly no danger of that at the moment. I couldn't even get his attention, because Turk had just come clattering into the house and jumped up on the table in front of him. She was now prowling around on the table and sniffing at the Harrods bag. The Colonel was grinning at her.

"This is Turk, isn't it?" he said. "She's got a lighter coat. And the nose is different."

"And she's got a scar," I said. "She's a fighter."

"So is your friend. What's his name? Tinker?"

"Tinkler?" I said. "I don't think I'd describe him as a fighter…"

"Really?" snarled the Colonel. "Wouldn't you? Well, it sounds to me like he did a terrific job of getting you out of a very nasty situation just in the nick of time."

"Trust me, nobody's more surprised than he is."

Nevada came in with coffee, and while the Colonel was stroking both cats, one with each hand—I had to admire his coordination—I tried to update him about what we'd found when we went back to Canterbury. We had located the house again and met the woman who actually owned it. She'd been away on holiday in Sardinia and had just returned. She was quite eager to talk to us, not least because at first she thought we had been sent by the insurance company.

"She was having quite a bit of trouble with the insurance company. It seems they only expect people to try and claim after they've successfully managed to burn their house down with cans of petrol, not to claim for a failed attempt."

"It's totally baffled their system," said Nevada.

The Colonel nodded as if he was listening closely, which he might well have been, despite the fact that he now had both Fanny and Turk on the table in front of him, circling the Harrods bag in fascination, and he was still deftly stroking them both.

"So after she found out we weren't with the insurance people she was quite happy to have us there to complain about the insurance people *to*," said Nevada.

"She never did get around to asking us who we were," I said.

"She was very preoccupied with her claim for damages," added Nevada.

"What damages?" said the Colonel. "Nothing burned, did it?"

"No, but they poured petrol all over everything. It soaked into the floor and furniture and ruined the rugs in the hallway, according to her."

"Yes," said Nevada, "and yet what really got her upset was that they'd cut some of her roses." This was true. But what had got her dander up even more was the fact of her missing Penguin paperbacks. Ironically, and presumably coincidentally, there had been a large collection of these in the house. It was the one instance where 'Mrs Beatty' had not been lying.

"Someone cherry-picked all of the best titles," the woman had said. Both Nevada and I had our suspicions about what had happened to these, but we kept our mouths firmly shut.

I said, "She certainly had no idea who tried to kill us."

The Colonel looked up from the cats. "Did you report what happened to the police?"

"She reported the break-in. And the petrol being poured everywhere."

"But you didn't report the attempt on your life?"

I shrugged. "What could we prove? If they took a sample of our blood now it might show a trace of the LSD—or whatever it was—or it might not. We don't have a copy of any of the handbills. We asked the woman who owned the house and she hadn't seen any trace of them. It seems the would-be arsonists were very scrupulous about removing those before they took off." I looked at Nevada. "About all we could prove was that we were there, in the house that had been broken into."

"And you can see the problem with that," she said, turning to the Colonel. "We might have ended up getting arrested ourselves."

He nodded. "And you don't think she might have been in on it?" he said. "The woman who actually owned the house."

Nevada shook her head. "She was genuinely pissed off about those roses."

And the Penguins.

"You should be paying us danger money," said Nevada, smiling at the Colonel, "since we seem to be dealing with dangerous people."

"I will," he said. "Consider your fee doubled as of now." Then he grinned. "But you know what it means if you're dealing with dangerous people?"

"It means they're trying to hide something," said Nevada.

"Which means there's something to hide," I said.

He nodded. "And now you can find out what it is."

The bag from Harrods Food Hall turned out to contain

diced lamb for the cats. While we were feeding it to them, the doorbell rang. Nevada went to answer it, and let Lucille Tegmark in. "Lucy," she said.

The Colonel's face fell as he saw her. I suspected that one reason he'd come here to talk to us was to get the hell away from his unwanted companion. She glanced into the kitchen, then joined us in the living room. "Lamb," she said. "I wondered what you'd bought." She sat down at the table beside the Colonel, who pointedly moved his chair away. Lucy looked at him. "You do realise that some poor little lamb had to be taken bleating and screaming from its mother? A lamb to the slaughter." She suddenly looked at me. "Isn't that what they tried to make of you?" She looked at Nevada. "Lambs to the slaughter."

"Oh, Jesus, Mary and Joseph," said the Colonel. He sighed and leaned back in his chair, looking at Lucy. "Have you worked out what happened to your documents yet?"

"We know what happened to them," she said.

He turned to us. "Of all the print shops in London, she has to choose that one," he said.

Lucy's face took on a ruddy tone and her eyes grew bright. "It didn't matter which one I chose," she said. "Obviously someone was watching and waiting and went in and stole our material."

The Colonel looked at us, shaking his head. "She chose the sort of place where that could happen."

Lucy looked at us. It seemed we were supposed to referee this. "I didn't know anything was *going* to happen. How could I have known?"

"Simple, basic precautions," said the Colonel. "The kind anybody would take. Any sensible person."

Lucy stood up, turning away from him. She smiled at us, but it was clear his remarks had stung. "Well, if you'll excuse me, I have to be going."

"Really, must you?" said Nevada. "You've only just got here."

"I have a lot of research to do. For the book. At the British Library."

Nevada showed her to the door. As soon as she was gone—while the door was still being closed behind her, in fact—the Colonel said, "She won't even be able to *find* the British Library." He was still staring angrily after her when Nevada came back into the room. Lucy's visit seemed to have definitively soured his mood, not that it had ever needed much souring.

Sensing the change, Nevada became determined to cheer him up. "Can we offer you a glass of wine, John? We've got rather a nice old vine Syrah on the go." To my surprise, he accepted. I had him pegged as a man who was against all pleasure, especially his own. But maybe I'd got it wrong. He sniffed the wine when Nevada brought him a glass, and began to sip at it steadily, with reluctant satisfaction.

Nevada put out cheese and figs and some bread and we picked away at it as we drank. We finished the bottle and I looked at Nevada and we decided silently to open another one. Turk climbed onto the coffee table to have a nap and Fanny fell asleep on the sofa. I served supper and we chatted in a desultory manner, mostly about how pissed off the Colonel was with Lucy.

We were about halfway through the third bottle of wine when the Colonel suddenly said, "It's her."

"I beg your pardon?" said Nevada.

"I got the results of the DNA test. That thing in Canterbury living with the gold-toothed shyster. It is my sister."

"God, John," said Nevada. When had she got on first name terms with him? He certainly didn't seem to mind. "That must be quite a feeling. I mean, to know for certain. After all these years."

He grunted something.

"Perhaps you feel a little... conflicted."

"Conflicted?" He snorted and took another sip of wine. "That human wreck is all I have left. That lobotomised mountain of dumb flesh. She's all that remains of my family." He looked up from his glass. "She's the remains." He chuckled coldly. "The human remains." The fact that Cecilia had spoken to us on that day in Canterbury seemed not to have moved him at all. When we'd reported it to him he hadn't even asked what she said.

He was a man who knew his mind, and his mind was made up. At least where Cecilia was concerned. He drained his glass and set it down. "No," he said. "My only hope is Valerian's son. If that little boy survived, he's a man now. And he's the only hope I have. For the future. For my family." For a moment his eyes glittered and I realised with a shock that the wine had brought him close to tears. Nevada gave me a look.

I went and put some music on, to lighten the mood. I

chose a Decca ten inch of Lita Roza. It was one of her few true jazz recordings. She was singing here with the Tony Kinsey quartet, including the mighty Joe Harriott on sax. The Colonel turned and listened for a minute and said, "Didn't this girl sing '(How Much Is That) Doggie in the Window'?"

"She did indeed," I said. "But not on this record, thank god."

We finally called for a taxi—not Clean Head, who was taking a few well-earned days off—and put the slightly squiffy Colonel in it and sent him back to his hotel. When we got back inside the house, Nevada looked at me and said, "The poor bastard. All he's got in this world is our cats."

"And he's not having them."

"So we've got to try and find out what happened to his nephew."

"I've got an idea." I picked up the phone.

Nevada glanced at the clock. "It's late. It's one in the morning."

"That's okay. He lives the rock and roll lifestyle." I dialled Erik Make Loud's number.

He answered right away. "Hello?"

"Hello."

"Yeah, hello."

I said, "Do you know who this is?"

A pause. "Tinkler's mate." Now that he'd established who I was, he started to sound sleepy. He yawned loudly and said, "How is he, by the way? Old Tinkler?"

"Great," I said. "On fine form. In fact a few days ago he saved my life."

"Really?" said Erik. He sounded intrigued. "What happened?"

"Someone tried to burn down a house with me in it." Nevada was pointing at herself and mouthing silently, *And me*. "And Nevada," I said.

"Holy shit." Suddenly Erik was wide awake. "Tell me all about it."

"Some other time," I said. "It's late."

"But Tinkler saved you, did he?" said Erik. He sounded impressed. I reassured him this was indeed the case, we said our goodbyes and I hung up. I'd had a cover story ready, but he hadn't asked why I'd rung him. Perhaps as a rock star he expected random calls from adoring fans. Just to hear his voice.

Nevada was looking at me sceptically. "What was all that about?"

"Erik didn't know anything about what happened to us in Canterbury. He was genuinely surprised."

"Either that or he's a very good actor."

"He's not that good an actor," I said. "He's not even that good a guitarist."

19. ICED BOTTLE

My next step was to talk to Nic Vardy.

This proved far from simple. He was impossible to reach on any of his many phone numbers, and text and Twitter proved equally ineffectual. Finally I resorted to email and eventually elicited a reply by this medium. It seemed the famous and suddenly very busy photographer was unable to schedule a phone conversation with us—no explanation why—but if we wanted to go to the trouble and inconvenience of travelling all the way out to Docklands again to see him, he was quite willing to grant us another interview in his bijou flat overlooking the marina.

I turned up five minutes early and watched the ducks, or rather the moorhens, until it was time for my appointment. I was on my own, having deliberately chosen a time when Nevada was busy. I didn't like the way Vardy looked at her.

As I approached the glass and steel flat I studied the windows. The pattern of them was randomised by the bright red, yellow and blue Mondrian blinds. The place looked deserted.

I wondered glumly if Vardy had sensed my hostility, or perhaps just the absence of Nevada, and decided to be out when I called.

When I rang the bell, however, I was instantly rewarded with the thumping of feet descending a staircase with emphatic, jaunty urgency. The door sprang open in a waft of warm air and expensive aftershave. It was Erik Make Loud.

"Hello, sport. Didn't bring Tinkler with you, then?"

"Had I known you were going to be here..."

He laughed and thumped me on the arm as I came in. "So what are you doing in Docklands?" I said.

"I've been seeing a lot of old Vardy since he came to the Half Moon for the gig that night. You're responsible for a bit of a reunion."

I took off my coat and we went up the minimalist wooden staircase—basically polished planks of wood set on iron bars jutting out of the wall. Vardy was waiting in the living room, sitting on a sofa. I entered the room and was instantly disoriented by a wave of déjà vu.

I had been in this room before, yet I hadn't. I remembered this place, yet I didn't. It was so powerful that I wondered if it was some kind of hideous flashback aftermath of the LSD, blasting into my brain days later. What a cheering notion—that my mind might have been damaged permanently by the stuff.

But then I realised what it was. I was standing in the same room, with the same view out the window of a pale afternoon reflected in the marina water. But the furniture in the room had been moved around—and some of it had actually changed. One of the armchairs, which had been a bit faded and worn last time, now looked paradoxically brand new. Maybe he'd had it refurbished in some way. Or maybe he'd upgraded to a better model and casually discarded the old one.

Even now, somewhere in Docklands, a devotee of modern furniture might be looking into a skip and shrieking with pleasure.

The crucial things, though, were the pictures.

All the pictures on the walls were changed. Gone were the charming colour images of wildlife, birds spreading their bright plumage against sky or water. They had been replaced by black and white photos from the 1960s. Mostly of rock stars, some of fashion models. Iconic faces of the day. And some surprisingly gritty reportage, all achingly redolent of the era.

The bastard could take a photograph, I'll give him that.

There were quite a few pictures of Valerian and her band.

Even more shots of them, unframed prints, were spread out on two long, black padded benches that hadn't been there before. They were situated in front of the sofa so that you could sit there and inspect a wide spread of photographs, completely filling your span of vision.

Erik sat down on the sofa, Vardy making room for him, as he picked up a glass from the floor. Vardy picked up his own glass. They both sipped and looked at me. I saw the bottle, standing on an elegant little cherry wood table. I couldn't actually see what they were drinking, though, because the bottle was encased in a solid block of ice. The ice was beginning to melt and in a little while the water was going to start ruining that nice polished wood.

But worrying about such a thing wouldn't have been very rock and roll.

Erik picked up one of the photos, a dramatic black and white shot of himself, shirtless and muscular and predatory, in a rock god posture. I wondered if it had been posed. On the whole I suspected not. Nic Vardy had a gift for capturing the moment. I wondered if it was his only gift.

"God, I was beautiful," said Erik.

Vardy laughed and swigged his drink. "You great ponce," he said. They were both in full laddish swing. He turned and grinned at me. "Hello there, by the way."

"Hello."

"What's all this bollocks I hear about someone trying to burn down a house with you in it?"

I was annoyed that Erik had told him about this, but I suppose I shouldn't have expected anything else. "Me, Nevada and couple friends of ours."

"Luckily old Tinkler got them out," said Erik.

Vardy blinked and said, "Where did this happen?"

"Canterbury."

"What were you doing there?"

"Seeing Cecilia."

Erik and Vardy both went quiet at the mention of her name. "How is she?" said Vardy.

"We had a chat with her."

"I didn't think she spoke to anyone."

"I think she speaks to Ambrose," said Erik. "I've always had that impression. Or at least he speaks to her."

"As long as that's all he's doing to her," said Vardy, elbowing Erik in the ribs. They both chuckled. "Can you imagine climbing around on that flesh mountain, looking for a way in?"

"How would you know it when you found it?" said Erik.

"And what if she rolled over in a moment of passion?" said Vardy. "You'd be squashed flat."

"All that meat and no potatoes!" They laughed, slapped their thighs, and laughed some more. It was a boys' night out, no mistake. Nic Vardy caught my eye and, apparently, something of my disapproval.

"You think we're being cruel?" he said.

I shrugged. "I'm not the one who knew her. I'm not the one who thinks she might have been a greater singer than Valerian, if she hadn't been stuck in her sister's shadow." I was looking at Erik as I said this and his grin slowly faded.

"I never said she was a greater singer, sport." He picked up his glass and stared into it. There was still a perilous amount of clear liquid there. He drained it. I was wondering how drunk the two of them were, and how drunk they intended to get. "I said she was a greater *talent*. Potentially a greater talent. She had a good voice. But she never had the balls, the guts. Her sister seized the spotlight. Cessie always hung about in the shadows." He searched for the words to sum it up. "She lacked *bottle*."

"But we don't," said Vardy. "We've got a bottle that still needs to be drunk. Let me refill your glass." He stood up, taking his own glass, which was still half-full and Erik's, which was predictably empty. He seemed to be pacing himself. Maybe he wasn't as taken by drink as he seemed. I didn't think he was going to have the courtesy to offer me anything, but as he walked towards the table with the bottle on it he turned and said to me, "How about you?"

"I'll take a beer." I wasn't going to get into competitive drinking with these two. And I was still feeling a little frail after the onslaught of psychic chemistry in Canterbury.

Erik Make Loud laughed at me. "Pussy," he said.

Vardy disappeared and came back with a cold silver can of Sapporo and a bowl of green olives. He handed me the beer and took the olives over to set on the sofa between himself and Erik. He sat down and smiled at me insultingly. "You think we're wrong to laugh about Cecilia? About what she's become?"

"You don't know what she was, mate," said Erik. "What she was like, back in the day."

"Exactly," said Nic Vardy. He got up and picked up one of the prints and brought it over to me. A black and white shot of Cecilia, looking fresh and young and lovely, giggling at something just out of shot. "Look at that and then look at what she turned into."

"It's a crime," said Erik.

"It's a crime against nature," said Vardy, rejoining him on the sofa. They both howled with laughter. I got up and put the photo back in the spot that he'd taken it from. I looked at some of the other prints. Erik wiped tears from his face and picked up his drink.

"We're laughing to keep from crying, mate," he said.

I was looking at a series of shots of Cecilia and Valerian. I said, "They look a lot alike, don't they?"

Nic Vardy got up. He came over and stood beside me, looking down at the photos, smiling. "If you use the right makeup," he said. "And in those days they used *big* makeup. Eye shadow like you wouldn't believe. It was that whole *Cleopatra* thing. Add the right clothes… a big floppy hat used to work quite well." He winked at me. "Let me let you in on a little secret. We sometimes used Cecilia to stand in for Valerian at photo shoots when Valerian was late or she was busy, or…"

"Too hung over or too drunk or too bloody stoned," offered Erik.

"All of those things, yes."

"Or too busy being shagged senseless by her latest toy boy."

"That too, yes."

"So there were pictures in circulation that were supposedly of Valerian, but they were actually of her sister?" I said.

Erik leaned forward on the sofa. "Yeah. So what, sport?"

"So, any attempt to identify either of them, Valerian or Cecilia, using a photograph is liable to be a somewhat dodgy business."

Erik stared at me silently. This never seemed to have occurred to him. And Vardy was watching me now with something resembling interest. "Where are you going with this?" he said. "What is it you think you know?"

I shrugged. "Valerian was always in the limelight and—you said it yourself—Cecilia was always in the shadows. Maybe she resented it." I looked at them. "Maybe she did something about it."

"Did something about it?" said Erik. "You've lost me, sport."

"Maybe she killed Valerian."

There was silence, then both of them howled with laughter. They made a big production of rolling around on the sofa in mirth. When they finally quieted down a bit, I said, "It would explain why she is the way she is."

"You mean she's gone insane with grief?"

"Something like that."

Erik shook his head decisively. "No, she went crazy because she was supposed to be looking after the little boy and he disappeared on her watch."

"That's right," said Vardy. They both seemed quite intent, for whatever individual reasons, to cling to this version of events. "Anyway, nobody killed Valerian," he said.

Erik nodded. "That's right. Valerian killed herself, mate. She topped herself because her little boy was gone forever."

I said, "The same reason her sister went insane? This is your all-purpose explanation?"

"You don't think it was an important event?" said Nic Vardy coldly. "The disappearance?"

"On the contrary, I think it's the key event."

"But you don't think it explains everything?"

"Actually," I said, shifting around so I could look at them, "maybe it does." The three of us looked at each other like a trio of poker players. I hoped nobody would ask me what I meant, because I had no idea. They picked up their drinks in unison and took synchronised sips.

I said, "Just out of purely idle interest, where were the rest of the band then?"

"When?"

"When Valerian died. When the little boy went missing."

Erik rolled his eyes wearily. "I told you. We were in London, at Olympic Studios. Busy laying down tracks while her ladyship took her ease in the countryside."

"You were all there?"

"Yeah." He looked at Vardy. "You were there too, weren't you, mate?"

Vardy smiled at me. "That's right." He picked up the glasses and went to the bottle for refills. He didn't bother asking me how my beer was doing. In fact, I hadn't touched it. I found I was a little wary of any refreshments offered to me these days. I wondered if this might turn out to be a permanent attitude.

Vardy returned to the sofa. He looked at me and said, "But if anything like that did happen—if somebody was behind it all, the little boy's disappearance, or even what happened to Valerian—you should take a look at John Blacklock."

Sitting beside him, Erik Make Loud's demeanour changed instantly. All the good cheer drained out of him and his face went hard and cold. "That's right, that fucking snake."

"Yeah, take a good look at him," said Nic Vardy.

"Definitely," said Erik. "I told you that myself, didn't I? I've always had my suspicions about him."

"Get the dirt on Blacklock."

"I'd love to," I said. "Where do I start?"

They looked at each other. "Well, you know, that might not be so easy," said Erik. *No, of course not*, I thought. "He was a bit of a mysterious character. Or at least he wanted us all to think he was a bit of a mysterious character. Covered his tracks. Never let on what his real name was, or where he was from."

"I thought you said he was Irish."

"Oh, he was definitely Irish," said Erik. "No question about that. And he was a total fucking chancer."

"And he was fucking her," said Vardy.

"Who," I said. "Valerian or Cecilia?"

"Probably both of them." He leered at Erik, and they laughed. "Anyway, he was a sleazebag."

"And a slippery character," said Erik. "That journalist who was hanging about did a story on him. Researched him. Or at least he tried to."

I said, "What journalist?"

Erik shook his head in irritation. "I can't remember his name. Do you remember him, Nic?"

"No."

I said, "Do you remember what newspaper the story ran in?"

"I don't know if it ever even came out. There was some talk of Blacklock calling in his libel lawyers. That always tickled me. John Blacklock, mysterious otherworldly master of the dark arts, just happened to have a libel lawyer on standby."

"He was a strange bastard, though," said Vardy.

"He certainly was. Refused to ever be photographed. He said it would steal his soul."

Vardy laughed. "Reveal his double chins, more like. You're so full of crap, you silly bugger. That might have been a line he tried on you. But he loved to be photographed if he could guarantee he would look dark and majestic. I took a bunch of pictures of him myself." He looked at me. "I can get you some prints if you like."

"Yes, please," I said.

"I took quite a few shots of him. Some approved, some not. I was always trying to catch him on the bog."

Erik chortled and sipped his drink. Then he paused. "You know what?" he said. "You should speak to the shrink. What's his name? Osterleigh? Osterloh."

"Bill Osterloh," said Vardy, nodding.

I didn't tell them that I'd met him. "Really? Who's he?"

"The shrink who was hanging around with the band. Valerian's shrink. But Nic knows more about him than I do. I mean, it was Nic who put us onto him." He looked at Vardy. "Wasn't it?"

"That's right. I was photographing this model. You'd call her a supermodel these days." He stared out the window, looking into a distant year. "She was a skinny little thing. You'd call *that* anorexic these days. She'd had a nervous breakdown, or she thought she had and that amounted to the same thing. So she started going to Dr Osterloh. And it did her a lot of good. We started noticing the difference, the people who worked with her. We saw how she changed and we clocked his name. It made a change to run across one of these witch doctors who actually knew what he was doing."

"By sheer law of averages there must be one or two of them out there," said Erik. They looked at each other and nodded. I found myself wondering how much I believed of this encomium. I looked at Erik Make Loud and said, "Did he sleep with her? The shrink? You said everybody did."

He shifted uncomfortably on the sofa. "Yeah, I might have said that. But I suspect he might have been one of the few and far between. One of the select company. We happy few. There weren't many of us who *didn't* fuck her." He perked up and turned to Nic Vardy. "You fucked her, didn't you, Nic?"

"I might have gone there, once or twice."

"How was it?"

By way of response, Nic held his hand out horizontally, flat in front of him and moved it minimally in a so-so gesture. They both roared with laughter.

When I made my excuses and departed, they were busy comparing graphic notes about the groupies they'd known. As I left I noticed that there was now a folded towel under the bottle in its melting block of ice, to catch and neutralise the growing pool of moisture. He must have put it there when he came back with my beer.

Nic Vardy wasn't so rock and roll after all.

20. MISSION: MOROCCO

While I was rubbing shoulders with rock stars and famous photographers, Nevada was having a coffee with the Colonel in Mayfair. "Green Park, actually," she said. "Near his hotel. It was quite nice coffee. I suspect even you would have approved. We must go there sometime, just you and me. Anyway, what he wants to do next is retrieve the documents."

"The ones that were stolen from the print shop?" I said. "How the hell does he propose to do that?"

"Did I say retrieve? Maybe that isn't exactly the right word. He wants to get the originals. You remember the ones that were stolen were just photocopies? He wants to get the originals from Morocco where Lucy left them. Actually, what he wants to do is go to Morocco, get the originals copied—digitally scanned, he's obsessed with that—and then lock up the originals in a bank, in a safety deposit box, and return here with the digital scans on a dongle or whatever the hell they call it."

"Good idea."

"But he doesn't want to go to Morocco himself. And

he certainly doesn't want to entrust the job to Lucy—for obvious reasons."

"For very obvious reasons."

"So he's asked us to sort it out for him."

"Do you want to go to Morocco?" I said.

Nevada smiled at me. "No. I thought we'd delegate."

"Well, we can't use Tinkler."

"Why not?"

I said, "Send Tinkler to Morocco? That would be like asking Jack the Ripper to babysit."

"Why? I mean, in what way?"

"The world's finest, or at least most potent, hashish is found in Morocco."

"Ah, I take your point."

"If he went there we'd probably never see him again."

"We wouldn't want that." Nevada snapped her fingers and pointed at me happily. "I know what to do," she said. "Clean Head, of course. She's even met the Colonel. They've bonded over cat feeding. It's perfect."

"Do you think she's up for it? After recent events?"

"She's a boon companion and a great girl. She's just a bit of a klepto where the rare Penguins are concerned."

"Clearly," I said. "Do you remember how angry the poor woman in Canterbury was?"

"Well, I suppose Clean Head felt those Penguins were owed to her after what they put us through. You know, almost burned at the stake, so to speak, while on acid."

"Except it's not the lady they were stolen from who actually tried to kill us."

Nevada looked at me, eyebrows angled sceptically. "A bit of a nuanced philosophical distinction, don't you think? Especially when poor Clean Head's head was buzzing with a huge amount of LS fucking D?"

"I suppose so," I said. "Do you know what's interesting about that whole situation? They didn't expect Clean Head to be with us in Canterbury that day."

"Why do you say that?"

"Well, the flyer they left on our car. It mentioned records, to hook me and, presumably, Tinkler. And it mentioned vintage clothes. To hook you."

"Yes, the bastards. I don't suppose you have any fresh idea about who said bastards are? It would be nice to know. Since they're trying to kill us and all."

I shook my head. "I keep going round in circles. I suppose Ambrose could conceivably have hired them. He had motive, and proximity. But what he didn't have was…"

"Knowledge of what bait to put on the handbill for us," said Nevada. "Clothes and records."

"But there was no mention of paperbacks. 'Mrs Beatty' just improvised that when we arrived. And luckily for her, they actually had some in the house."

"Is that significant?" said Nevada.

"It means that whoever set us up didn't know about Clean Head. Or didn't know much about her."

"They do now," said Nevada. "Unfortunately." The cat flap rattled open and Turk came scurrying in and peered at us proudly. "Ah," said Nevada. "I've been looking for you, young lady." She made kissing noises and Turk came over and hopped up onto the sofa between us. Her fur was wet from the recent rain and, as I stroked her, it grew rapidly dry under my fingers. Nature's finest weather proofing.

While I was patting Turk, Nevada went to fetch a piece of paper. When she'd visited the Colonel she'd also dropped by Stinky Stanmer's office in Soho. Part of our agreement with Stinky was that we'd pass the occasional 'vital message' back to him from his business people. Initially I'd been concerned that this would prove an endless and onerous task. But Nevada had put her foot down and we now had Stinky's people quite well trained. They even provided the messages on small pieces of paper especially designed to fit neatly under Turk's collar.

As soon as she saw the piece of paper, Turk lifted her head so Nevada could get easy access to her collar. She was a clever cat and she knew this routine meant a luxury fish meal was waiting for her, just on the other side of the wall.

The note was no sooner in place than Turk squirmed out of my grasp, hopped off the sofa, and rattled briskly out through the cat flap again. I went to the window and watched her move through the garden, hop onto the wall and disappear over it. "I'm going to time her," I said.

"And I'll ring Clean Head. About Mission: Morocco."

I went out into the garden. The air was clean and cool after the rain. Soaked red and yellow leaves lay thick across the ground. I told myself that once the trees had finally finished shedding their autumn load I was going to make a concerted effort to rake up the leaves and generally tidy the place. I'm the first to admit that such tasks don't come naturally to me. Give me a difficult-to-set-up cartridge any day. I'm more comfortable with a stylus protractor and alignment gauge than a rake and a black bin bag.

I was still staring at the graceful white façade of the Abbey, and trying to work out whether the window I'd imagined was Stinky's might actually be Stinky's, when Turk came bounding back over the wall. The note was gone from under her collar. I checked the time. Just under three minutes. She was a fast eater. And Stinky must have had a fridge in his room stocked with seafood treats.

We went back inside together, Turk waiting for me to open the door for her. Despite the presence of cat flaps in every available portal, the little fiends still liked to have doors opened for them. I guess it was a luxury.

Nevada was grinning at me as I stepped inside. She held up the phone. "Well, I spoke to her and, not surprisingly, Clean Head is up for an all-expenses-paid weekend in Morocco. I also rang the Colonel and cleared it with him. So it's full speed ahead! Clean Head asked if she could bring us back a present for sending a free holiday her way, and I said she'd bloody well better." Nevada nodded with satisfaction. "So she will get us something nice in the way of wine. I've given her a list. She might be able to get Chateau Musar cheap over there. It's that part of the world."

"Good thinking."

"And you'll also be pleased to hear that Clean Head has made restitution."

"How so?"

Nevada smiled. "She sent some money to that poor woman in Canterbury."

"The woman whose books she stole?"

"Stole is such a harsh word." Turk was writhing with pleasure as Nevada scratched her tummy. "She sent a generous cash settlement by courier, strictly anonymously."

"So there's no chance of her actually returning the books?"

"Are you kidding? She's raving that she got all the Iris Murdochs she was looking for. The ones with the wild cover photos."

I dug out the business card that Dr Osterloh had given to us when we had so memorably crossed paths in Canterbury. I saw on the back of it he had printed an ad for his book. At the bottom it said, *First editions still available—but going fast.*

I tried to ring the number on the card but all I got was voicemail. I considered leaving a message but instead I thought I'd try again later. I wanted a chance to think, anyway, about what approach to use with the good doctor. I called again later that day. Still voicemail. I wanted to speak to him in person, if at all possible.

I tried intermittently over the next few days, always getting voicemail.

I decided if I did leave a message it would be to say that I wished to buy a signed hardcover of *The Sovereignty of the Self*. That ought to flush him out of the undergrowth.

Clean Head came back from Morocco with a bottle—a magnum, actually—of Chateau Musar for us in an attractive wooden box. And the documents. She was looking chic in tight black leggings, pink Converse high tops and a leather jacket. When she unzipped the jacket it revealed a stylishly baggy white t-shirt with a legend in bold, black letters that read, I WENT TO CANTERBURY AND ALL I GOT WAS THIS LOUSY MURDER ATTEMPT.

"It's a present from Tinkler," she said. "What do you think?"

I was speechless.

Nevada said, "It's reminiscent of Katharine Hamnett."

"I understand your Iris Murdoch collection has improved recently," I said.

Clean Head smiled at me, eyes gleaming with enthusiasm. "Yes, I've now got all the ones with Harri Peccinotti covers. I've been looking for some of those for years." Then she went next door with Nevada to talk about whatever it is women talk about when they slip away to strategise.

I spent the afternoon going through the cache of documents about Valerian. I had imagined it would be handwritten papers such as letters and journals, and there were indeed a lot of those. But there were also newspaper clippings, tear-sheets from magazines, photographs and even drawings. Among the photographs was one of Monty Tegmark. He looked just like his daughter. They had identical pug noses set in matching potato faces. I didn't even need to find the scan of the back of the photo and read the typed caption to identify him—although I did, and saw the photo was credited to one Nicholas Vardy.

I showed it to Nevada. "Lucille takes after her father."

"Doesn't she just? Poor thing."

In the evening Tinkler came over for supper and to assist. He'd brought his laptop to help try and organise the Valerian documents into some kind of a database. "This is where my spectrum disorder side comes in really handy," he said, peering cheerfully into the computer screen. "Actually you're really lucky."

"Why?"

"Clean Head has done an amazing job."

Nevada looked in from the kitchen where she was theoretically doing the washing up but was actually playing with the cats. "As if you'd say anything else, love-struck boy."

"No, really," said Tinkler, studying the screen. "She hasn't just scanned the documents optically, she's actually taken all the printed material—all the material that is in the form of printed text—"

"Yes, yes, we get it."

"Well, she has scanned all that stuff in using OCR software."

"You're sure it's not OCD software?" said Nevada.

"Optical character *recognition*," said Tinkler. "And it's a very sophisticated algorithm. It's managed to make sense of the rather blurry type on the faded newspaper clippings, of which there are several hundred in the archive."

"So why does that help us?" said Nevada.

"Because it's searchable," I said.

The next morning I got up early, fed the cats, put some music on—Lucy Ann Polk—and went to sit at the computer.

I fired up the database Tinkler had prepared.

I typed in the name 'John Blacklock'.

Sure enough, several documents were immediately selected. I clicked on them and started to read.

John Blacklock, real name Neville Stimping, was indeed Irish. He had been an orphan—parents unknown—and had been raised in a church orphanage: not a fate I would have wished on anyone in rural Ireland in the 1940s and 1950s. In the late 1950s he had run away, and eventually managed to stay away, from these institutions. He had then been at the centre of a bohemian set in Dublin. There had always been a mystical tendency in Irish literary circles and, at its extremes, this had led to people who should have known better dabbling in the 'dark arts'. Like his illustrious predecessor Aleister Crowley, Blacklock had seen a marketing opportunity here and had proceeded to peddle his own particular brand of snake oil to the well heeled and gullible.

The arrival of the swinging 1960s, with its soft-headed enthusiasm for drugs and the occult, had pretty much represented a gold rush for people such as Blacklock and he had wasted no time moving to London and taking advantage of folk like Valerian.

There were photographs of him in the archive. He was clean-shaven, slightly soft-looking, all dressed in black with carefully coiffured black hair. In one shot he was holding a human skull, like some hack actor playing Hamlet. It was a head and shoulders shot of him, holding the skull against his chest. The jagged whiteness of the bone was strikingly in contrast to the soft, black garment he wore. His black eyes peered out intently. It was hard to deny him some charisma, at least in this arresting shot. I checked the photo credit, in small print at the bottom right edge of the picture.

Photograph by Nic Vardy.

Ah, Nic, I thought. *You didn't catch him just getting off the crapper here, did you? No attempt to minimise the subject's magnetism in this case.*

At that moment the doorbell rang and one of the cats came hammering excitedly through the cat flap. They sometimes did this when people arrived, rushing past the visitor and disappearing inside. They'd almost given one postman a heart attack.

It was Fanny. She came trotting into the room and started washing herself as Nevada answered the door. I heard voices. Lucy and the Colonel. Unusual to hear them together. And it didn't even sound like they were fighting. At least not yet.

The Colonel bustled in and immediately came and stared over my shoulder at the computer screen. "Very good," he said. "Tinkler Dropboxed us a copy of the archive, all organised on his database. It's useful, isn't it?"

"Very," I said.

Nevada came through and took the Colonel's coat. "What, no lamb from Harrods?" she said, and he chuckled. Lucy came in and also looked over my shoulder.

"That's my father's article," she said proudly. I checked the by-line on it—which embarrassingly I hadn't bothered to look at, despite carefully scrutinising the provenance of the accompanying photo. She was right. *A special report by Monty Tegmark.*

It had been published in one of the Sunday tabloids, in the same year that Valerian had died.

The Colonel was marching around the room, peering out the window, pretending that he wasn't going to end up sitting beside the cat. "We're going to Ireland," he said. *Ireland?* I thought. Then, *we?* I wondered if there had been some sort of rapprochement between the two of them.

"We're getting separate flights," said Lucy. "And staying in separate hotels. Apparently I'm going to foot my own bills, too." This sounded a lot more like it.

"I'm quite happy to pay for your hotel if you remain in London," said the Colonel, sitting down beside Fanny. "But if you insist on coming with me to Dublin—"

"I *need* to go," said Lucy.

"You are to have absolutely no involvement with any of my activities while I am over there." The Colonel reached down and scratched Fanny behind the ear. She lifted her head to give him better access.

"I don't *want* any involvement in your activities. I just need to soak up the atmosphere. For the book."

"Dublin," I said. "Have you been reading about Blacklock?"

The Colonel nodded. "And Nevada told me about your suspicions concerning the possible paternity of Valerie's son."

"We don't know anything for certain," I said, or started to say. He immediately waved his hands in the air in protest. Fanny yelped at the sudden cessation of the stroking and he immediately resumed it, properly rebuked.

"I'm going to see what I can do to confirm or deny the

rumour. I will be making use of local sources, researchers and investigators."

"He's going to hire a private eye," said Lucy contemptuously.

"You don't want me to look into it?" I felt both relieved and obscurely offended. The Colonel shook his head vigorously, as he continued to caress Fanny's little head with both hands.

"I want you to stay here and continue making progress," he said.

"We're making progress?" I said, surprised and pleased.

He gave me a sardonic look. "Number one, my sister who had been presumed dead for twenty years, turns out to be alive. Number two, she has been talking to you when we thought she wasn't capable of speech. Number three, we might have found the identity of the father of Valerie Anne's son." He looked down, rubbing his hands on Fanny's whiskers. "Yes, I would say you were making progress."

The following day I rang Dr Osterloh's number again and finally got an answer. It was his secretary, who told me he was at a conference in Zurich and wouldn't be back until the end of the week. She promised she'd get him to ring me immediately on his return. She sounded very Scandinavian and very efficient. I didn't even have to offer to buy his book.

Despite her promises I hung up feeling thwarted. I would have to wait days before I could speak to Osterloh. It was all very frustrating. Surprisingly so. I felt anxious and tense. Then I realised why I was so eager to talk to him.

It was so I could avoid thinking about the other possibility.

But there was no dodging it now. I sat staring out the window, not registering the familiar view. I thought it over and decided I was right. We'd have to pursue it. Nevada came in and immediately realised something was wrong. Maybe I just looked miserable.

"What is it?" she said. She sat down beside me, looking at me with concern. "What's the matter?"

"Do you remember what Cecilia said to us in Canterbury, just before we left?"

"I'm hardly likely to forget it."

"But do you remember exactly what she said? 'Do you want to know the truth about my sister? She took it to the grave with her. That's where it is. All of it. That's where it is now.'"

Nevada looked at me.

She said, "You don't think…"

21. CINEPHILE

Valerian's grave was in a little churchyard in Canterbury.

"Back to bloody Canterbury," said Nevada, as we sat on the train.

"It was the family home," I said. "This is where her father, the Colonel—the real Colonel—lived. So it makes sense that they brought her back here to bury her."

"Oh it makes sense, all right. But it's still the same poxy place to have to visit again. I mean, if we were going buzzing around the UK enjoying its diverse cultural heritage, that's one thing. But always going to sodding Canterbury, that's quite another."

I said, "You're just not wild about the place because we were almost lured to our doom in its sunny streets."

"True," said Nevada. "I went to Canterbury and all I got was almost burned alive." She looked at me. "Maybe I should print my own t-shirt."

"You have to have the word 'lousy' in there, or it doesn't qualify."

She peered out the window at the speedily unfurling countryside, which was just then obscured by a passing train, thundering by in the opposite direction. We had caught the 11:22 from Victoria that morning. "That business about her father explains why Valerian is buried there, but it doesn't explain why Cecilia is *living* there."

"Presumably when she went mad they slung her into the nearest loony bin."

"Don't think the insensitivity of your language has escaped notice."

"I'm laughing to keep from crying," I said. "All right, let's call it her nervous breakdown. That was the jargon at the time. And she had her first nervous breakdown just after she buried her sister." I'd been reading about the incident in newspaper accounts in the archive. Very lurid newspaper accounts. I suppose it invited that. It was a huge, juicy story. Little boy disappears. Pop princess hangs self. Now sister goes insane. The cash registers just kept on ringing.

"And so she spent all the intervening years at a psychiatric hospital in Canterbury?" said Nevada.

"Various hospitals. In and around the city." I shrugged. "This was as far as Cecilia got. It's weird to think about. She was a schoolgirl in Canterbury, dreaming about the big wide world. And sure enough, off she went with her sister and the band and they did go everywhere, Australia, Japan, Brazil, Mexico, the States and Singapore, but she ends up back here in Canterbury. Back where she started, stuck here for all the remaining years. Just like it never happened. Just like she never went away."

"You know what," said Nevada. She leaned over in the seat towards me, eyes bright. She was genuinely quite excited. "That would be a wonderful angle for the documentary."

"It would," I said. "If we were actually making a documentary."

There was a pause while our train rattled past Rochester.

"Good point," she said, at last. "But I'm still the producer. You still have to fetch coffee for me."

"What else is new?"

We came into Canterbury East railway station and got a taxi the rest of the way. It took us past Boleyn Court, the wide green tree-lined grounds of St Augustine's College and—I must admit I felt a little pang of apprehension as we passed it—HM Prison Canterbury.

The taxi turned down a little lane beside the church. We paid off our driver and arranged for him to collect us at this spot in exactly an hour. The taxi pulled away and we turned to the church gate, an antique structure of dark, worn wood with a funny little triangular roof. As you stepped through there were wooden walls and small benches on either side of a flagstone path and a second gate inside. It was like a tiny little house, open at the front and back.

"I always like a good lychgate," said Nevada.

"You know what lych means?"

"Oh yes." We walked through it hand in hand and we were in the churchyard. Or the graveyard if you wanted to call it that. It was a couple of acres of greenery that surrounded the church—a handsome rectangular building with a tall bell tower made of honey-coloured stone. There were flowerbeds and shrubs planted among the graves—many of which were ancient, with moss-covered ragged-edged stones that looked like time had chewed on them.

The rich green grass was neatly trimmed and I noted the hard work that must be involved with the detached relief and awe of a man who had no intention of switching on a lawnmower any time soon.

The wide flagstone path divided into three narrower paths that wound among the graves. The one in the middle led towards the door of the church. The other two weaved around the building to the left and right. We took the left-hand path and began to study the gravestones.

"It's around the back," called a man's voice. "In the far corner on your right." We turned around to see the vicar standing in the church door. He was wearing a dog collar and a long black cassock with, incongruously, a lime-green tweed sports jacket pulled on over it. He came out of the shadow of the church doorway and approached us. I noticed his black shoes were scuffed and muddy.

The bell in the tower above us began to ring as he entered the churchyard, as if on cue. I wondered if he had a remote control. He walked briskly up to us, unsmiling and, to be frank, looking a little pissed off. I would have thought he could have been a touch more welcoming, given the level of church attendance these days. "If you follow the other path it will get you there more quickly," he said, his tone somewhere between resignation and impatience. He had red hair and a salt and pepper beard. His eyes looked weary behind gold wire-rimmed spectacles. Up close I saw he was younger than I'd first thought.

"Get where more quickly?" I said.

He sighed and studied the toes of his shoes. Maybe he was thinking he'd better clean them before the evening service. "To her grave. Valerian's grave."

I said, "Who's Valerian?"

He looked up at me, startled and a little wary. "I'm sorry," he said. "I just assumed you were here to see her grave. Almost everyone usually is." He suddenly sounded a lot more civil.

"Oh no," said Nevada. "We just came in to have a look because it's so beautiful." He squinted at her with suspicion and I wondered if she'd overdone it. She turned quickly to a grave beside her with a single pink rose lying on it. "This one for instance."

The vicar frowned at her. "You know the Endures?"

The inscription on the headstone read:

MARNIE VALMOND ENDURE
1908–1968

"No, no, no," said Nevada casually. "I was just admiring the rose on it." She hurriedly took out her phone and began taking photos, as if in support of her claim. "Isn't it a lovely thought that someone cares so much that they go to the trouble of putting flowers on a grave, and making sure that they're always fresh and new."

"It's artificial," said the vicar, smiling thinly. "The rose is artificial." I looked more closely and saw that he was right. Poor old Marnie Valmond Endure deserved better, if only for the heroic proportions of her name.

"And it's so peaceful," added Nevada hastily. She looked around us and smiled. "In places like these. They always remind me of Thomas Gray's poem."

The vicar relaxed a little. "The 'Ode to a Country Churchyard'," he said.

"The 'Elegy Written in a Country Churchyard', actually," said Nevada primly. She took a deep, appreciative breath of the air, which was indeed cleaner than London air, and worth savouring. It smelled of damp and green growth. "'The curfew tolls the knell of parting day,'" quoted Nevada. "Though of course the most famous line in the poem is 'The paths of glory lead but to the grave.'"

The vicar tried a smile. "Which provided the title of a very good film," he said.

"*Paths of Glory*," said Nevada. "A masterpiece. You know, I'm not sure it's not Kubrick's finest picture."

"You know it?"

"Know it? I've never been able to get it out of my head. Do you remember those scenes in the trenches?"

"The tracking shots," said the vicar excitedly. "They're magnificent!" He was now officially eating out of her hand.

"And the sequence at the end with the girl—"

"The singer, yes!"

"Singing to the troops," said Nevada. "What a great film. Certainly one of his best." There then ensued a brief but enthusiastic discussion of the films of Stanley Kubrick in which it was immediately agreed that the black and white ones were the most interesting, with detailed reference to *Dr. Strangelove*, which then veered off into a symposium of vociferous agreement about the merits of a banned film by Peter Watkins, broadening out into an analysis of the whole anti-nuclear movement in the 1960s that was in danger of getting profound.

So I said, "Who is this Valerian?"

Nevada flashed me a look of annoyance. I was risking spoiling the rapport she had so painstakingly built up. But in fact, as I suspected, the vicar seemed quite happy to talk to us about Valerian—providing we weren't the usual sick sensation seekers. "Oh, a rock singer," he said. "Rather notorious and very famous. I understand she was actually quite good, extremely talented." He smiled thinly. "A bit heavy for my taste, I fear. Her music, I mean. Bob Dylan is more my speed. The pre-electric Dylan." I repressed the urge to ask if he had any records he might want to get rid of. Some mint vintage albums by, say, the post-electric Dylan. Tinkler would have chewed his leg off.

"Anyway, she was a local girl and she died tragically at the height of her fame. It's entirely understandable that people are so fascinated by her, I suppose." He sighed. "It's terrible to say something like this, but I rather wish she hadn't been. A local girl, I mean. If only she had lived elsewhere, just a few miles away, in someone else's parish."

And then it would be someone else's problem, he didn't need to say.

"I suppose you have a lot of riffraff coming to look at it," said Nevada. "Rock riffraff. Rock and roll riffraff."

"There are a lot of... visitors," conceded the vicar. "Far too many for a small churchyard like this. And they *leave* things. On her grave. Sometimes very inappropriate things." I could see we weren't just talking about artificial roses here. "It really is quite a problem. I've even been in touch with the people at Père Lachaise in Paris, to see how they cope."

"Père Lachaise," I said. "That's where Jim Morrison's buried, isn't it?"

"Yes." He shook his head fretfully. "Now, they *really* have a problem. Vandalism, desecration, graffiti." He glanced over his shoulder at the far side of the churchyard. "At least here we've managed to keep matters relatively under control."

We followed him along the right-hand path around the church tower. The vicar said, "Luckily there is a trust fund set up by Valerian's father. He had seen what had happened to the tree."

I remembered just in the nick of time that I wasn't supposed to know anything about this. "What tree?"

"She hanged herself from a tree, the poor creature, and it was almost immediately mobbed by fans. So he knew what to expect with her last resting place. Hence the fund administers a small amount to care for the grave each year, in perpetuity. And it yielded enough money to pay for things." The path led us to an area at the back in the shadow of several large and rather healthy-looking pines. They provided shelter and a sense of restfulness.

The rural calm of the place was somewhat spoiled by the brutalist slab of concrete that he led us to, an enormous grey rectangle the size of a double bed. There was a withered bouquet of flowers lying on it. "Including the recent renovations," said the vicar.

"Renovations?" I said.

"Yes." He nodded happily.

In a notch at the top of the concrete slab, a modest headstone barely protruded with the name *Valerie Anne Drummond* chiselled on it, and below this *'Valerian'* and the dates of her birth and death. I noticed those quotation marks and sensed the angry old man behind them, her father. I looked at Nevada.

She was staring at the slab of stone that covered the grave. The vicar followed her gaze and said, "See how it's been done?" He looked down at it fondly. "We used wooden forms that guided the flow of the concrete, neatly avoiding the headstone itself. And it remains low enough not to interfere with any of the inscription on the stone." He shook his head, smiling affectionately. "I am rather proud of it."

"That's certainly... a large slab of concrete," said Nevada.

The vicar nodded. "Several tons. It had to be." He glanced at her. "Somebody kept trying to dig up the grave."

"Really?" said Nevada. "How awful. What sort of people would even think of doing such a thing?"

22. BLACKLOCK

I must admit, my first reaction was a feeling of considerable relief. It seemed I wasn't going to end up in Canterbury prison for grave robbing after all.

Nevada, on the other hand, was extremely pissed off. She'd spent hours on the Internet researching the tools we'd need for the job, including a sophisticated turf cutter that would have allowed us to remove the layer of grass on top of the grave and replace it afterwards so that it would appear that nothing had been disturbed. "I even found one that operated virtually silently," she said, sulkily. "So we could go in at the dead of night."

I felt a little disloyal that I didn't share her disgruntlement but, after a while, as we stared at the water flashing below us as the train carried us through Chatham on our way back to London, my relief began to give way to disappointment and frustration.

We had literally hit a dead end, an unbreakable obstacle. I thought about the giant concrete slab on Valerian's grave.

What would we do now? I'd been so sure that this was the right next step, and that we would learn something crucial.

Now it was all gone.

I forced myself to count my blessings; at least Nevada wasn't online researching concrete-breaking machines that operated silently, by the dead of night.

We got into Victoria just as the rush hour was beginning in earnest and rode back to Hammersmith on a packed Tube train, then got off and squeezed onto an equally packed bus that sat endlessly in traffic before working its way cautiously across the bridge and gradually trundling south, homewards. Nevada only perked up when she found Fanny and Turk waiting for us in the kitchen and making affronted noises about not having been fed yet. While she was pouring out some stopgap cat biscuits I checked our landline.

There was a message from Dr Osterloh, inviting me to come and visit him at his office tomorrow.

Bayswater is an intriguing neighbourhood. There's a lot of money there, and a great deal of it from the Middle East. Hence the presence of the Islamic bookshop, mosque and assorted interesting restaurants. I came out of the Tube station and walked up Queensway. I'd deliberately got here early, so I could hit the charity shops. An unusual and cosmopolitan neighbourhood like this could yield some remarkable finds on vinyl. The first two shops didn't have any LPs, but in the third I found some nice recordings of Glenn Miller's Army Air Force Band with arrangements by Eddie Sauter.

I thought it would be unprofessional of me to turn up with a bundle of LPs under my arm, so I paid for them and got the girl to put them behind the counter to pick up later.

I left the shop with the sense of a job well done already and walked past the Whiteley's shopping centre towards Westbourne Grove. I turned off at the old art deco swimming baths, down a shady side street lined with trees. On the corner was a house, huge by London standards, and painted bright pink. It was the end of a terraced row of dwellings, all with the same flat-faced three-storey facades and shallow front gardens. Judging by the long wall that ran around the right side of the house, there appeared to be a very large back garden indeed.

I went up the steps and rang the bell, well aware that a house like this in a neighbourhood like this was worth a few million at least. It was Osterloh's office, but also his home.

The doctor's secretary let me in. Her name was Adela, and after speaking to her on the phone I wasn't surprised to learn that she was Swedish. I was surprised, however, to see she was six feet tall and had a black Mohawk that added considerably to her height.

Call me a sad victim of stereotype, but I'd been expecting a blonde.

She led me down the hall to a doorway on the left. Inside was a tiny sunlit lounge with two grey silk sofas facing each other. "I'll go and get the doctor," she said. "Can I offer you anything to drink? Coffee? Tea?"

"Coffee, please."

"Please sit down."

She went and I sat down on one of the sofas. The walls were painted white and hung with bright, cheerful posters. Most of them were by the Belgian graphic artist Folon, though one was a Chagall. It was a friendly, welcoming room. Or at least it was until I noticed, standing in the corner, a life-sized cardboard cut-out of Dr Osterloh clutching his book. He was grinning toothily like a proud father holding his newborn. I was staring at it when he came in and he immediately registered the direction of my gaze.

"I told her not to put that in here," he said crossly. "Adela!" He looked up to see that Adela was clinking through the doorway with coffee cups on a tray. "Thank you, Adela." We each took a cup from her. "Now, would you mind taking that away, please?" Adela nodded and picked up the cardboard cut-out. It grinned over her shoulder as she carried it out. It looked like she was wrestling with him.

Dr Osterloh sat down opposite me. He was wearing a black roll-neck sweater and baggy, expensive-looking charcoal-grey trousers. On his feet were a pair of gleaming mahogany-brown brogues. He looked very relaxed, but then he was at home. "Sorry about that. Underneath the shambolic exterior Adela is actually highly organised. And very good with the clients." He smiled at me. "I always enjoy the reaction of people who have spoken to her on the phone but never actually met her before. They're always expecting some kind of little blonde. And they get..." He didn't bother to complete his thought but just shook his head fondly. "I find it charming, her appearance. But quite inexplicable."

I thought it was charming, but highly explicable. I said,

"I imagine it's the influence of Stieg Larsson."

He looked at me with interest. "Ah, is that what it is? I'm afraid I've never heard of him, but then I don't follow modern music. Indeed, the last time I took any interest in popular recording artists is when Valerian was my client."

"You haven't had any musicians as clients since then?"

"Not in the same sense." He smiled. "People come here and talk to me. I operate my practice out of this house. People come to me; I no longer go to them."

"But you were actually on tour with Valerian."

"Oh yes." He shrugged. "I had more energy in those days."

"How did you happen to end up with her as a client?" I already knew one version of this story, but I wanted to hear his.

He frowned. "Hmm. I must have been recommended by a friend. Someone in the band? No, they were all fearless, loveable extroverts who were innocent of any appetite for self-analysis." As an assessment of the only member of the band I actually knew, Erik Make Loud, I thought this stood up pretty well, even after all these years. "No, it must have been someone in her management or some person like that," he said. "But the important thing is that we did meet, and we hit it off, and I knew we could work together."

I nodded and took a sip of the coffee. It was shockingly bad, watery and bitter. I thought I concealed my reaction pretty well, but he must have picked up on something because he said, "How is the coffee?" He actually made it sound like a genuine question instead of the usual bit of social white noise. "Is it really that dreadful?"

"No, it's fine, I just—"

He held up his hand. "I would consider it a personal favour if you were candid with me. You see, I don't drink the stuff, so I have no idea."

"Well… it's not great."

"Excellent, thank you. That's very useful to know. In future I will get Adela to go out and buy some fresh from one of the dozens of coffee bars that have sprung up in the main road."

I said, "She'll hate me for making all the extra work for her."

He grinned. "On the contrary she will be delighted to have the chance to get out and meet her many friends among the local students and young mothers who throng those places. She will be *grateful* to you. Now, where were we?"

I set the coffee aside, relieved not to have to maintain the pretence of drinking the swill. "You were telling me about how you met Valerian and started… working with her."

He nodded. "Yes, that's what we call it." He smiled. "Work. Because that's what it is."

"From everything I read about her she didn't seem the type to have a…"

"Shrink?" He chuckled. "Maybe she wasn't." He spread his hands. "And yet there we were. I suppose we just hit it off. I think she only saw me because someone had talked her into it, but when we met we got along." He looked at me. "It was as simple as that. I don't think I was quite what she expected."

I said, "Viennese couch and all that?"

"Exactly. With a lot of theory and lecturing. But that's not my approach. I'm very down to earth and practical." He examined his hands, as though expecting to find the dirt of honest labour under his fingernails. "I began by making some very simple practical suggestions about how she could make life easier on herself."

"For example?"

He leaned back on the sofa, folding his hands together. "Ah, for example the whole question of domestic help." He chuckled. "It seems that the Drummond girls had grown up thinking that it was the height of sophistication to have an au pair. So when they became wealthy rock stars and needed waiting on hand and foot, nothing would do but to have an au pair. It was a badge of status, I suppose, and of course they did need someone to make the tea and toast, run the bath, crucial things like that. In an earlier age it would have been a butler or a maid, but given the period they were living in and their particular social aspirations, it had to be an au pair. But when hiring these girls, Valerian felt she had an image to keep up, which I suppose she did. A public image. So she insisted on hiring the most exquisite creatures imaginable." He smiled at me. "I wonder if you can guess what happened?"

I thought of Erik Make Loud and Nic Vardy sitting on a sofa, drunk and comparing notes. "The guys in the band wouldn't leave them alone?"

"Exactly! It became a point of honour to see who could be the first to seduce the new au pair. And since we're talking about men who were young, handsome, famous and rich, it never took them very long. So the inevitable complications would ensue. The poor girls would not only get distracted from their primary task..."

"Tea and toast."

"And running the bath. You mustn't forget about running the bath. Yes, they would also inevitably end up leaving in tears when whichever bloke in the band had seduced them moved on to his next conquest. Which never took long. So it was my humble suggestion that she stop hiring these ravishing, glamorous creatures and instead employ less comely but equally efficient girls." He chuckled. "And of course, that did the trick."

I could well imagine Erik Make Loud's horror at the suddenly changed situation and his disgusted utter reluctance to lower his standards. "Smart move," I said.

He nodded. "Interestingly, when Valerian had the baby she got rid of all the domestic help. Just when you would have thought she'd need it most, she decided she had to be a proper old-fashioned hands-on mother. No au pairs or nannies. She looked after the little boy herself." He smiled. "Although of course looking after him herself really meant delegating his care to Cecilia." He sighed nostalgically. "She was a nice girl."

"Cecilia or Valerian?"

"Both of them. Though of course it was Valerian I knew best." He smiled again. "I like to think that I did help her." The smile faded. "Although of course in the end it turns out that perhaps I was no help to her at all." He looked down at his shoes.

I said, "You don't blame yourself for what happened, do you?"

"The suicide of a client is the most emphatic failure possible for someone in my profession."

"Perhaps she didn't commit suicide."

He looked up and stared at me for a long time with increasing interest. "What makes you say that?"

I leaned forward. "There are two big question marks about the life of Valerian. The circumstances of her death and the disappearance of her child." He nodded. I said, "I'm wondering if the two are somehow connected."

"How might they be connected?"

"What do you know about John Blacklock?" I asked.

He sagged back on the sofa, nodding. "Ah. Blacklock. Of course." He shifted uneasily. "He was already on the scene when I met Valerian. Unfortunately." He glanced at me. "I like to think that I managed to diminish his influence over her, at least."

"What was he like?"

Osterloh shrugged. "Do you know what cold reading is?"

"It's when you make guesses about someone you've just met."

"Yes, exactly, and you act on these guesses to try and make the person think you know more about them, and their situation, than you actually do." He gave a chilly little smile. "Mind readers, fortune tellers, con men. There are all sorts of people who apply this method, to awe the credulous and advance their own ends."

"And that's what John Blacklock did?"

Osterloh considered carefully. "That wasn't all he did. He also possessed a certain acuteness. A perceptiveness. About people. Let me give you an example. When we first met in Canterbury, and you were with the young lady."

"Nevada," I said.

"Yes. It was instantly obvious you two were what we used to call 'an item'. Now, there is no way John Blacklock would have failed to notice something like that, and no way he would have failed to make use of it, whether it was by trying to drive a wedge between you, or exploiting the bond to his own profit. The only sure thing is that, whatever he did, it would be to his own profit."

"Could he have been the father of Valerian's baby?"

He fell silent. At first I thought I'd shocked him, but then I realised he was thinking carefully. "The dates work," he said. "Blacklock was certainly seeing her around the time the child must have been conceived. It's also true that their tryst seemed unusually monogamous, and exclusive. At least on Valerian's side…" He shook his head. "And do you know what, he was around a great deal after the boy was born. Much more than before."

"Could he have taken the kid?"

"A custody snatch?" he said. Again he was silent for a moment. "Do you know…" he said thoughtfully, "he *did* go back to Ireland at just about the time the boy disappeared." He began to nod his head as if confirming something to himself. "Yes. And Blacklock himself vanished from the scene, at least the scene here in Britain, for some years after that." He looked up at me. "So the answer is yes, potentially, to both your questions."

"Is he still alive?" I said, "Blacklock?"

Osterloh blinked at me in surprise. "Of course. I think so. Why do you ask?"

"I've tried to find out, but it isn't that easy. I've looked at his entry on Wikipedia, and it seems to depend on the time of day whether it says he's alive or dead."

The doctor chuckled. "Yes, that makes sense."

"Does it?"

"Yes, you see Blacklock has his devoted followers. But he also has sworn enemies. They would both be trying to alter his page, each to their own ends. Distorting the truth. When you add that to the Wikipedia people themselves, trying to maintain accuracy, and the public relations firm that I suspect Blacklock employs—he used to employ one back in the 1960s and I hardly see him changing his ways—that makes for a total of at least four interested parties, very interested, all changing the entry on Blacklock to suit their agenda." He thought for a moment and then hooted with laughter. "I imagine it's changing with almost stroboscopic frequency."

I said, "Well, that explains why sometimes it says he's alive, sometimes that he's dead and occasionally has a message from some colourful individual that he's eternal and is never going to die."

Osterloh laughed again and said, "You see, this is why the printed page is superior to the Internet. Have I told you about my book?"

Here it comes, I thought. I considered myself very lucky to have eluded the sales pitch so far. Now I tried to head it off at the pass. "Actually, you did. You also mentioned that there was nothing about Valerian in it."

He nodded glumly. "That's true."

"Is there anything about Blacklock in it?"

He sighed. "Unfortunately, no."

"Maybe you should write a book about him. There's obviously a need for some hard facts about the man, and as you say, in a medium less subject to distortion than the Internet. And there are probably few people as well qualified to write one."

He stared at me, then suddenly dug out a pen and a small red notebook. He flipped it open and started scribbling. "What a splendid idea!" he said. "That's a truly wonderful idea. Why did I never think of it? And it will very probably be a substantial bestseller." He shut the notebook. "Thank you for that. I shall make a point of thanking you again, properly, on the acknowledgements page when the book is published."

I considered asking for a signed first edition but decided that he was all too likely to spot the sarcasm. He put the pen and notebook away. "Of course," he said, "to avoid the inevitable libel suit I shall have to wait until after he dies."

"Assuming he doesn't live forever," I said.

On the way back I stopped at the charity shop to pick up my records. The girl who'd served me was no longer behind the counter. She'd been replaced by a surly young guy with a beard. It took a lot of explaining to get across what I wanted, and when I finally did, he made a big deal of looking for the records and failing to find them. If he'd had his way, that would have been that, but I made him go to get the girl who was sorting stock in the back room. She wasn't pleased to be disturbed but she looked for the records and, again, drew a blank.

After much discussion the girl and the bloke finally came to the conclusion that someone else must have taken them. In any case, they were gone.

After considerable argument they finally refunded what I'd paid; luckily I'd kept the receipt with me. I left the shop with my money, but a cold feeling in my stomach.

23. BLACK EYE

From Bayswater I headed to the Colonel's hotel in Mayfair, where I was supposed to meet Nevada. She was waiting for me in a small bar just off the lobby. The bar was full of gleaming brass fixtures and leather sofas and it was very dimly lit. Not so dimly lit that I didn't immediately see the familiar figure sitting at the table beside her.

"Tinkler, what are you doing here?"

He grinned at me. "John wanted to see me."

"John?" I said.

"The Colonel," provided Nevada.

Tinkler wagged his finger in a scolding gesture. "You have to stop calling him that. It really pisses him off."

"Yes, poor bloke," she said.

I kissed Nevada and sat down with them. There were two coffees already on the table and a mangled pile of wrappers that had once contained expensive chocolate biscuits. The spoor of Tinkler. "But why did he want to see you?" I said.

Tinkler puffed up with pride. "Well, John used to have a

big real estate business back in the States."

"Before he got divorced," said Nevada. "Then he packed it all in. Sold up, split it fifty-fifty with the ex-wife and then retired."

I said, "Are we getting any nearer an answer here?"

"The thing is," said Tinkler, "John still keeps his hand in. He operates a small property portfolio. And he wants me to help him with it."

"Help him?"

"He's witnessed my breathtaking database skills."

I sighed and sat back in my chair, looking at the cups in front of them. "Is this the place with the good coffee?"

Nevada shook her head. "No, we left the hotel for that. But today John wanted to meet in here. Said he didn't want to go far. So please don't complain and make a scene if it's not up to scratch. The coffee, I mean."

"Do I ever?" A waitress took my order and the coffee came with suspicious speed. But it wasn't bad. Considerably better than at Dr Osterloh's—though that wasn't saying much.

"Oh, by the way," said Tinkler. "I've booked us a visit with the Evil Elves." It took me a moment to think who the hell he was talking about. Then I remembered those gnarled, red hands hovering over the jigsaw puzzle.

I said, "The Trevertons. Timothy and Gordon Treverton."

"The Alpine Twins," said Tinkler.

"I think we're sticking with Evil Elves," said Nevada, sipping her coffee.

"You remember we worked out that they were more than likely to have a stash of rare vinyl? Stuff that Valerian and her entourage left at the house? Well, I could hardly sleep thinking about it, so I got in touch with them—"

I said, "How did you get in touch with them? We never had their phone number."

"They have a Facebook page."

"They're on Facebook?"

Tinkler nodded. "A whole load of family photos. Actually, to be honest, just photos of the brothers. In the great outdoors. Mountain climbing, canoeing, doing archery. Mostly with their shirts off and revealing rippling torsos. I sent a link to Clean Head because I thought she'd appreciate it. And she got quite excited."

"Why didn't you send me a link?" said Nevada.

"Oh, for Christ's sake," I said.

"Sending it to you now," said Tinkler, taking out his smartphone.

"Where the hell is the Colonel?" I said.

"Just coming down from his room. He—"

"I'm here." I turned around to see the Colonel standing there. He had a livid purple bruise under his left eye, and a small dressing taped just above his left eyebrow. The battered appearance of his face was seriously at odds with his fastidious clothing. Perhaps he'd dressed with extra care, to compensate.

"My god," said Nevada. "What happened to you?"

"Mugged," said the Colonel succinctly. He pulled up a chair and sat down with us. We were all staring at him.

"Your poor face," said Nevada.

"You were mugged?" I said. He nodded, smiling a tight,

bitter little smile. If anything he seemed quietly proud of the revelation. The waitress came over and took his order. She showed no reaction to his appearance. Working in the hotel, she'd probably seen him already.

"This was the day I got back from Ireland. I was coming out of the Tube at Piccadilly Circus, heading along Regent Street and this little…" He searched for a suitable word, "This little scumbag came along on a bicycle. One with a lot of gears. And he grabbed the package I was holding…"

"What was the package?" I said.

"Some shoes I'd bought. But they weren't in a bag from the shoe shop." He stared at me, his wounded eye gleaming oddly. "They were in another bag, a plastic shopping bag I was using."

"Very good for the environment," said Tinkler brightly. We all ignored him.

"There was nothing on the bag to indicate what was inside," said the Colonel. "But from the size of the parcel I think they believed it was documents." He gave me a little smile. "In fact I think they thought it was the documents that your friend Agatha went to Morocco to collect." He looked at Nevada. "She did an excellent job, by the way."

"Of course," said Nevada, who had recovered her composure. She had been genuinely shocked at the sight of the Colonel, though. "We only use the finest."

"Of course, the documents are all safe in a bank in Morocco, the originals." The Colonel glanced at Tinkler. "With copies on our computers thanks to Jordon here." Tinkler beamed modestly. "But they don't know that," said the Colonel.

"So this cyclist grabbed the bag from you," I said. It didn't explain his injuries.

"I wouldn't let go of it. So he stopped and hit me with something. I think it was a bicycle pump."

"Ouch," said Nevada.

"Or something of that nature," said the Colonel. He shook his head, as though dismissing the whole incident. "Anyway, never mind any of that. I haven't spoken to you properly since I got back from Ireland, so I thought we should meet."

"Where's Lucy?" I said.

"Still in Dublin. Decided to stay over for a few days. She found a pub where she liked the Guinness. In Dublin I imagine even she could manage to achieve that."

"So she doesn't know you were attacked?" said Nevada.

"Or care," said the Colonel. He turned to me. "Have you made any progress while I was away?"

I nodded. "John Blacklock is definitely our top contender."

The Colonel stared at me pityingly. "You're sure of that?"

"He was around when the kid disappeared. He is a strong candidate for the father—"

"And you're certain of your facts?" said the Colonel.

I looked at him. Obviously he knew something I didn't. "I was," I said. "Up until now. What did you find out in Ireland?"

"I employed a local investigation firm to look into Blacklock. They already had a detailed dossier on him, which I suppose makes sense. Given the kind of man that he is." He stared at me, eyes pale and cold. "I gave them the relevant dates. And it turns out on the day the boy disappeared Blacklock was in Ireland. In prison."

We looked at him. So much for that theory. "He could have got someone else to do it for him," I said.

The Colonel nodded happily. "Sure, he could have. But the most likely candidates, all his close associates, were also in prison. It seems that Blacklock's group—cult, commune, whatever you want to call it—were squatting in a building that was church property. The authorities, both church and civil, had been waiting for the chance to apprehend him there and arrest the lot of them. Which they did about a week before Tom was taken. They remained in prison for almost a month."

"Still," said Nevada, "someone else could have kidnapped the boy on Blacklock's behalf. Someone who wasn't behind bars."

The Colonel shrugged. "It's possible," he said. He sounded far from convinced.

"And he's still the most likely candidate to be Tom's father," I said.

The Colonel smiled happily. This was apparently the statement he'd been waiting for. He now proceeded to explain with bitter relish why I was wrong.

Blacklock had a longstanding and, it has to be said, quite justifiable grudge against the clergy of his country. He had been raised in church institutions where he had been subject to violent abuse. His story was far from unique, but it was an extreme example. As he had got older and stronger Blacklock had begun to fight back against his tormentors.

So the priests had decided to teach him a lesson. This had involved holding him down and giving him such a savage kicking that, in one sense, he had never recovered. "He was effectively castrated," said the Colonel. "There was no way he could ever have fathered a child after that."

"So he was a eunuch?" said Tinkler, who, I noticed, was clutching his groin protectively.

"I suppose you could call him that," said the Colonel.

Tinkler looked at me. "But he was supposed to have had an affair with Valerian."

Nevada shrugged. "He still could have done."

"But how? He was a eunuch."

"That just means his testicles are gone," said Nevada. "He can't produce spermatozoa but, if it happened after puberty, he can still do everything else."

"Everything else?" said Tinkler.

"Yes."

"How do you *know* these things?"

"The further benefits of a classical education," said Nevada. "Anyway, that's why those calls you occasionally hear for castration of rapists are such spectacular nonsense."

Tinkler shifted uneasily in his chair, crossing his legs. "Let's just agree not to use the word 'castration' again for a while, okay?" he said.

So, scratch one suspect.

Tinkler and I stayed in the West End to visit Styli while Nevada headed home. Styli was a record store just off

Tottenham Court Road. It wasn't the same since its owner, Jerry, had died, but it still offered up the occasional treasure. Not today, though. I came home empty-handed.

And found that my reception from Nevada was distinctly icy. She turned her mouth away when I tried to kiss her and offered only the most perfunctory greeting. Then frosty silence. "What have I done now?" I said.

"Have you listened to your messages?"

I went into the sitting room and dialled up voicemail on our landline. There was one message, from Adela at Dr Osterloh's office. But it wasn't concerning Osterloh. Instead she said how nice it was to have met me today and asked if I'd like to get together for a drink sometime. I hung up and looked at Nevada, who was watching me with a scowl.

"Why is she ringing you?"

"I have no idea." I could have said that I was just naturally irresistible, but I decided this wouldn't go down well. "She probably doesn't meet many people," I offered. "She's at work all day, and the people she does meet are the patients of a psychiatrist. So not necessarily the most enticing bunch. Then I come along…"

"Then you come along."

"I just mean, I wasn't there as a patient, I must have seemed a bit different…"

"What did you *say* to her?"

"I didn't say anything. Wait a minute, I said her coffee was terrible. That's probably why she wants to meet. Because she wants revenge. She probably wants to kill me. When we meet she's going to kill me with a knife. An axe.

Whatever they use in Sweden. A ski pole."

"*When* you meet?"

"*If* we meet," I said hastily. "We're not going to meet. It's not going to happen."

That night Nevada slept on the far side of the bed, twisted away from me. Fanny, the turncoat little trollop, snuggled up tight beside her. I was left all alone on my side and it was a cold night. I could have done with all that extra body heat. I lay awake for what seemed like half the night, reduced to hoping that Turk might come in, with or without a disembowelled mouse, and curl up beside me.

The next morning while Nevada and Fanny were in the bath—or rather while Nevada was in the bath and Fanny was sitting on the wicker chair we keep in the bathroom, enjoying the steam—I made a phone call. I rang Dr Osterloh's surgery, wanting to speak to Adela. I was going to tell her that I wouldn't be able to meet up with her, because although that was a charming prospect, I was already spoken for.

But Osterloh himself answered. He sounded hurried and harassed, although he became much more civil when he realised who I was. "Sorry if I was a bit abrupt," he said. "What can I do for you?"

I was a bit wrong-footed by not having Adela answer the phone. I couldn't quite bring myself to ask to speak to her, though. So I made up some story about wanting to talk to him further. To check on some details. "Well, it won't be for a few days, I'm afraid," said Osterloh. "We've had a bit of trouble here."

"Trouble?"

"Yes, I'm afraid there's been a break-in." I went cold. "Last night," said Osterloh. "The worst thing about it was that I was right here in the house when the intruder entered. They were downstairs while I was upstairs."

"Jesus."

"Yes. I must say it gives one a very strange feeling indeed. And they must have known I was here. I was making plenty of noise. And yet they came in anyway. This is suggestive of a certain type of personality, a bold sociopath—the sort of human being I am in no way eager to have a closer acquaintance with."

"Shit."

"Yes. Needless to say I'm going to have a new security system put in. So everything's a bit chaotic. I hope you'll understand if I'm not available for a little while."

"What exactly did they take?"

"I'm sorry?"

I said, "They broke in. What did they steal?"

"Ah, yes. We're still trying to ascertain that, exactly." His voice changed, taking on a note of pride. "I think they might have got some copies of my book."

After I hung up Nevada came and sat on the sofa beside me. She was wearing her dressing gown and her hair was still wet. I told her what had happened to Osterloh, but she didn't seem particularly interested. "Why did you ring him?" she said.

"I didn't. Not really. I was ringing his secretary."

"The Scandinavian Amazon?"

"Yes."

"The Swedish Stalker?"

"Yes, I was going to explain to her gently that I'm already seeing someone."

Nevada smiled and kissed me. "You didn't have to do that," she said. *I did if I knew what was good for me*, I thought. But I didn't say anything. She relaxed against me, folding her legs up on the sofa, and I put my arms around her. Her hair was damp and fragrant. Fanny came in and saw us sitting together and promptly hopped onto the sofa to join us. Having spent all night nestled beside a warm body obviously wasn't enough. She found a little spot where she could lie fairly comfortably across both of us and settled down for the long haul. As if sensing she was being left out of something, Turk ambled in, yowled, and hopped up on the back of the sofa to join us. She reclined there, her thick fur tickling the back of my neck.

We all sat there together, my little family unit, in a moment of total peace. Or it would have been if I could have stopped thinking. Blacklock was a dead end because there was nothing there. The grave in Canterbury was an even more frustrating dead end because there *might* be something there, but we couldn't get at it.

We were nowhere, and it looked as though it was going to stay that way. I was beginning to wish I'd never got involved. I'd *told* them I didn't do missing persons.

All I was good at was finding records.

I remembered what Tinkler had said about the Evil Elves. He'd arranged for us to go there on a weekend and look through their vinyl, of which they apparently had quite a lot. And much of it had indeed been acquired during Valerian's stay in the house. So who knew what gems were lurking?

I felt the old excitement beginning again, moderated a little by the memory of the gloomy house with the tree outside, falsely receiving offerings for the poor dead girl.

I thought about the brothers and the tree. The way it had become a shrine. Like Valerian's grave in Canterbury.

I remembered what the vicar had said. The old man, Valerian's father, had known about the tree and what had happened to it. And he had taken measures accordingly.

A tremor ran through me.

The cats were the first to sense it. Stirring restlessly then getting up and moving off us. Nevada turned and gave me a curious look. I eased myself up, disentangling myself. "What's up?" she said. "You ruined a perfectly good communal cuddle."

I said, "You remember, in the churchyard in Canterbury, were there any other graves with flowers on them?"

"Any *other* graves?"

"Besides Valerian's and that one with the artificial rose."

She was staring at me. "No, just Valerian's and that one with the extraordinary name. What was it? Endure. I remember because that's what I thought was going to happen to us. That we were going to have to *endure* a bollocking from the vicar about coming there into his lovely peaceful churchyard to gawp at Valerian's grave. Until luckily I tapped into his cineaste side with my lively dissertation about the films of Stanley Kubrick. Wasn't that brilliant?"

"It certainly was," I said. "But it's just those two graves. Valerian and…"

"Mrs Endure's. Or I suppose it could be Miss Endure's. But somehow I see her as a married woman."

"Marnie something Endure." I felt the anticipation growing.

"Valmont. I remember it because of *Les Liaisons Dangereuses*. He's the hero, though I suppose you can't actually call him a hero. Or, hang on, was it Valmond with a 'd'? Wait a minute." She took out her phone. "I took a picture. Yes. With a 'd'."

The laptop was on the dining room table. I went over and sat down and switched it on. I typed the name.

MARNIE VALMOND ENDURE

Then I sat and stared. Within a few seconds I felt a warm shock of triumph. Nevada came over and sat down beside me. She looked at it. She got it immediately.

"It's an anagram," she said.

VALERIE ANNE DRUMMOND

24. THE PATHS OF GLORY

"You mean we get to desecrate someone's last resting place after all?" said Tinkler. "Stupendous. For a moment there I thought I was going to miss out." He was sitting opposite me at our dining room table, which is a somewhat grand name for a rather scarred item of furniture obtained from the Ikea sale. But at least it's circular and has just one central pillar leg to support it, rather than four of them, one at each corner, so as to provide maximum opportunities for knee-bruising by long-legged people like me.

Sitting either side of Tinkler and myself were Nevada and Clean Head. We were all wearing dark clothing, as had previously been agreed.

Cats have a way of sensing when people are discussing something important or serious, and they seem to want to be part of these discussions. At any rate, Turk did. She jumped up and sat on the table in the exact centre of our small group. As we talked, Clean Head thoughtfully stroked Turk's back, running her long fingers through the thick, dark fur. Tinkler watched the two of them, quite obviously wishing it was him that was being stroked. I considered kicking him under the table, but Nevada might well have done that for me because he suddenly pulled himself together, looked away and got serious.

"I almost forgot," he said. "Look what I brought."

He reached down on the floor and picked up a bag. I'd been hoping it contained food to take with us. Not that I was certain I'd have much of an appetite before, during or after tonight's activities. But it didn't contain food. Instead Tinkler proudly reached into it and drew out a stack of t-shirts. All of them black this time.

With bold white lettering that read, I WENT TO CANTERBURY AND ALL I ROBBED WAS THIS LOUSY GRAVE.

"Jesus," I snarled, "Tinkler!"

He looked nonplussed. "Steady on, big fella."

Nevada immediately intervened, putting a hand on my shoulder. "He's just a little stressed out," she said to Tinkler. "We all are, getting ready for the big night."

"The big night," I said.

Tinkler fingered the stack of t-shirts. "I got one for everybody this time. It's like a bonding thing. Team spirit."

Clean Head studied the shirts with interest. "Are they organic cotton?" she said.

"But of course."

By common consent (three out of four) we left the t-shirts behind and set off just after midnight in Tinkler's car, humming down an empty motorway at high speed. With

Clean Head at the wheel it took us less than an hour to get to Canterbury, cut through the town, and find the lane leading to the churchyard. Clean Head stopped just past the turning for the lane and reversed into it.

I remembered what she'd said about the car's reverse gear as she drove smoothly and swiftly down the lane, backwards. We came to a stop by the church gate, the front of the car pointing back in the direction we'd come.

She was just showing off, of course, although her reasoning was sound enough. "Now we're ready for a quick getaway," she said.

We all got out and began to unpack our equipment, using the small halogen torches Nevada had bought for us. The light from them was a lurid red. Nevada was under the impression that red light was much less likely to be noticed at night than the usual white beams. She might well have been right about this, although all I knew was that it was favoured by the military because it didn't spoil your night vision.

We moved our kit, of which there was a lot, into the lychgate, setting it on the benches on either side. "This is handy," whispered Tinkler. "What is it, like a mini-church for outdoor sermons?"

"It's a lychgate," I said.

"What's a lych?"

"It's an Old English word for corpse," said Nevada. That shut him up.

I went to help Clean Head wrestle the tent out of the car. We manoeuvred it carefully through the outer gate into the alcove where Nevada and Tinkler waited.

"This is a lychgate," said Tinkler to Clean Head. "Lych is an Old English word for corpse."

"What the hell?" she said. "Why would anyone want a gate for their corpse?"

"It's to keep them out," said Tinkler blithely. "The walking dead. It was a medieval anti-zombie measure."

Nevada immediately put a stop to this nonsense. "It's a place for pall bearers to wait, out of the weather," she said. "And it's where the cleric would meet the corpse."

"Meet?" I said.

"Maybe that's not the best word choice."

"Be formally introduced to," suggested Tinkler.

We began to gather our gear and transfer it from the gate into the churchyard. But just as we stepped into the yard there was a sound, very loud and very near at hand.

An unearthly scream.

We all froze, looking at each other.

"Fox?" said Tinkler. His voice trembled.

"Owl, city boy," said Clean Head, moving forward with one end of the tent. I followed, carrying the other end. It wasn't heavy, but it was unwieldy. Definitely a two-person lift. Maybe that's one reason Nevada had been able to get a deal on it. She had gone to a lot of trouble researching tents. We had decided we couldn't risk just digging up a grave, even if it was the middle of the night, without our activities being somehow screened. So, to stop any late night passer-by or dog walker glimpsing our lights, we would set up a tent around the grave and work inside it.

"What is that thing?" said Tinkler. His voice had

steadied and he was back to normal, if any of his states can be said to be normal.

"Tent," said Nevada.

"Tent?"

"And, because nobody fancies hammering tent pegs into the ground and wrestling with guy ropes in a darkened graveyard, it had to be one of those handy new self-erecting ones." Nevada had spent hours poring over the computer, comparing makes and models. The idea was to buy a tent and cut the fabric out of the bottom of it, so it would be open to the ground and we could get at the grave.

This meant some of the self-opening designs were out of the question because they depended on being airtight, and cutting the bottom out of the thing would tend to compromise that. Also, they required an electric air pump to inflate them, with the concomitant noise factor.

All these considerations had led Nevada to very reluctantly forego the Ninja Jump tent—she just loved the name—and go with something else instead. The model she'd chosen depended on the operation of curved metal uprights that were folded under tension to cause it to spring open.

"Self-erecting tent," Tinkler chortled.

"A pop-up tent," said Nevada hastily.

"That's no better!"

"You have a filthy mind, boy," said Clean Head. She sounded amused, and for a moment there was a sense of happy intimacy among our little crew as we stood there in the darkness. For all I knew Tinkler and Clean Head might have been holding hands. I reached out and found Nevada's hand and took it.

"Or we could have used night-vision goggles," she said. "Why am I only thinking of that now?"

"No, I like the tent," said Clean Head. "Keeping prying eyes off us."

I thought that if prying eyes were to be turned in our direction then it was already too late and a tent would be no help at all. But I kept this to myself. We moved deeper into the graveyard. Tinkler looked up at the large cross adorning the church spire above us. It obviously put him in mind of his deeply religious sister, because he said, "Maggie must never hear about this night's doings. All right?"

"That's a pity, because I was going to text her," said Nevada. "Now, let's get started."

We had previously cut the floor out of the tent, but we had retained the piece of material and divided it into two. Each strip thus created was spread out on either side of the grave. We'd put the dug-up earth onto these strips of fabric. This would, theoretically, make it easier to return the dirt to the hole when we were finished, and also had the advantage of keeping the ground around the hole clean, and hopefully not leaving too many telltale marks on the grass.

I found that I was a lot more comfortable thinking of it as a hole than a grave.

Nevada had reasoned that, while ordinary white light might have shone through the tent walls, the material would certainly be thick enough to screen the red lights we were using. She was entirely correct about this, but what we'd failed to anticipate was the hellish mood this ruddy glow would lend to proceedings.

So we set up the tent, lay the strips of fabric on either side, cut the turf with the turf cutter and carefully stacked it in neat squares behind Marnie Valmond Endure's headstone. Then we got out our shovels and, with a light that looked like it came straight from Satan's personal cook stove, we started digging.

If you ever decide to dig up a grave in a lonely cemetery in the dead of night allow me to suggest that you really don't need a ghoulish and unearthly lighting scheme to lend additional drama and atmosphere to the proceedings. I don't think Tinkler even noticed it, though. It soon got quite warm in the tent and Clean Head stripped down to a tank top, which gave frequent glimpses of her bra as she dug. Tinkler couldn't conceal his spectacular delight at this turn of events, so Nevada hustled him out of the tent because, as she put it later, it would have been creepy on a night not short of creepiness.

So Nevada and Tinkler went off, ostensibly to keep watch. The notion was that if anyone rumbled us they would give warning. Although how much we could do to make good our escape, even if we abandoned all our gear, was a debatable point. Anyway, it was left to Clean Head and me to do the digging.

Nevada had carefully chosen the biggest tent she could find, but whoever had designed it had been envisioning its happy occupants spending most of their time sitting or lying down. There wasn't a lot of room for standing upright and wielding a shovel. It was uncomfortable bending and crouching as we worked, and this added to the infernal aspect of our labours.

Luckily it was too early for frost, and there had been several days of recent rain, so the ground was relatively soft. It only took us about two hours before we hit something.

Nevada and Tinkler stood expectantly at the entrance to the tent where we'd summoned them. "There's a box in there," I said.

"Of course there's a box in there," said Tinkler. "It's called a coffin."

"No," said Clean Head. "On top of the coffin. A smaller, separate wooden box." My relief at this discovery was indescribable. Someone had buried something else in the grave. This meant that I wouldn't necessarily have to open Valerian's casket itself. But then, as we excavated the box, my sense of relief drained away.

It was a solid, wooden box with cast-iron handles on either side. Rectangular and deep, it was quite large.

Just the right size for a child's coffin.

25. WHITE MICE

I must be mistaken, but my memory is that no one said a word the entire duration of the drive back to London. We were all too aware of the box in the back of the car, jammed in there with all our gear.

We had refilled the grave in record time. The principle that there's always somehow too much earth to fit back into the hole you dug up being usefully nullified by the fact that, in this case, there was now a large object missing inside the grave and therefore more space to fill. The hole filled up neatly and we quickly reassembled the squares of turf over it and even lay the artificial rose back in place. It all looked pretty good when we were finished with it.

But then we were working by unearthly tinted light in the middle of the night, with an urgent impulse to get out of there as quickly as possible. So who knows what it really looked like?

When we got back to our house the first pink light of dawn was just showing in ragged bands across the sky beyond the Abbey. We took all the gear out of the car and carried it in through our garden gate, leaving the box until last. Clean Head helped me carry it, which was good of her because I could see she just wanted to get the hell away from here. On the other hand, she could afford to be magnanimous because she was indeed able to just get the hell away from here. It wasn't her home.

"Hey," said Tinkler. "The t-shirts! I left them in your living room. Should I get them and hand them out now?"

No one said anything. No one even looked at him. So he just got back in the car. Clean Head said goodnight, although it was now more like good morning, and got into the car with him. They drove off. We closed the garden gate. Nevada looked at me. We put everything in the garden shed, just about managing to wedge the tent in there among the watering cans and cobwebs. The only thing we left out was the box. We looked at it, and then looked at each other.

"I don't want it in the house," said Nevada. "I'm sorry."

"I understand," I said. She went inside and left me alone with it. I put the box down on the decking outside the back door and kneeled beside it. Fanny peered out of the cat flap, then came out to see what I was doing. Turk followed her. I went back to the shed and searched among the tools and chose a short, steel pry bar. I went back to the decking where the box lay and set to work. Fanny and Turk swarmed around me, fascinated. I tried to shoo them away, but they wouldn't go.

Cecilia Drummond had hinted that all the answers to our questions would be here.

I looked at the box. I had to do it. We had to know.

I prised the lid off. It screeched like a stricken living thing. The cats flinched and retreated for a moment and then came nosing forward. With the opening of the lid the dark recesses of the box were exposed, an intense smell of cold, damp earth rising from it. Inside was a long, greyish bundle wrapped in what looked like muslin. My heart pinched at the sight of it. The cats stuck their noses into the box and I quickly lifted it up, out of their reach.

I moved so abruptly and jerkily that the contents of the box shifted. It grew suddenly heavier at one end, shifting in my grasp. I lost my grip on it and nearly dropped it. It twisted in my hands and something spilled out, to land on the decking at my feet. The cats shot forward to inspect it.

A notebook.

I set the box back down and hooked a cautious finger inside the muslin. It contained a heavy-duty plastic bag of some kind, which had been sealed with adhesive tape that had long since let go. The plastic bag was jammed full of dozens of notebooks. This explained the weight of the box. Most of the notebooks, like the one that had fallen out, were the kind I used to use in school. A few were more elaborate and expensive. One was even leather-bound. But that was all, just notebooks.

Fanny sniffed at the one on the ground, then wandered back into the house. Turk followed her. Move along now, folks, there's nothing to see here…

* * *

The Colonel looked at the notebooks piled on the table in front of him. "So am I supposed to pretend that I don't know where you got these?"

"From a legal point of view that would probably be the best and smartest move," I said.

He sighed. The bruise on his face had faded to a brownish yellow, still unsightly but less painful-looking. "What happened to the box they were in?"

"Tinkler wanted it for a souvenir." The Colonel grunted and nodded, presumably indicating that this was all right. I didn't feel I had to mention that Tinkler planned to turn it into a drinks cabinet.

The Colonel leafed through the notebooks. "What's in them?"

Nevada came in from the kitchen, "Songs, mostly," she said. "Lyrics and poetry. Some drawings. Jottings. Daydreams on paper. The sort of thing you'd expect from an artistic and musical young woman." She sat down with us. "From two artistic and musical young women."

The Colonel gently prodded the notebooks with his finger, as if he expected them to somehow respond or retaliate. "So they're not all by Valerian?"

"They're about half Valerian and half Cecilia," I said.

"Sometimes they share a notebook," said Nevada, "writing on alternate pages."

I picked one up. It was yellow with age but intact and legible. Nearly half a century underground had done it no perceptible harm. "All of their songs are here. The original lyrics. Sometimes in multiple versions, so you can trace their development. Plus some notes about chords and musical sketches. There's even a few fully written compositions."

"It's a treasure trove," said Nevada.

I nodded. "It's priceless. Our friend Tinkler…"

"Jordon."

"Yes. He reckons these will fetch at least seven figures at auction." He'd actually said it was like finding John Lennon's original sketchbook or Jim Morrison's poems. But I felt the point was made.

"I see," said the Colonel, picking up a notebook and looking at it with new respect.

"However," I said, "what is *not* there is any kind of journal or diary or letter. Not even a newspaper clipping. So from the point of view of information, the whole thing was a complete bust."

The Colonel set down the notebook and looked at me. "A complete bust?"

Nevada said, "He just means—"

I said, "I just mean we are no nearer working out the exact circumstances of Valerian's death, or what happened to her little boy."

"I wouldn't call it a complete bust," said Nevada.

The Colonel shook his head briskly. "Neither would I." He set the notebook back on top of the nearest stack and began to carefully straighten it, neatly aligning the notebooks. "These are going to prove very useful."

"How?" I said.

"If Jordon is correct about what they're worth, and I'm sure he is, then I am going to be able to put a plan into action much sooner than I'd anticipated."

"What plan?" said Nevada.

The Colonel smiled with grim satisfaction. "To rescue my sister from the clutches of that gold-toothed ghoul."

The gold-toothed ghoul, by all accounts, shed more than a few tears when Cecilia walked out of his little house in Castle Row in Canterbury for the last time. They were apparently quite sincere tears, but then he was saying goodbye to his meal ticket.

I didn't witness the spectacle because I was at her new flat, supervising the installation of a baby grand piano. Its finish was black lacquer, not bright red, but it would have to do. It was a modest, self-contained garden flat with a small lounge and bedroom, a galley kitchen and a bathroom. There was an L-shaped section of garden that was exclusive to the property, and sliding glass doors in the lounge looked out on this. The garden was a strip of grass bordered with flowerbeds and a brick wall providing privacy from the street beyond.

It was part of a complex of similar dwellings, all designed to strike a balance between independence and assisted living for the residents. There was a team on site to look in on and, if necessary, look after the inhabitants. The other units were mostly occupied by the elderly or the seriously invalided. The flat immediately next door housed an old lady who was profoundly deaf.

Very handy, considering the baby grand piano that now stood facing the garden doors.

Nevada and the Colonel and Cecilia arrived just after the piano delivery guys cleared out. The Colonel and Cecilia had been to some kind of induction meeting with the people who operated the residence, and Nevada had tagged along. I wondered how that had gone. Cecilia looked blankly at me as she came through the door and said nothing as the Colonel showed her the place, leading her from room to room in an intricate dance as he manoeuvred around her bulk in the small spaces.

Nevada filled me in on the dissolution of the happy couple and their final farewell. Apparently Cecilia had said goodbye to Ambrose Smith as though he was someone she'd met at a bus stop and exchanged a few words with until her bus had finally come. *Good for her*, I thought.

Then she showed me the suitcase that contained all Cecilia's worldly belongings. It was a small suitcase and, despite the bulkiness of the clothing required by a woman of her size, it wasn't even full.

The Colonel came back into the lounge with his sister, their tour complete. She looked at the piano and promptly sat down at it without comment and began to play. At first I thought she was just playing fragments, but it gradually came together into a sparse, haunting melody. "Satie," said Nevada. "Erik Satie."

At the piano Cecilia nodded. "*Gymnopédies*," she said. "Number three." She kept playing. It was as though we weren't there.

The Colonel gestured for us to come with him and we stepped out through the sliding glass doors into the cool air of the garden. He peered at us so intently that I wondered if I had traces of my breakfast on my face. But Nevada was immaculate as usual and he was gazing at her with equal intensity.

Finally he said, "I'm not sure I've done the right thing." He wasn't a man given to self-doubt, and certainly not to voicing it, so I was impressed by this disclosure.

"Of course you have," said Nevada. She gestured at the little flat. "It's a beautiful place. You've chosen really well." He had, actually. Cecilia would be looked after here only to the extent that she needed or wanted to be, while being granted as much freedom as she could cope with. It was the best possible solution for someone like her and it sure as hell didn't come cheap. He would have had to drastically restructure his finances to foot her bills here. The discovery of the notebooks and their potential cash value had suddenly moved it from a plan to a fact.

It made me glad I'd found them.

The Colonel shook his head, "I don't know, I feel like perhaps I shouldn't have separated them."

I stared at him. "Who? Her and Ambrose?" He nodded. "You have to be kidding," I said. "You're having second thoughts?"

"Not about getting that bastard out of the picture. He was just a leech. Somebody else can pay for his fancy dentistry from now on."

I was glad to hear this. "How did that go, by the way? What did he say when you threatened him with a restraining order?"

The Colonel gave a thin little smile, remembering. "I didn't even have to go that far. I just threatened him with a legal challenge to his custody of my sister. He folded immediately."

"He was a paper tiger," said Nevada happily. "You completely made him your bitch."

The Colonel shook his head. "I'm still not sure it was a smart move. I mean, he was a shit. But he was all she had. He was a bastard and a shit and a leech. But he was *her* bastard and shit and leech. Maybe I shouldn't have pulled them apart." He turned and looked through the glass doors at Cecilia bent over the piano, absorbed in her playing. "Now she's completely alone." He looked at us. "Maybe all I've achieved is to isolate her."

Nevada suddenly gave a little chuckle. "Wait a minute," she said. "I have an idea."

Cecilia was still playing the piano when we came back an hour later. She didn't even look up as we filed in. And she paid no attention to the shopping bags or the large cardboard box that Nevada set on the floor.

Until the box moved.

Cecilia got up from the piano and stared at it. Then she came over and squatted by the box, inert on her great hams of legs. She hesitated before abruptly leaning forward and pushing open the top of the box. She peered inside for a moment and then looked up at us. We opened the bags and took out the cat biscuits, the kitty litter, the green plastic tray and the two purple and white polka dot plastic bowls.

She took them from us, stacking everything carefully into the tray, which she carried out of the room. We all filed after her, to the bathroom where she set the tray on the floor with the two bowls nearby. We watched from the doorway as Cecilia hefted the bag of kitty litter. It was a ten-kilo bag but she lifted it in one hand as if it were a sachet of sugar. For some reason it's a matter of policy that bags of kitty litter aren't just glued, sealed or folded shut but instead are stitched with a piece of twine and involve a painstaking operation to unthread and open them.

Cecilia just tore the bag open as if she were opening an envelope.

She poured the grey granules of litter into the tray in a dusty plume. Then she opened the bag of biscuits and filled one of the bowls. The other bowl she filled with water from the tap in the sink. Meanwhile Nevada went and got the cardboard box, which she plonked gently down in the middle of the bathroom floor.

She stepped back and waited for Cecilia to open it again. As soon as she did so, the kitten pushed its head out, peered around, then jumped from the box. It was a black kitten with white socks and an asymmetric white smudge on its face. It went immediately to the litter tray, hopped in and took a long, blissful piss. Then it kicked its paws to bury the wet patch under fresh litter. It hopped out, took a long drink from the water bowl, then set about the biscuits with enthusiasm.

We're three for three, I thought.

Having eaten and drunk its fill the kitten wandered out of the bathroom and back through the flat, starting comically when it saw its reflection in a floor-length mirror. While it explored, Cecilia went back to the piano and started playing again. She seemed to have forgotten all about the kitten and I wondered if we'd made a terrible mistake.

But the sound of the music drew the kitten into the lounge. It peered curiously up at the piano and then, with the astounding agility of its species, hopped up onto it. It came to the edge of the piano lid above the keyboard and peered down at Cecilia's hands moving nimbly across the keys. It watched for a while then suddenly stretched its paw out, pursuing the moving hands as if they were big, white mice. It moved back and forth, chasing the hands and reaching down for them.

Cecilia's big shoulders started heaving and she blurted out a strange sound.

I realised she was laughing.

When we left, she was sitting in a chair with the kitten perched on her chest. They were gazing contentedly at each other, the huge woman and the tiny animal. We said our goodbyes and Cecilia suddenly shot us a fearful look.

"Wait," she said.

We paused. "What?" said the Colonel.

She nodded at the kitten on her chest. "What am I going to call him?" Her voice was tight with anxiety.

"It's a her," said Nevada.

Cecilia relaxed. "Then I'll call her Nevada," she said.

On the train back to London the Colonel looked at us speculatively and said, "That was a smart move."

"Plus we found a furry little fiend a good home," said Nevada.

The Colonel looked at me. "I have a question for you. If Valerie is buried in Marnie Valmond Endure's grave, what do you think is in Valerie's grave? I mean her official one."

I shrugged. "I don't know. Rocks? If you want us to find out we're going to have to dig through a rather thick slab of concrete."

"There are ways and means," said Nevada with what I thought was altogether too much eagerness. But he shook his head.

"It doesn't matter. Forget it."

"Now I have a question for you," I said. "Do you think the vicar at the time was in on it? The whole fake burial and decoy grave? Not to mention the real grave with a pseudonym on the head stone?"

"I don't see why not," said the Colonel. "The old man was good friends with our vicar. They were as thick as thieves. They used to tell each other lies about their heroic exploits in the war. The vicar parachuted into Antwerp, apparently. My father's lies principally pertained to the war in North Africa. Anyway I don't see any problem there, especially since you said he donated a large sum of money to the church."

"For maintaining the grave," I said.

"Yes, they probably did a bit of that in return for getting their hands on the money." Not a big fan of the Church, evidently, the Colonel.

We were all silent for a while as the train swept along.

The speeding view of the Kentish countryside had faded from the window as daylight fled, to be replaced by our own reflections. Finally the Colonel said, "The old man wasn't so bad. You can't imagine the abuse that was aimed at Valerie when she had a child out of wedlock—and didn't even try to hide the fact. It was like she was the whore of Babylon." He gave us a mirthless smile. "But when it turned out to be a little boy, our father was willing to let bygones be bygones. At least where Valerie and Cecilia were concerned. There wasn't going to be any reconciliation with me." He shook his head and peered fiercely at his reflection. "I guess he didn't need me. There was going to be another male Drummond for him to pass the torch to."

He suddenly looked at us. "That's why I want to find him," he said. "To find Tom. Because now it's me who needs to pass the torch to him."

I was surprised that this hard-headed man was letting himself open up to such a distant hope. There was virtually no chance we'd find out what became of the boy, and even less chance that he was still alive.

He must have sensed what I was thinking because he said, "At least I have to know what *happened* to him."

26. CARD TABLE

The initial list of likely prospects I'd been given by the Colonel and Lucy had featured eleven names. Four of these had proved stubbornly untraceable, four of them had died—one, Jack Welland, suffocated under a pillow at his hospice just days before I'd managed to interview him—and three had proved both alive and traceable. Of this lucky trio I'd so far managed to speak to Nic Vardy and Erik Make Loud. The remaining name was Penny Sheridan, Valerian's business manager. I'd never actually succeeded in getting a phone number for her but, after much persistence and hassle, I'd eventually elicited an email address.

I got hold of it just after our grave-robbing adventure and, following a rather guarded exchange of emails, at least guarded on her part, I'd finally managed to get her to agree to talk to us. I had mostly achieved this through the stratagem of buttering her up about her rare, possibly even unique, position as a female business manager of one of the leading rock bands of the 1960s. No doubt this gave her all sorts of unique—that word again—perspective and insights and so forth.

Nevada would reliably help me enlarge on this blarney when we met with the unique Mrs Sheridan this Friday, on her houseboat in Twickenham.

The night before, I sent an email confirming our meeting. On Friday morning, Nevada was feeding the cats and choosing her outfit—the fantasy of being a producer had led her to begin acquiring what amounted to a whole new wardrobe—when I got the reply. The subject line was just a repeat of the one I'd used—*Confirming our meeting tomorrow*—so the actual contents of the message came as quite a shock.

> This is Penny's husband using her computer. I am
> wrapping up her affairs. I'm afraid Penny has died.
> So as you can see there isn't a great deal of point
> you coming to speak to us. I don't think I can tell you
> any of the things you would want to know for your
> documentary and, as you can imagine, I have a great
> deal else on my mind.

I emailed back saying how terribly sorry I was to hear the news and asking him, quite legitimately and naturally I thought, what had so suddenly happened to her. I held my breath, waiting for a reply. It came in the form of six words.

> Traffic accident. Hit-and-run driver.

I went into the bedroom to tell Nevada to forget about choosing her producer's costume and I showed her the emails. She looked at them, then looked at me. She said, "I went to Paranoia Heights and all I got was this lousy suspicion and anxiety."

"Very good," I said.

"I managed to get 'lousy' in there this time."

"So I noticed."

The following day had been appointed by Tinkler for our visit to the Evil Elves to look through their collection of records, including the ones left behind by Valerian's entourage. Tinkler himself had been looking forward to it with considerable excitement. This manifested itself in a number of exuberant phone calls, texts and tweets, the most recent and least obscene of which was *We're going to fleece those yokels for their vinyl!* His only regret was that Clean Head was working on the weekend and wouldn't be able to join us.

Then, late that evening, he called to say he couldn't make it.

"What do you mean, you can't make it? You set the whole thing in motion."

"I know, I know, but Henry, my boss, wants me to go into the office tomorrow and look at something."

"Not another emergency repair job?"

"Just as long as I go in tomorrow it won't be an emergency. Anyway, there's no way out of it."

"So do you want us to postpone it?"

"Fleecing the Evil Elves of their rare vinyl? Don't talk crazy. Strike while the iron is hot. They might suddenly realise they're sitting on a treasure trove and jack the prices up. No, what I want you to do is go up there as my proxy, hoover up anything of any value and rob them blind. Is that quite clear?"

"I think I've got it."

"In particular I want you to look for a copy of—"

"The original Decca pressing of the Artwoods," I said. "Yes."

"The one with the Mod cover."

"Yes, yes, yes. You do realise that just talking about it doesn't make it any more likely for us to find it."

"It doesn't make it any less likely, either," he said, with irrefutable logic. I hung up as Nevada came into the room. "We're going without Tinkler tomorrow," I said.

"What? After he set it all up?"

"That's what I said."

Nevada shook her head. "Typical."

"He's going to lend us the car, though."

"It's the least he can do."

Before we turned in that night I got in touch with Timothy Treverton, the more ambulatory of the Evil Elves. I didn't have his phone number or email address so I contacted him the same way Tinkler had done, via his Facebook page. I felt a sick little lurch of anticipatory fear in my stomach when I sent him a message confirming our meeting the following day.

But I got a reply almost immediately, assuring me that

everything was okay. He must have been online right then. It seemed like a serendipitous coincidence, but for all I knew he was a social networking obsessive and never away from the keyboard.

That being the case, I decided to send him another message. It was a question I had intended to ask him tomorrow, but since he seemed to be online now and downright chatty I didn't see any point in delaying.

I mentioned how clever I thought it was, shifting Valerian's tree the way they had. And I asked him whether they'd got the idea from Colonel Drummond.

The thing was, the decoy principle involved was virtually identical to that of the false grave in Canterbury. And it had been bothering me.

It just seemed like too much of a coincidence.

But his reply was terse and perhaps even a little offended.

No, we thought of it ourselves.

I shrugged and decided to call it a day before I ruffled any more feathers. I was reaching out my hand to shut the laptop when a pinging noise told me another message had arrived. It was from Timothy Treverton. I had a second of worry that he was cancelling our visit. But instead, it read:

Actually Gordon says it was Colonel Drummond's idea.

So that at least explained that. And it made the shrewd old man take on a further dimension of reality in my mind.

I wondered if maybe he was the key to this whole thing. Could he have snatched the little boy? Why? Because he didn't approve of the way his daughters were bringing the child up? It was a motive of sorts.

But if so, what had happened to the kid?

I went to bed more full of questions than ever, and I was barely awake when Nevada threw me a curveball. She did it very nicely over breakfast—I should have suspected something when she offered to prepare the coffee and croissants—but a curveball, nonetheless. "I was on the Internet yesterday," she said.

"Always a bad thing," I said.

"Don't be so cynical. I was just doing some research, since we are driving off to hell and gone today."

"If by 'hell and gone' you mean in the general direction of Cambridge…"

"I do. And as it happens I have found a vintage clothes shop nearby."

"Nearby where?"

"Close to where the Evil Elves dwell. Very close. Well, quite close."

"Okay," I said cautiously.

"And it looks like it really is wonderful, this shop. Potentially wonderful. Full of great stuff. But, as you know with these intriguing bohemian-type places, it's almost a legal requirement for them to keep irregular and inconvenient hours. To cut a long story short, it will be closed by the time we get there, if we stick to our original plan." She leaned over and kissed me. "So I was thinking

we could go to the Evil Elves early. Then we can do both."
She checked the clock. "But we need to set off soon."

So we left some biscuits for the cats along with a road atlas
of Great Britain open to the correct page, in case they wanted
to see where we were going. We caught a bus to Putney and
went around to Tinkler's house. He had long since gone to
work but as he had promised the car was parked outside.

And, also as promised, the keys were tucked behind the
rear number plate, which hinged cunningly down to reveal
the concealed cap of the fuel tank. This arrangement had
given Tinkler conniptions when he'd taken the car in for
the first time to fill it up. He had searched frantically for
somewhere to stick the nozzle, wondering if somehow his
sister had managed to buy him a car that you couldn't put
petrol into. "I wouldn't put anything past Maggie," he'd said.

We started the car and turned onto the Upper Richmond
Road, heading for Kew and points north. I had sent a message
by Facebook before we'd set off, telling Timothy Treverton
to expect us a couple of hours earlier than previously
arranged and hoping this wouldn't be a problem. I couldn't
see that it would be, largely because I couldn't see the Evil
Elves having gone anywhere this morning, or indeed ever
leaving their house. Although I supposed they must do from
time to time, if only to buy new jigsaw puzzles.

I hadn't received a reply, though, and when we were
on the road Nevada tried to contact him again using her
smartphone but the coverage was intermittent and we didn't
get a response. Finally we were so close to our destination I
told her to give up trying.

Approaching the house and seeing that tree covered with memorials felt very different this time, knowing it to be a fraud. Strange—the way this utterly altered everything. I wondered how the thousands of adherents who had visited over the years and left their offerings to Valerian would feel if they knew the truth.

"I hope nobody fucking well calls me Snowball this time," said Nevada, staring ahead at the house.

The flagstones of the driveway were covered ankle-deep with a rustling carpet of windblown leaves, but other than that the place looked much the same. The house itself appeared deserted, but it had last time as well so I didn't necessarily let that worry me. We parked Tinkler's little car and walked up to the green front door.

It was open.

We looked at each other. "Maybe they're expecting us," said Nevada.

"And they just want us to walk in? They just leave the door open?"

She shrugged. "Well, they certainly don't have to worry about the heat escaping. The place was like a crypt last time, do you remember?" I did. I also remembered that the doorbell didn't seem to work, so there was no point trying that. So we walked into the house. There were leaves on the floor inside, blown in by the autumn wind. The place was dark and might have been untenanted for years. We walked along the hall. Working from memory and, I suppose, precedent, we made our way towards the kitchen. Leaning against the wall by the doorway was the folding card table that I recognised as the one Gordon had used for his jigsaw puzzles. I wondered what it was doing down here.

"Hello," we called as we stepped through the open door of the kitchen.

There was a flurry of movement from the shadowed recesses of the room, a strange high-pitched sound, and then something came flickering towards us, moving too fast for the eye to identify.

A sharp *chunking* sound registered an emphatic impact. I turned my head to look at what had made the sound and for one hallucinatory instant I thought some kind of living feathered creature had buried itself into the wall between us.

It was an arrow.

The thing about a bow and arrow is that, as an indoor weapon, it is virtually useless. Of course, it is equally true that if you turn your back on someone wielding such a weapon and proceed to flee you could end up in the embarrassing situation of having an arrow sticking in your back in a potentially lethal manner.

Which is why we did what we did, instead.

We picked up the card table and, holding it in front of us, walked rapidly into the kitchen, moving *towards* rather than away from our assailant. An abrupt rapping sound and the sudden appearance of a gleaming triangle of metal poking through the table announced the arrival of another arrow. It also confirmed we were heading in exactly the right direction. So we picked up speed and drove the table in front of us like a battering ram.

Its effectiveness was indicated by the thud of collision and the cry of pain that instantly followed. Nevada suddenly dropped her end of the table and reached down to scrabble on the floor for something. She stood up, grinning at me fiercely and clutching the bow, a long, wicked curve of dark wood with yellow tape in the middle to form a hand grip. Good girl. We'd neutralised our opponent.

Who turned out to be Timothy Treverton.

He was dressed in a tatty, yellow dressing gown with white trim. His bony legs were bare and he was wearing grubby tartan slippers. All of which made the leather quiver of arrows slung over his shoulder even more absurd—not so absurd that he hadn't almost killed us, though. He stared at me wildly.

"It's you," he said.

"What the fuck were you doing shooting arrows at us?" I said. We might have walked in uninvited, but as far as I was concerned, nothing warranted his potentially murderous and vastly stupid behaviour. Now that I had got over being scared I was suddenly very angry.

Treverton's voice dropped. "There's someone in the house. Someone else. I heard them talking. They're going to kill us. They've got guns." His eyes weren't any less wild, and I was on the point of deciding that he must be on something, or simply off his rocker, when Nevada called out sharply.

"Look!"

She was standing at the window staring out. I went to the window and then hurried past it to the back door, which

I flung open. Outside, the big open back yard of the house stretched towards a grey stone wall. Running across the leaf-strewn lawn among the trees was a man. He was going hell for leather and very clearly wanted to get away from us.

He was already at a considerable distance but I could see he was heavily built and had dark hair. When he glanced back over his shoulder I saw the heavy black-rimmed glasses he was wearing. Behind me Nevada said, "Does he look like the bloke from the house in Canterbury? The one with the petrol?"

I stared after him. He had almost reached the wall, but I'd got a pretty good look. "He does," I said.

Close by my ear there was a sharp, not-quite-musical sound and—almost as if in response to the sound—the man suddenly fell onto the leaf-strewn lawn. It was only when he staggered to his feet that I saw the feathered shaft sticking out of his shoulder. I turned around to see Timothy Treverton staring in astonishment and Nevada holding the bow and nodding.

"I told you I was rather good," she said with satisfaction. "Nice to know I haven't lost my touch."

At the far end of the garden, at the top of the stone wall, another man appeared. He was young and thin, dressed in what looked like blue overalls. As far as I could tell, he was no one I'd ever seen before. His wounded companion staggered towards him and, between them, they managed to drag him over the wall, despite the arrow in his shoulder.

We went out and approached the wall. Timothy Treverton had said something about guns, so we approached with great caution. But even before we got there we heard an engine start and speed away. It sounded like something bigger than a car. A van, maybe. I peered carefully over the wall, but all I could see was an empty country lane with a little ring of dried leaves dancing in the middle of it in the wake of a departed vehicle. I dropped back into the garden and looked at Nevada. We both shivered, in response to the cold wind and perhaps also in simple reaction to what had happened.

We went back inside to find Timothy, bizarrely, making a pot of tea. His hands were shaking, though, and so was his voice as he called out, "You can come out now, Gordie. They're gone." There was the rattling of a latch and then the pantry door sprang open and Gordon Treverton rolled out in his wheelchair. He glanced at me, and then at Nevada.

"Oh look," he said. "It's Snowball!"

27. WEEDING

"You didn't forget to look at the records," said Tinkler. "Just because somebody tried to kill you?"

"No, actually," I said, pouring him a coffee. "I looked at them."

"That's the spirit. Ignore these irrelevancies."

"But it was a complete bust." I poured myself a coffee. Tinkler's face fell.

"Why? I thought Valerian's crew would have left a load of stuff there."

"They did. But this material was divided neatly into two categories. First, records that belonged to the blokes in the band and various hangers on, all of which were invariably completely trashed. It wasn't just a case of them having rolled joints on the covers. In some cases it looked like someone had tried to smoke the vinyl itself. Pity, because there would have been some nice items otherwise."

"Shit," said Tinkler. "So what was the second category?"

"A collection of several hundred LPs that were in really

nice shape. But all classical. If you were looking for the masterworks of some joker called Beethoven on a record label called Deutsche Grammophon, you would have been in luck."

"Whose record collection was that?"

"Cecilia's, of course."

"Not Valerian's?"

I said, "As far as I can tell, Valerian didn't listen to records. Maybe she didn't like music."

"So you didn't find anything at all?"

"I found a photo," I said. "In the Evil Elf family album." I showed it to him. It was a faded Polaroid of Valerian and Cecilia in bathing suits. They were splashing around in a kids' paddling pool, but they were both clearly in their twenties—at the height of their brief fame and young power. The pool was full of inflatable toys and bobbing wine bottles. The sisters were laughing and larking about, and it was clear that it was the Summer of Love and certain substances had been smoked.

Tinkler studied it. "Bathing suit shot. So were the Evil Elfs perving over this? Is it Evil Elfs or Elves?"

"Elves," called Nevada from the kitchen. "It's like wolf and wolves."

"It's like wolf and wolves," said Tinkler, handing me back the photo. He seemed a little despondent. Perhaps at the prospect of hundreds of records that weren't early British R&B or rock but classical instead. What right did they have to exist? But then he perked up. "Boy was I relieved when it turned out there wasn't a dead child in that box after all. Do you know why?"

"By 'that box' you mean your drinks cabinet."

"Yes, it's coming on nicely, by the way. I'm going to have strip lighting inside it. What was I saying?"

"You were really relieved."

"That's right. And not just for all the obvious reasons, but also because—"

"Because it meant you could distribute your tasteless t-shirts."

Tinkler nodded happily. "That's right!"

Nevada came in from the kitchen. "And by 'distribute' we mean give one to Clean Head." She sat down beside me and I poured her a coffee.

"You two got yours!" said Tinkler. "And while we're on the subject, I want to see you wearing them."

"Not when we're expecting Lucy and the Colonel," I said.

"Maybe you're right," said Tinkler. "Not entirely appropriate."

Nevada went to the window, sipping her coffee, and stared out, tapping her foot restlessly. "Where is Turk? Where has that girl got to?"

"She's probably hunting for mice," I said.

"But she does that at night. It's daytime."

I shrugged. "It's a full-time job, I guess."

"Why are you so worried about Turk's comings and goings?" said Tinkler.

"We need her to take a message to Stinky." I looked at Nevada. "A rather important message." Nevada nodded and sat down again, but continued tapping her foot. I considered pouring her some more coffee, but concluded that was the last thing she needed.

"A very important message," she said.

"You see," I said, "we've concluded that someone is opposed to our line of research and is willing to kill us." We didn't know who that someone was, but Nevada and I had been discussing it, and one candidate who seemed increasingly plausible was Erik Make Loud. We had no idea why he might want us dead, but he was very well aware of us and our mission. And, crucially, he'd become chummy with Tinkler. Enough so to glean crucial information about us, and our vulnerabilities. So he could have, for example, set the trap for us in Canterbury.

But I wanted a little more certainty about this theory before I effectively accused Tinkler of nearly getting his best friends killed. He was looking at me now, all smiling and innocent. I said, "This unknown party wants to prevent us finding something out. We don't know what that something might be, but we know they're willing to kill."

"Well, duh," said Tinkler.

"But you see," said Nevada, "that creates quite a serious problem."

"Apart from the fact that someone is trying to kill us," I said.

"Apart from that, yes. You see, Tinkler, we've been blithely going around telling everyone that we're doing this research on behalf of Stinky Stanmer. And they have no particular reason not to believe that."

I saw the dawning comprehension on Tinkler's face.

"So you see," said Nevada, "if they're willing to try and kill us, how much more willing would they be to kill the person they believe is *really* responsible? The person who supposedly hired us." Tinkler turned and stared out the window towards the Abbey.

"Stinky," said Tinkler.

"Yes," said Nevada.

He turned back to us and roared with laughter. "But that's great!" he said. "You can just not tell him."

"No, Tinkler," said Nevada firmly. "We can't do that."

"No, I guess not," said Tinkler wistfully.

I gave him back his car keys. He'd had to come over to collect them because yesterday, by the time we'd returned from the Trevertons' house and our adventures with archery, we'd been feeling far too frazzled to drop his car in Putney and limp home on public transport.

Nevada saw Tinkler out, following him through the front door and hanging around by the gate for a moment. She came back, looking anxious. "Still no sign of Turk." Her face brightened. "I know. I'll give Fanny some biscuits." Nevada had a theory that if one of the cats was having a nice meal the other one would sense it, no matter how far away she was, and come racing home. The nicer the meal, the quicker she'd come. I'd had to convince her on several occasions not to write a letter to Rupert Sheldrake, an expert on strange animal phenomena, describing this wonder of nature and inviting him to come and investigate. I was afraid he might agree.

Nevada opened the cupboard beside the sink and took

out the bag of high-end cat biscuits. At the first telltale sounds Fanny came racing in from the sitting room where she'd been lolling. But there was a simultaneous stirring behind the kitchen curtain and Turk suddenly appeared.

"You sly girl!" said Nevada. "You were here all along. But you were hiding!" Nevada put the biscuits back in the cupboard, much to the frustration of Fanny, and instead slipped the note we had prepared under Turk's collar. She knew what this meant. A fish dinner. She jumped down from the counter and hurried out the cat flap into the garden and over the back wall.

She was back in just over five minutes. Very slow by her standards. We fished out Stinky's response.

HEY HIPSTERS,

THANK YOU FOR YOUR KIND WARNING. I DIDN'T KNOW YOU CARED! HA HA. I SPOKE TO BARNEY WHO IS IN CHARGE OF SECURITY HERE AT THE ABBEY AND TOLD HIM WHAT YOU SAID. BARNEY IS EX-POLICE AND HE IS GOING TO ARRANGE FOR A COUPLE OF HIS MATES TO TAKE A LEAVE OF ABSENCE FROM CO19 (THE BRIT EQUIVALENT OF SWAT) AND THEY WILL STAY IN A ROOM IN THE ABBEY AND KEEP AN EYE ON ME. MY OWN PERSONAL SWAT TEAM! IT WILL BE HEINOUSLY EXPENSIVE, OF COURSE. BUT WE CAN WRITE IT OFF AGAINST THE BUDGET FOR THE DOCUMENTARY. THANKS AGAIN FOR THINKING OF ME. LOVE TO NIRVANA.

Nevada set the note down. "Documentary?" she said.

I shrugged. "Apparently he's going to actually proceed with a programme about Valerian."

"And steal all our ideas. Tinkler was right. We *shouldn't* have warned him."

Any debate about the morality of such a course of action was cut short by the doorbell announcing the arrival of the Colonel and Lucy. The Colonel was quite obviously more pissed off with Lucy than usual. As he strode in I saw a vein was throbbing dangerously in his forehead. The black eye, however, was completely gone. He had healed thoroughly. Good genes, I thought.

Nevada diplomatically hustled Lucy off, allegedly to show her some clothes she'd found in her trawl of the charity shops that she thought might appeal. I later found out that this actually wasn't an inspired lie made up on the spur of the moment, but Nevada had in fact found some clothes for Lucy, and indeed made a number of cash sales to her.

Meanwhile I was left to report to the Colonel. "And I suppose it never crossed your mind to go to the police with any of this?" he said.

"Well, the Trevertons," I said, making a conscious effort not to call them the Evil Elves, "were none too eager to do so. And there was the slight complicating factor that Nevada had fired an arrow into someone."

He nodded. "Yes, that might cause some complications." Fanny jumped up on the table in front of him and he tried to disguise his pleasure as he stroked her. "What else have you got for me?"

"This," I said, switching on the laptop. "It's one of the photos scanned in from the archive of documents we got from Lucy."

"You can hardly say we got them from *her*," he said. "Your friend did more than she did in terms of getting them for us. Do you know what she brought back from Dublin?" I realised that we were talking about Lucy again now. I shook my head. "Guinness," he said. He didn't bother lowering his voice. "She brought back Guinness. As though we don't have it here. And she is swilling the stuff down. Sluicing it down her gullet."

"Seems sober enough."

He shook his head angrily. "Oh, she doesn't get *drunk*. That's not the problem. It makes her *fart*. Vile, reeking farts. So when I'm on public transport with her or, god help us, in a *taxi*—"

"Anyway," I said, eager to stem any further disclosures, "this picture." I showed it to him. It was a black and white shot from a magazine depicting Valerian at the piano. It was stylish and well composed, and it was hard to tell whether it was posed or a candid shot. There was no credit but I wouldn't have been surprised to learn that it was by Nic Vardy.

The Colonel studied it. "What about it?" he said.

"I didn't know she played the piano. Valerian."

"Oh yes."

"So it's not just a pose for the sake of the picture? She could actually play?"

"Oh yes. She wasn't quite in the same league as Cecilia but she still played to a professional standard. The old man saw to that." He looked at me. "What are you driving at?"

I handed him the Polaroid I'd got from the Trevertons. He examined it with more curiosity than the other one, then looked up at me expectantly. "Yes?"

"That's Valerian and Cecilia."

"Yes."

"Cecilia on the left."

"Yes."

"There's a mark on Cecilia's shoulder." It was a brown mark, shaped like a crudely drawn hourglass. The swimsuit she wore clearly revealed it. "Do you think it's some kind of stain or wound—"

"It's a birthmark," said the Colonel tersely. "Cecilia was always a little embarrassed about it. I'm surprised to see she has it on display here." I hardly heard this last bit. I was savouring a warm flash of triumph. This was exactly what I'd been hoping. "Excellent," I said.

"Why is it excellent?"

"You remember that DNA test you did? All it proved was that the test subject is your sister."

He stared at me. He'd got it.

He said, "Not which sister it is."

It was late afternoon by the time we reached Canterbury, but the sun was still shining into the little L-shaped garden. I opened the gate and followed Nevada and the Colonel inside. We'd been expecting to find Cecilia in her flat and were startled to see her outside. She was kneeling beside one of the flowerbeds, busy with a fork and trowel. There was a sack of compost at her elbow. Delving among the plants, there was a look of happy interest on her face, a lively engagement with the world, which vanished when she saw us—to be replaced by the frightened blankness that I had come to accept as her habitual expression.

She got to her feet, her big face staring at us, pinched with worry. "Do I have to go now?"

We explained that we hadn't come to take her away from her new flat, and she began to relax. She gathered up her gardening things, picking up the sack of compost with one hand. It weighed twenty kilos, I knew because it said so on the side, but she picked it up as though it was nothing. Once again I was impressed by the strength lurking in that large, shapeless body.

We all went inside and, as soon as the gardening things were put away, Cecilia made a beeline for the piano.

"Wait a minute," said the Colonel. "Please." She stood and stared at us. She didn't seem to know what to do with herself if she couldn't play the piano and lose herself in the music. "Listen, Cessie," said the Colonel. "Could you show us your birthmark?"

"My birthmark?" She looked at us helplessly.

"Yes, please. Just show us your shoulder. Please."

Big tears began to well up in her eyes and roll down her plump cheeks. But she lifted her hand to the strap of her dress and loosened it. She slipped the strap down and exposed a big roll of smooth, white flesh.

In the middle of it, a brown mark in the shape of an hourglass.

The Colonel sighed. "All right, Cessie. Thank you. You can put your dress back on now. Thank you." Cecilia obeyed. As she did so there was a small, rapid drumming sound and the kitten came racing into the room. It headed straight for Cecilia, came to a dramatic halt and looked up at her, squeaking peremptorily. A smile lit up her face and she bent down to scoop the creature up, holding it to her extensive bosom. The kitten squeaked again, acknowledging that things were ordered according to its satisfaction.

The Colonel looked at me. "So much for that theory," he murmured. He glanced at his watch. "If we get a move on, we can catch the fast train back to London." Nevada cleared her throat loudly. We looked at her.

"I think Cecilia wants to say something," she said.

Cecilia had set the kitten down on the piano where it was washing itself. She was looking at us, wringing her hands. Then she peered fearfully at the ceiling as if she was trying to remember some complex formulation in a foreign tongue. "Would you like," she said hesitantly, "to stay for a cup of tea?"

The Colonel stared at her, then sat down abruptly in the nearest chair.

"Yes, Cecilia," he said. "We'd like to stay for a cup of tea."

28. THE SIDE ENTRANCE

Strange as it sounds, with everything that had happened, my greatest concern around this time was that Osterloh's secretary Adela—the Scandinavian Stalker—might ring me up again asking for a date before I had a chance to head her off at the pass, and that Nevada would find out about it. I knew that she had only given me a conditional discharge, so to speak.

Worryingly, despite all my good intentions I hadn't actually managed to speak to Adela, Osterloh himself having inconveniently decided to start answering his own phone. So I went back to Bayswater and did the charity shops—finding nothing—and then just happened to drop in at Osterloh's place, since I was in the neighbourhood.

I approached the pink house with apprehension, wondering if the doctor himself would open the door. My fear of having to explain my errand to him was matched only by the possibility of being asked once more to buy his book.

I started up the steps, but before I reached the front door a voice called to me. I looked around to see Adela standing below me in a kind of sunken concrete alleyway that ran around the side of the house. She looked pleased to see me, which made my heart sink. I came down and joined her.

I felt a further pang of guilt when I saw that she was holding a cardboard cup of takeaway coffee.

"Is that for the doctor?" I asked.

"No, for me," she grinned. "And these too." She held up a bag of pastries. "But I can share them with you." She turned and walked along the alleyway, obviously expecting me to follow. I followed. "The doctor is out," she said. "He is lecturing at Queen Mary's University today." She stopped. We had come to a small alcove containing a side door, which evidently led into the basement of the house.

There was a light in an art-nouveau glass shade beside the door and Adela now reached into this, fished out a key and opened the door with it. This seemed to me a terribly lax arrangement, especially in light of recent events.

I said, "So he hasn't got the new security system installed yet?"

She turned and looked at me in the open doorway. "Security system?"

"You know, there was the break-in…"

"Oh, yes, that." She went inside and I followed. "He moaned about that for a few days and then forgot all about it."

This sounded dangerously careless to me but not uncharacteristic of the good doctor, from what little I knew of him. Maybe he'd decided the intruder had indeed pinched some copies of his book and was therefore a person to be cultivated. We walked past a small, tiled room with a gleaming new washing machine and dryer standing in it and went through an inner door into a large and surprisingly bright kitchen that seemed to occupy about half of the basement of the big house.

To our left there was a long pine table with placemats on it depicting engravings of Victorian London. Adela set the coffee and the bag of pastries down between Crystal Palace and the Houses of Parliament. I could smell the pastries now. They smelled good. She turned to me and smiled and I began to wish I hadn't come in with her. But I didn't feel I could have made my little speech outside.

I took a deep breath and said, "Listen, Adela, about your phone call. It was really nice to hear from you and I was terribly flattered, but—"

"You have a girlfriend."

I paused, relieved. "Yes," I said.

She smiled at me. "That isn't necessarily an obstacle."

"Isn't it?"

"She may not mind. Your girlfriend may not mind you seeing me."

"No, actually I think she will. I strongly suspect she will. I'm pretty sure she will."

"Then maybe she could be a participant."

"A participant?"

"Yes, you know, you, me and her…"

"Oh yes, of course."

"You hadn't thought of that?"

"No I hadn't," I said. "How old-fashioned of me."

"So you didn't ask her if she might be interested? In the three of us? Together?"

"No."

"But you will ask her?"

"Yes." *When hell freezes over*, I added silently.

"Okay." She smiled at me. "Help yourself to a pastry."

"Okay, thanks," I said.

She walked across the room towards the staircase. "I'll be back in a moment."

I looked at her coffee on the table. "Do you want me to open that and pour it into a real cup?" No one should have to drink their coffee out of cardboard.

"No thank you, that's fine. I'm going to drink it in the car." She disappeared up the stairs. I inspected the bag of pastries. They were warm and there was the rich fragrance of cinnamon rising from them. I was sorely tempted, but worried that if I ate one I'd be somehow committing myself and Nevada to participation in a string of orgies arranged by Scandinavian swingers.

Adela came back in carrying a large cardboard box that had the logo of a book distribution firm on the side. It was full of men's shoes. "We're having a clear out."

"So I see." The shoes looked new to me, and hellishly expensive.

She saw my look and shrugged. "He never wears them. I'm taking them to donate at one of the local charity shops." I could have given her a map of these establishments, but I didn't think she needed it. "There's already a load of stuff in the car. I was just about to pack up and go when you arrived."

"Don't let me keep you."

"It's fine, I can give you a lift." She scooped up the bag

of pastries and the coffee and carefully put them in the box among the shoes. I followed her back out of the kitchen, wondering how I could politely decline the lift. She locked the door and put the key back in the lampshade. I offered to carry the box but she shook her head. I followed her out to the street where a dusty black Citroen was parked under a cluster of trees. The back seat was full of boxes, with some jackets and trousers draped over them. It looked like she'd purloined half his wardrobe.

There was also a pile of hardcover copies of *The Sovereignty of the Self.* I looked at her. "He's getting rid of his books?"

She shrugged. "Nobody ever buys them. We have hundreds of copies. The house is full of junk. He asked me to do a clear out." She smiled and handed me the box. "Put that in the back. I'll tidy the front seat for you."

I opened the back door of the car. "It's okay," I said. "I can catch the Tube home."

"I will take you to the Tube station." She was rooting around in the front, clearing maps and other clutter off the passenger seat.

I delved among the clothing and books in the back, looking for a place to put the box of shoes. I lifted a brown and white check jacket and underneath it was a pile of records. My heart instantly raced—a purely reflex reaction. I quickly set the box down and had a look through them.

"Help yourself to anything you want from back there," said Adela.

I went cold from throat to groin. The LPs all featured

Glenn Miller's Army Air Force Band.

They were the same ones that I had bought the other day. The ones that had disappeared.

Adela drove me to the Tube station, which wasn't at all awkward until she put on the brakes and turned to me, leaning forward, obviously expecting a kiss. I gave her a chaste peck on the cheek and got the hell out of there.

With the Glenn Miller records.

I headed home as fast as I could. I had to tell Nevada—not about the peck on the cheek, I thought we could safely omit that—and consider the implications thrown up by the fact that Dr Osterloh had these records in his possession.

I came through the front door to find Nevada racing towards me from the living room, smiling and saying, "Darling, we've got company. Lucy has dropped in for a visit." She added, mouthing silently, something that eventually I realised was, *She's pregnant.*

Pregnant? I silently mouthed back. She nodded her head impatiently towards the front room and I went down the corridor and inside, preparing a big and hopefully convincing smile for our guest.

I instantly saw that our charades in the hallway had been redundant. Lucy had her open purse on the table in front of her. While Fanny was nosing around inside it, Lucy was holding in her hand the bright packaging of a commercial pregnancy testing kit. She set it down and looked at me and said, "I'm going to have a baby."

Also on the table, in addition to the cat, the purse and the pregnancy test, were seven cans of Guinness. Six of them were in front of Lucy—three already open—and one in front of the chair where Nevada had presumably been sitting.

"Congratulations," I said.

Lucy was looking rather smarter than previous times I'd seen her—I put this down to Nevada's recent benign, though no doubt expensive, influence on her wardrobe—but her face was red and blotchy. She looked like she'd been crying.

She opened another Guinness and offered it to me. "Thank you," I said, accepting it. What I really wanted was a cup of coffee and I was going to disappear as soon as possible into the kitchen to make myself some of the proper stuff. I gestured at the cans on the table.

"Are you sure you should be... I mean, in your current..."

"Guinness is good for the baby," snarled Lucy.

"Well, okay," I said.

"It's all the *iron* that's in it."

Nevada came in and sat beside me. She picked up her can of Guinness and sipped.

"But isn't that much later, during breastfeeding..." I said.

"What would you know about breastfeeding?" said Lucy with rising truculence. I decided this would be a good time to fix myself that coffee and went through to the kitchen. When I came back Lucy was talking about Rory. Rory apparently was the father. She'd met him when she'd arrived in London. That was fast work, I thought.

"He's a journalist. His father was a journalist. He knew *my* father. So when I got here I got in touch with him and we met and it just happened."

I bet it did, I thought.

"Now the important thing is the baby," said Lucy. "That's all that matters. So the book is more crucial than ever."

For a moment I couldn't even remember what book she was talking about. Then I got it. She was supposed to be researching the definitive story of Valerian.

"Isn't it funny? I started work on this book for my father. It was the book he was always saying he was going to write. The book that he could write better than anyone in the world. He knew Valerian better than anyone in the world. And it's a tragedy, a genuine tragedy, that he never wrote it. That's why I have to write it. For him. Isn't it funny? I started writing the book for *him* and now I'm writing it for *my* child." She looked at me owlishly. "It costs a lot of money to raise a child," she said.

After the earlier shredding I'd got for mentioning breastfeeding, I wasn't sure I was supposed to even have an opinion on this subject, but I cautiously nodded.

"So I need to get a lot of money," said Lucy. I nodded. "So the book must be a huge success."

No pressure there, then, I thought.

Lucy then proceeded to speculate on whether she'd first receive a seven- or eight-figure advance for this putative masterpiece. She discussed film rights, television rights, radio and book club rights and whether she would be able to get it on *Oprah*. She conjured vast fortunes pouring in for this purely hypothetical book of which she had yet, to my knowledge, to write one word. Perhaps I was being unduly influenced by the Colonel's cynicism on the subject. But maybe he was right.

He was certainly right about the Guinness-induced flatulence.

Eventually she left. We had called Clean Head to come and pick her up and make sure she got safely home—or at least back to the hotel in Mayfair—with her newly acquired precious cargo. After many goodbyes, Nevada shut the door behind her—a welcome blast of fresh, frigid wind blew through the house—and came back in and sat down.

"My god," she said. We stared at the Guinness cans on the table in front of us. One of them was still unopened. I lifted it and shook it, listening to the widget rattle around inside.

"She left one," I said.

The doorbell rang. "She's come back for it," said Nevada, and she giggled and went to answer the door. I tried to piece my thoughts back together after the barrage of information, sentiment and lunatic speculation that had been Lucy's visit. I had to tell Nevada about my suspicions concerning Dr Osterloh.

"Oh, hello," said Nevada. Then she fell silent and the front door shut. I looked up as she came back into the room. Her face was white. A man followed her into the room.

It was Nic Vardy.

And he was pointing a shotgun at us.

29. RED BUTTERFLY

I recognised the shotgun. It was one of the collection I'd seen at Vardy's Docklands flat, safely locked away behind glass. I wished it was there now. It wavered in the air as he pointed it first at me then at Nevada. I estimated the chances of grabbing it away from him without running the risk of one or both of us getting blasted into a red mess and decided that there was no hope.

Sighting along the twin barrels of the gun, his eyes were bloodshot and brightly raw-looking as if he'd been drinking a great deal. This was not a comforting thought.

"Get back," he said. "Back into the room." We did as he said.

I said, "What the hell…"

"Shut up." He moved the shotgun from Nevada and pointed it at me. My whole body went cold. "Don't say anything."

"Nic," said Nevada. "What on earth are you doing?" She spoke in an amazingly calm and casual voice, as if we were all just having a conversation. Mind you, she didn't have a shotgun pointed at her just at this instant. That must have helped, but nonetheless I had to admire her coolness. I was still trying to wrap my head around what was happening. I had been sitting in my living room thinking about doing the washing up, and now this.

"Please be quiet," said Vardy. There was a note of pleading in his voice.

"Nic," said Nevada. I noticed how she kept using his first name. Clever. "What on earth?"

"Please don't make this any harder than it has to be." He was talking to Nevada but kept the gun pointed at me, which was very unpleasant. Better than him pointing it at her, but unpleasant nonetheless. I made a deliberate effort to stop staring into the dark twin tunnels of the barrels and lifted my gaze to his face. I was startled, in so far as I still had the capacity to be startled, to see that there were tears flowing down his cheeks and I realised that his eyes weren't bloodshot from drinking but from crying.

"Don't make what any harder? Why are you doing this, for heaven's sake? Why not just put the gun down and let me make you a cup of tea." Nevada was the sweet voice of reason. But Vardy wasn't listening. Or he wasn't letting himself listen. He shook his head stubbornly.

"No, it has to be done. I'm sorry, but it has to be done."

"What has to be done? Why?"

More tears flowed down his face. They were splashing on the floor. "Why did you have to do it?" he said.

"Do what?"

"Stick your nose in. Go nosing around. Digging things

up. Why couldn't you just have let the past be the past?"

"You mean about Valerian?" said Nevada with convincing innocence.

"Yes."

"We honestly haven't found anything," said Nevada. "About Valerian or anything else." And she was so sincere that I believed her. In fact, I suddenly began to believe, with a deep and searing frankness, that we *hadn't* found anything. Such is the pedagogical power of having a gun pointed at you.

"Yes you have," said Vardy. "Or if you haven't found out anything, you're about to." He shook his head obstinately. "I'm sorry. But it has to be done."

"Look, Nic, we promise to drop it. To drop the whole thing. We'll never ask anyone another question about Valerian, and we'll never even think about her again. Whatever it is you think we've uncovered or you think we might uncover, we haven't and we don't care. We don't care about any of it. We'll just leave it all alone and never give it another thought."

"I wish I could believe you." His tears kept flowing, copious and continuous. They ran down his face and splashed on the floor. But the shotgun remained steady, aimed squarely at me.

"Nic, this just isn't you," said Nevada. "You don't even like to shoot birds."

"It has to be done," he repeated, as if it was a phrase he'd learned by rote.

"But, Nic," said Nevada. Her voice was gentle,

reasonable, oozing with sympathy. "You told us how you'd given up hunting because you couldn't bear the bloodshed, the cruelty, the foolish waste." I couldn't remember if he had actually said anything remotely resembling any of this, but it all sounded good to me.

"I know," said Vardy. "I wish it didn't have to be this way."

"But it doesn't, Nic, it really doesn't."

He turned his tear-stained face to her. "Doesn't it?" He began to lower the shotgun and Nevada took a slow step towards him, her arms extended carefully at her sides, a smile on her face. She moved towards him and held out her hands for the gun. He lowered it further, his face starting to look slack and beaten, but somehow relieved beyond description.

There was an abrupt rattling sound from the other side of the house.

Vardy stepped back and the shotgun went up again, clutched tightly in his hands, shaking with tension, pointing at me. I stared at the twin barrels jerking in little circles, aimed point blank at my face. His finger curled around the trigger and Nevada said, her voice high and tight with fear, "It's just the cat flap. *It's just the cat flap.*"

Vardy relaxed a fraction and his finger eased off the trigger and Turk came trotting into the room. She looked up at us and then at Vardy, then circled him warily.

"You have a cat," said Vardy stupidly.

"We have two of them," said Nevada.

Turk sniffed at the wet spot on the floor that had been formed by Vardy's tears, then jumped up onto the table beside me. "Now, Nic," said Nevada, "we were just saying…"

"It doesn't matter what we were saying." His hands were steady again.

"You're right, it doesn't, Nic, but you were just about to give me the gun."

For the first time the shotgun moved away from me and pointed at Nevada. "No," he said. "Get back." I considered jumping him, but I couldn't take the risk that the gun would go off while it was pointing at Nevada. Presumably, though, he would turn and point it at me again. And if I could just move while he was in the act of turning, while he was pointing at neither of us...

It was sickeningly as if he'd read my mind, because as soon as Nevada had backed away from him, he turned towards me so sharply and suddenly that I had no chance to move. He walked away from her but kept pointing the gun at me. I realised what he was doing. He was making sure she wasn't close enough to him to try anything. And meanwhile he had me utterly neutralised. I could almost *feel* the gun barrels pointing at my face, as though chilled air was flowing from them.

The shotgun was steady in his hands, ready for action, and somehow I didn't see him setting it down again. There was a tortured resolve on his face that told me he wouldn't soften now. But Nevada kept at it, persistent and gentle. "That's Turk there on the table, Nic. We have two cats, Fanny and Turk. They're lovely little creatures, and I'd hate to have anything happen to them. It would break my heart. You would never hurt a cat, would you, Nic?"

"Of course not," said Vardy thickly.

"Of course you wouldn't."

He frowned, his brows knotting. "Hurting animals is a disgusting idea."

"And you'd never hurt a person, either, would you?"

"I'm sorry. I have to. This is different. It has to be done." That phrase again.

"Nothing has to be done," said Nevada, gently and reasonably.

"This does."

Moving restlessly on the table at my elbow, Turk suddenly howled for attention. She had no comprehension of the situation and didn't understand why no one was petting her. "What's the matter with her?" said Vardy. "Is she hungry?"

When he said this, I thought of something, and Nevada must have had exactly the same thought. I could see it in her eyes. "That's right," said Nevada carefully. "She's hungry. Please let me feed her, Nic. Whatever happens, whatever you have to do, let me at least give Turk her meal."

Vardy glanced at her suspiciously. I noticed with a sinking feeling that his face was dry now, all tears gone. "It's all right," said Nevada soothingly. "There's no way out from the kitchen. Only this door that leads back in here. I'm not going anywhere." Vardy kept the gun pointed at me but took a step backward and turned his head to glance into the kitchen. "And the curtains are drawn," said Nevada. "No one can see me." Vardy turned back to me just as I was deciding that now was the time to go for him—and the moment passed.

"Please just let me go into the kitchen and feed my little girl," said Nevada beseechingly.

"Where's your phone?" said Vardy, and I knew we had him. He was going to let her do it. Nevada gave him her phone. He took it and put it in his pocket, then he turned to me. "Where's yours?" I gave it to him. He put my phone in his pocket then went to the landline and unplugged it. "Okay, go in the kitchen and feed her," he said.

Nevada moved to the kitchen, giving the little whistle that signified food, and Turk promptly hopped off the table and went scrambling after her.

Vardy took the landline and carried it away from the sofa where it normally resided. I thought for a surreal second that he was going to try and fit this in his pocket, too, but he contented himself with going to the bookshelf at the other end of the room and tucking it away on the highest shelf. All the while he was doing this he kept twisting around so he was still pointing the shotgun at me. I prayed his contortions wouldn't cause it to go off.

There was the sound of Nevada opening a cupboard in the kitchen. The dry rattle of cat biscuits in their box. I assumed she was shaking the box with one hand while writing with the other. Vardy wasn't even looking in her direction. He was staring at me over the shotgun barrels. I tried not to let anything I was thinking or feeling show in my eyes. The sounds from the kitchen stopped. Nevada appeared in the doorway.

"I'm back," she said mildly. Turk came trotting after her.

"All done?" said Vardy.

"All done," said Nevada.

Turk dashed through the room and out the cat flap in the back door, moving so quickly that I barely glimpsed the note tucked under her collar. She went through the garden and over the back wall in one lithe leap, and I prayed with all my soul that she'd move quickly.

"All right," said Vardy. There was a hint of finality in his voice. A suggestion that something had to happen now, which Nevada immediately recognised and set about attempting to counter.

"Nic, I just wanted to say…"

"The time for talking is over," he said. His voice was hard and I felt a horrid cold thrill. He meant business. But Nevada ignored him and just kept going, soft and gentle and relentless.

"I just wanted to thank you."

His eyes flickered towards her. "Thank me?"

"For letting us feed Turk. That was so kind of you. You're a good bloke." There was such warmth in her voice that even I almost believed her.

"You think so?" His voice shook but his hands were steady. The gun pointed at me without wavering. He snatched a quick glance at her, too fast for me to do anything.

"You're such a lovely girl," he said. "I liked you the moment I saw you. Believe me, I've known a lot of beautiful women. But you have something special." My stomach turned over queasily. I didn't like the way this was tending.

"You have a special quality," he said. "A special warmth. Has anyone ever told you that before?"

"That's a very interesting question," said Nevada. "Why don't we talk about it? Why don't you put the gun down and we can talk about it. Just talk."

He shook his head. "Sorry. I can't. It has to be done."

"You keep saying that."

"I know. Because it has to be done." His eyes moved shiftily. "But we can do something else first." He was looking at her and I recognised the look. He'd had it in his eyes when we'd met before, every time he looked at her, and I didn't like it then. Now it caused a wave of cold, hard hatred in me, followed by a fear so intense that I could hardly think.

We all knew what he was talking about, but none of us was willing to say it aloud.

Just then, Turk came back in. She nosed through the cat flap and trotted back into the centre of the room.

The note was still under her collar, exactly where we'd put it.

Nevada saw it too and I saw the shock register in her eyes. This had never happened before. Turk wandered off into the bedroom, probably to have a nap. I wondered how long she'd sleep before the sound of the shotgun sent her fleeing in terror.

But maybe there would be other noises first.

"I liked you as soon as I saw you," said Vardy hoarsely.

"I liked you too," said Nevada cautiously, as if she was stepping through a minefield.

"I don't want you to die." His voice was thick now and the tears were gleaming in his eyes again.

"And I don't want to die. I don't want anyone to die. And no one has to."

"It has to be done," said Vardy, softly. "I'm sorry. It's such a waste." He glanced at her. "But it doesn't have to be."

"That's right," said Nevada, her voice as soft as his. "It doesn't have to be."

"Not a complete waste," said Vardy. "*That* has to happen. But we can do something else first." Nevada didn't say anything. "One last burst of life," said Vardy. "An affirmation. Life and pleasure, the pleasure of the flesh."

The air temperature in the room felt like it had suddenly dropped ten degrees. "And I promise you'll like it," said Vardy, his voice soft and oily. "I'll see that you like it. I know what to do. I'm a very good lover. I'm very experienced. I promise you things that you've never felt before. Tantric sensations." He looked at me. "But we'll have to tie him up. To make sure he doesn't interfere."

There was real hatred in his eyes when he looked at me. And the shotgun never wavered. But I began to feel a strange elation. I could see a way out of this.

If Nevada could get within reach of Vardy I'm sure it wouldn't be a Tantric sensation that she gave him.

"Of course, I'll have to tie you up as well," he said, glancing at Nevada. And all hope died. At that moment I felt us, and our situation, descending into hell. "I'll have to tie you to the bed first," he said.

Just then a curious thing happened.

Somehow a butterfly had got into the room and it fluttered past Vardy. It was bright red. Its vivid red wings fluttered as it moved swiftly back and forth, then settled on his chest, and I saw that it wasn't a butterfly at all but an intense spot of red light.

Laser light.

Outside an electronically amplified voice called out. "Armed police. Put down your weapon."

30. POSTMARKED CANTERBURY

Tinkler shook his head. "Tsk tsk." He folded the newspaper and showed us the front page. The headline read: FAMOUS PHOTOGRAPHER DIES IN POLICE CUSTODY. "I guess this means that I don't get my autographed print after all." He shoved the paper aside despondently and picked up the menu.

"Cheer up," said Nevada. "Your favourite people on Earth are still alive and well."

"A small consolation."

The girl from behind the bar came and took our orders. We'd only recently discovered that our local gastro-pub did breakfasts, and we'd been coming here every day since. We weren't spending much time at home at the moment. What had once been our sanctuary had been transformed into a place with some very vivid and recent bad memories. I couldn't go into my own living room without thinking about the madman with the shotgun. Nevada felt much the same.

So we were spending as much time as possible outside the house. In fact we only went home to sleep and feed the cats.

Today Tinkler had decided to join us for breakfast. The pub did a particularly good one, with all organic, locally sourced ingredients—much of it from the nearby allotments cultivated by local environmental nuts. The Spanish omelette was especially nice and all three of us had ordered it.

"So the police didn't shoot him," said Tinkler.

"No."

"He died in the police station."

I sighed. "Here's what happened. He put down his gun when the cops arrived outside—"

"You mean Stinky's SWAT team."

"Yes. His police bodyguards were living on site at the Abbey."

"Thank god," said Nevada.

"So Stinky actually came good?" said Tinkler.

"I suppose I have to say yes," I said. " But being Stinky he had to add a little characteristic twist to things."

"How so?" said Tinkler. "My god, that omelette smells good. Where are ours? Do you suppose those people would mind if I took some of theirs?"

"In an answer to your question," I said, "when Stinky got the note he acted immediately. But he also felt he had to write an acknowledgement on the note, put it back exactly where it had been and send it back to us."

Nevada nodded. "So when poor Turk came in with the note still under her collar, we thought the message hadn't got through." She looked at me. I knew what she was thinking. We were both still having nightmares.

Nevada said, "Stinky, that maniac, had actually written

back to us, suggesting we sit tight. As if we could read this while some fucker is pointing a gun at us."

"Whoops," said Tinkler. "Typical Stinky. Still the SWAT team came through. So what did they do? Take Vardy back to the police station and kill him there?"

"Nobody killed him," I said. "Look, this is what happened. He put down his shotgun and they took us to the police station and put us all in separate interview rooms. I was left sitting in mine for hours, waiting for something to happen, no one talking to me—I later found out exactly the same thing had happened to Nevada."

"Exactly," said Nevada.

"Then eventually someone came and told us we could go home. We later found out that Vardy had died shortly after they brought him in. At first everyone thought it was a heart attack."

"But now," said Nevada, "everyone thinks he took something."

"Took something?" said Tinkler. He paused in wiping his cutlery with a paper napkin. Restaurant cutlery was never quite clean enough for Tinkler. "You mean like a suicide pill? Like cyanide?"

"Not cyanide," I said. "But something equally effective."

"Bummer." Tinkler breathed on a fork and began polishing it.

"Call me small-minded and vindictive," I said, "but I couldn't be more pleased."

"I mean from the point of view of you not getting closure. I mean, now he's dead he can never tell us what the hell was going on."

"The very fact that he came in pointing a shotgun at us tends to tell us something," said Nevada.

Tinkler reached for my knife and fork and I moved them away from him. "I don't want you polishing my cutlery."

"Touchy. I was just offering. Anyhow, so concerning Vardy, he might have been Valerian's killer—always assuming she didn't actually kill herself."

"Yes," I said. "He might have been."

"And now we'll never know. Like I said, bummer. And he also might have been the missing boy's father."

"He might have been."

"And we'll never know," said Tinkler. "But wait a minute. Can't you do a DNA test? I mean, sure Vardy's dead, but you could get a post-mortem sample. The DNA would be viable."

"Viable?" said Nevada. "Have you been watching *CSI* again?"

"We could get a sample all right," I said. "But what would we compare it against?"

"The kid's," said Tinkler. Then he stopped. "But of course we don't have any trace of the kid."

"That's kind of the difficulty."

Our omelettes came and we all got stuck in. "So anyway," said Tinkler, "now you're completely screwed in terms of your investigation. This omelette's stupendous. What is this, coriander?"

We got back to the house late that night, having been to see a movie—we'd been to a lot of movies lately—and while

Nevada fed the cats I went through the mail on the doormat. The only interesting item was a letter addressed to Nevada in looping feminine handwriting and postmarked Canterbury.

I gave it to her and she ripped it open.

Dear Nevada,

My brother has now told me the truth. There is no documentary and there never was one. You should not have lied to me and misled me. However I am now sitting here looking out at my little garden with Nevada (the kitten) purring in my lap and I am feeling inclined to be magnanimous. I forgive you. More than that, since you seem to be so eager to solve the mysteries in our family, I shall make a compact with you.

If you find out who really killed my sister I will tell you what happened to her child.

Yours faithfully,
Cecilia Drummond

31. SOAP BUBBLES

I went up the steps and rang the doorbell of the pink house. I had left Tinkler's car parked around the corner and I glanced back in that direction while I waited. I didn't have to wait long. There were footsteps and then the door was opened by Dr Osterloh, as I knew it would be. It was late on a cool, autumn night and Adela would be long gone, off to wherever omnivorously sexual Swedes go at the end of their working day.

Osterloh was wearing a dark green sweater, white shirt and grey trousers. He didn't have shoes on, just black socks, and he was clutching what looked like a half-eaten smoked salmon and cream cheese bagel in one hand; well, it was his house and his working day was over, too.

I said, "Thank you for seeing me at such short notice."

"Not a problem."

"And out of office hours."

"Come in." He gestured with the remains of the bagel and I followed him inside. We went past the room where we'd talked previously and up the stairs and along a thickly carpeted corridor. He daintily finished the bagel as we walked, then took a tissue out of his pocket and wiped his hands. Putting the tissue away, he opened a door on our right and we went into a small office dominated by a desk with a comfortable-looking armchair in front of it. Behind the desk was a high narrow window with the shadowy shape of a tree dividing the faint amber light that came from the street.

He sat behind the desk and I sat in the armchair. "Since this is something resembling an official consultation," he said, "I thought we'd conduct it in my office."

"Right," I said. I laced my fingers around my left knee and stared down at the navy-blue carpet. "Well…"

"Take your time." He leaned back in his chair, relaxed and professional. Suddenly the bagel-eater was quite gone. "Just let me make sure all the phones are off." He opened a drawer in his desk and frowned down into it as he consulted an unseen piece of technology and pushed buttons. After a moment he smiled and closed the drawer. "There. All ready." He looked at me expectantly.

"So," I said, "since the recent incident I've been having certain… difficulties."

His face became grave. "I'm not surprised. What a terrible thing to happen. It must have been profoundly unsettling."

"It was."

"I knew Nic Vardy," said Osterloh.

"I know," I said. "All you guys knew each other."

"You were saying?"

"Well, since it happened both my girlfriend and I find it

hard to be around the house. We go out as much as we can because we just don't feel safe there anymore. It was our home. We used to be happy there. Comfortable. We used to enjoy just being there. Now we avoid it as much as we can."

He leaned towards me across the desk, hands clasped in front of him. "That's entirely natural of course. And you mustn't worry too much. I imagine at the moment you're bleakly prognosticating that your feelings about your home have changed forever, that you'll never feel safe or comfortable there again. Perhaps you're thinking of selling the house and moving."

"That's right."

Osterloh smiled. "Of course. But trite as it sounds, you will find that the passage of time will allow your feelings to change, to return to normal. And it need not even take long for that to happen."

"What if we can't wait?" I said.

He nodded as if he understood. "I think you'll find that any major new event in your life will tend to push this into the background, emotionally speaking. In a sense you can hasten the return to normality by deliberately creating a major new event. For example, by doing something as simple as going on holiday. Visiting a country where you've never been before." He smiled.

"A holiday," I said. "Now there's an idea."

Osterloh folded his arms and leaned back in the chair. "But this wasn't really what you came to talk about, was it?"

I said, "No. I came to ask you why you killed Valerian."

He peered at me for a moment and then chuckled.

"Is that dramatic accusation supposed to elicit an equally dramatic response?"

"It's not an accusation. It's a deduction based on facts."

"Well, then it's a deeply flawed deduction," he said. "Because I did not kill her." He glanced at me. "What facts?"

"Some Glenn Miller records."

He seemed taken aback. "What?"

"The last time I came to see you I bought some records from a charity shop. Or rather I paid for them and left them there. But before I could go back to collect the records, somebody stole them. Or maybe they bought them."

"Why would anyone want to steal some Glenn Miller records? Or indeed buy them?"

"They wouldn't," I said. "But they didn't know that's all they were. For all the thief knew, they represented some vital piece of information."

"Relating to what?"

"To the fact that you killed Valerian."

He shook his head. "You keep coming back to that. But it seems to be circular reasoning, with no actual input of fact."

"How's this for an input of fact? Those records ended up here, in your house. Someone working for you got hold of them when they saw me choose them at the charity shop. And they brought them here to you. Presumably you just stuck them in a closet or something, when you realised they weren't important after all. And that's where Adela found them."

"Adela?"

"Yes. She had a clear out. Took a load of things that she

said you never use. To a charity shop, ironically. And the records were amongst these things. As were several copies of your book."

There was a long pause, then he said, "The little bitch. Copies of my book?"

"She said there were hundreds of them, and nobody ever buys any. She said you'd never notice."

"Well, she's wrong there," he said triumphantly. "And I knew some had gone missing."

I'd had enough of this. I said, "You did it, didn't you?"

He sighed and looked at me. "Let me tell you something interesting. I know you don't have any kind of recording device on you. You're not even carrying a phone. Do you know how I know that?"

I said, "Because you've got a bug buster in that drawer. Quite possibly a Stone Circle 10, sold to you by a guy at Spook Store with some very dodgy stubble shaved in the shape of a Maori tattoo."

For the first time, Osterloh looked utterly wrong-footed and unsure of himself. "How did you know that?"

I shrugged. "There's only so many places in London where you can buy those things. What is it with that guy and his stubble?"

He smiled. He'd regained his composure. "An ignored child, perhaps," he said. "The important point is that I can deny anything that is said in this room and you have no way of proving otherwise."

I crossed my legs and tried to relax. "In that case you have no reason not to talk to me."

He gave me a long, speculative look. "What do you want to know?"

"You sent Nic Vardy to kill us, didn't you?"

He smiled. "If I did, I would be very upset with the job he did. Or didn't do, rather."

"But it wasn't just Nic Vardy, was it?" I remembered the old woman and the man with the glasses in the house in Canterbury. And the man who'd helped his friend with the glasses over the Trevertons' back wall, with an arrow in his shoulder. One of these was my candidate for the idiot who'd thought the Glenn Miller records were a vital clue, and had triumphantly scooped them up. I wish I could have seen the look on Osterloh's face when he'd been presented with this proud find.

Osterloh spread his hands. "I've met many interesting people over the years. Some socially, like Nic Vardy. Some in a professional capacity. For example in the course of my visits to prisons." He grinned at me. "I get to know them. Their strengths and weaknesses and foibles. And I keep track of them."

"What about Vardy? What were his foibles?"

"Throughout his long career Nic did many questionable things. Usually involving women, girls who wanted to be famous. He did many things he came to regret. And he told me about them. Discussed them with me at our regular weekly sessions. I would offer him advice. Make suggestions."

I said, "You blackmailed him."

He looked annoyed. "All I did was encourage him to do what he wanted to do anyway. In any case, the key to Nic

Vardy was not his predatory treatment of young women. It was his response to hunting." He looked at me to make sure I was following his monologue. "He was conflicted about killing birds."

"He hated doing it," I said.

"He hated it because he loved it so much. He hated what it revealed to him about himself. So he tried to repress it, to deny it. But of course that didn't work."

"Not with you as his shrink," I said.

"I merely told him to explore his own possibilities. Essentially, to do what he wanted to do anyway." He made a clucking sound and shook his head. "But he never had the courage to fully embrace that aspect of himself. Look at what happened when he killed the goose—"

"The goose?" I said. *Gwenevere?*

Osterloh nodded. "He strangled it with a piece of wire. And greatly enjoyed the experience, I'm sure. But then what does he do afterwards? Does he make use of what he has discovered about himself, and build on it? No. The weakling has such a crisis of conscience that he has to take down all of the photographs of birds on his wall. Because he can't bear to look at them."

"Why did you have him kill the goose?" I said.

"Oh, that was only a means to an end. When you went to your friend who sold the rare singles it was obvious that you were going after that record by Valerian. The one with the supposed secret message on it."

"And you thought that message might be something about you?"

He shrugged. "The goose merely got in the way. Of course, once I had a chance to listen to the record—luckily I still have my Bang and Olufsen turntable—I realised that it was irrelevant. So I made Vardy put it back. I sent him back the next night to plant it among the debris he'd created the first time, when he was looking for it. It was all very straightforward." He smiled at me.

"Because there was no longer a goose to get past."

"Yes. So he returned the record for your friend to find, and to cover our tracks. I assume your friend did find it?"

"Yes, he did," I said, repressing the ridiculous urge to thank him.

"But Nic Vardy just couldn't face what was within himself. So I had to take him by the hand and lead him, so to speak."

"Right up to our front door," I said.

"If you like. As I said, it was his slobbering affection for all manner of birdlife that was the key to the man. I knew he had a deep-seated longing to explore his penchant for animal cruelty and I—" He looked at me. "I might say *we* gave him the opportunity to do so. But after he had killed that goose he manifested such tedious and protracted regret that I began to wonder if he was actually contemplating suicide. I decided then that I must act quickly if I was to make use of him. I wanted him to deal with you. You and your friend Nevada were becoming a real problem. So I told him what he had to do. He was reluctant, so I simply told him he was hypnotised and had no choice in the matter. He was under a compulsion he couldn't resist. And whenever he felt himself weakening he was to repeat the phrase I had given him."

"'It has to be done'," I said.

"Precisely."

"Was he hypnotised?"

"Of course not. I just gave him an excuse to express the terrible sadism and savagery that was boiling away at the base of his psyche. I gave him permission to be who he was. I suspected it would destroy him in the process, and that was all to the good. But I was counting on him to polish the two of you off before he made his suicide attempt." He nodded thoughtfully, as though confirming something to himself. "Which I have to confess he carried off quite well. Very dramatic, in the police station like that. He'd probably seen films depicting heroic World War II freedom fighters who took poison just before the Gestapo interrogators got them to divulge the vital secret." He looked at me. "That's why I gave him the capsule. I'm sure he saw such films when he was at an impressionable age."

"Perhaps he didn't see any films about blowing two fellow human beings apart with a shotgun," I said. "When he was at an impressionable age. Which is why in the end he couldn't do it."

"Yes, that may well have been part of the problem. Still, as I say, he carried off the suicide quite well, and tidied things up in that respect."

"Did he know too much to live?"

Osterloh's eyes narrowed. "You're being remarkably snotty for someone in your position."

"What exactly is my position?"

He seemed to make an effort to recover his temper and once again became smooth and civil and professional. "Was that all you wanted to know?"

"No. What about the other people you used, besides Vardy?"

"I told you about them. They're just various folk of my acquaintance. I employed assorted forms of persuasion to enlist their help. Some feel they are under an obligation to me. Others are happy to do what comes naturally. Still others expected to be paid."

"What about those two in Canterbury?"

"I must admit they weren't my finest choices. I gave them money for the petrol to burn the house down and they pocketed most of it. Then they discovered they didn't have enough petrol, *quelle surprise*, and they had to go back and buy some more." He shook his head despairingly. "It was just a nightmare."

"For us, too," I said. He gave me a look of polite inquiry. "Being locked in a house," I said, "out of our minds on drugs while someone tries to burn it down around us."

He leaned forward with real interest. "How did you find the LSD? What was your impression?"

"I can take it or leave it."

"That's a shame. It's a pity you couldn't appreciate its value. It was the most pure, finest grade Swiss pharmaceutical standard, identical to the kind first synthesised by Albert Hofmann." He began to get quite animated. I think he'd forgotten the context of our conversation, and the implications of it. Or maybe he was just beyond caring. "I have had considerable experience of LSD and the other hallucinogens, sometimes at extremely high doses." He chuckled reminiscently. "I almost had a 'bad trip' once." He looked up at me, eyes bright. "You know what I did? *I exerted my will.* I simply took charge of myself and calmed myself, and restored the experience to its proper therapeutic norms. It is a very beautiful and powerful drug. But it's not for everyone. Or perhaps I should say, not everyone is for it. Some people are simply inadequate, unworthy of the psychedelic experience. So you might argue that the ordeal of the bad trip acts as a kind of gatekeeper, filtering out those who are unfit and only allowing those who have the requisite psychological robustness to move on."

"To the sunlit uplands," I said.

"Despite your sarcasm, yes, that is exactly what they are. And since you asked about Valerian, she was one of those who tried but failed. She was found wanting."

"You killed her," I said.

He leaned back in his chair and studied me. "Of course I killed her."

"Why?"

"In the course of my work I had encountered some extraordinary individuals, such as Charles Sobhraj, the so-called Charles Manson of India. People who don't acknowledge the existence of the boundaries and conventions that stifle most human beings. They have experiences beyond your imagining." He tapped his finger on the desk as if indicating a point. "I wanted to see what it felt like. So I talked Valerian into the noose and I talked her out of the window. I just wanted to see if I could do it, and I could. I don't think I even needed the acid, although I made sure she'd taken plenty. She just went and did what I told her to do." He looked up. "It was certainly a first for me."

"You were supposed to be helping her. She trusted you."

He shrugged. "If someone can't maintain the sovereignty of self, preserve the most basic of psychic defences, if they don't even have that most fundamental level of self-love, then they deserve whatever the world throws at them. They are as evanescent, as ephemeral and as vulnerable as soap bubbles." He smiled at me. "And there's no shame in bursting them."

"Nobody knew you'd done it?"

"Don't be absurd. The place was a circus. No one ever knew what was going on. The only one who might conceivably have put two and two together was her sister. So after Valerian died, when she was grieving, I gave Cecilia what she thought was a sedative. But it was the most powerful LSD I could source." Once again his voice grew rich with nostalgia. "I remember watching her when it took hold, at the funeral. It was extraordinary. I thought her head might pop like a light bulb blowing. Of course, the drug was interacting with all sorts of underlying mental pathologies and weaknesses. It opened up a seismic fault that had always been there, and triggered a psychic earthquake, so to speak. One that had been waiting to happen." He nodded, deep in thought. "It's very impressive that you managed to get her back as much as you have. A testament to the toughness of the human psyche."

"The sovereignty of the self," I said.

He flashed me a look of annoyance. "I did the world a favour with Valerian. I improved the gene pool, or rather the mind pool. You have no idea how screwed up that girl was. And if she'd remained alive who knows how many others she would have messed up with her neuroses and her obsessions?"

"Is that really why you killed her?" I said. "As an altruistic act for mankind? I don't think so."

He placed his hands on the desk in front of him and studied them as though checking his manicure. "All right then, what do *you* think?"

"Erik Make Loud said you were one of the few men in her circle she didn't have sex with."

"True."

"But I don't think that was your choice."

He looked up and studied me for a long moment. "Why do you say that?"

"I've seen pictures of a lot of the lucky guys. They were all big, impressive, charismatic. Jolly jock types. There wasn't a little shrimp of an academic among them."

If I'd made him angry, he did a good job of concealing it. "I was right to think you were dangerous," he said. "It's true. She dispensed her favours far and wide. She would have slept with the postman if he'd asked her nicely. But she wouldn't sleep with me. Too bad. Who knows? If she had, she might still be with us." He stood up, signalling that our interview was at an end.

"So, congratulations," he said. "You worked it out. But what have you achieved, really? You can't prove anything.

If you try to repeat what I've said, I shall merely deny it. And in any case, I don't anticipate you being a problem for long." He smiled at me. "When you walk out the door I shall simply make a phone call and arrange for you to be dealt with. And regrettably your lady friend too. It will cost several thousand pounds to have it done properly. But I know it will be a thorough, professional job because I have met some very thorough, professional people as patients in the course of my career. Indeed they have offered just this kind of assistance, should I ever need it. I have never availed myself of these kind offers, until now."

"So you're going to kill us?"

He spread his hands in a gesture of polite helplessness. "What other choice do I have? I am who I am, and you are who you are. For example, I know you won't try and do anything to me, despite what I've said. You could no more physically attack me than you could swim the Atlantic Ocean. We are all, ultimately, victims of who we are."

He concluded on a rising note, with a nice air of finality, which I assumed he'd learned from years of giving lectures. I rather spoiled the effect by turning to the open door and saying, "So what do you think of all that bullshit?"

Nevada stepped in.

Followed by Cecilia.

I turned to Osterloh and said, "You shouldn't keep a key in the lamp by the back door. Not all your intruders are going to be imaginary."

Cecilia was staring at Osterloh. "You killed Valerie," she said. He must have seen something in her face, because he made a break for the door. But she lunged powerfully and pinned him down, like a cat catching a mouse by the tail.

He struggled, but she held him tight in a cruel parody of a lover's embrace. "Cecilia," he said, "Cessie—"

She looked at us and said, "Go. Get out of here now. I'll deal with him."

Nevada and I turned and started for the door.

He called out. "Please don't go," he said. "Don't leave me with her."

I said, "It has to be done," and we walked out the door.

We went and got the car and drove away into the night. We covered about half a mile in silence and then I slowed down, my foot drifting off the accelerator almost of its own volition. I hit the indicator and we coasted to the side of the road. I was gripping the steering wheel so tightly that my hands hurt. I stared out the windscreen, straight ahead.

"I can't do it," I said.

"I'm so glad you said that," said Nevada. I turned to look at her. Her face was strained and pale in the unearthly glow of the streetlight.

"I can't just leave him there like that."

"I know," said Nevada.

"Even him."

"I know."

"We can turn him over to the police. Between the three of us we'll be able to hang something on him." I threw the car into a U-turn and we headed back the way we came. Because of the one-way system, progress was maddeningly slow.

And, long before we got there, we saw the flames.

By the time we arrived the fire was pouring into the sky from the roof of the pink house as though from a giant chimney. The underside of the clouds had taken on a coppery glow and the autumn chill had given way locally to a furnace warmth. There were people standing in the street, neighbours, some of them in pyjamas and slippers.

There was no sign of Cecilia.

We drove around looking for her, but in the end we had to give up. As we turned towards home three fire engines passed us, going the other way.

32. DRINKS

"So the bastard is dead," said the Colonel. "He killed Valerie, but now he's dead."

Nevada nodded. "He died in the fire."

"And the authorities are treating it all as purely accidental," I said. "Just one of those things."

We were sitting in the same hotel bar where we'd met before. The only difference this time was that Lucy was with us. As usual, she and the Colonel were sitting as far apart as they could without actually being at separate tables. Lucy was wearing a rather natty houndstooth jacket that Nevada had sold her, over a bright pink sweatshirt with blue cartoon lettering that read BABY ON BOARD. The Colonel was, as ever, resplendent in L.L.Bean.

Lucy said, "Do we know what actually happened, in the house? How the fire started?"

"No," I said. "And I don't imagine we ever will. Once we saw the place going up in flames, and we couldn't find Cecilia, we didn't know what to do. We spent a couple of hours trying to figure out our next move."

"And in the end," said Nevada, "we decided the best thing was to drive down to Canterbury, even though by then it was the middle of the night."

The Colonel nodded. "You went looking for Cessie. That was very good of you."

I didn't correct him, but in fact at that point we'd begun to assume that Cecilia had died in the conflagration. So we'd driven down to Canterbury with a cat carrier in the car for what we assumed was the now-orphaned kitten named Nevada. Appalling as it may sound, our main worry at the time had been how Fanny and Turk would adjust to another cat in the house.

"But when we arrived," I said, "Cecilia was already there. She'd beaten us down to Canterbury. Despite the fact that she had hitch-hiked."

"She seems to have a knack for it," said Nevada.

"Cecilia didn't volunteer any information about exactly what happened between her and Osterloh in the house, and we didn't press her on it."

"So what did you talk about?" the Colonel asked.

"We promised to bring her back her record collection. All her classical LPs. The Trevertons had them in storage. And I'll set up a system for her to play them on." I'd chosen some good bookshelf speakers, a solid-state amp and a semi-automatic turntable with a decent budget Ortofon cartridge. Not a bad little system.

The Colonel frowned. "Wouldn't she be better off with a CD player?"

I said, "Nobody's better off with a CD player." Under the table Nevada nudged me. We were getting off the topic here.

Suddenly Lucy gave an elaborate shudder. "That's so dangerous."

We all looked at her. "What's so dangerous?" said Nevada.

"Hitch-hiking," said Lucy.

The Colonel gave her a disgusted look. "Hitch-hiking? Cecilia had a confrontation with the psychopathic murderer who killed our sister, and you think the dangerous part of the evening was hitch-hiking?"

"I was just saying…"

"Well, don't," said the Colonel. "Don't say anything." He turned to me. "Why didn't you tell us all this right away? When it all happened?" His alert, intelligent eyes glinted in the dimness of the bar. "Instead, you waited a few days."

This was true. We had seen both the Colonel and Lucy, separately, since the incident and had drinks with them and had deliberately said nothing. "I'll get to that in a minute," I said. "First I need to tell you about Cecilia's promise."

"Her promise?"

Nevada nodded. "She said that if we could find her sister's killer—"

The Colonel nodded energetically. "Which you have done. And for which you have my thanks."

"You have closure," said Lucy.

"Oh, for Christ's sake." The Colonel glared at her. "I thought I told you not to say anything." He leaned aggressively towards her as he spoke, and I realised that the only time they grew close physically was when they argued.

Lucy started to say something, but Nevada hastily intervened. "Cecilia said if we found the killer she would tell us what happened to Valerian's child."

That shut both of them up. They turned to look at us. The Colonel spoke softly. "She knew?"

"Yes."

"All these years?"

"Yes."

"And kept quiet about it?"

I shrugged. "I suppose she didn't feel she had anyone to tell. Until now."

He stared at me, his gaze drilling into me. "And you know now? What happened to the little boy?"

"Yes."

He sighed and sank back in his chair. Then he leaned forward again and I could see him literally bracing himself, as if for a physical impact. "All right," he said. "You can tell me. But first I want to say that I know that it's going to be bad news. I'm not a fool. But also I want to say that every cloud has a silver lining." He glanced at Lucy. "At least now I'll be rid of you. Now that it's over I'll never have to see you again."

"Likewise," said Lucy. "The feeling couldn't be more mutual."

Nevada and I looked at each other. I cleared my throat. I didn't quite know where to start. I said, "You remember how your father disowned your sisters?"

The Colonel nodded. "He swore he'd never speak to them. And not long before that, he'd made the same declaration to me." He gave a little smile. "In my case he kept his promise."

I said, "Valerian professed not to be too bothered by the arrangement. But Cecilia was deeply upset by it. She couldn't stand being estranged from her father."

"She always was a daddy's girl."

"So when Valerian discovered that she was pregnant, at first they thought it would drive the old man even further away, make him even more angry at them."

"If that was possible," said the Colonel.

"If that was possible," I said. "But then Cecilia realised that the child could actually be an asset. If he was a boy, suddenly they would have a route back into the old man's affections."

The Colonel chuckled dryly. "He had a big thing about wanting a male heir. And I no longer counted, of course."

"It was a good plan," I said. "It was such a good plan that they decided to go ahead with it even when they discovered that the baby was a girl."

They stared at me.

I went on. "That was why, when she discovered she was pregnant, Valerian got rid of her au pairs and insisted on looking after the child herself. Which in practice meant Cecilia doing a great deal of the work and Valerian occasionally helping. But it also meant, during the first two years of her life, it was easy to maintain the fiction that the child was a boy. After all, your father was hardly the type to change a nappy."

The Colonel gave a humourless bark of laughter. "Well, that's certainly true."

"Anyway, the old man loved the kid. So Valerian and Cecilia figured that by the time he found out about their ruse, it would be too late. It wouldn't matter." I looked at the Colonel. "As it happened, no one ever found out about the ruse. Until now."

He nodded. He was still braced like a man getting ready for a physical blow, but he was brisk, businesslike. "So it was a little girl instead of a little boy. What happened to her?"

"Okay," I said. "As we suspected, it was a custody snatch. The father took her. He wrote a letter to Cecilia confessing what he'd done. And by then, with everything that had happened and Cecilia out of the picture one way or another, it seemed as good a place for the child as any. So the man and his girlfriend, later his wife, then raised the child as their own and no one ever knew. Even the girl herself, since she was too young to have any memories of her early life. Things were simplified by the fact that they left the country. And, it being the 1960s, it was relatively easy to pass a child off as their own and acquire the various documentation. Crossing borders was a lot simpler then than it is now, and it helped that they set up house in Morocco."

"Morocco?" said Lucy.

I nodded. "The girl's father was Monty Tegmark—your father."

It took a moment for the implications of this to sink in. Then Lucy and the Colonel looked at each other. "Wait a minute," said the Colonel in a strangled voice.

"Lucy," said Nevada, "meet your uncle. John, meet your niece."

They stared at us with identical aghast expressions. It was easy now, with the benefit of hindsight, to see all kinds of family resemblance.

"There must be a mistake," said the Colonel.

"That's why we didn't tell you right away," I said. "We had to be sure. So we invited you both around for drinks, on separate occasions. And pretended it was a purely social occasion."

"Sorry about the deception," said Nevada.

"And I'm sorry about what else we did," I said, "but I had to be sure before we told you. So we kept your drinking glasses and took DNA samples and got them tested. It's definite." I didn't mention that I'd also be sending him an invoice for the tests, which hadn't been cheap.

Lucy and the Colonel stared at me. And then at each other.

I could have gone on. I could have said that as a journalist writing a book about the band and touring with them, Monty Tegmark had plenty of access to Valerian—in every imaginable sense. She and Monty must have had a long-standing affair. Certainly they had been close enough for him to be certain that the child was his—a fact easily verified later in life by the resemblance I'd seen in photographs.

And close enough for Monty to be able to snatch the infant Lucy shortly after her mother died.

But I don't think either of them wanted, or needed, to hear any of this. They were still staring at each other. Disbelief was beginning to be replaced by some dawning emotion. I wasn't sure I wanted to stick around and find out what it was.

Evidently Nevada felt the same way. She cleared her throat and we stood up. "We'll leave the two of you to get acquainted."

We walked out of the hotel through a revolving glass door, into the bright, autumn day. We turned towards Green Park Tube station. The sun was shining but it was bitingly cold. Winter was approaching at speed. We were walking into a chill, driving wind. Nevada took my arm and huddled beside me.

"I brought their bill with me," she said. "But somehow it didn't seem like the right moment to present them with it. Never mind. I'll attach it to an email."

EPILOGUE

That was the end of it, except for three small incidents.

Some months later we were just finishing dinner when we got an excited phone call from Tinkler. "Turn on your television. Right away."

We went into the bedroom and switched on the designated channel, then we settled on the bed. The cats came in to join us. We turned up the volume on the remote, providing sound for what turned out to be the annual British Academy of Film and Television Arts award ceremony.

The award for Best Documentary was being presented, and receiving it was Stinky Stanmer, managing to look badly dressed even in a very expensive and no doubt tailor-made tuxedo. He accepted the statuette and made his speech—all bulging eyes, moist fish lips and feigned sincerity. "Making *In Search of Valerian* was a deeply moving experience," he said.

Nevada got off the bed, disturbing Fanny who had curled up beside us, and began restlessly pacing the room in front of the television, periodically cutting off my view.

On the screen Stinky was saying, "It's hard to express the poignancy of what happened to the Drummond sisters and the universal message it conveys to all of us. It's a modern fairy tale, about a schoolgirl full of dreams who sets out into the big world, travelling to every corner of the globe, but who finds that dream turns into a nightmare and then, ironically, ends up back in the same small town she came from, forever. As if nothing ever happened. As if she never went away."

He gave his serious look, which made him look like a dairy cow receiving the abrupt attentions of a bull, but there was thunderous applause from the audience of assembled dignitaries. There was, of course, the added emotional dimension of the award-winner's recent well-publicised battle with, and presumed conquest of, his cocaine addiction. All the more reason to pour on the plaudits.

By this point Nevada was getting so agitated that I thought I'd better switch the television off, before she put her foot through the screen. I pressed the button on the remote, and the image died. She turned and glared at me.

"That was our idea! That was exactly our idea! Yours and mine. Virtually word for word. How did the bastard even *know* about it?" She snapped her fingers. "I know. I told his office about it so they'd know what we were telling people. So that if anyone checked up on us, their cover story would match ours. And they stole it. They told Stinky and *he* stole it. The bastard stole our idea and made our documentary."

"Well, it wasn't really our documentary."

"Yes it was. And now he's getting awards for it. And is he giving us any credit?"

"Knowing Stinky," I said, "I suspect not."

"He stole our idea and didn't give us any credit!"

"That's Stinky," I said. "Come back to bed."

The next development was rather more pleasant. We received a letter from Lucy, written in a somewhat florid hand and overheated prose style. In it she told us she'd had an ultrasound and the baby was fine. And he was a boy. When I read this I couldn't help thinking that the Colonel—the real Colonel, the crusty old patriarch—had somehow triumphed after all. I said, "There's going to be a male heir at last."

"And that's the main thing," said Nevada.

The last incident began soon after the death of Dr Osterloh.

Somewhat forgotten in recent years, Osterloh had apparently been well known in the 1960s as a celebrity shrink. So the obituary writers suddenly discovered that they had quite an interesting figure to resurrect, an angle to exploit, and lots of material to examine.

I don't know who was the first to get hold of his self-published book, but there was certainly no shortage of copies. Maybe they found it in a charity shop. In any case, they actually read it and decided to argue that it was, like its author, unjustly neglected. Excerpts were printed in one of the Sunday papers and then a proper publisher decided to release a new edition, with an introduction about Osterloh and his tragic demise. Then Radio 4 ran a serialisation of the book and it began to pick up momentum. Now judged a forgotten classic, it was reprinted, then reprinted again, then again, triggering its inexorable climb up the international bestseller lists.

I began to wish I'd bought a signed first edition after all.

READ ON FOR AN EXCLUSIVE EXTRACT FROM
THE NEXT IN ANDREW CARTMEL'S BRILLIANT

VINYL DETECTIVE SERIES

VICTORY DISC

Available May 2018

1. HIDDEN TREASURE

We were in the kitchen. I was making coffee and Nevada was feeding the cats, when suddenly she looked out the window and said, "There he is now. At last."

"Who?" I said, measuring the ground beans as I poured them into the filter.

"Your friend Tinkler."

"I see," I said. "So he's *my* friend now."

"Finish feeding these two, would you? I'm going to deal with him." She wiped her hands and hurried out of the kitchen just as the front gate clanged, signalling Tinkler's arrival. Nevada had been waiting for days for just this moment—her chance to pounce—but now it had arrived, she played it very cool. Opening the door before he had a chance to ring the bell, she was as nice as pie. "Tinkler! Hello." There was the sound of her smooching him on the cheek and then she led him into the kitchen, her arm twined around his. "Darling, look who's here."

She was laying it on a bit thick, I thought. But I knew what she was up to.

"Hello, Tinkler," I said. I'd finished giving the cats their breakfast—Aberdeen Angus ox cheek, served raw and laboriously chopped up with the kitchen scissors while Turk tried to snag pieces from me, with her razor sharp claws and great dexterity, and Fanny merely contented herself by getting underfoot and making lots of imploring noises—and returned to making the coffee. "You want some coffee? It's the good stuff."

"I'd expect nothing less," said Tinkler. His face had an unaccustomed touch of suntan and he was grinning happily. He had no idea what was in store for him.

"How was France?" said Nevada.

"Great. It was just Mum and Dad and Maggie and me in this huge *gite*. That's a kind of farmhouse—"

"Of course it is," said Nevada, who was fluent in more languages than Tinkler had had hot baths. "But why don't you come in and sit down and tell us all about it?" Tinkler made a move towards a kitchen chair, but Nevada steered him away from it. "No, come into the *sitting* room," she said.

Here it comes, I thought. She took him by the arm again and guided him out of the kitchen. He was beaming, enjoying all the attention, the poor sap. "And while you're at it," said Nevada from the next room, still at this point appearing to be the sweet voice of reason, "*perhaps you can tell us what the fuck this is.*"

I left the coffee and hurried through. I wasn't going to miss this for the world.

Nevada and Tinkler were standing there looking at a tall black object that dominated the room.

It was taller than an upright piano, and deeper. A vast, grim-looking box of unvarnished wood painted a matte, obdurate black, its top third consisted of a broad rectangular opening. It completely dominated the lounge, taking up most of the space between the dining table and the sofa and blotting out a great swathe of light from our high, sunny, south-facing windows.

The object was almost as tall as I was. It was big, and it was ugly.

"What is this thing?" said Nevada. "And what is it doing in my living room?"

But if she'd expected contrition or remorse from Tinkler, she was out of luck. He stared at the black monolith and sank down on his knees before it, like one of the hairy humanoids in *Space Odyssey*, a look of beatific satisfaction on his face. "It came," he murmured, almost prayerfully. "It's here."

"Of course it bloody came," said Nevada. "Of course it's frigging here. The question is, *why* did it come? *Why* is it here? As opposed to being around at your place. Taking up all the room there."

"It had to be delivered while I was away," said Tinkler. He had risen from his knees now and was standing beside the huge black box, caressing the side of it as if it were the flanks of some monstrous black horse. "And somebody had to be at home to accept it and sign for it. Which was you guys. I told you to expect it."

"Actually," said Nevada, "you told Agatha to tell us to expect it." It was an index of her anger that she was using

Clean Head's real name here. "And she duly told us."

Tinkler looked at us, all innocence. "So what's the problem?"

"So the problem is that she told us to expect a small package which was being sent here for you. Which we were more than happy to do. *A small package.*" Nevada's extravagant hand gesture in the direction of the black behemoth was entirely redundant.

"I didn't say that to her."

"No," said Nevada, shaking her head. "You didn't. You told her that we should expect a speaker for your hi-fi. A speaker!"

Tinkler patted the crudely painted black wood with the pride of new ownership. "That's right. A speaker. And here it is."

"But she thought that you meant what any normal person would have meant by a speaker. And she translated that into a small package, and that's what she told us to expect."

Tinkler shrugged. "Well, that girl just doesn't know her exponential horn-loaded loudspeakers, then, does she?" His nonchalance fooled no one. We all knew he was talking about the girl he loved, or at least lusted after, with a longstanding and no doubt hopeless passion.

Turk came wandering into the room, having devoured her breakfast, and jumped up with an effortless leap onto the top of the black box, where she crouched peering up at Tinkler. "Hello, Turk," he said, rubbing her under the chin. "Do you like my new speaker? I know you prefer the horn-loaded designs. All the girls do." Then he smiled brightly at us. "At least it gives the cats a new place to play."

Nevada nodded at me. "I thought *his* speakers were ridiculously gigantic. But compared to yours they are just dainty adornments." I gazed fondly at the Quads in question. Just looking at them made me want to listen to music.

"That's because the sorry fool prefers electrostatic technology to the noble horn," said Tinkler.

Nevada headed for the kitchen to serve the coffee, which was beginning to smell good. As she went, she said, "Come away from there before I give you the noble horn."

"Sounds attractive," said Tinkler. But he moved briskly away from the speaker and followed her out. I found my Luis Bonfa album—on Verve, with arrangements by Lalo Schifrin—and put it on loud enough to be heard in the kitchen. It was one that Nevada loved and it always chilled her out. Sure enough, by the time they returned with the coffee, she had begun to mellow. Luis's guitar was working its magic. She and Tinkler set the coffee things down on the table and I went to join them, sitting in the sunshine. This took a certain amount of careful manoeuvring of the chairs—to avoid the baleful shadow of the monster speaker.

Tinkler finished stirring sugar into his coffee and said, casually, "So where are the cables?"

"What cables?"

He frowned at me. "Don't tease me. You know I can't stand it where serious matters like hi-fi are concerned."

"I'm not teasing you," I said. "What cables?"

"They were part of the deal."

"What do you mean?"

"The deal. On eBay. When I bought the speaker for what

I let this guy think was an extortionate price but actually, although of course I didn't let on to him, was a snip."

"A snip," said Nevada staring at the giant ugly black box.

"That's right. This beauty here is worth a couple of grand more than I paid for her." Tinkler sipped his coffee, discovered it was still too hot, and set it aside.

"This beauty," repeated Nevada, shaking her head. "There's something creepy about you referring to it as 'her', too."

Tinkler ignored her and kept on with his story. "I even convinced this guy to throw in a set of cables, too. It was a really sweet deal. And I want my cables!"

Nevada shrugged. "So what's a set of cables more or less?"

Tinkler sighed the long-suffering sigh of an audiophile having to explain things to a civilian. "They were *silver* cables. Solid silver. They were worth almost as much as the speaker. And he threw them in for nothing."

"Or perhaps didn't," I said, and Tinkler winced.

"Silver?" said Nevada. "You mean silver wire instead of copper?"

"Yes."

She looked at me. "Does that make a difference? To the sound, I mean?"

"Christ, yes," I said. I'd gone from thinking Tinkler was making a fuss about nothing concerning these cables to suddenly and poignantly sharing his pain. I turned and looked at the speaker. "You're sure the guy's not sending them separately?"

"No, he said they were definitely coming with the speaker."

"Maybe the blokes pinched them," said Nevada. "The

blokes who delivered the speaker. They looked like ruffians. Would they have known how valuable they were?"

"I don't see how," I said. "They looked like ruffians."

"But couldn't they have seen that they were silver?"

"No." Tinkler shook his head sadly. "On the outside they just looked like boring ordinary cables with a red and blue dielectric."

"Dialectic?" said Nevada.

"*Dielectric*," I said. "It's the insulator."

A mournful silence ensued as we all contemplated the loss of Tinkler's silver cables. "There was nothing else?" he said. "Nothing else with the speaker?"

"Nope," I said.

"Not an envelope, or—"

"Nothing at all." Then I thought about it. I stood up and went over to the speaker and inspected the top of it where Fanny, ever the opportunist, had supplanted her sister and was lying in a patch of sunlight. I put my hand on the warm black wood. Nevada and Tinkler were staring at me. "What is it?" said Nevada.

I ran my hand over the wood. Fanny feinted at me with her paw. She thought I was playing.

Then I found it.

Or felt it, rather. A small scrap of adhesive tape. It was black electrical tape and almost invisible against the black wood. The tape was at the front edge of the top of the speaker, and ran down over the lip of the large opening. My fingers traced it inside. "There was something taped here," I said.

Tinkler was already on his feet. He came over and inspected it. "If the cables were in there…"

I said, "Hanging in the mouth of the speaker…"

Nevada came over and joined us, peering into the shadowy maw of the giant box. "You think they're *in* there?"

Tinkler murmured, "They fell inside…"

I nodded. "It's possible. If the clowns who delivered it were careless."

"Of course they were careless," said Tinkler. I could see he had seized onto this hope and was clinging to it for dear life. "They were ruffians. They were clowns. They were ruffian clowns." We all stared into the mouth of the speaker. And saw nothing staring back at us but darkness.

I went into the spare room to look for a torch and came back with two small, powerful LED flashlights, which gave off an intense red beam. For reasons too complex to go into here, we'd once had to rob a grave in the middle of the night and Nevada had purchased a large amount of ancillary equipment for the endeavour, including these.

"I recognise these babies," said Tinkler happily, taking one of the flashlights. He'd been there in the graveyard with us, in the cold dark Kent night. Though he'd done precious little of the digging. But he was a keen participant now, as we shone the red beams of light down into the mouth of the speaker.

We could still see nothing, except the smooth tapering flare of the horn. "They could be at the bottom of the enclosure." Tinkler looked at me. The childlike eagerness in his face was touching.

So, while Nevada sat blithely drinking coffee and watching us with a slightly superior smile, we got down on our hands and knees on the floor in a grovelling posture and inspected the base of the speaker. On three sides the wood was a solid, flawless piece of cabinetry without so much as an indentation.

But on the fourth was a small access panel about the size of a magazine cover. Recessed in each corner of the panel was a screw with a Phillips cross-head. I went back into the spare room and got my tools, including an electric screwdriver and a drill, in case we had to drill out one of the screws. Tinkler began to sweat at the very suggestion of this—drilling a hole in his beloved. But it looked to me like the screws hadn't been turned for decades and might be hopelessly frozen in place.

"How old is this speaker?" I said, lying on the floor with a manual screwdriver in my hand, trying to find an angle where I both had access to the screws and room to manipulate the tools.

"Over fifty years," said Tinkler. "Be careful there. You'll spoil the paintwork."

"Spoil the paintwork? It looks like a blind man with a brush in his mouth did it in half an hour while drunk."

"But it's still the original paint job."

I got the head of the screwdriver seated in the top left screw and moved around on the floor to free my elbow so I could begin twisting it. Nothing. No give at all. I moved on to the next one. I worked each of the screws in turn and on the second attempt they started to rotate. With a warm feeling of triumph, and Tinkler crooning encouragement, I switched to the electric screwdriver. At the sound of it, the cats peered down apprehensively from the top of the speaker. Then, when they realised that the noise wasn't actually coming from an electric cat-killing machine, they both hopped down to study it more closely. Tinkler was on his knees beside me and the cats were crouching between us.

Nevada came over and regarded us ironically. "Need any help there, boys?" she said. Then she bent down and caressed the cats. "And girls."

"Could you get the Hoover, please," I said. There was sweat running down from my hairline onto my face, and I considered asking my beloved to get a towel and swab my brow for me while I laboured nobly, like a surgeon in an operating theatre with his loyal nurse at his side.

But I decided I'd better not press my luck, and just settled for the Hoover.

The first screw came free and fell ringing onto the floor. Fanny pounced on it instantly and batted it across the floor, chasing it and moving like quicksilver. Tinkler in turn was chasing her. "That's the original screw!" he cried. While he was retrieving it I got the other three original screws out, falling one after the other musically onto the floor. Unlike her sister, Turk made no move to intercept the little bouncing objects. Instead, evidently bored by the whole enterprise, she disappeared out the cat flap into the garden.

Tinkler came back with the rogue screw and I gave him the other three. Then I swapped the full-sized Phillips screwdriver for a miniature, flat-headed one and carefully inserted the narrow leading edge of the flat blade into the line in the wood where the panel met the rest of the speaker. Tinkler said, "Be careful not to—"

"Damage the original paintwork," I said. "Yes, I know." I used the screwdriver to gently pry the panel open. It gave way with a pop and a stale smell of dust, revealing a large hole in the base of the speaker cabinet. Tinkler aimed the flashlight inside.

We saw it right away. There in the thick dust of decades, a fat blue curl of cable like a nesting snake, and the gleam of a phono plug. "Where's that Hoover?" I said.

Nevada bustled in. "Coming right up."

We switched it on and Fanny fled from the noise. Nevada held the nozzle by the base of the speaker as we drew the cable out, catching a rich flow of dirty grey dust and fuzz. The vacuum cleaner consumed it cheerfully, preventing it from becoming an airborne health hazard. As a result of these ministrations, the cables arrived shiny and pristine in Tinkler's eager hands.

"Are they the right ones?" said Nevada. "Your precious silver cables?"

"Oh, yes," said Tinkler happily, stroking them. "My pretties."

Nevada switched off the Hoover and Tinkler and I were just discussing the possibility of giving the cables a test run in my system—"They've never been used. We'll have to run them in for a few hours before they start to sound good"—when Fanny came streaking into the room.

She took one look at the inviting new opening in the

bottom of the big black box and, before we could stop her, shot straight inside.

Our cat was inside the speaker.

"Fanny!"

"Wonderful," said Nevada. "Now we've lost one of the cats." She turned to Tinkler. "Your speaker has *eaten* her."

ACKNOWLEDGEMENTS

Thanks, as ever, to Ben Aaronovitch for advice and support and to Guy Adams for setting the ball rolling in the first place. To John Berlyne for stepping into the breach; to Celeste Bronfman-Nadas for enlightening discussions of story technique, and for taking the Vinyl Detective to the Caribbean; to Scott Cochrane for a lifetime of friendship and for reading first drafts; to Linda Kissick, crime fiction connoisseur, for early enthusiasm; to David Quantick for reading and coming up with a blazing blurb; to Jeff Stephen for reading and for letting me play my Bill Evans record on his tasty system; to Martin Stiff for another great cover design; to Gregg Tonn and all the staff at Into the Music in Winnipeg for putting up with me as I ransacked their stock of vinyl. To all the readers, reviewers and bloggers who made the first book a success. And to everyone at Titan Books, especially Miranda Jewess for brilliant editing and having faith in the project and Lydia Gittins for doing such a superb job on publicity ("Not cheap advertising. Tube advertising").

ABOUT THE AUTHOR

Andrew Cartmel is a novelist and screenwriter. He is the author of *Written in Dead Wax*, the first Vinyl Detective novel, which was hailed as "marvelously inventive and endlessly fascinating" by *Publishers Weekly* and received a starred review from *Kirkus*. His work for television includes commissions for *Midsomer Murders* and *Torchwood*, and a legendary stint as script editor on *Doctor Who*. He has also written plays for the London Fringe, toured as a stand-up comedian, and is currently co-writing a series of comics with Ben Aaronovitch based on the bestselling *Rivers of London* books. He lives in London with too much vinyl and just enough cats.